Ice Crash: Antarctica

Other novels by Lynda Engler:

Into the Outside

Into the Yellow Zone

Under the Mountain

Novella:

Time's Anchor

Ice Crash: Antarctica

By Lynda Engler

ICE CRASH: ANTARCTICA
Copyright © 2022 Lynda Engler.

All rights reserved.
Printed in the United States of America

Cover art by Rachel Bostwick.

ISBN: 979-8-401-98849-2

This book is dedicated to all the climate change activists who have worked tirelessly to raise the public's awareness of the state of our planet, and more importantly, what we can do about it.

Ice Crash: Antarctica

Fast Facts

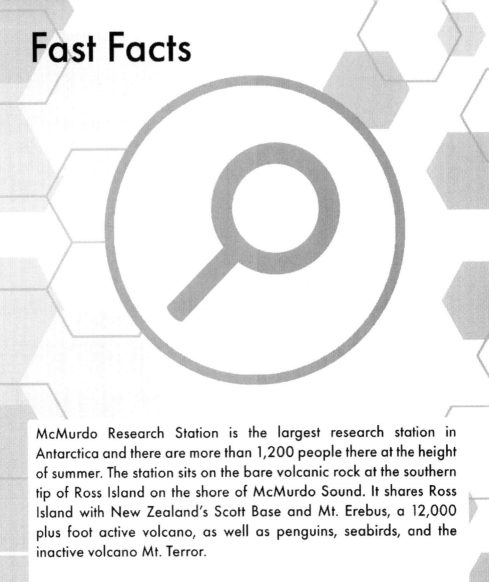

McMurdo Research Station is the largest research station in Antarctica and there are more than 1,200 people there at the height of summer. The station sits on the bare volcanic rock at the southern tip of Ross Island on the shore of McMurdo Sound. It shares Ross Island with New Zealand's Scott Base and Mt. Erebus, a 12,000 plus foot active volcano, as well as penguins, seabirds, and the inactive volcano Mt. Terror.

McMurdo has a range of labs, offices, living spaces, food, and amenities. There are three ice runways and a floating dock made artificially of frozen freshwater. The base spreads out over 160 acres.

Chapter 1

March 2030

Kathryn – Antarctica

Antarctica was bitterly cold and just brutal on the human body. Humans weren't meant to survive here. But we are curious creatures who insisted on stepping outside of our comfort zones to explore the unknown. So here we were.

I sat outside McMurdo Station, and breathed in the frigid air, gazing across the bay at the glacier flowing imperceptibly down from the heights of the Transantarctic Mountains. The only sound was the wind blowing past the hood of my parka. The Ross Ice Shelf is a floating area of freshwater ice fed by glaciers spilling off the Antarctic continent that filled a huge bay roughly the size of France. Watching the ice was my daily meditation.

It was this or yoga, and I was terrible at yoga.

The people here called this place *Mac-Town*, and it was a crazy, diverse, and hectic little town. Though much smaller than most major cities, it was an international center where people of different backgrounds met and exchanged ideas. That was why I was here – I loved the vibrant exchange of scientific ideas.

A loud *PING!* startled me. It was my tablet, tucked into the large inside pocket of my heavy-duty parka. Unable to access it outdoors, I activated my earpiece. "Read message alert."

The soothing voice from the tablet belied the grave news. "New seismograph reading available from off-shore sensors. Shall I read the data?"

I answered affirmatively and listened. Each reading was a higher magnitude than the one before it, and there had been three small undersea quakes this morning alone. Seismographs climbing in magnitude made me nervous.

I stared out at the ice-clogged McMurdo Sound. After eight months the last of the summer crew was packing to go home. The last ship would arrive in two days to pick up my group of fifty. About two-hundred people would winter over on this ice-cold continent.

Cold was a relative term. Growing up in Boston, I thought I'd always known what cold was. I was wrong. While every month in Antarctica was below freezing, December and January – high summer – occasionally pushed the mercury above freezing. They told me that McMurdo was lucky. It sat on an island off the coast and those same mountains that forced the glaciers onto the sea protected the base from frigid air from the interior of Antarctica. Temperatures below minus 40 degrees were rare at McMurdo Station.

I was glad to be *lucky,* but I disagreed with the Antarctic definition of the term.

Sound traveled exceptionally well in the frozen south, but McMurdo could often be a noisy place, and my quietude was broken by the rumble of large equipment moving about the town, staging items for the *R/V Richard E. Byrd* that was en route. Beginning in January, icebreakers carved a shipping channel for supply ships to reach the station. It was damned difficult for the icebreakers to get through the floating ice pack. Helicopters used to guide them, but since the crash of a Canadian helicopter in 2013, drones did the reconnaissance, so it was not unusual for the arrival of an icebreaker to be heralded by the sound of a drone up in the sky.

"Kathryn?" I almost jumped out of my skin as Joshua Levy placed a hand on my shoulder. I had not heard our Chief Evacuation Officer come up behind me.

"Yes, Josh?" I managed to squeak out, trying to gain my composure. Every noise had been making me tense the last few days. I was coming down to the wire on my research, my entire career at stake. My life's worth of seismologic research, my theories, my thoughts, and work needed to be wrapped up into a concise paper I would submit to a professional journal for publication.

"Are you ready to break down your equipment today?"

My eyes teared up against the cold wind as I squinted at him and replied, "I need a couple more days. I'm still in the middle of my observations."

"No need to cry about it," he laughed. Josh was also Chief Joker at McMurdo. He was funny – at least *he* thought he was.

"I need two more days to observe the tectonic activity beneath the Antarctic Plate before we pack up. Seismic activity has been increasing and I need to know if it's simply random activity or if there is a pattern." I mashed my gloved hands deeper into my pockets and wiggled my fingers to keep the circulation going.

He shrugged. "Will 48 hours make that big a difference, Kathryn? I mean, you've been recording data for seven months."

The first two weeks I'd been in Antarctica had been out at sea, dropping submerged sensors along a thousand miles of open water along the coast. The sensors would pick up seismic activity at the edge of the plate. Since then, I'd recorded that data along with the figures from the seismic station I had erected on the mainland, across the sound from McMurdo.

"I know what you are implying, but the changes have only been occurring for the last week. I need a couple more days to figure out if it's an indication of a larger quake, or if it's a short-term event. Give me two days, and then I promise I'll pack up my gear and get it on the *Richard Byrd* when it arrives."

Josh swore. "Kathryn, you try my patience. Alright, you have two days, but if you and your gear aren't ready, you become a winterer – or your gear does. I really don't care."

He stormed off in a visible huff, his exhalations forming small clouds around his rapidly receding form. Josh had plenty to keep him busy over the next two days and I hoped he would stay out of my way.

Josh was a pain in the ass. If he hadn't come to bug me, I would already be back inside the Crary Science and Engineering Center taking down more readings instead of out here freezing my extremities off. Now I rushed across the station, past the dorms and the common building that contained the dining hall, and into the CSEC, yanking gloves and hat off as I walked. I stuffed them into the sleeve of my parka and hung it on the wall hook in my office and scrolled back through the seismic readings on my screen.

What I saw chilled me more than the sub-zero weather outside.

Fourteen million years ago, the Antarctic Plate began its slow dive under South America. For the last three decades, this borderland of plates has had about twenty earthquakes a year. Nothing remarkable as fault lines go. They were out at sea, ten kilometers down, nothing above magnitude-5.8. That's why I placed my new sensors off the coast. That sensor data now appeared on my screen, and it clearly showed three quakes in the last 24 hours. All three were over magnitude-6 and each slightly stronger than the one before.

Earthquakes were not unusual in Antarctica, but they didn't happen often. There had been a couple big ones, including a magnitude-8 in the

Balleny Islands. I could picture the Scotia Plate meeting the Antarctic Plate where it grazed the tip of the continent, a seismic map stuck in my head since college. There was a line of seismic activity at the plate boundary, but fewer in the interior. I suspected there were more quakes in the interior than we knew about because with only twenty seismograph stations operating on the entire continent, you'd miss a lot of activity. Before I arrived, only one of those twenty was on the continent, at the South Pole. My station brought the grand total to a whopping two, but that was still too few for such a vast territory. You could hide a lot of little earthquakes in a place this big.

The current readings left no doubt that the frequency and magnitude were both increasing. Instead of answers, I had more questions. Were they statistically relevant and would they get stronger?

I had two days to find out.

Fast Facts

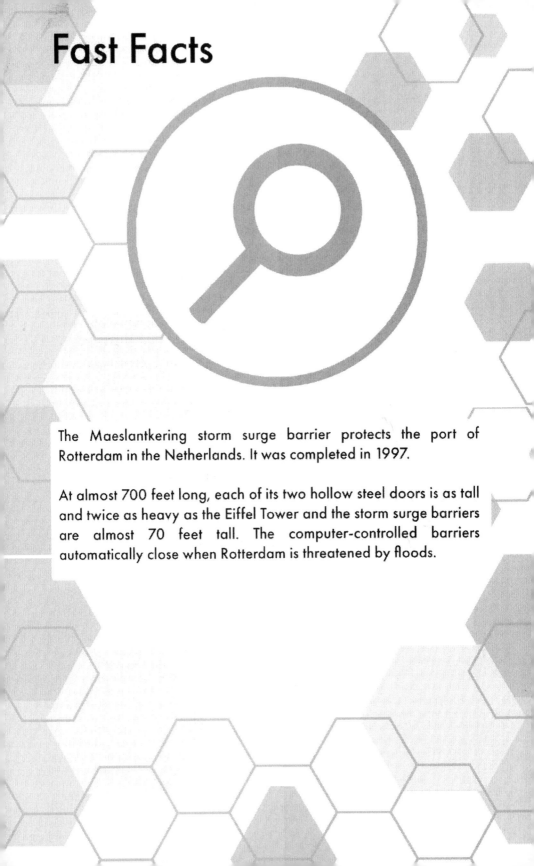

The Maeslantkering storm surge barrier protects the port of Rotterdam in the Netherlands. It was completed in 1997.

At almost 700 feet long, each of its two hollow steel doors is as tall and twice as heavy as the Eiffel Tower and the storm surge barriers are almost 70 feet tall. The computer-controlled barriers automatically close when Rotterdam is threatened by floods.

Chapter 2

Inga – Boston

I looked at the clock in the bottom corner of my tablet for the hundredth time in the last thirty minutes. How could this class be this long? It was my last before spring break and even though I had two papers to write during my time off, my mind was on our flight out of Logan in just a few hours. Zoe would be ready way before I was, as usual, and as soon as I got back to my dorm, she would be pestering me to get my suitcase together and get our asses to the airport.

Zoe was one of my three roommates, and the only one with a car. Growing up in Cambridge, I had gotten my license in high school, but as a freshman in Boston, I was terrified to drive in the city. Zoe suffered no such fears. She had grown up in New Jersey and had plenty of experience driving in New York City. Driving in New York was a different kind of crazy than driving in Boston, but still, she was good at it. She was a year ahead of me and shared my major and we became close friends as soon as we moved in together.

The professor's voice drew my faltering attention back to the class. "When we get back from break, we will move on to the next section of the course: political connections. Don't forget to submit your cultural globalization paper by Sunday at midnight."

Although I'm a music major, my college believed in a liberal arts tradition, which meant I had to suffer through this course to fulfill a history requirement. It was boring but not the worst course I had taken.

"Really?" I heard someone nearby murmur. I wanted to call him a dumbass for not reading the syllabus. This wasn't high school anymore. Just because we had a week off did not mean we didn't have classwork to complete. But I kept my mouth shut as always and headed for the exit, hoping to beat Zoe back to the dorm. No such luck.

"Hey Zoe," I announced before she could start in on me. "I've got everything pre-packed, so just give me a sec to go pee, and then I'll get ready to go."

"Pre-packed, Inga? What on Earth is 'pre-packed?'" she said, her vowels drawn out, Jersey style.

"You know...out and organized in piles on my bed. It's all ready to go into my suitcase."

"Then why isn't it *in* your suitcase?" Zoe rolled her eyes at me in irritation.

"Didn't want it to get any more wrinkled than necessary," I said, closing the bathroom door behind me.

"Wrinkled?" Even with the wooden plank between us, I could *see* her in my mind's eye, throwing her hands in the air in frustration. I was neat. She was a slob. Such was life.

The running water drowned out whatever she said next, and I only opened the door once my hands were dry. Without a word, I carefully arranged my clothes, sandals, bathing suits, toiletries bag, and sunscreen into my suitcase, and zipped it shut. Standing it up, I pulled the travel handle out the top, dropped my tablet into my backpack, threw a couple of bags of chips and chocolate bars in for good measure, and shoved the suitcase's handle up through the arm straps of my backpack.

"Ready," I announced, shoving my arms into my heavy winter jacket, and dreaming of south Florida sunshine. By the second week of

March in Boston, everyone wanted out of winter and the roads would be jammed.

"Finally," Zoe huffed, grabbing her coat and pulling her suitcase toward the front door. We lived in an apartment-style dorm with two double bedrooms and two bathrooms. We shared a kitchen and living room with two juniors, Avery, and Madison. I didn't know much about either of them other than Madison had turned twenty-one early in the semester and now that she was legal to buy alcohol, she frequently did. Keeping it in our communal fridge was a no-no since the rest of us could be held accountable for underage drinking. I confronted her on it only once. I got a short retort and I never asked her again. But Zoe was a force of nature and threatened to pour her expensive purchases down the drain. Now Madison – never *Maddie* – kept the crap in her own room.

I'm not a prude or anything, but this was an expensive private school, and it was run by the Jesuits, so their rules were a bit stricter than public colleges. My family wasn't made of money, and they were paying a lot for this education. I didn't want to get expelled. I liked it here.

Despite that, I was quite adept at breaking rules and being a rebel. Like this trip to Miami. My parents didn't have a clue and, while dad might not care too much, mom would absolutely freak. My mom was the *famous* researcher, Kathryn Whitson, from MIT's Earth, Atmosphere, and Planetary Sciences Department. Well, famous in academic circles anyway. All my professors knew who she was, even though she didn't teach at our school. She studied seismology and was in Antarctica researching earthquakes. It was her first time there and she was due back in two weeks, which was the end of summer at the ass-end of the world. Antarctica was so far down under that even the Aussies called it Way Down Under.

Zoe was already at the front door. She huffed and yelled over her shoulder, "Come on, Inga! Grab your *cawfee* cup and get *moooving!*" Boston had a bad enough accent, but here was this Jersey girl with her weird way of saying things and it always cracked me up. I followed orders and raced to the door before it slammed.

Zoe was halfway to the student parking deck before I caught up. My suitcase dragged behind me through the slush. I'd have to scrub the dirt off the purple roller-case once we arrived.

"Oh, man, Florida!" I exhaled. I could see my breath. "I cannot *wait* to get out of this sub-freakin-zero climate." I sighed, and Zoe nodded in agreement as we took the elevator to the fifth level.

Zoe reached her beat-up old car and yanked its cable out, letting it retract into the charging station. It was fifteen years old, had peeling paint and one black door from a junk yard, and only went 200 miles on a charge. Even though she had to plug it in more often than a newer car, Zoe didn't care. She didn't drive it that often, except to New Jersey to see her folks once in a while, which was why they paid to keep the old cranker on campus.

The airport was only twelve miles from our school and shouldn't take more than twenty-five minutes, but it was the last day before a hundred thousand college students fled Boston for spring break.

After securing our suitcases in the trunk and ourselves in the car, Zoe zoomed down the garage ramp and headed for the airport. She said, "I'll bet your mother is frozen after her eight-months in Antarctica. She'd probably cringe to hear us whine about the weather here."

I didn't know how many traffic lights there were between the campus and the entrance to I-90, but if they were all red, we'd miss our flight. We lucked out and only half were, allowing Zoe to get onto the highway and curse her way to the airport.

"She'd be more pissed about us going to Miami than our weather complaints." I drank my coffee carefully, trying to finish it without wearing it. I couldn't take it through airport security.

"Why doesn't she want you to go to Florida? Too much money?" asked Zoe as she saw the sign for the Ted Williams Tunnel. Zoe performed a Jersey slide, the rude and frightening act of traveling quickly from the left lane all the way to the exit ramp in one fell swoop. I grabbed the panic handle but didn't miss a beat in our conversation. This was normal for Zoe.

"No, that's not it. I have the money. The earthquakes she's been studying at McMurdo have gotten worse over the last six months. She's convinced 'the big one' is coming and, well, you can imagine what that means if ice starts falling off that damned frozen continent. Miami is too far south and too low in elevation, so if the sea level goes up any further, it's not gonna' do well. She doesn't want me in danger. You know, over-protective mom."

"You remember that food riot in Indonesia last week? Did you see that on the news? The news said something like half the island was now under the ocean. Think she's worried that could happen here?" asked Zoe.

"I mean, I'm not stupid. I know rising seas have created food shortages and started wars and stuff, but sheesh! Those are in third world countries, not here. And really, none of this is going to happen in the next week."

I looked at the signs and continued, "We need the left side for Departures." I always hoped that if Zoe knew which lane to be in earlier, she might not need to drive like a lunatic.

One always needed hope.

It was dark when we arrived in Miami so I was disappointed I couldn't see any palm trees outside the terminal windows. While we walked toward the airport exit, my phone beeped announcing a voicemail. No one ever left me voicemail, since all my friends texted me, so I knew who it had to be.

"Hey, walk slower," I called out to Zoe. "I need to check this voicemail. It's probably from my mom. She's the only one I know who is stuck with nothing but a landline."

"No cell Way Down Under?" she said, but I didn't answer since I assumed that was a rhetorical question.

I keyed a button on my earpiece that brought up a holographic virtual menu floating in front of me that projected out of the almost invisible plastic device in my right ear. Operating a phone in visual mode while walking was like talking and chewing gum at the same time. Some people were fantastic at it, but I was as likely to bite the inside of my cheek as to chew the gum. I would walk into something as I accessed the visual controls, so I stopped at a bank of chairs near the bathrooms.

"No problem," said Zoe. "Watch my bag a minute." She parked her suitcase at my side and disappeared into the restroom.

I could have voice-activated my digital personal assistant, Lilith, who I had named after a robot from a steampunk sci-fi novel and had her play me the message. Lilith was a great DPA, but it was too noisy in the terminal for audio controls, so I used the virtual screen. My eyes tracked to the voicemail icon in my field of vision. I blinked once to access it and then again for it to play the recording.

The message was not from my mother at all but the inn. I blinked away the voicemail to the trash just as Zoe returned.

"Everything okay?" she asked, smoothing her hands dry on her jeans.

"Yep. It was the hotel letting us know our shuttle is on the way." I was glad I'd given them our flight information so they could track it.

Lilith had all the current rideshare apps, but the hotel shuttle was way easier.

Sure enough, when we left the terminal downstairs at baggage claim, there was a purple van with a picture of the hotel's palm tree logo emblazoned across its side, back, and even the darkly tinted windows. I wheeled my suitcase toward it with Zoe so close on my heels that when I stopped in front of it, she almost ran into me. A handsome dark-skinned man of indeterminate age stepped out of the vehicle and greeted us.

"Ms. Whitson and Ms. Walsh?" he asked with an accent. Cuban, maybe? It sounded lyrical and exotic to my New England ears.

"That's us," I said and nodded. "I'm Inga and this is Zoe."

I started toward the shuttle's steps with my bag, but he took my suitcase off my hands and said, "Welcome to Miami, ladies. Please watch your step."

Zoe and I boarded the shuttle bus empty-handed, our suitcases and backpacks safely stowed on the van's luggage rack behind the driver's seat.

The city lights flickered outside the van windows as we left the airport. We were the only passengers, although it was not that late at night. I was pulled back from my thoughts as the driver asked a question, but Zoe was already answering.

"Is this your first time in our lovely city?"

"Yes!" Zoe's smile conveyed her excitement. "We flew down from Boston to get out of the cold for spring break, but I guess we are only two out of thousands doing that." She giggled in an uncharacteristically shy way. I guess she liked the driver, too. Plus, he was easy on the eyes. If everyone in Miami looked this good, it was going to be one hell of a vacation.

"Ah, yes, it is the sun and fun capital of the world. Miami has hundreds of thousands of visitors here during March and April. It is a busy place." He pronounced it *bee-zee* and I could see that Zoe was enthralled by the handsome Latino. I think she may have actually batted her eyelashes at him.

"How far is downtown from the hotel?" she asked, even though she already knew. We had thoroughly researched the hotel, the beach, and the area to make sure it was safe. Zoe's parents knew where we were, even though mine didn't, and her mother had specifically required her to make sure our affordable hotel was not in a crap area before she gave her permission – and money – for the trip.

The driver, whose license tag above the dashboard said his name was Carlos Martinez, gave us the rundown. I'm not sure if he did that with all guests, or was simply responding to Zoe's friendly request, but I conceded that it was a good idea to have a local perspective in a strange place. Google knowledge could only get you so far.

"Downtown is four miles across the bay. There is a city bus from the hotel. Once you are there, you can get around on the Metromover train. It's free and has twenty stops around the city, so it's the best way to see downtown. Of course, you can walk to the beach from the hotel, which I think is what most college students come here for. The sand, the water, and the parties." His eyes lit up, and it seemed like partying, and beach-going were his favorite leisure activities as well. Now that I got a better look at him, I placed him in his late twenties, which made him out of Zoe's preferred age range, but that wouldn't stop her from flirting.

"Oh yeah, we love the water," replied Zoe, her pronunciation of *worter* giving away her New Jersey roots and making me smirk, as always.

I jumped in with my own questions. "Thanks, Carlos, we really appreciate your advice. Besides the beach, we – well at least *I* – would like to experience the ocean from a different perspective. As in *on it*. What's the best way to get offshore to see Fisher Gate?"

Eight years ago, a Dutch company built the immense sea gate to protect Biscayne Bay. Without it, the western shore of Miami Beach and the eastern shore of the city proper would probably have been engulfed by now. It was no secret that sea level had risen three feet in the last decade. Fisher Gate was a popular attraction for people who wanted to see what coastal cities had to do to protect themselves.

"Oh yes!" said Carlos. "Take the speedboat sightseeing tour. It is not too expensive. Besides the sea gate, the tour takes you past luxurious multi-million-dollar homes and cruises up the coast of South Beach lined with art deco homes. It is *magneeficient!*"

His accent was charming, and I thought Zoe would explode from joy. "Of all the tourist attractions in Miami, that is one you should not miss. Oh, and the Everglades airboat adventure is worthwhile if you like alligators or wandering along a jungle-walking trail. There is a zoo, too. If you like art, the Wynwood arts district is about a mile north of the last Metromover stop. It's an easy walk, with lots of local street art and multiple galleries along it."

The van pulled silently into the parking lot of our hotel, and Carlos wrapped up his impromptu tour monologue. "If you have any questions about the city, any at all, come see Carlos. If we don't have anyone needing to go to or from the airport, I can drop you off with the van, which is much quicker than the bus."

The Miami Inn was not exactly a dive, but it was low budget, or as I prefer to think of it, *student budget*. A mere seven stories, it was petite by Miami Beach standards. A black and white checkered floor and art deco styling greeted us in the lobby. Most importantly, it was one block from the boardwalk and beach, and it had free Wi-Fi and breakfast. We could have stayed in a hostel for half the money, but the free food and shuttle made up for the extra cost, and we got a nice place with a view of the ocean, if not right on it.

Carlos deposited our bags on a cart and wheeled it into the lobby, wished us good night, and gave Zoe a wink before departing. Was *swoon* still a word? If it was, she did it. "God, Zoe, I'm gonna puke. He's like a million years older than you!" I grabbed her by the arm, the luggage trolley with my other hand, and walked to the reception desk to check-in.

"Oh, this is awesome," she murmured, looking around at the lobby as if she had never seen a hotel before. Zoe must have had Spring Fever. Being stuck in Massachusetts for her second winter might have caused permanent damage to her brain.

"Warm weather, a retro hotel, a cute driver, and there's a party on the beach. Can life get *any* better?"

I rolled my eyes before addressing the desk clerk. Once the check-in was complete, she handed me our key cards and said, "Welcome to Miami Beach. Is this your first time here?"

"Are we that obvious?" I winced.

She smiled kindly. "There are a few things you should be aware of to make your stay as pleasant as possible. The main beachfront road is sometimes shut down on Friday and Saturday as crowds fill the sand and streets. The city does a lot of planning for the season, allocating extra officers on foot, bicycles, and ATVs, but please be careful in the crowds. Also, certain traffic routes are reserved only for locals with permits and business patrons. Do you have a rental car?"

I shook my head and she continued. "Good. This place is best enjoyed on foot. The city wants everyone to have a good time but do it safely and responsibly. The officers are there to make sure everyone follows the rules. It is forbidden to consume alcohol on the beach, play heavily amplified music, or bring tents, tables, or coolers onto the sand. There are locker rental locations along the beach for valuables. Do you have any questions?"

Zoe replied, "No thank you, ma'am." She turned to me. "Let's drop our stuff in the room and go out to the beach. I know it's dark out, but I want to feel the sand between my toes."

Her gleeful giggle was starting to freak me out. If we didn't get out there soon, she might have an aneurysm.

Fast Facts

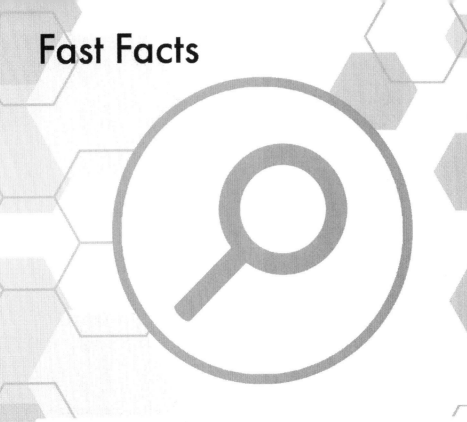

McMurdo's Crary Science and Engineering Center (CSEC) began operations during the 1994-1995 season. It supports biological, earth science, atmospheric sciences, and an aquarium under one roof. It was named for Albert P. Crary (1911-1987) who was the first person to set foot on both the North and South Poles.

Commonly referred to as the Crary Lab, the building consists of five pods: Core and Biology, Earth and Atmospheric Sciences, and the Aquarium Pod. The lab contains state-of-the-art instruments and equipment to facilitate research and to advance science, technology, and education.

Chapter 3
Kathryn – Antarctica

I spent the entire night at my workstation in the CSEC. About a decade ago, over one hundred buildings were re-engineered into a 300,000 square foot campus composed of six interconnected structures, allowing 21st century McMurdo to be a model of scientific leadership, sustainability, and engineering.

McMurdo's new layout, completed in 2024, had public spaces designed to combat the isolation of a remote location. The complex gave residents fresh air, natural light, and views of the landscape while also linking the facilities to avoid unnecessary exposure to the elements and decrease energy usage.

We had everything here, including the only ATM on the continent. Cash had no official use in Antarctica, but there was always the odd poker game and other forms of vice where cash was still king. Though the area was small, I had pretty much anything and everything that I needed.

The only thing missing was my family. I was a long way from home.

My workstation sat in one of the five research offices in the Earth Sciences pod. Besides my computer, I had various screens to monitor my remote equipment, an extra chair, and the best part – a cot. Too tired to walk back to my quarters last night, I had used the cot for a few hours of sleep. It wasn't uncomfortable, yet I woke with a crick in my neck. I brushed my teeth, and then headed over to the dining hall for breakfast. Passageways connected the Central Services Building to the CSEC on the east and the six dorm pods on the west. We still had to battle the elements to get to the data support center, waste-handling building, vehicle maintenance, and equipment storage, but at least the daily live-and-work facilities were interconnected.

McMurdo Station was a center for all manner of scientific programs and experiments. Terrestrial and marine biology, geology, glaciology, sea-ice studies, meteorology, atmospheric physics, and cosmic radiation were just a handful of the scientific research activities that went on. The station even had recompression chambers for diving accident victims. Mars probes and landers had been tested on Antarctica's dry valleys – areas where glaciers flowed but then wind caused the ice to evaporate leaving dry, permanently frigid land. It was the closest thing on Earth to the surface of Mars.

My seismology and oceanography studies fit in perfectly here.

I wasn't the only first-timer at the station this summer and I had made quite a few friends over the last eight months. It wasn't hard to get to know people here. We ate three meals a day together unless you were off base conducting experiments. The food was amazingly good, and everyone would have gained a lot of weight if we didn't burn so many calories in this climate just staying alive. The kitchen had at least a dozen chefs and they brought in fresh food from New Zealand regularly. Keeping perishables cold wasn't a challenge, after all.

My stomach grumbled loudly as I hurried through the passageway, barely noticing the view through the heavy-duty glass. I marched straight to the coffee and then filled my tray with a scrambled egg and vegetable dish, fresh bread, and bacon, before seeking out my regular table. Marnie and Sylvia were already there, looking like they were close to leaving.

"Morning ladies." My tray clanked as I put it down next to Marnie, our resident marine biologist.

"Were you up all night packing?" asked Sylvia from across the table. She was a glaciologist from New Brunswick, Canada and had spent months telling me about her research and comparing notes on kids since we both had two of almost the same age. Like my Liam, her son was fourteen and just finishing middle school, while her daughter was in college, like Inga.

I shook my head and then sipped my coffee before answering. "No. Haven't even started. I was up most of the night analyzing new readings from my sensors. Barely got any sleep at all."

"Tell me about it," replied Sylvia. "I'm up to my ears in data from Thwaites and we have to leave tomorrow night. I have half a mind to just stay for the winter and keep working."

I had been thinking the same thing myself because of the seismic readings. Most of the summer crew had left by plane or on the last two ships, but like me, Marnie and Sylvia had volunteered to be on the last ship out. We all needed as much time as we could get for our research.

Sylvia's glacier was as perplexing a problem as my seismic data. Thwaites was one of the largest glaciers on the planet and was what Sylvia called a *threshold system*, which meant that instead of melting slowly like an ice cube on a summer day, it was more like a house of cards. It was completely stable until it wasn't, then it would collapse. When a chunk of ice the size of Ohio falls apart, that's a big problem. Its loss would destabilize the rest of the West Antarctic ice, and that would collapse too.

Sylvia had been extolling the issues of climate change and how it had been affecting the Thwaites glacier to us all summer. It was nothing like the Larsen ice shelf calvings over the years. Larsen A, B, and C had been breaking up in chunks since 1995, but because they were already floating, they did not affect sea level when they drifted into warmer waters and melted.

Thwaites was different – it sat on land. If it collapsed, sea levels would rise three to four meters in many parts of the world. Because of the way gravity pushed water around the planet, the waters in New York, Boston, and Miami would rise even higher, as much as five meters. It was a terrifying thought.

Sylvia continued as I ate. "Here's the thing. I can't just leave this data all winter. What if Thwaites collapses during that time?"

I swallowed and replied, "If Thwaites collapses, the whole world is in danger, but the most dangerous place will be right here. You would be at ground zero."

"Yes and no. I'd have to be quick about it, but we can evacuate by helo to higher ground, well above the high-water mark, even with the tsunamis that it would cause locally."

She was right. Ross Island had two extremely high peaks: Mt. Erebus topped out at 3,657 meters, about 12,000 feet, but as an active volcano, it wouldn't be anyone's first choice. However, the inactive volcano Mt. Terror was certainly high enough.

"Can a helicopter evacuate all the winter staff to Mt. Terror fast enough if the shit hits the fan down here?" Over 200 people would be staying at McMurdo after the *Richard Byrd* left, and they would be isolated until about October 1.

Sylvia nodded. "I think so."

Marnie swept her gaze between me and Sylvia and finally stared dumbfounded at us. "Are you really going to winter over? Seriously?"

I looked at Sylvia because, honestly, I wasn't sure what my answer was. How could I leave Nick at home with our two kids for another half a year? But how could I leave my research unfinished? My grant was for one season, and I'd never get another one. No matter what, I was never coming back to Antarctica.

Sylvia gave me the tiniest of nods, throwing the final decision in my court. I sighed. "Yeah. I think so."

I was going to winter over at the bottom of the world.

Fast Facts

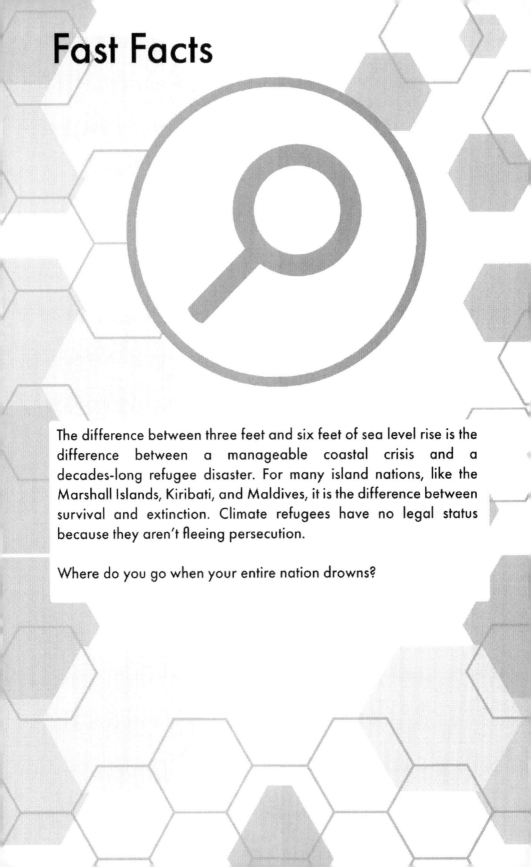

The difference between three feet and six feet of sea level rise is the difference between a manageable coastal crisis and a decades-long refugee disaster. For many island nations, like the Marshall Islands, Kiribati, and Maldives, it is the difference between survival and extinction. Climate refugees have no legal status because they aren't fleeing persecution.

Where do you go when your entire nation drowns?

Chapter 4
Inga – Miami

The warm light streaked through the plantation blinds and filtered through my eyelids, awakening me much earlier than I would have liked on vacation. Golden rays cast rectangular shapes onto the carpet and the simple furnishings of our cheap hotel room. I blinked a few times in an attempt to adjust to the early morning sun.

Then I threw my pillow at Zoe, hitting her square in the head. "Get up, you lazy ass. It's time to hit the beach."

She growled at me and mumbled something not for polite company.

Grinning like a sadistic Cheshire cat, I knew I had the single bathroom to myself for as long as I wanted. Zoe would sleep another hour, giving me time to take a nice, hot shower before dressing and hitting the breakfast bar in the lobby for coffee, food, and some much-needed sunshine at an outdoor table.

By the time Zoe joined me, I was well into my second cup and three chapters into a new novel on my phone. I could hear the surf but couldn't see the water from my seat, but with my feet propped up on the chair next to me, my legs were gaining some color. Apparently, 'beach view' in the hotel's description meant you could see it if you stood at a certain angle, craned your neck, and then used your imagination.

"Hey," said Zoe, standing above me with a cup in one hand and a plate in the other.

"Sit. You're blocking my sun," I scolded. She sat and dove into her free breakfast like a ravenous hyena...or a college student on a limited budget. Pretty much the same thing.

I put my phone down on the table, leaned back in my chair, and closed my eyes. The golden sun warmed my face. My fair skin and flame-colored hair betrayed my half-Scottish ancestry, so I was caked in SPF 70. I'd still tan, but at a pace that wouldn't create an Inga-lobster.

Through a mouthful of bagel and cream cheese, Zoe said, "Taking a nap? Interesting factoid: If you hadn't woken up so early, you wouldn't need one."

I knew she wasn't really angry with me, even if she was trying extremely hard to sound that way. This was not a new argument between us. I always woke up early, and she liked to sleep in. We had managed not to kill each other since August. Besides, I knew she always fell back to sleep after I got up, and she knew she would get the bathroom all to herself because of my earlier body clock.

"Just taking in all this sunshine while I can. In a week, we'll be back in the frozen north. Worse, the thawing and soggy north." Without opening my eyes or leaning forward, I added, "Tell me when you're done eating so we can head to the beach. I've reserved two beach loungers and an umbrella. Don't worry, I tipped the attendant already, *and* I got towels from the lobby, *plus* have sunscreen in my bag." I was nothing if not a full-service vacation planner.

I could hear Zoe chewing and waited for her to finish. She could take all the time she wanted. Other than moving from a chair on the patio to a chair on the sand, I had no plans for the day other than relaxation. Playing tourist would wait until tomorrow, and those two papers I had to write were both started, courtesy of yesterday's four-hour flight.

I almost did fall asleep leaning back in my chair, the soft sigh of the wind and surf lulling me into complete relaxation. It wasn't until I felt Zoe's hand on my shoulder, that I stretched like a cat waking from a sunny dozing spot and followed her down the long path to the oceanfront.

Zoe scanned the surf. "The tide chart in the lobby says the fun stuff isn't until early afternoon. Shame."

Halfway between low tide and high, the waves were just right for me. Maybe these weren't the rough waves she'd hoped for, but that didn't stop her from running right out into the marginal surf the minute she dropped her cover-up on her lounge chair.

Bostonians aren't quite as comfortable with open ocean, not having grown up with one nearby, so I waded in slower, letting the water hit my knees as each wave rolled over the sand, white-fringed and chaotic. I had been to beaches before. Boston sat on the coast, but it was all bays and sounds, not open water. My family went to Cape Cod almost every summer, but even the Cape sat on a bay, with no direct waves like the Jersey Shore that Zoe was so familiar with. The only time I had been on a beach where uninterrupted waves hit it twenty-four seven was on Nantucket Island when I was twelve.

The foaming crests swirled around my feet, mesmerizing me with their rhythmic movement and their slight chill. The air was warm, but the sea was not. I locked my eyes on the horizon, hearing the crashing of the waves, tasting the air as much as smelling it. Pure perfection.

Perfection interrupted as a volleyball crashed into my butt.

"Sorry," said a husky voice from behind me as a twenty-something guy raced to grab his ball before the sea claimed it.

He seized the volleyball and I turned to face him. His eyes were almost as golden as his skin, every flawless muscle toned to precision. "No problem," I muttered to the vision of Apollo, standing two feet from my throbbing heart.

He smiled, turned, and ran out of my life. I sighed, enjoying his backside recede from view.

A giant wave came in and almost knocked me over and Zoe laughed as her soaking wet form washed up next to me. "Geez, Inga, stop watching the local wildlife and come in the water. I'll teach you how to body surf."

Regaining my balance, I carefully walked into the ocean, bracing as each wave hit the dry parts of my body until I was finally bobbing up and down in the salty sea. Treading water each time a wave lifted me, I asked, "How do you know he's a local? He could be here for spring break like us."

Rolling your eyes while almost entirely submerged in the Atlantic Ocean was a skill that until that moment, I had no idea Zoe possessed, but she mastered it brilliantly. "Oh, Inga. Just look at him. Tan, buff, and athletic. Only native beach bums look like that." Then she splashed water in my face.

I couldn't help but laugh at myself.

We spent the next hour studying the easy yet respectable subject of throwing oneself on top of the perfect crest as it curled above our heads, launching into a front crawl, paddling as fast as we could, and building as much speed as possible. I watched Zoe as a wave lifted her up and she put her head down in line with her right arm and copied her.

The wave came at me, and I tucked down, my head and arm lined up. Lifted by the wave, I stiffened and streamlined my body. Desperately trying not to drown, I pushed all my weight onto my arm and created the perfect forward and downward momentum. I had it! I actually had it. I was in the curl, if just for a moment. The rushing water rewarded me by bearing me onto the beach, the sand scouring my legs as I struggled to stand. It was fun, simple, and probably the most natural sport ever invented. With or without your bathing suit, as mine tried to leave several times.

After five good rides, my muscles were bunched like taught cords and I hit my lounge chair hard and closed my eyes for some length of time, I wasn't sure how long. I was in the shade of the umbrella when I closed my eyes, but eventually, the sun shifted and shone brightly through my eyelids, simultaneously awakening me and my stomach. I rolled to my right and saw Zoe fast asleep, but without a pillow to chuck at her, I had to improvise. I threw the bottle of sunscreen instead.

"Ooof!" She exclaimed and threw it back at me but missed and it fell harmlessly to the sand. "Well, now that you've woken me for the second time today, my choices are to kill you or get food. I'm starved so I'll wait on that act of murder."

I gathered my bag and flip-flops, pulled on my cover-up, and plopped a wide-brimmed hat on my head, and off we went in search of lunch. The problem with the area we were staying in was that it wasn't South Beach, and it wasn't North Beach. We were somewhat stuck in the middle, which meant we had to walk several blocks north or south to get to shops and eateries. The boardwalk meandered up and down the entire length of the beach, palm trees lining the circuitous paths leading from the beach to the road at any given point.

Zoe grumbled. "I want pizza. At home, pizza places, arcades, and clubs line every inch of the boards. I guess palm trees instead of noisy arcades have some charm too. But my stomach would appreciate crappy boardwalk food."

Realizing we would have to walk down a side street and get back to the main road for anything to eat, we set off south. I stuck my DPA in my ear and asked, "Lilith, where is the nearest place for pizza that's not a chain?" I preferred to spend what little money I had at small businesses rather than Conglomerated 'R Us.

Her disembodied voice came through the earpiece and said, "Happily, Inga." Lilith brought up a holographic screen with a map in my field of vision. A red map pin three blocks down Florida State Road A1A tagged *Giovanni's Home Slice*. My eyes tracked to the icon and blinked to open up the description.

"I've found a place that says it's real New York style pizza. We turn off the boardwalk right after that five-star resort with the jungle theme. You remember – the one we couldn't afford even if we won the lottery?" I enjoyed the four-block walk, the breeze blowing slightly through my damp hair and watching the 'local wildlife' as Zoe called it, plus the throngs of other spring breakers like us.

The desk clerk at our hotel had been right about the extra cops. They were everywhere, on both bikes and foot, which made me feel more secure. They patrolled the beach, the boardwalk, and the streets. They were the reason why I hadn't put my stuff in a locker but rather had left my phone in my bag under my lounge chair on the beach when we had gone in the water. I didn't like to be cut off from my phone, especially from my digital personal assistant, but if someone did steal my phone, all my data was backed up online. Besides, with security these days, no one could unlock my phone to use it anyway.

Giovanni's was sandwiched between a national drug store chain and a huge beachwear store. It had an art deco facade with café tables lining the sidewalk. We seated ourselves.

"It's weird the way you can't see the ocean from the main drag here. Not like down the shore where everything sits on the boardwalk so you can't get away from the water," said Zoe. Her dark brown hair had dried in unruly curls during the walk and now hung in her face. She swatted it behind her ears in annoyance.

"Almost like people here are so used to the ocean that they don't care to see it at every given moment," I agreed. The ocean was a scary place, truth be told. Especially in the last ten years since sea level had risen by three feet after one of the largest glaciers in Greenland collapsed into the sea. It was worse in South America, where waters had risen almost five feet. Some weird thing about what melted at one pole had more effect on the opposite side of the world, because of the way gravity moved the water around as the planet spun. Much of the western shore of South Florida – the Everglades – was underwater. The Keys had drowned. North of Homestead, Florida had implemented Dutch-style sea walls that would protect parts of the coast for maybe another two- or three-foot rise.

A server brought us glasses of water and menus, but Zoe didn't let her get away. "I hear you've got the best pizza south of the Bronx," she said with a disbelieving faux smile.

"That's right," she replied. "It's real New York pizza. The owner is from Manhattan, and he replicated his old place here. What would you like?"

Zoe chewed on her lower lip, the gears of her brain churning, and replied, "We'll take a medium Classico, with extra cheese, green peppers, and mushrooms. And two Cokes." She knew my tastes in toppings as well as my mother did. Better. Zoe was around more.

As soon as the server departed, Zoe smiled at me and said, "She's full of crap. The best pizza south of New York is in New Jersey."

I nodded and said, "She's probably never been to New York. She's a local. Give her a break. Doubtless, she's lived in Florida her entire life. She doesn't care about the ocean, or the food, just making a living."

"Well, let's hope she's right about the food because I'm starving. And before you mention it again, yes, we'll go see that sea gate while we are here."

"Sure," I replied, as if it were no big deal, but the truth was, I was dying to see Fisher Gate. If not for the sea walls, at another three feet of sea level rise, Miami Beach would be gone, as would most of the coast from Boca Raton to Homestead, as far as two miles inland. The city of Miami would survive because it sat up higher, but the gates and sea walls around the lower half of the state were the only things protecting south Florida now.

Ten minutes later our pie arrived, and while Zoe wasn't that impressed, I loved it. Boston had damn fine pizza, but this stuff was a close second for me.

The boardwalk was much more crowded in the late afternoon. We weaved between slow-moving people and tried not to get run over by skaters and long-boarders, all forms of personal wheeled transportation being legal on Miami's boardwalk. As we neared our spot on the beach, we could see our umbrella blowing in a stiff wind that had picked up in the last few minutes.

"Geez, looks like it's trying to take off like a rocket!" I exclaimed, taking off at a run toward it.

Two guys were walking toward us across the hot sand. The taller one reached under our flailing umbrella and started lowering it. "Just to be safe," he said as we reached it.

His friend stuck out his hand to me and I shook it by reflex. "I'm Jason and that's Caleb. Sorry, didn't mean to intrude. We saw your umbrella blowing around and no one here so we thought we'd do a good deed for the day and secure it."

"Well, we are back now," Zoe said, indignantly. Her face took on a flat look, her eyes narrowed, whenever she felt injured or insulted. "We are perfectly capable of lowering our own umbrella."

"Of course! As I said, we didn't see anyone here. We're sitting right down at those chairs there." Jason pointed about fifty feet up the beach. "Um, I think we got off on the wrong foot. Can we start over?"

Nodding, I put my hand on Zoe's shoulder and said, "We thank you for your help. Zoe does, too. Ignore her rudeness. I'm Inga."

Jason smiled, clearly glad to no longer be punished for their act of kindness. "Are you here on spring break? We go to school in Delaware.

Where are you ladies from?"

Zoe remained mute, purposely ignoring their conciliatory efforts.

"Boston College. We're music majors. Nice to meet you," I replied.

Jason said, "Cool. What do you play?"

"Woodwinds mostly, but besides the flute, piccolo, and sax, I've got passable piano skills. Zoe is a wiz at anything with strings. Guitar, cello, upright bass."

I'm not sure if Jason was impressed, intimidated, or horrified.

The tall but silent guy, Caleb, revealed that his mouth did indeed work and said, "Um, if you don't have plans, there is a party here on the beach tonight. Starts at sundown. We'll be here, um, if you want to come and hang out with us."

"Sounds fun." I was thrilled. They were both cute, and as much as I adored Zoe, I wanted more company for the week than just her. Preferably male.

Neither of them was Zoe's type, physically, but I would be happy with a spring break fling with either. Neither the tall skinny one who saved the umbrella or the shorter guy, Jason, would interest Zoe. Both were too skinny and average. Athletic physiques, especially those that leaned toward brawny, were more her style.

"So, we'll meet you guys here?" It was a statement, but I phrased it like a question because I wasn't sure where they wanted to meet up and I sure as hell was not giving out our hotel address to complete strangers, no matter how attractive.

Jason nodded happily and said, "Yeah. Like, sevenish. Last year people barbequed on the beach and shared, but you can bring food or get something from one of the food trucks on the side streets off the boardwalk. You can't bring a cooler, but plastic drink bottles are good as long as there isn't alcohol in it."

I nodded. We knew the beach rules. "See you then."

They said their goodbyes and headed up the beach.

Jason was incredibly good-looking and the other one wasn't bad either, in a gawky, geeky sort of way. I was looking forward to tonight, but for now, I was beat. Zoe and I packed up our belongings, let the rental kiosk know we were done with our chairs and crashed in our hotel room for an hour.

By seven that evening, we had showered, picked up burritos and drinks, and were sitting on colorful towels on the sand. A DJ was spinning a mix of Caribbean salsa and dance music, and crowds thronged the oceanfront. The sun set around 6:30 this time of year, and twilight was fast becoming true dark, making it hard to spot the guys who invited us here. I hoped they wouldn't be a no-show, but really, what did it matter? We had good food, music, and people dancing on the beach to watch.

"Hey," said a voice behind us. "Sorry, we're late. Getting through the crowd is murder!"

It was the silent one, Caleb, who turned out not to be so quiet after all. As the night wore on, I found out just how much he could talk. Oddly, I originally thought Jason was more my type, but the skinny blue-eyed boy with the immigrant Russian parents loved music, was majoring in digital art design, and had the same taste in books as me.

"Hey, Zoe," I shouted to her over the noisy music. "Caleb and I are going for a walk on the beach. I'll catch up with you back at the hotel later."

She nodded, engrossed in the music, and maybe just a little interested in Jason, after all.

I followed Caleb down to the water where the surf packed the sand hard, and walking was easier. He reached down and took my hand and we walked in silence for a couple of minutes. It was blissful listening to the waves crash and breathing the warm, salty air.

Caleb squeezed my hand and asked, "I like your name. Are you Norwegian or something?"

I laughed because he was hardly the first person to think that. "Only partly. My father is half Scottish, half Norwegian, and my mom is German. My name is Danish, but mom just liked it."

No reason to confirm what a total egghead my mother was by telling him she named me after Inge Lehmann, a famous Danish seismologist, simply because Mom admired her. My father had the sense to spell my name with an 'a' at the end so Americans could pronounce it properly.

So far, we were hitting it off. I wasn't going to ruin a good start.

Fast Facts

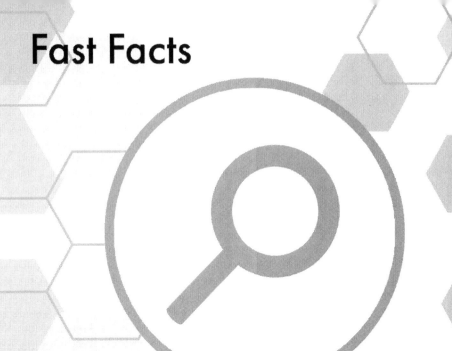

Antarctica's population varies from approximately 4,400 in summer to 1,100 in winter. This population is spread across approximately 40 year-round stations and a range of summer-only stations, camps, and refuges.

The most populated place on the continent is McMurdo Base with about 1,500 summer residents and roughly 200 in the winter. New Zealand's Scott Base is 1.25 mile (2 km) from McMurdo and has about 25 personnel in the summer and 12-15 over the winter. It has been occupied since 1957.

The South Pole Traverse, a.k.a. the McMurdo-South Pole Highway, is a 995 mile (1,600 km) compacted snow road that links McMurdo Station to the Amundsen-Scott South Pole Station.

Chapter 5

Kathryn – Antarctica

I scanned Winter Quarters Bay, my eyes searching for the ice breaker that would guide in the *R/V Richard E. Byrd.* A narrow peninsula on the southern tip of Ross Island created the cove that provided the natural harbor for those few ships that could penetrate the two- to four-meter-thick ice cover. The floating ice pier was getting wider as the winter ice began to encroach. The Coast Guard icebreaker had arrived yesterday and cleared a path into the dock, cut a turning basin in McMurdo Sound, then went back out to the Ross Sea to escort the *Byrd.*

It was getting past time for that ship, and I wondered what was keeping it.

Most of the summer people had already left, beginning with the staff and crew at the Amundsen-Scott South Pole Station. Being at the pole, they got locked in earlier than the rest of the continent, and only about fifty people wintered over at Amundsen. Between McMurdo, Scott Base, and the hardy winter staff at the pole, 312 people were waiting on that ship for the supplies they would need for the next six months. Needless to say, I was getting anxious.

That and I was freezing my ever-loving tail off.

Joshua Levy was an ass. He figured, since I was staying and messing up his evacuation tally numbers, he would conscript me to work unloading, seeing as how I wasn't expected elsewhere on the base. Damn him. I wanted to get back to my seismology research, not play longshoreman.

A voice to my right called out, "I see it. The *Byrd* is landing." Another joker. The station was full of them. The best news of the day though was that many of these jokers, including Chief Evacuation Officer Joshua Levy, would be shipping out on the *Richard E. Byrd* tomorrow.

Until then, however, Josh would do his best to make my life a living hell.

The ice breaker had to stay within 1,000 yards ahead of the *Byrd* to protect the ship from the brash ice, the smaller chunks that float after the ice has been broken. It was a delicate dance between the ships until the Coast Guard vessel turned away and the *Byrd* made its final approach on its own.

As the ship pulled along the ice dock, I prepared for the eventuality of a screaming backache and blisters even through my double-layered gloves.

Two hours later, we had off-loaded all the pallets and brought them into McMurdo's large supply warehouse. Working outside in sub-zero temps was not something you wanted to do for long, so the five of us, with the aid of two forklifts, made as quick work of it as possible. Dakota O'Sullivan, who was one of our chefs but was also cross trained to operate forklifts, directed the unloading operations. Dakota was an interesting person. I really liked them.

Once inside the warehouse, the heat brought the room up a couple of degrees above freezing, which was quite tolerable for unloading crates and unpacking boxes. The crates held everything from construction materials, truck and tractor parts, to mail parcels, dry and frozen food, and scientific instruments. Dakota directed the lift-shlep-unpack process and by lunchtime, all I could do was groan.

No time to nurse aching muscles, I spent the afternoon moving. Lodging at Mac-Town included dorms provided for most of the civilians traveling through the base in the summer. Each pod supported 200 people but only one dorm remained open for the winter, and it wasn't mine. I had to box up my personal gear and bedding and lug them one building over to the winter dorm Josh had assigned me. Sylvia was in the room next door.

I had just finished making up the bed in my new room and crashed on top of it when Sylvia came in. We had an unspoken agreement that if the door was not locked, friends would just enter. After all, it's not like either one of us needed privacy. With our husbands back home, we weren't exactly entertaining.

"Hey," said Sylvia from the doorway. I turned to look at her but was too exhausted even to groan a response, so she went on. "Just a heads up, the ship is pulling out at five o'clock. You going to the pier to wish Marnie and the rest of the summer people off?"

In my experience, ships set off in the morning, but at the ass-end of the world, at this time of year, it was daylight until almost 10 p.m., so it hardly mattered. It was a misconception that Antarctica was all day or all-night fifty percent of the year. It wasn't like the sun flipped a switch.

During this second week of March, our day was almost fourteen hours long. By early-April, that would shorten to nine hours, and then every day in April would lose half an hour until April 24th when the sun would finally set an hour after it rose. From then on, we would have darkness all day until three weeks into September when the sun gloriously rose again. That first day – even though there would be only an hour and a half of sunshine – would be heralded with a party like no one outside of Antarctica had ever seen. That's because Mac-Town's inhabitants took pride in being just a little bit weird. As the saying went, "When you shake the world, the most interesting people fall to the bottom." We had a turkey trot in full costume every Thanksgiving. We were a strange lot.

"Coming." I flung my feet onto the floor and hauled myself to a standing position. Coat, glove liners pushed into gloves, hat, scarf...going outside at McMurdo took so much effort, I almost wondered if it was worth it.

I pulled on all my cold-weather outerwear and followed Sylvia down the hall and through the vestibule door to the walkway that ran alongside the dormitory buildings and led to the pier. Plenty of others were already there doling out hugs and farewells to those leaving. I spied Marnie in the crowd and pulled her aside and into my parka-shrouded arms. I had to shout over the collective din of the well-wishers and the wind. "Damn, woman, I'm going to miss you."

Sylvia was beside me and wrapped her Michelin Man attired self around as much of Marnie as she could. The three of us just stood there, saying nothing, until a blast from the ship's horn made us pull apart. We had planned so many fun things for that voyage home – drinking, sleeping late, and relaxing in the ship's sauna. Now, two of us were staying on the frozen continent.

Without another word, Marnie turned and walked up the gangway. She turned back just as she reached the top and waved. Her weak smile was forced. I knew she was disappointed that we both decided to winter over.

Sylvia and I smiled and waved, and then once Marnie was out of view, we headed back to the station.

"Hey, I'm going to go check some seismic readings at the CSEC. Meet you for dinner in half an hour?" I asked. I was exhausted but could not end my day just yet.

She just nodded and left for the dorm.

Reaching the Crary Science and Engineering Center, I entered a building that usually had a dozen people working in it, but today stood empty. I wasn't the only researcher staying, but apparently, everyone else was either down at the dock, in the dining hall, or somewhere else. It was well after 5:30, but we didn't follow nine to five work hours here.

I removed my outdoor gear and dropped it on the floor of my cubicle. I would be carrying it all to the lockers outside the dining hall shortly or taking it back to my room before eating, but I could not stay in it for even five minutes in the lab. I would quickly overheat. I sat down at my workstation and pulled up the recorded sensor data on my screen. Yesterday it had shown three quakes over 24 hours, but since then, the seismic sensors had picked up another five quakes. All were over magnitude-5, and one of them was 6.2.

Damn. A frequency increase, even if not consistently incremental magnitudes, meant what I feared. My fingers twitched over my keyboard, as if typing something could change the facts on the screen. I wasn't sure how long they would last, if they would continue, or increase, but what I did know was that these seismic readings were not an aberration. These readings were statistically relevant.

I pulled up my email and composed a long message to my daughter, Inga, who was visiting with her roommate in New Jersey for the week off from school and then another message to my husband Nicholas and our 14-year-old son Liam back in Cambridge. I wasn't exactly sure how to tell them that I wouldn't be home for another six months, and I knew I should make phone calls instead, but I chickened out, convincing myself that the seventeen-hour time difference would make it an inconvenient time to call home. It was almost midnight there. Yesterday.

The emails were a cop out and I knew it. I felt like a horrible mother and wife, but I just couldn't let go of my unfinished research. The earthquakes were getting worse, and if the Antarctic Plate destabilized severely enough, entire glaciers could collapse.

Surely they would understand.

My finger hovered over SEND, trembling slightly. I chewed my lower lip, then finally hit the button, picked up my parka, and marched to the dining hall.

Fast Facts

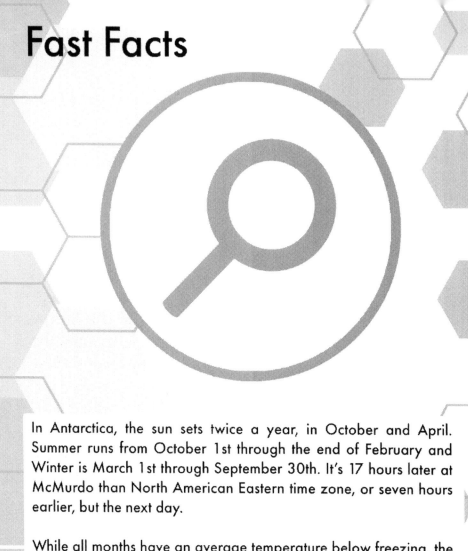

In Antarctica, the sun sets twice a year, in October and April. Summer runs from October 1st through the end of February and Winter is March 1st through September 30th. It's 17 hours later at McMurdo than North American Eastern time zone, or seven hours earlier, but the next day.

While all months have an average temperature below freezing, the warmest months (December and January) may occasionally be above freezing. The place is protected from cold waves from the interior of Antarctica by the Transantarctic Mountains, so temperatures rarely fall below −40°. The highest temperature ever recorded at McMurdo was 51°F (10.8°C) on December 21, 1987.

Chapter 6

Nick – Boston

I woke to pandemonium. *BANG!* Something exploded in the living room. *Oh, damn it,* I thought and looked at the clock. It was 2 a.m. I heaved a sigh as I hauled my tired body from the bed and slipped my feet into the house shoes on the floor. I knew what the noises were and tried to calm myself as I walked down the hall and stepped into the family room.

"Liam!" I shouted. I took a deep breath and held it in before continuing. "Is that really necessary?" This kid had the innate ability to frustrate the crap out of me. After single-parenting for eight months, I could not wait until Kathryn got home.

My son was a video game addict. "Dad, it's break week. I don't have to get up early for school, so what's wrong with playing a game?"

"What's wrong? It's the middle of the night, for Pete's sake! Just because you don't have to get up early doesn't mean you are allowed to stay up all night. And more importantly, *I* don't want to be awake. Turn that thing off before I throw it in the trash. I'm serious. Enough is enough." I rubbed my brow in a vain attempt to ward off the headache building behind my skull.

At that moment, the evil monster on the screen spewed green liquid across Liam's avatar, which uttered an inhuman wail as it melted down to a virtual neon puddle. Liam grumbled. "Now look what you did! You got me killed! Game over."

He turned off the game and continued, "Might as well go to bed. G'night Dad." My son sauntered down the hall and up the stairs to his room, almost gleefully. Even though I could not see his face, I knew he was smiling.

That kid was never going to grow up. Weren't they supposed to start maturing around fourteen? I swore, shut off the manual-switch lights in our house, and aimed my tired body toward the first-floor master bedroom. I crawled back into bed, but now that I was awake, I couldn't shut off my brain.

My thoughts turned to the projects I had been putting off – modernizing some of the things this old house needed. It was an updated 19th century Colonial Revival in the Berkeley Street historic district. It was on the National Register of Historic Places, and as such, every change needed to be approved before it could be done. Still, it was the house I dreamed of growing up, and now I had it, even if the paint was peeling and I'd never be approved to put up siding. I would only be able to get niggling things approved – automatic lights, interfacing with a house AI to control alarms, heating, and air conditioning. Things like that I could get approved. But not at 2 a.m.

I tried to go back to sleep but finally gave up and reached for my tablet to check my email. My eyes had trouble focusing on the screen. At forty-five, they were getting old from decades of staring at monitors. Soon I would have to emulate my daughter and join the world of digital personal assistants. Then, I could have my email read to me instead of trying to force astigmatic eyes to do work cut out for the young.

A flashing email icon from Kathryn made me smile. I couldn't wait for her to get home. She would be leaving Antarctica today, her time, and the ship would be pulling into a New Zealand port two days later, then the long flight back to Boston. I really missed her.

I opened the email eagerly, but it wasn't long before my joy soured. My fingers touched my parted lips as I read more of her letter. My expression grew tight as my surprise turned to anger.

Her research was that important that she was staying there through the Antarctic winter? I could feel my jaw clenching.

Did she ever think of anyone but herself when she made these decisions? First, to disappear for more than half a year, and now to stay there? Geez, we might as well be divorced at this point. Between my full-time graduate teaching at MIT, the housework, parenting Liam, and being available for a somewhat-but-not-quite grown daughter, this was getting to be too much. I'd hung on this long because I knew she would be home soon. But damn, I'd done more than my share of the work for the last eight months, and now I must deal with being a single parent for another six.

I felt abandoned. Hurt. Angry. But mostly, I felt betrayed by the woman I loved.

Fast Facts

Warm ocean water is carving an enormous channel into the underside of the Dotson ice shelf, one of the key floating ice shelves of West Antarctica. The warm water flows into the deep cavity beneath the ice shelf, and then streams upward toward the floating ice as it mixes with buoyant meltwater. The warm water constantly melts just one part of the shelf, creating the channel.

Dotson has been thinning at about eight feet per year since 1994, but the ice flowing outward through the shelf has sped up by 180 percent. Forty-five feet of ice thickness is lost every year. As a result of this highly uneven melting, the Dotson ice shelf could be melted all the way through in 40 years, rather than 170 years, which would be the time it would take if the melt occurred evenly. As the thinning continues, the shelf may break up dramatically.

The undermining of the shelf will increase the flow of ice outward from the glaciers behind it, which contributes to sea level rise. If the ice shelf collapsed, sea level rise would speed up radically.

Chapter 7

Inga – Miami

I woke up way too early again, so I went for a run on the beach. I dressed in warm sweatpants and a jacket because although this was Florida, the morning temperature wasn't exactly tropical.

It was so calming to hear the surf breaking on the sand. I was impressed by the lack of debris on the beach as well, considering the number of late-night revelers. The beach was almost deserted this early in the morning, just a couple walking holding hands, and a few joggers. After about a mile, I turned back and retraced my steps. A two-mile run wasn't terribly long, but on the beach, it probably burned as many calories as three times that distance on pavement. Besides, after the long winter, I was out of shape.

I ran directly to the hotel lobby for a cup of coffee and then walked the block back to the waterfront to sit in the sand and drink it. As I watched the waves break, my phone buzzed. Not sure who would call me at 7 a.m., I said, "Lilith, answer call."

There was no video transmission, only voice. It was Caleb. "Hi, Inga. Are you out running on the beach?"

"I was. Why? Did you see me?" Was he stalking me? I hadn't even told him what hotel we were staying in.

"I'm sitting on a deck chair in front of the Palms, and you ran right by me. I didn't know you were a runner."

I wondered if he could hear the smirk on my face. "I'm not much of one, obviously, since I've given up in favor of a cup of coffee instead. Wanna join me?" The Palms was less than half a mile south. It was a four-star oceanfront resort, something Zoe and I could not afford during the high season.

"Sure. Give me ten minutes to slog through the sand. I'm not a runner, so forgive me. It will take me more time than it took you. But I'm walking now. I've got on a navy-blue t-shirt. Can you see me yet? I would wave, but then I'd look more like a dork than I usually do." Caleb laughed at his own joke. He was kind of cute, and the goofy laugh was endearing.

I did see him coming and told him so. Meanwhile, I pulled up my email to check that quickly before he got to my spot on the beach and saw one from my mother just as he arrived. "You see me now, right? I'm hanging up. Have a family crisis by email to attend to."

He said that was fine and before I was done reading the email, he had arrived. "Eeew, wet sand. My favorite," said Caleb as he plopped down beside me in the damp sand. "What's the emergency?"

I closed the email, which Lilith had presented in my heads-up display. The angle of HUDs was such that it was difficult for anyone else to see it, even if they were next to you. It was totally antisocial.

Caleb was dressed in tight jeans that were such a light blue, they were almost white. The air had warmed up substantially, as had I from my run and my jacket was lying next to me where I had unceremoniously dropped it on the sand. I pulled it toward him and spread it out. "Here, sit on this. Those jeans won't stay that color sitting here."

"Isn't it the guy that's supposed to be chivalrous?" He winked. I just groaned in response, so he asked again, "What's the emergency?"

I sighed. "Not an emergency, just a crisis. Well, not even that, for me. My dad, on the other hand, will see it as a crisis. My mom has opted to stay in Antarctica for another six months."

"Whoa, Antarctica! What's she doing there?" The look on Caleb's face was *exactly* the reason why I never told anyone what my mom did for a living.

Forced to tell him the whole story, I had to let him in on my embarrassing family dynamic: my mother was Supreme Geek Extraordinaire, and my father was only slightly behind her as a college prof. "So, who's the dork now? As if being a music major isn't bad enough – I mean, at least that has some band geek cred – my parents are the world's biggest geeks. Nerds. Dorks. Whatever you want to call it, I am hopelessly, genetically, uncool."

In response, he leaned over and kissed me. A long, deep, passionate kiss. When I came up for air, sweating and flustered, I stammered, "Wha...what was that for?"

"Inga, you are anything but uncool. You are amazing, and now I know where you get it."

I was speechless – a rarity for me. I also didn't have a whole lot of experience with men and wasn't sure if he was genuine or just trying to sleep with me. Probably both. That's what everyone did here during spring break, right? I mean, I'd had boyfriends before, in high school. Well, truth be told, neither of those two had lasted long. I was a band geek and honor student and most of the guys I spent time with were either taken or gay. I had lots of male friends, but precious few that led to romantic encounters. I wasn't inexperienced, just not actually *experienced*.

And yes, it *was* spring break, and I was going to get the most out of it, even if I never saw this guy again once the week was over. I put my hand behind his head and pulled him in for another kiss. I wasn't sure how long we one-upped each other on kisses, but I enjoyed every moment of it. We made out and watched the surf, sharing my impromptu jacket-blanket, until finally, my stomach rumbled louder than the Atlantic Ocean.

"Breakfast?" I asked.

Caleb nodded, stood, and finally getting the opportunity to be chivalrous, reached out his hand to help me up. I took it, grabbing my jacket from the sand in one fluid motion, and stood. "I get free breakfast with my room. Let's go back to the Palms."

"Won't they notice you've brought a guest?" I asked, following him down near the water. Our bare feet made imprints in the sand until the surf washed them away.

"They will, but I'll give my room number and they don't care who the second person is. Jason isn't much for breakfast or being up early, so it would go to waste anyway."

I laughed. "He's absolutely perfect for Zoe."

The Palms had an outdoor eating area, encircled by a bamboo fence and exquisite landscaping. Aloe bushes, palm trees, and exotic flowers ringed the verandah. The buffet was much more extensive than our cheap hotel and even had an omelet station with a chef. I took full advantage. One thing I learned from my few experiences with the male half of the population was to be myself. A lot of girls ate like shy little birds around men, but I didn't. I was starved, and I wasn't going to let some possible relationship with a guy stop me from being me. I didn't care what he thought of my weight.

All the tables with the best water views were taken so we sat in the center of the terrace, surrounded by people. Vacationers, families with kids, and students alike, yet somehow it felt like we were the only two people on the planet.

How cliché.

"So, do you want to go play tourist in the city today? Or are you planning to spend the whole week on the beach, picking up girls?" I was hedging my emotional bets in case he said no. I'd given him an easy out if he wanted it. I was also hoping Zoe wouldn't mind if I invited him to tag along on our planned trip, if he agreed.

Caleb didn't disappoint me. "I'd love to go. I've been to Miami a few times before. Have you?"

I shook my head.

"I can play tour guide if you want. I'd love to show you one of my favorite parts of Miami – the Wynwood arts district. It's got some fantastic galleries and loads of street art. Or we could head over to Little River. It's a quiet enclave wedged between Little Haiti and El Porto Village. Full of old boat building warehouses that are now eclectic shops, restaurants, and art galleries. Catch some jazz streaming from open-air eateries."

I liked this guy. I'm not sure how I thought that Jason was more my type at first, and silently chided myself for ogling the guy with the striking good looks rather than the plain one.

We made plans to meet at our hotel lobby at 9:30. The galleries didn't open until ten, and I was fairly certain we could get Carlos to drop us off downtown in the hotel van. Caleb offered to walk me home – sweet, but corny – so I declined, saying I'd get in another short run along the beach before getting ready for the day.

I was still whistling happy tunes as I stepped into the shower.

I was pleasantly surprised to find Zoe awake and setting out clothes when I emerged from the bathroom. "Good morning, late sleeping roommate."

She grunted. "Need coffee."

"I've been up for hours. Took a run, had breakfast at the Palms with Caleb, and got a second run on my way back. Grabbed you a coffee from the lobby, too. It's on the dresser."

That brightened her usual morning gloom and inspired her to speak actual words, rather than grunts. "I love you, Inga."

I laughed. "I arranged for Carlos to drive us downtown in the hotel van at 9:30. You have time to shower and grab some food downstairs before, if you want it."

She took another sip from the paper cup before saying, "Then get outta my way so I can get ready."

I stepped aside and as she entered the bathroom I added, "Hope you don't mind, but Caleb and Jason are going to join us to play tourist today."

"Great!" Her sarcasm seeped through the bathroom door. "So happy to be of service as your wingman. Wingwoman. Whatever."

Caleb and Jason were waiting in the lobby when the elevator door opened, and we rushed outside to meet the hotel van.

"Good morning, Carlos," said Zoe, in a voice that was way too flirtatious. I could tell she still had some weird crush on this older guy and wondered why she was more interested in him than the perfectly good college guy standing next to her. But that's Zoe.

"Good morning, ladies, and good morning to your gentlemen friends." His accent made every word sound exotic. That's probably what Zoe liked – not the guy, but the voice. "The concierge tells me you wish to go downtown. I am headed to the airport to pick up guests, so I can drop you on the way. Do you have a location in mind or just the middle of downtown?"

Caleb answered since he knew the area. "If you take the I-195 causeway over, you can drive through Wynwood and drop us there on your way to the airport. It won't even take you much out of the way."

"Yes, that will be fine. You will enjoy the art galleries. Do the art walk tour as well. I will take you to one of the galleries that opens early. Oh, and some galleries aren't open on Sunday. No guarantees."

"Thank you so much, Carlos," she replied as she squeezed across the middle row of seats to the far side.

"So, what's the deal with your mom anyway?" asked Caleb. "You told me so much about her and your family over breakfast, but not the reason why she's in Antarctica or why she's staying."

"Wait, your mom's not coming home?!" exclaimed Zoe. With rushing around to get ready this morning, I hadn't told her.

"I got an email from her this morning."

I took a breath before launching into her message. "My mom is studying earthquakes down there because Antarctica is one of the only places in the world with truly quiet surroundings and no environmental noise. The seismometer readings there are directly joined to the continent itself. She's *staying* because the earthquakes along the Antarctic Plate have been happening more often and getting stronger. She's worried that since the activity has grown so much in just the last couple of weeks, that leaving now would mean she would miss measurements that are crucial to her research."

"But if it's important, isn't it better she stays?" asked Jason. "I mean it's not like you can't survive another half a year without her. You aren't a kid."

"Yeah, not really the issue. I have a 14-year-old brother and my dad's been doing the single parent thing while mom is away. He's doing okay with it, but I'm sure he was counting down the days until he wasn't the only one in charge of riding herd on my pain in the ass brother. It takes two parents to team up against that one." Everyone laughed, but I could tell they knew exactly what I meant. Every family had someone like Liam.

My father comes down to campus once a week to have dinner with me, usually dropping Liam off at a friend's beforehand, except for once when he brought the kid along. That one time was all it took for Zoe to figure out what a pain my little brother was.

"Your dad will survive it, Inga. What I want to know is what happens if those earthquakes down there get worse? Won't everyone at McMurdo be in danger? I mean, staying is a big risk, isn't it?" asked Zoe.

"Yeah, it's a risk. Mom said that most of the quakes are happening off the coast, at the edge of the Antarctic Plate. Most of the continent is in the interior of the tectonic plate. It was all in her email. She's explained this to me before, but my mom knows I don't pay attention to the science stuff. Anyway, she says the risk from earthquakes isn't really the issue. It's what happens to the glaciers when they occur."

"What do you mean?" asked Caleb, looking confused. "Will an earthquake melt the ice?"

So, this guy may know even less about science than I do. One point in the negative for him. Not that I'm keeping score.

"Of course not, but they could shake glaciers apart. People have been studying the ice for decades, especially with global warming. Mom's got a glaciologist friend there, Sylvia, who is worried that the warming ocean water is melting glaciers from underneath and could destabilize the entire ice sheet. The biggest glaciers are huge, like the size of Pennsylvania. When the underside of the glacier melts, it leaves the rest floating on top of the ocean, so only part of it is on land anymore, and the rest looks like a giant fingernail. If those fingernails break off, the floating ice shelves don't raise sea level any more than an ice cube melting in a drink doesn't change how much liquid is in the glass, but, and here's the kicker, those ice shelves hold the rest of the glacier back. The ice shelf is the part on land – and that's a *lot* of ice. If they collapse, mountains of ice will slide into the ocean." I felt like a college professor. That was more knowledge than I even knew I had on the subject.

No one said anything for a moment until finally Caleb finished my lecture for me. "If an earthquake shakes apart a really big glacier, it's going to cause all kinds of shit storms."

"Yup."

"Does your mom have any idea how long it would take for all that ice to melt if one of those giant fingernails lets loose a mountain of ice? I mean, forget about the three feet of ocean rise over the past ten years. I imagine chunks of ice that big would raise the sea level higher than anyone is prepared to deal with."

"Not sure, but I'm more worried about her being down there if a quake like that hit. I wasn't worried about her during the summer because there were ships and planes and ways to get out. But now? The last ship left, and the planes are few and far between during the winter. Where is she going to go if an earthquake shakes them up, and then a giant glacier collapses? Shit. It's too much to think about."

I turned to look out the window of the van. We had crossed the causeway over Biscayne Bay. Back in the late twenty-tens, the city of Miami started a study on sea-level rise and found out that the interstate and three causeways linking Miami Beach and the rest of the city were vulnerable with even just one or two feet of sea level rise. That would have cut Miami Beach off from the mainland, so, in the twenties, they got funding to raise the roadbed by five feet on all four roadways. Since then, the water had risen three feet, and even though climatologists had been saying that the water would continue to rise, I guess Miami figured the ocean couldn't go up by much more. Besides, these roads were good for another two feet.

Any idiot could see that the beach wasn't as wide as it used to be. None of those fancy hotels started at almost the water's edge, after all, but I guess the real estate people and tourism experts had no choice. What could they do, move a hotel? Then in the late twenties, the city built the Fisher Gate and Dodge Island barrier wall. When the gate was closed, it was totally cut off from the Atlantic Ocean. Since the gate was only opened at low tide, allowing the ships in and out twice a day, the water was at pre-Greenland glacier collapse level for all but two hours a day. Biscayne Bay was more a giant lake than a bay. There was only so much humanity could do to stop the ocean.

I watched the sailboats on the bay and thought how lovely it was. No matter what was happening to the ocean, Miami was still the city of pleasure. It had no industry to speak of, just tourism. For me and hundreds of thousands just like me, that meant cool beaches, hotels, restaurants, shopping and art, plus magnificent cruise ships to gawk at.

I was jolted out of my musing by the van slowing. As he pulled up to the curb, Carlos announced, "I can't park here, so you'll need to get going. Have a fun day and watch yourselves in this city. Not all of Miami is good. Away from the beach, it is poor and gritty. There are many poor people here and tourists just don't go to some neighborhoods. If you find yourself on a street where every house or building is behind locked, chain link fences, and the walls are covered in graffiti, turn around and walk back to better areas. Please watch yourselves, and when you are ready to come back, call the hotel. If I can swing by, I will, or you can get a rideshare."

We thanked him profusely for the free ride and went straight to the contemporary art gallery three blocks from the Wynwood Walls, an outdoor museum with huge, colorful street art. But that didn't open until 10:30, so we figured a quick walk through this gallery first, then grab a cup of coffee and walk the three blocks to the outdoor art gallery.

Nursing my third cup of coffee for the day, I turned my face into the sun and closed my eyes. Caleb asked, "Something wrong, Inga?"

"No." I looked at him and smiled. "Just enjoying a perfect day. I'm so glad you like art, Caleb."

"Hey, don't paint me as one-dimensional. I like music, too."

It was a picture-perfect day. After the Wynwood Walls, we walked downtown and picked up the Metromover. The train was standing room only, but growing up in a Boston suburb, I'd gotten good at strap hanging by the time I was tall enough to reach the handholds. Still, it was nice that Caleb held my arm to support me.

Zoe stood across from me and said, "Don't you two look cute

together." Then she rolled her eyes in typical Zoe sarcasm. I didn't care. We were having a great time.

"Hey, there's that sushi place with the five-star reviews and two-star prices," said Zoe, swinging her head sideways to get a better view. "Want to hop off the next stop for lunch?"

As it turned out, Jason didn't like sushi. He called it bait, but we enjoyed the restaurant anyway, and he was able to get a nice plate of *cooked* fish. We sat outside at a sidewalk table and watched all the people. Downtown had a different vibe than the beach did; more cosmo, less bikini. After lunch, we spent the afternoon wandering through a couple more galleries and a bunch of stores we couldn't afford. By 6 o'clock, we were starved, but we had spent so much on lunch that we just grabbed street food and ate as we walked.

I called the hotel, but just missed Carlos and they said it could be an hour before he got to us, so I had Lilith arrange a rideshare for us. Since Lilith knew where we were, where we wanted to go, and had my payment info, it was much easier than using my phone to decide which rideshare app had the quickest time, best rating, and lowest price. My parents called me lazy for using the DPA. Back in their day, they had to actually download apps to their phones and do it all manually. I wasn't lazy; that was just a pain in the ass.

Our car arrived – an electric blue compact that was a tight fit for all four of us, plus the driver, but I didn't mind being mashed up between Zoe and Caleb. I edged closer to Caleb, just because.

Ten minutes later, the driver delivered us to the Palms, and rather than continue to our hotel, Zoe announced that she was getting out there to hang out with Jason, so I decided to stay as well. I wasn't surprised when she went into the hotel with Jason and headed for the elevator.

Seeing I was a bit uncomfortable with my shameless roommate, Caleb asked, "Want to take a walk on the beach? We can head up to your hotel and, if you've had enough of me by then, I'll say good night and walk you to your door."

"How gallant of you." I may have sounded sarcastic, but I did think it was chivalrous of Caleb to do that.

He smiled as if he understood my mask of sarcasm and said, "I'm glad I dared to finally speak to you, Inga. You might have noticed that I'm a little quiet at first." He took my hand and led me to the beach where we took off our shoes and began strolling north. It was crowded, forcing us to thread our way through the people. I breathed in the salty aroma and felt the softness of the sand between my toes. The setting sun was fading behind us, cascading apricot and turquoise shades across the sand and fading into brilliant gold across the overlapping waves. White bubbles reached toward us as waves crested onto the shore.

"There is nothing wrong with quiet," I replied finally.

"There is when it's caused by shyness bordering on paralysis. I was overwhelmingly shy as a kid, like hiding behind my mother's skirts shy. I *literally* hid behind her, using her as a shield between me and the world. In elementary school, I wanted to talk to the other kids but was always worried about what to say and how to say it. What if I got it wrong? I worked at it slowly over the years, but still only had one good friend, and I used him as a buffer from the world too, especially with girls. My nerves were so bad about asking a girl out that I shook at just the thought. Social situations scared the pants off me."

His hand was getting sweaty in mine, but I didn't want to point that out. Instead, I asked, "So what happened? You're talking to me."

He laughed a short, snort of a laugh. "College happened. Suddenly, I was one of thousands. Hiding was a given. Everyone ignored me at UD. Delaware may be a small state, but the University of Delaware is not. You have to work to be noticed. I guess I just figured that if I didn't try to stand out, I'd be fine, and by Christmas of freshman year, I got over being shy."

He angled his face down a bit to look into my eyes and finished. "Mostly."

I stopped walking and repositioned my shoes under my arm and as I did so, Caleb paused next to me. I stretched up on my toes, sinking a bit into the wet sand as I did, and pressed my lips onto his. They were sweet and silken, and I lost myself in the moment. His arms wrapped around me and ventured over my curves, exploring. I let out a soft whimper of anticipation as his fingers touched the small of my back.

And then a rogue wave knocked us both over.

Soaking wet and laughing hysterically, Caleb stood and reached out a hand to pull me up, but instead, I pulled him back down to the sand and rolled on top of his thin yet muscular body. I brushed sand away from his neck with my fingertips, then ran my lips up the side of it, back to his face, and landed an intense kiss on his lips. His very smell was flooding my senses now and I got lost in him.

A moment later, some obnoxious spring breaker tripped over us in the growing darkness as he rushed to rescue a Frisbee before the ocean consumed it. Caleb helped me to my feet, and we retrieved our shoes and phones from higher along the beach and walked silently north, hand in hand. When we reached the high-rise hotel that was my landmark for finding my hotel a block off the ocean, I said, "You should come in with me and get dry. There is laundry on the first floor. We can throw your shorts and shirt in the dryer."

He followed me across the boardwalk and down the narrow road to my meager seven-story budget accommodations and asked, "What will I wear while my clothes are drying?"

We entered the lobby and got to the elevator, and I pushed the up button. I looked appreciatively at his squared shoulders and muscled upper arms visible in the wet t-shirt. "Why do you need to wear anything?"

Caleb smiled and I saw the shyness behind the false confidence. Perhaps he had not outgrown that emotion yet. It was endearing.

Fast Facts

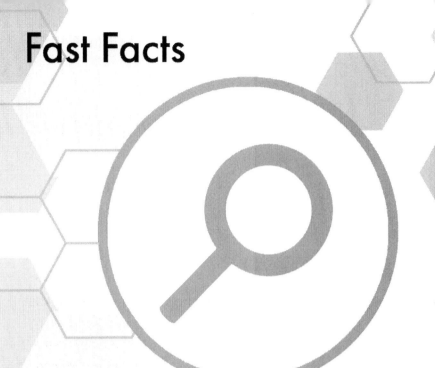

The Antarctic Plate is made up of 13 distinct areas of seismicity, with the three on the continent the least active and the 10 in the surrounding ocean the most. East Antarctica is the most seismically active area on the continent, while the oceanic region has considerable tectonic stress between the Antarctic Plate, the Pacific Plate, and the Nazuca micro-Plate. There is also a lot of seismic activity in the three volcanic areas of Deception Island, Mt. Erebus, and Melbourn — the one in Antarctica, not Australia.

For many decades, Antarctica had been considered one of the least seismic regions of the planet, but since the development of global networks measuring seismic activity, the number of earthquakes detected around the Antarctic continent has increased exponentially, in no small part due to the equipment to measure it, rather than the actual seismic activity.

Chapter 8
Kathryn – Antarctica

I woke up early and walked over to the lab before breakfast. The Crary Lab looked like a giant "H" with an extra half-letter hook jutting off the right side. It was designed as three pods, divided into the earth science and atmospheric science pod; the aquarium pod; and the biology and core pod, which had a second floor. My office was in the middle pod, in the earth sciences half, and my office sat next door to the Mt. Erebus Volcano Observatory, which made sense since volcanism and seismic activity were often linked.

I had access to all twenty-one seismographs on the continent, plus those offshore. The instruments were housed in an orange box and buried deep in holes in the snow, and a framework tower stood above them not only to mark their locations but to house the aboveground equipment. Solar power ran the seismic stations during the summer, and batteries kept them going during the dark winter months.

Those dark months would be starting soon so I had to get everything done before the summer season ended.

Seismographs had been operating in Antarctica since the first one was installed at the South Pole in 1957. I had been evaluating seismicity in the Antarctic, including the ocean surrounding it, based on compiled data from the International Seismological Center (ISC) and my readings during my tenure here.

We had records of seismic observations from the summit of Mt. Erebus going back to 1981, especially during its phase of volcanic eruptions between 1984 and 1990. Those eruptions were ejection of incandescent cinder and lava bombs to altitudes of up to a few hundred meters, but they were small to medium in volume, with only sporadic violence. The curious thing about the current readings of seismic activity I was recording was that it was equivalent to the eruptions during that period, yet Mt. Erebus was not currently active.

That meant that the current seismic activity was shifting the continental plates rather than blowing the top off the mountain.

That was not good.

I blew air out the gap in my front teeth in a half-hearted whistle and gathered up my data tablet, trying to walk toward the dining hall without bumping into any walls as I continued to read the overnight sensor data. Luckily, there were so few people here for the winter that I didn't physically run into anyone on the way. Once I had my coffee and breakfast, I sat at my usual table, beating Sylvia by only five minutes.

She sat down across from me and said something.

"Huh," I replied.

"Take your nose out of the tablet and pay attention, Kathryn," replied Sylvia.

I did as ordered, and sipped coffee silently.

"Listen. I'm going to head up to Thwaites today while we still have daylight. The helo is heading out at 9 a.m. Want to come along? It might be the last look we get at the doomsday glacier before the long night."

I looked at my watch. It was a few minutes past seven, giving me almost two hours before her helicopter transport left. I nodded my head. "I could do some analysis on these troubling seismic readings before we leave. Yeah, I'll go."

Sylvia raised one eyebrow. "How troubling? Different than before, or have you just obtained more data to substantiate your previous readings?"

"Both. I've got more data but I'm also looking at the old data with new methodologies. My theory is that there is an impending quake of high magnitude, but at this point, I can't predict the time frame. That's why I need more analysis."

Sylvia asked, "Could the seismic readings be from glacial earthquakes, rather than actual seismic activity?"

Glacial earthquakes generated surface waves that lasted longer than twenty-five seconds and were comparable in strength to those radiated by standard magnitude-5 earthquakes. Glacial earthquakes were the one place where Sylvia's expertise and mine overlapped.

I chewed my lower lip, thinking, before replying. "It's always a possibility. Glacial earthquakes radiate almost no high-frequency energy, which is why they weren't detected or located by traditional earthquake monitoring systems."

"Until you installed your sensors here," finished Sylvia. She knew the logic behind my research better than most seismologists did, her focus on glaciers helping her recognize the relevance.

"Yes, but those readings could not only be from true plate tectonic activity or glacial earthquakes, but there is also a slight probability that they arise from ice quakes."

Ice quakes were vibrations in glaciers and ice sheets that ranged from small creaks and groans to abrupt slips equivalent to a magnitude-7 earthquake, the shaking indicating movement in the ice.

Ice quakes terrified Sylvia. Nothing could disrupt an ice sheet more violently or suddenly than an ice quake.

She nodded and said, "Not for nothing, but that's why I'm asking you to go up to Thwaites with me. We can make a visual inspection of the glacier and determine if there has been any slippage in the month since I last took readings. I could use your help with the cameras. It's helpful to have images from multiple angles."

"You don't have to sell me. I already agreed. Let me tie up a few loose ends and get my cold-weather gear and an overnight bag," I told her.

"That works for me. Meet me at the Field Science Support building at 8:15. I've got a crawler arranged to get us to the Helicopter Operations and Passenger Terminal. Try not to be late. There are only so many hours in a day." She ate silently, waved goodbye, and left me sitting in the dining hall alone.

There are only so many hours in a day. That was never truer than the beginning of winter in the Antarctic. West Antarctica would have fourteen hours of daylight today, but since the sun rose four hours ago, we would only have eight hours from the time we ascended in the helo, and it took six to seven hours to fly to Thwaites from McMurdo depending on weather and winds. There was an overnight base camp there, with a helicopter landing pad and a weeks' worth of supplies in the shelter and fuel for the helicopter. We would sleep there then inspect the glacier tomorrow morning, and then take the rest of the day returning to McMurdo.

Thwaites was so remote that only a couple dozen people had ever been up close and personal with it. It was in West Antarctica, like McMurdo, but almost 1,600 kilometers up the coast. Antarctica was so vast it boggled the mind. Few people had any idea that the continent was 50 percent larger than Europe, the U.S., or Canada.

I finished eating and carried my coffee back to my lab and checked my email first. There was a message from Marnie, still on the ship carrying her home. She said that the trip out had been horrible, and we were lucky to still be at Mac-Town. Antarctica had a circumpolar current, a band of deep water that insulated the continent from the outside, but it was driven by winds, so the seas were rough, and there were strong gusts at the surface. Marnie had thrown up the entire voyage out of the continent. She was glad to be into the southern sea now and heading for New Zealand, where the ship was finally able to pick up satellite signal for phone and email. A big part of me wanted to be onboard that ship with her, even if it was a literal gut-wrenching experience.

I backed up all my data and copied the latest recordings to my laptop. Being stuck on a helicopter for seven hours each way over the next two days would give me plenty of time to analyze it all. I put all my equipment into the insulated thermal laptop carrier that was standard issue at McMurdo. You couldn't walk outside any distance without severe damage to electronics. Batteries didn't like frigid temps, neither did LCD screens, not to mention what condensation could do to circuits and memory platters. Computers were remarkably resilient dealing with low temperatures, but only down to about zero Fahrenheit, or negative seventeen Celsius.

That was a warm day in Antarctica.

Humans weren't built for this crap either, I reminded myself as I gathered my things and walked across the passageway to the Central Services Building, and from there, through another passageway to the six interconnected dorm pods. The winter dorm was the closest pod as the other five had been sealed off for the next six months. As much as I disliked the inconvenience of moving, these quarters were much more convenient than my summer accommodations had been.

Packing in Antarctica was easy, but bulky. The helicopter would have emergency tents, sleeping bags, food, and water, in case we had to land unexpectedly, but I still needed my personal stuff. Besides my toiletries bag, pared down to just a toothbrush, toothpaste, deodorant, and a hairbrush – I'd be a thousand miles from the nearest shower, so I didn't pack shampoo – I also included undergarments and a change of clothes.

Here, that didn't mean panties and a bra. Antarctic undergarments included full length double-thermal long johns and long sleeve undershirt. The pants I had on would do, but I brought extra shirts and sweaters. Layers were the key to survival.

Another key to survival at McMurdo was the good old-fashioned wagon. Carrying all my gear plus my clothes would have been exhausting, but a few years ago, someone in Procurement had ordered two hundred red plastic wagons. Moms and kids around the world pulled these carts loaded down with children or toys, but at McMurdo, they were convenient, stackable, and unbreakable everything-haulers. Plus, they were charmingly kitschy. You had to have a sense of humor to work here.

I pulled my little red wagon through the passage to Central Services, walked through the massive building to Field Science Support to the airlock-style exit. Sylvia wasn't there yet so I waited. The new campus of McMurdo Station had been built over five years, with prefabricated components brought by ship and constructed on-site. The building was a highly insulated envelope that improved energy management and reduced unnecessary exposure to harsh elements outside. It also had floor to ceiling windows, making good use of natural light for half the year. The windows were triple insulated to avoid heat loss, and also had built-in micro-louvers that could be turned to close off the view. For the last six months, the louvers had been closed at night to block out the midnight sun. During the dark winter, the base would use massive halogen lights in the courtyard outside – not precisely simulating day, but close – for ten hours, and the louvers would open and close on a timer to let in the light. It was a practical scheme to deal with the perpetual darkness and its psychological effects.

"Hey, Kathryn, how the hell did you beat me here?" Sylvia said, coming up behind me.

"It's more a question of 'why' than 'how.' I didn't want you to rib me again about always being late," I responded.

Without another word, we went through the airlock, into the vast foyer between the base proper and the outer door and helped each other into our outdoor clothing. It was a bit like I imagined an astronaut dressing for a spacewalk, but without the air tanks. The crawler driver was already dressed and checking his gear by the time we finished. I thought it was Pieter Nordling, but until he spoke, I wasn't sure. Everyone looked alike covered in Antarctic outerwear.

Hauling our wagons, we exited the building. I didn't think I would ever get over the blast that hit you full in the face in Antarctica. The driver led us to the crawler, a lightweight, personal tracked vehicle that we used to navigate between buildings and outer facilities. The crawlers were designed to traverse the worst conditions Antarctica could dish out.

Once inside the cab, and out of the wind, I was able to confirm that our driver was indeed Pieter. He was a Dutch construction worker, wintering at McMurdo. Unlike me, this was his fifth year here. Those who come for only one season were called "the one and done-ers." I had planned to be one myself.

Pieter had retired at fifty-five and being a single man with grown children, he enjoyed the half-year break from home. He spent the other half of the year split between three separate sets of children and grandchildren, who never tired of hearing their *Grootvader's* stories.

Pieter had a slight accent, somewhat Germanic but if you didn't know he was from the Netherlands, you might have thought he was from the Midwest. "Your helicopter is waiting at the passenger terminal. I just drove Rothan and Phil up there half an hour ago. I think they are as eager to see that doomsday glacier as you gals are. Wish I could go, but right now there are only two of us on crawler duty and I can't leave the base. But I'll be here to pick you up the minute you return. The pilots will radio ahead as soon as you are close to landing. I want to get you out of the deep freeze as quickly as possible after that long return flight."

"Thanks, Pieter," said Sylvia. "I'll say this much; we appreciate all you do for the base." She flashed him a bright smile that, if I didn't know better, said that she appreciated more than his work.

Crawlers did not move fast but that was the norm for this continent. From the ice to animals, things moved slowly Way Down Under. The only thing that ever moved fast on this continent was the wind, but luckily today, it was within acceptable levels, or we would not be going anywhere.

As we approached the passenger terminal, I saw the helo being readied on the pad. All the helicopters at McMurdo were red with white and blue insignia. It wasn't some patriotic American thing – red was the easiest to see in the white world that was Antarctica. Most of the arctic-rated helicopters sat eight passengers, but it was usually more like four, plus gear and two pilots. We also had two larger ones that carried up to twenty-four passengers. Our flying tour buses.

Pieter parked the crawler and helped us get our gear into the helo before wishing us well and pulling away. Sylvia waved goodbye to him, although I was fairly sure he couldn't see her inside the helicopter from the interior of the crawler.

This wasn't my first helicopter trip in Antarctica. I had been to Amundsen-Scott Station, better known as the South Pole, a few weeks after arriving at McMurdo, to check on their seismograph, plus I'd planted another seismograph inland. In general, I did not mind flying, but helicopters always made me a bit nervous. Realistically, things made of steel should not fly or float, yet I flew in jets, turboprops, and cruised on the ocean in floating steel. So far, so good.

"What was that all about?" I asked her, settling myself into my seat and belting in even before Rothan or Phil could instruct us to do just that.

"What? He's a good-looking guy, and it's been eight months since I've seen my charming husband. Nothing wrong with making conversation with a nice guy." Her stupid-looking smile befitted a teenager, not a woman in her forties.

"Uh-huh." I let the subject drop, preferring to talk with the pilots over our headsets. Phil gave us a running narration of the sights below us and Rothan flew the helicopter. They would switch off every ninety minutes, landing at a designated area and quickly changing sides, before taking off again. By 4 p.m. we should be landing at the base camp just south of the glacier in the Amundsen Sea. Researchers had established the base a few years ago. It could hardly be called a 'base,' being only one lone shelter almost entirely covered by snow. But it had heat, electricity, a latrine, kitchen, and four bunk beds. Cozy.

An hour into the trip I lost interest in the scenery and opened my laptop to get some work done. Antarctica was a spectacular place, but there was only so much white desolation I could handle.

As I read through the charts of seismic data, I thought back to what Sylvia had surmised about glacial earthquakes. "I thought about those ice quakes of yours. Nominally, I know what they are, but you know more about glaciers."

"Duh."

Alright, so she was still a bit annoyed about my quip about her advances toward Pieter. I rolled my eyes at her. "Grow up."

Now she was laughing. "Okay, so what can I tell you about the earth shaking that *you* don't already know?"

"Not the earth. The ice. We pick up signals from ice quakes, and I know to dismiss them, but I'm not sure I understand exactly how ice can mimic what the earth does."

"You have to understand tabular icebergs. When the edges of two icebergs rub together during glancing, they create a 'strike-slip' collision.

Iceberg-originated harmonics happen during extended episodes of strike-slip ice quakes."

"Of course! And those ice quakes show up on seismic sensors as tremors," I exclaimed.

"Yep. The thing is, harmonic tremors could provide useful information for the study of iceberg behavior, and a possible method for remotely monitoring iceberg activity," replied Sylvia.

We made our first landing and Phil took the controls, which were on the right side of the helicopter's cockpit. As co-pilot, Rothan was now able to play tourist himself and was eagerly looking at the undulating ice beneath us. Our headsets were all on the same channel, and even though the pilots had not been participating in our conversation, they had been listening. Rothan asked, "Dr. Rapp, I was wondering something about icebergs."

Without the radio headsets, we would not be able to converse over the noise of the helicopter, but with them, we could talk without needing to raise our voice, even from the front seats of the helo to the passenger compartment in the back. Sylvia answered, "Yes, of course, Rothan. What do you want to know?"

"A few weeks ago, I took one of the oceanographers out and he was talking about how the ocean floor is deeper toward the center around this part of Antarctica, so as each iceberg breaks away, it exposes taller and taller ice cliffs until the ice gets so heavy that the taller cliffs can't support their own weight and they crumble. He said that once that crumbling begins, the destruction can become unstoppable. He called it marine ice cliff instability. I know floating ice doesn't raise sea levels when it falls into the ocean – but some of those cliffs are on land. What happens if that instability keeps happening, and more ice cliffs collapse?"

Rothan had a German accent and pronounced his name "rot-han." It took me months to figure out that it wasn't actually his name. His given name was Johannes, but when he was a kid, he had red hair, so his friends nicknamed him "red Han." The name had stuck and now that his reddish-brown hair was almost always covered in a hat, even if I had spoken more German, I wouldn't have figured out the derivation of his name. I liked it. Rothan was unique, curious, and intelligent. Everyone in Antarctica was either brilliant or crazy. Why else come here?

Sylvia was in her element now. She loved explaining icebergs and glaciers and all things frozen to anyone who would listen.

"As far as I'm concerned, the collapse of more ice cliffs is a distinct possibility. In the past decade, glaciologists have identified marine ice cliff instability as a potential cause of the disintegration of the entire West Antarctic ice sheet this century. It's a feedback loop – the ice cliff collapses, which in turn creates taller cliffs, which could kick start complete disintegration. Huge skyscraper-sized shards of ice crumbling into the sea, some as deep underwater as the Statue of Liberty, would create a global catastrophe.

"But those ice cliffs are borne of ice shelves – floating ice. Land-based ice is much more troublesome. When that falls into the sea, it adds to the overall volume of liquid in the oceans and sea level rises. That's one of the reasons we are going out to Thwaites to check on it. A complete collapse of the doomsday glacier would set off a catastrophe. That's how it got its name. Giant icebergs are plunged into the ocean and the currents carry them away from Antarctica, into warmer water where they will melt. Tides will creep higher all over the planet, slowly burying every shoreline and flooding coastal cities."

Rothan groaned and then asked, "Ice skyscrapers are big, but really, how much water is there in those glaciers? Sea level has already gone up a meter in the last decade, and it has been bad, but the world has been adapting. How much more water would Thwaites put into the sea?"

"A lot. But it isn't just that Thwaites holds a lot of water. Thwaites holds back a lot more ice on the continent. If Thwaites crashes, the ice cliffs behind it become more unstable and they fracture and fall into the sea, putting pretty much all the ice in West Antarctica at risk of sliding into the ocean. More than 70 percent of the fresh water on the planet is locked up on this frozen continent. A runaway collapse of the ice sheet would be catastrophic. A meter of sea level rise will be laughable at that point. If the ice sheet collapsed, it would raise sea levels faster than ever seen before. Short of a meteor strike, it's the quickest way to reshape the Earth." Sylvia's excitement about lecturing on her favorite topic turned to dismay as the last words left her mouth. This was reality, not esoteric data.

The helicopter suddenly shifted sideways, and I grabbed the nearest security handle with both hands. "Hold on!" said Phil loudly from the cockpit. "We've got a bit of turbulence."

His voice was calm, but the helicopter pitched at an angle I didn't think was possible for a vehicle propelled by rotors. My seatbelt grabbed tight, and Sylvia and I exchanged terrified glances.

Fear splintered my heart, and I was barely able to breathe. The helo momentarily caught an updraft and righted itself before pitching down another twenty meters or so. I bit back a scream, grabbed Sylvia's hand, and squeezed it hard.

A moment that felt like forever passed, and the helicopter was once again flying straight, and more importantly, upright. My heart was still pounding, and I couldn't do anything about that, but I tried to stop the alarm bells ringing in my head. I could control my thoughts, if not my organs.

"Sorry for the unexpected katabatics, ladies," said Rothan.

Katabatic winds were something I was aware of in a theoretical sense, because out on Ross Island, we were spared them. But on the continent, most winds were katabatic. They dropped down 2,700 meters from the tops of mountains, gathering speed as they flowed across the land, sending cold air speeding along the continent toward the ocean. Those winds could be as cold as one hundred below. Besides being frigid, they created impressive amounts of turbulence.

"For the rest of the flight, we will try to keep the rotors up and our asses down. But no promises." He laughed his best mad-scientist-dragging-unsuspecting-victims-to-a-secret-lab laugh.

For the rest of the trip, I alternated between looking out the window, chewing gum, and sleeping, but I was never able to get my mind on my work again until we landed at the base a little after four. Rothan and Phil refueled the helicopter from fuel stored at the shelter before joining us inside to unpack and pick our sleeping bunks in the hut. Sylvia volunteered to thaw out food, so I set up my laptop on a tabletop and settled in to work on my research.

Not only did I have a lot of data to process, but I also still had to organize all of it into some form of academic paper which I could present later to other seismologists. As they said in academia, publish or perish. As I stared at my screen, a tremor hit the hut. It lasted over twenty seconds and shook everything off every horizontal surface, but it subsided, and we were none the worse for wear.

"Well, that's a perfect end to a weird day," said Rothan. "The first quake I've felt in five winters here. Do they happen often?"

I looked at Sylvia and back again at Rothan. "No, actually, they don't. Like ever. Quakes here happen far offshore, and we seldom feel anything from them on land."

Sylvia shook her head, agreeing with me. "Believe me, that is not normal."

Fast Facts

If sea level were to rise 10 to 13 feet, most of South Florida would become an underwater theme park, including Miami, Fort Lauderdale, and Tampa.

In downtown Boston, the only thing that would not be underwater are the historic houses on Beacon Hill. For anyone living in low-lying coastal neighborhoods like Boston's Back Bay, Miami Beach, or Brooklyn, the difference between a three- and six-foot sea-level rise is the difference between a wet city and a submerged city – and billions of dollars' worth of coastal real estate gone.

At 10 or more feet, hundreds of millions of people's land worldwide would wind up underwater. Low-lying South Florida would become uninhabitable; floods like those from Hurricane Sandy would strike twice a month in New Jersey and New York, as tides from the tug of the moon would be enough to submerge homes and buildings twice a day.

Chapter 9
Nick – Boston

I woke groggily and looked at the clock. It was almost 9 a.m. My internal clock generally woke me at 6:15 on weekdays and I did not normally sleep this late on weekends. But after lying awake most of the night, I was going to be off schedule all day. The last time I glanced at the clock it was 5 a.m., so I was thankful I got at least four hours of sleep. Oh, plus the three hours I slept before being awoken by Liam's video game. I was tired if I couldn't add three plus four.

The more I thought about it, I realized I wasn't so much tired as angry at Kathryn. I would need to deal with that. I ambled into the bathroom and added my warm robe to my flannel pajamas and slippers, and finally headed to the kitchen for coffee and breakfast. Liam would sleep as long as I let him, and I deliberated over letting him so I could have some peace and quiet versus waking him, so he would be tired enough to go to sleep tonight at an hour that suited me.

I was still deliberating when the coffee finished brewing. A steaming cup in hand, I stared at the front yard from the den window. The Massachusetts winter was ending, and the ground was more slush than snow. Patches of brown grass stuck up out of it, heralding spring. The streets were clear except for piles where the plows had compressed it into icy, dirt-colored mounds.

Sipping my mug of highly caffeinated black miracle, I thought about the predicament logically.

First, there wasn't anything I could do about the situation. Second, Kathryn sent an email instead of calling, which means she knew I would disapprove of her staying and did not want a confrontation. So basically, she bailed. Lastly, I would have to live with it. I had no choice.

Six more months started with today. Both my son and I had the week off from school. I would have to figure out activities for us to do or he would just play ear-shattering video games all week. I had some chores around the house I had been putting off, like organizing the garage, and I needed to get those done, but perhaps I could spend a couple of days with Liam doing things he enjoyed, like the science museum or planetarium. This was his last year before high school, if he survived.

At the rate he was going, I might kill him myself if his teachers didn't beat me to it.

I loved Liam with all my heart, but he could be exasperating.

Liam used to be such a wonderful child. I remembered when he delighted in being pushed on the swings at the park and the free and generous smiles he bestowed on the world. As he grew, he became adventurous and outgoing. Then the teen years started and first he became moody, then distant. I chalked it up to hormones and hoped that soon his remoteness would end and perhaps he would be the boy I remembered once again.

Until that day came, I needed to refrain from strangling him and do my best to understand this time in his young life. I had a vague recollection of being fourteen myself. Inga was not like this four years ago, but perhaps being a girl, her 'difficult teen years' manifested differently. Or perhaps she had directed her anger at the world toward her mother instead of me.

After I showered, I would need to reply to Kathryn's email. I thought about my response while the warm water massaged my stiff neck and decided to be okay with her decision. I didn't like being angry at my wife.

Kathryn had always made me want to be a better person. Being angry at her, or at anyone, wasn't me being my best self.

Dried and dressed, I sat down at my desk in the den with my tablet and poured my heart out, including my frustration. I told her first how angry I was, and that I felt she had abandoned not only me but our kids. I told her that she should have called to discuss it with me. Then I typed the words 'I love you,' and toned down my anger. Kathryn and I were always honest with each other, and we never pulled punches. We said what we had to.

I finished up the email with some updates on our 'problem child' Liam's recent mood swings and anger issues. "But all in all, I guess it could be worse. Let him have the Angry Young Man badge – it's better than the drug-addict badge or the juvie badge. With any luck, that wonderful person I knew will return once his teenage hormones die down. I just have to keep him on the right track until then."

Fast Facts

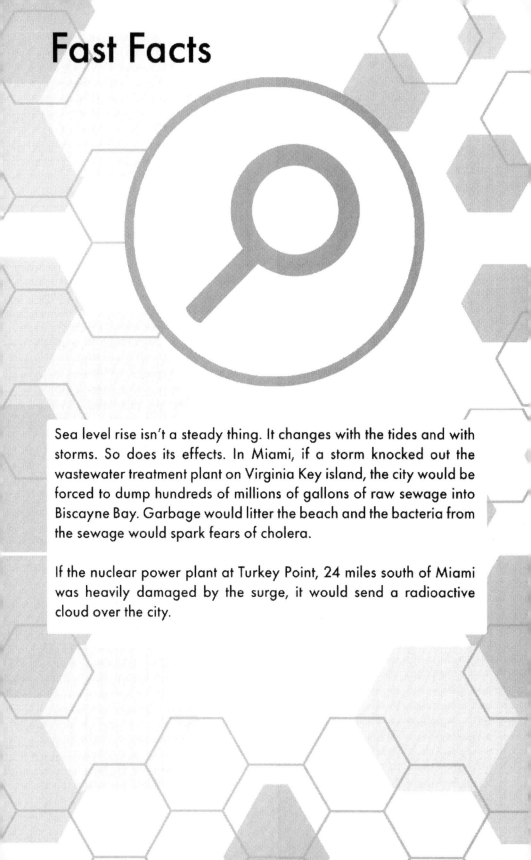

Sea level rise isn't a steady thing. It changes with the tides and with storms. So does its effects. In Miami, if a storm knocked out the wastewater treatment plant on Virginia Key island, the city would be forced to dump hundreds of millions of gallons of raw sewage into Biscayne Bay. Garbage would litter the beach and the bacteria from the sewage would spark fears of cholera.

If the nuclear power plant at Turkey Point, 24 miles south of Miami was heavily damaged by the surge, it would send a radioactive cloud over the city.

Chapter 10

Inga – Miami

There was no sun to wake me through the blinds today, but I woke instead to a warm body smashed up against me and realized Caleb had never left last night. I laid there for a long while but eventually I couldn't deny it anymore: I needed the bathroom. I rolled over quietly, trying to keep the mattress from shifting, but before I could extricate myself, Caleb woke.

I smiled sheepishly at him and got out of bed. "I was trying not to disturb you. Good morning." I felt self-conscious standing next to the bed, looking at this guy who I had just spent the night with. Not knowing what to do, I ran off to the bathroom, reemerging only after answering the call of nature and brushing my teeth. Twice. I was a bit over paranoid about bad breath.

"I didn't plan to spend the night, I just...umm," began Caleb awkwardly.

"We fell asleep. It's okay. I'm glad you stayed."

I *was* glad he had stayed. I liked him, a lot.

His smile was enchanting, but somehow, he still seemed worried.

"What is it?" I asked, confused. "I thought we had a wonderful night. At least, *I* enjoyed it."

Affection glowed in his eyes. "Oh, Inga, I enjoyed it! It was wonderful. *You* are wonderful. I just worry about what people will think. What will Zoe think? What if she came back to your room and saw us?"

I almost laughed out loud. "Caleb, you might have noticed, Zoe didn't come back. She sent me a message late last night that she was staying with Jason. But even if she had come back, why would you worry about what she would think?"

He looked confused, but then a corner of his mouth lifted. "You've got a point. She hasn't made any secret of what her intentions are for spring break! Guess I'm just kind of old school. Russian parents and all. I worry about reputations. Mostly yours."

I thought that was charmingly quaint. I almost said so. Instead, I laughed, then said, "You shouldn't worry about my reputation. It's not like you are my first. Or second. Actually, not even third." I immediately regretted my words when his smile faded.

Before he could think any worse of me, I quickly added, "I *have* had boyfriends before."

I am not sure that made things any better.

Was I his first? No way. He seemed to know what he was doing. Actually, he knew his way around the female body quite well.

I waited for his reply and almost jumped in before he could speak to defend myself further, but luckily, he cut me off. "Inga, it's fine. It's spring break. Sex is what this week is all about. I guess I was somewhat worried that if this was your first time, that I wasn't everything you expected. Male insecurity." He should've laughed or something to lighten the mood, but instead, his face remained passive and expressionless.

I weighed my words carefully. Putting my foot in my mouth was one of my special talents, and I desperately wanted to avoid that. "Caleb. I'm eighteen. I had two boyfriends in high school, both lasted about four months, neither serious. I had another last semester that lasted exactly one night. I'm not especially proud of that, but I don't want to come across as promiscuous either. I really like you. If I didn't, I wouldn't have slept with you. I don't take sex lightly. So, can we start over?"

"Right now? Sure!" He pulled me onto the bed, and I laughed.

"Not what I meant!"

Well, maybe that was what I meant. I certainly didn't argue and within moments I was quite sure I never wanted spring break to end.

Soon, we were lying next to each other with him stroking my hair, and he reached down to kiss my forehead lightly. I sighed and rolled into him, closed my eyes, and started to drift off.

A short time later, Caleb's phone buzzed from the nightstand. So much for my lazy vacation day nap.

I murmured something inaudible as he grabbed his phone. "Jason says he and Zoe are eating breakfast and then they'll meet us here. He arranged a tour of Fisher Gate for all of us. Says to dress warmly because it's a windy ride. I texted him back to bring my sweatshirt and a pair of jeans from my suitcase."

"Really? I'm surprised Zoe mentioned that to him. She didn't seem that interested, but it was one of the top things on my To-Do list. Geez, just when I think I know Zoe, she surprises me all over again." I gave him a quick kiss and almost jumped out of bed to run for the shower first. After all, it *was* my hotel room.

I was glad that Caleb was as quick as I was at getting ready and before Zoe and Jason arrived, we were in the lobby with to-go cups of coffee and breakfast sandwiches in hand. A rideshare car pulled up in front of the hotel and Zoe rolled down the window and shouted. "Over here. Come on guys, we don't have all day!"

We ran to the vehicle and jumped in the back seat next to her. "Sheesh, Zoe, chill," I grumbled, balancing my cup between my knees, the sandwich on my lap, while putting on my seat belt. "What's the rush?"

She looked at me as if I had suddenly lost fifty IQ points. "Jason was nice enough to reserve us four seats on a speedboat tour – and paid for it too – and you are arguing? I thought this was what you wanted to do?

Anyway, it leaves at 9:30 from the downtown Marketplace pier. That's the only tour that allows us to see Fisher Gate in action. You are the one who told me that they only open it at low tide."

I knew that. All the cruise ships leaving from anywhere in Biscayne Bay had only one or two windows of opportunity to get out of the bay. Low tide happened at a different time each day, but generally, there were two of them, one in the morning and one at night. There was a tide chart in the lobby of our hotel.

"Zoe, I'm amazed you got up this early on vacation, just so I could go gawk at a giant floodgate."

"Yeah, well, I guess Jason is a good influence."

Jason snorted and turned around from the front seat to face us. "Someone has to be responsible, and as the oldest, and a legal adult at twenty-one, I claim that right."

"I'm responsible!" Zoe elbowed me in the ribs. "At least my parents know where I am. Inga is the one who didn't tell hers where she went."

"Seriously?" Caleb asked. I was seated between him and Zoe and though the car was roomy enough, suddenly I felt confined and crowded. I was feeling guilty for lying to my parents and I admitted as much to my new friends and explained to them why my mother never would have let me come to Miami.

"Oh man," said Caleb. "I'm not sure if you are a bad-ass rebel, or you just enjoy taking your life in your hands. Your mom is going to flip when she finds out where you are!"

Jason nodded affirmation.

They were right. My mom could never find out where I'd gone.

The car pulled into the drop-off lane at the Marketplace pier. The pier was not strictly speaking *inside* Biscayne Bay, at least not since they closed off the bay by building the seawalls that connected the cruise ship terminal to the bay on the west side and Fisher Island on the east.

While standing in line to board, a loudspeaker blared over our heads. "Welcome to Miami Beach Speedboat Adventures. The forty-five-minute ride is the ultimate tourist experience to see the city in style. Get ready for a thrill ride and view the celebrity mansions at Millionaires Row, the fabulous Fisher Gate that keeps the city safe from the rising ocean, and the remarkable art deco district of South Beach, all from the perspective of the Atlantic Ocean. No other tour can show you this much, this fast! The high-speed thrill of Miami Beach Speedboat Adventures is Miami's best offshore experience. Each catamaran holds thirty-six guests, so please line up according to the ship number on your electronic ticket." The recording went on to say that children under three were not allowed and a whole lot of legalese that everyone ignored.

We boarded the second catamaran, put on life jackets, and took our seats. The captain and tour guide introduced themselves and the guide gave final instructions before departing. "Please stay seated at all times unless told otherwise. We will make a few stops at which time you will be allowed to stand and take pictures. Today's tour has the added excitement of seeing Fisher Gate open for this morning's low tide. Let's go!"

The guide sat down, and the boat carefully edged out from the crowded pier, its sleek form angled toward the open water. We picked up speed as we passed the cruise ship terminal to our left and rounded the eastern side of Fisher Island, slowing so the guide could stand and talk. "Fisher Gate was installed eight years ago to protect Biscayne Bay. The barriers strengthen the seawall on the southern and eastern sides of Fisher Island, and the gate forms the southern end of the bay. The gates are about to open to let the ships out. You don't want to miss this, it's magnificent. Each of its two arms is as tall and twice as heavy as the Eiffel Tower and the storm surge barriers are over seventy feet tall."

The arms of the massive gate were mid-way separated already by the time we passed by the mouth of the Biscayne, and water rushed from the

Atlantic Ocean into the bay. My father was into engineering marvels and told me that they could not build a system of locks here because there wasn't enough room, so they built the gate instead. I had wanted to see this behemoth ever since.

I craned my neck to get a better view of it over the other passengers. The gate groaned loudly as the metal moved through the water, equalizing the water depth between the ocean and the bay.

As the arms neared the edge of the pier, the first of the giant cruise ships lumbered toward it, with three more behind it like a parade.

The crowd on board all four catamarans cheered and took pictures with the ships behind them.

"Smile!" shouted Jason, and Zoe and I simultaneously realized people on the other boats were taking pictures of us, as well as the cruise ships.

"Great," grumbled Zoe, but she smiled anyway. "I hate winding up in the background on someone else's post."

I stood to get a better view.

"It is fantastic, I'll give it that," said Zoe, standing at my side.

The tour guide announced, "If you'll please take your seats, we are going to take a quick tour around some small islands to our south before zooming up the coast."

I was still staring at the cruise ships, now moving freely through the entrance to the bay when I felt a tug beside me. Caleb was tugging at my shirt, reminding me to sit down.

The speedboat took off before I was settled when I felt Zoe shift. That was when I realized that she was still standing. A moment later she was falling toward the steel deck of the boat.

The world shifted into slow motion.

My hand jumped out in a flash, reaching for her.

Zoe's feet went out from under her, and her body tumbled to the floor.

I slid out of my seat to the deck and then Zoe was on top of me.

She let out a stream of curses before saying, "Thanks. A second later my head would have connected with the deck."

I exhaled long and hard, not realizing I'd been holding my breath.

As we bumped through the waves, the guide's amplified voice announced, "With the sea level so much higher than decades earlier, the smaller islands, such as historic Virginia Key and much of Key Biscayne before us now, have been partially submerged under the Atlantic Ocean, even at low tide, except for the water treatment plant, which is now protected by a sea wall."

We didn't make any stops as we circled the small bits of land poking through the water. After skirting past the islands, the captain turned our boat into the open ocean and the speedboat cruised up the coast. I braced my legs as the hull bounced higher and higher. High-rise towers soared into the gray sky on the beach as the boat knifed through the sea. Along the shore, iconic lifeguard stands stood alongside palm trees. Since it was a cloudy day and the water somewhat rough, the beach was not as crowded as it had been the last couple of days. Still, beach umbrellas dotted the sand. A long stretch of parkland separated the narrow beach from tall hotel and apartment buildings along Ocean Drive.

The boat sped past the twenty-three blocks that marked South Beach and raced along mid-beach. "I wonder if we can see our hotels?" shouted Caleb. The wind whipped our hair and almost swept away his words.

"Maybe yours, but ours isn't on the water. At this speed, I think it's a blink-and-you'll-miss-it kind of thing anyway!"

Caleb squeezed my hand in answer. Talking was pointless until we slowed. Here the hotels were almost on the water, with just a small strip of dune grass and sand separating them from the ocean. I wondered what it had been like twenty or fifty years ago when the sea level was lower. How glorious it must have been to have all that sand. I leaned into Caleb and enjoyed the rush of the speedboat.

Ten minutes later, the tour guide announced that we were nearing the northern end of Miami Beach and pointed to the sea wall that had been built to connect it to Sunny Isles Beach. "Inland, another steel-and-concrete wall seals off Miami from North Miami Beach, effectively turning Biscayne Bay into a lake. A lock allows ships to travel from the Intracoastal Waterway into Biscayne Bay. Without that wall, the interior islands between the mainland and the barrier islands would have been inundated by the sea years ago. We don't get political here," he laughed as if this was a truly funny statement, then continued, "but if Miami hadn't created a master plan to deal with the water rising by passing tax incentives to get people to move to higher ground, not to mention building Fisher Gate and the seawalls, we wouldn't be here today. This lively city might be gone if it hadn't been for the quick thinking of elected officials and engineers back at the end of the teens."

Everyone cheered for that as if the people he spoke of could hear them. For not getting political, his canned speech seemed rather political.

The boat slowed for another photo op at Pier Park. Quite a few people were fishing from the end of the jetty, the cloudy weather not deterring them. Maybe it was nicer fishing without the sun beating on you.

Soon, the captain turned the speedboat around and we sped south along the coast, loud music blaring from the speakers, making whatever conversation had been possible on the ride up no longer viable. The catamaran rose and fell with each wave, slapping them hard with each fall. What had taken half an hour with stops, now passed in fifteen minutes and we pulled into the Marketplace pier along with the other three speedboats.

Our boat was second in line to dock, so we had a few minutes. I said, "They always talk about Miami being so smart with all the engineering they did to save it from the sea but being from another major city also threatened by sea level rise – Zoe too, because her home state's shores lost almost 25,000 homes to the rising sea over the last decade – I wonder why we put so much money into saving something when we should just retreat to higher ground."

Caleb answered. "Delaware is in the same boat, but we don't have higher ground to move to. I guess after a place has sunk so much into buildings and monuments, concrete, and steel, it's just not that easy to pick up and move. Sure, on small scale, families have moved to new places, but they had to be ordered to, at least in Delaware. Our state declared entire sections of low-lying land disaster areas and gave grants to people to let the ocean swallow their homes. They built housing inland and many moved. There is an entire town in coastal Delaware that took their grant money and bought ten square miles of cornfields in Indiana and moved the entire town. They sold the corn and built houses, shops, a town hall, offices, you name it. But they are the exception. Most people don't just pick up and move like some nomadic tribe."

He was right. Miami wasn't the only city dealing with sea level rise these days. Millions of people around the world were, and most of them weren't fairing as well as the U.S. and Europe. Not all coastal communities had the money to elevate streets and other infrastructures like airports and sewer systems. There were climate refugees from a dozen island nations where they had no money to install pumps, build seawalls, or any of the countless things they needed to do to deal with the rising ocean.

"Anyone else hungry?" I asked.

"Worked up an appetite this morning?" asked Zoe with a wink.

"Haha," I replied, and then turned to Caleb. "See? I told you not to worry about my reputation."

Fast Facts

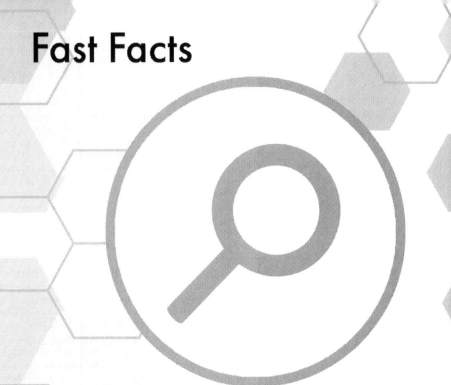

Thwaites Glacier in West Antarctica is one of the largest glaciers on the planet. It is so remote that only 28 people have ever set foot on it. Between 60 and 70% of the Earth's fresh water is frozen in Antarctic ice sheets that can be nearly 3 miles (5 km) thick.

The Transantarctic Mountains bisect the continent. East Antarctica is larger and colder than West Antarctica, which is more vulnerable to melting because the bases of many glaciers in West Antarctica lie below sea level, making them susceptible to changes in ocean temperatures.

An almost half-mile-tall ridge of rock helps anchor Twaites, slowing the glacier's slide into the ocean, but Twaites is also a threshold system. Instead of melting slowly like a glass of ice cubes on a warm day, it's unstable like a house of cards. It's perfectly fine, until it crashes.

Chapter 11
Kathryn – Antarctica

Wednesday morning, we woke early to fly out to the glacier. I slept in my double-thermal long johns and long sleeve undershirt, even though the overnight shelter was fairly warm, and my sub-zero insulated sleeping bag did an admirable job of keeping me from freezing to death.

Everyone slept with so much clothing on that it never mattered if there were mixed groups of men and women in a cabin. Who could tell what your body looked like covered in flannel and layers?

"Just so you know, I'm jealous of your legs," said Sylvia.

"What? What the hell are you talking about?" I stared at Sylvia as she extracted herself from her sleeping bag.

"You actually have ankles. Mine are tree trunks."

I looked down at her long john clad form and she was right. Sylvia was a thin woman, but her ankles were the same circumference as her calves. I laughed and said, "I never noticed. Did you come to Antarctica so you'd always have so much clothing on that no one would see your legs?"

She threw me a lopsided grin and then pulled on her pants and sweater. I beat her by about twelve seconds before shouting, "Wakey, wakey, rise and shine!"

My inane rooster call was greeted by groans from both Phil and Rothan.

"Seriously? The sun isn't even up yet," he whined.

Phil looked at his wrist. "Geeze, sunrise is at 6:42. How long do you intend to fly around the glacier taking pictures? Honestly, you did not need to get up *this* early."

As if he were one of my children, I gave him *the look* and said, "Then you shouldn't have snored all night and kept me awake. If I'm up, then everyone else might as well be."

Rothan had no wiseass comments to add to this ridiculous conversation worthy of middle schoolers and set off for the bathroom without another word.

While we slept – or not slept, in my case – my laptop had been hard at work compiling a model of the seismic data I had fed into it last night. Between my readings of seismic activity over almost eight months and the ISC data, there was a huge amount of information.

We left the shelter after everyone had eaten and packed up, and as Phil and Rothan flew our helicopter to the Thwaites glacier, it didn't take me long to review what the model had amassed.

It was based on the predictive algorithm developed by the Berkeley Seismology Lab because the national register did not incorporate Antarctic data.

UC Berkeley was perhaps the most advanced research center for earthquakes and had developed an early warning system that the entire west coast of the United States has used since the mid-teens, but my Antarctic data threw a monkey wrench into the works of established theory.

My current readings of seismic activity from the three volcanoes in Antarctica were too high for an area with no volcanic activity, indicating a shifting of the tectonic plates underneath it. Without the number-crunching ability of my new computer model, I would not be able to determine if the seismic readings were from glacial earthquakes, actual seismic activity, or ice quakes.

I stared at the results from the model and my heart galloped.

If what I was seeing was accurate, it meant that a quake of high magnitude loomed in Antarctica's near future, and based on the analysis, I estimated it would happen within the next month.

The model showed that it would occur at the boundary of the Scotia and Antarctic Plates, but that was a massive area. If it happened at sea, even a large magnitude quake could have little to no effect on the continent other than potential tidal waves. Since Antarctica was mostly uninhabited, a tidal wave would pose little safety risk.

If the quake happened along the continental edge, it would be devastating.

"This is bad," I said, almost to myself, but I forgot that my headset was on. Whispering into a microphone was the same as shouting when your voice carried directly to the earpieces of your companions.

Sylvia asked, "What's bad?"

Both pilots glanced back at me, and I saw Rothan raise an eyebrow quizzically.

"This data shows an imminent earthquake between the Scotia Plate and the Antarctic Plate. Like within a month. This isn't the type of data that you write an academic paper on. I won't have time. I'll need to send this directly to the USGS for dissemination," I replied.

The U.S. Geological Survey was the arm of the government that handled earthquakes, and along with FEMA and the National Science Foundation, made up a multi-agency program, the National Earthquake Hazards Reduction Program. The NEHRP couldn't predict earthquakes or prevent them, but they tried to minimize the damage they caused by providing preparedness data and funding research.

"How big a quake?" asked Rothan from the pilot's seat.

"I don't know the precise magnitude range, but greater than seven, by the model. The problem is, I can't pinpoint where along the plate boundary the slippage will occur. If it's deep at sea, the damage will be minimal, so warning the USGS is simply protocol."

"But if it's not out at sea," Sylvia began, "and it hits along the coastal boundary of Antarctica – the continent, not the plate – its damage could be extensive. It could trigger ice quake vibrations of great magnitude. It might even cause a sudden disruption of the ice sheet."

A line etched between Rothan's brows, and he looked at Sylvia. "If an earthquake shakes loose those ice cliffs, that could start the feedback loop you mentioned yesterday, no?"

Sylvia's expression hardened. "Yes, especially if Thwaites collapses and throws giant icebergs into the sea. But that is what today's visual inspection is for. Our aerial photos will reveal any slippage in the glacier. That will also let us know how reactive to a large quake the glacier might be."

She was right.

I interjected my only comment. "Even if a high magnitude quake does happen, it won't necessarily dislodge the Thwaites glacier. That's a worst-case scenario. The big problem on my end is that my timeline on my paper needs to be moved up. I don't know if I can publish it before the quake hits. Once we get back to McMurdo, I'll send my data to the USGS as is. Meanwhile, I'm going to dive headfirst into writing on our flight back today."

Writing research into a readable paper is not my favorite task as an academic. I was easily distracted by actual research, so the flight back would be the opportunity I needed to jump-start an arduous chore. I would be trapped with no distractions at that point, but right now the helicopter neared the doomsday glacier.

And oh, what a sight!

It was hard for the human brain to comprehend the vastness of the ice in Antarctica. The glacial valley shimmered in multitudes of shades making it look almost blue, as the ice beneath us flowed imperceptibly into the sea yet speeding up every year.

Sylvia handed me a camera and said, "See where the glacier is thinning inland? That's what we need to photograph. Phil! You have the coordinates set in?"

The pilot responded, "Roger that. Plotted and progressing on course."

I looked quizzically at Sylvia, and she answered my unasked question. "We have to follow the exact flight path to be sure we collect data from the same spot every month to measure the change. The summer crew knew this flight path because they did it every month with me, but this is a first for the winter pilots."

I focused my camera on the receding glacier, trying to ignore the unearthly Antarctic light.

This early in the morning it seemed as if we were on another planet, the blinding, glaring rays of an alien sun shining on us small human interlopers. In a few short weeks, the sun would set for the final time until southern hemisphere spring, so I tried to concentrate on taking the last photos of the season, but the dazzling sunlight was a challenging distraction.

Sylvia was better at multitasking than I was and spoke as her camera took image after image of blue-white ice. "Warm water flows in from the surrounding ocean and undercuts the glaciers in both the Arctic and in Antarctica. Untold tons of sea ice have melted in the last decade."

Rothan said, "That is what has caused the meter of sea level to rise around the globe."

I don't know if he meant it as a statement or question, but Sylvia nodded. "My research group has been tracking the major glaciers on the continent to record their size for decades, and the shrinkage has been incredible to witness first-hand. In 2017, researchers discovered that warm ocean water was carving an enormous channel into the underside of one of the key floating ice shelves of West Antarctica, the Dotson ice shelf, which dumps into the Amundsen Sea."

Her camera whirred and clicked as she spoke. "Because of uneven melting, the Dotson ice shelf could be melted all the way through by 2050. As the thinning continues, the shelf may not go quietly and something dramatic could occur."

"So, the whole ice shelf might break up?" asked Rothan.

More camera clicks as Sylvia turned her body to face the camera at a different angle. "It might. As warm ocean waters undermine the shelf, it would increase the flow of ice outward from the Smith and Kohler glaciers behind it. Smith ultimately connects to Thwaites, and Thwaites runs backward into the core of the West Antarctic ice sheet. If it were to all go, there is about a 3-meter sea level rise contained in the system."

Rothan and Phil whistled in stereo.

"But not in our lifetimes, right?" asked Rothan, tentatively.

"I can't really guess," replied Sylvia.

We flew around for two more hours, taking photos and staring into the mouth and body of Thwaites, the doomsday glacier. Other than periodic confirmation of the flight path from the pilot, the sheer awe of the spectacle silenced all of us.

The flight path complete, Phil turned the helo toward McMurdo, and I handed the camera back to Sylvia.

I needed to use the next seven hours to write up my research into something that would not only notify the USGS back home, but also be a powerful warning of the dangers the impending quake posed for the coastal cities if Thwaites glacier, or any other sizeable glacier in Antarctica, was dislodged.

I had been typing for over an hour and barely noticed that we had landed so the pilots could switch seats, but it was Sylvia who was, for once, more engrossed in her monitor than me. We were taking off, with Rothan at the controls when she looked up from her computer.

I saw the color drain from her face and asked, "What's wrong?"

"I've examined the photos we took and there is no doubt; the glacier has shifted significantly since my last measurements."

I was about to ask what that meant but she raised a hand to stop me. "It means it's becoming more unstable. It's being weakened by the warmer ocean water and the flow of the glacier is accelerating. Not going to lie, that has me worried. Thwaites may have entered the early stages of unstoppable disintegration."

Fast Facts

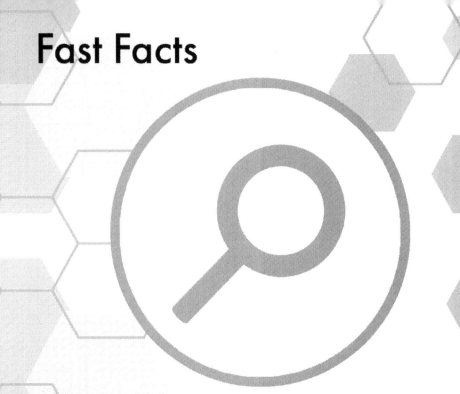

McMurdo Research Station receives three channels of the US Military's American Forces Network, the Australia Network, and New Zealand news broadcasts. Television broadcasts are received by satellite at Black Island and transmitted 25 miles (40 km) by digital microwave to McMurdo.

McMurdo gets both voice communications and internet by satellite relayed through Sydney, Australia. Voice communications are tied into the United States Antarctic Program (USAP) headquarters in Centennial, Colorado, providing inbound and outbound calls to McMurdo. Voice communications within McMurdo are conducted via VHF radio. Communications priority is calls first, then data transfer, then social media. YouTube has the lowest priority.

Chapter 12

Nick – Boston

I was sitting in my customary spot in the den when a glum voice behind me said, "Dad." Liam came around the love seat to stand in front of me. I looked at my son and wondered which one stood before me: the little boy that wanted me to make him breakfast, or the insolent adolescent who looked at the world with disdain.

"Morning, Liam," I replied, and my son surprised me by plopping onto the seat beside me and hugging me. One small victory. I'd take them where I could get them. "Hungry?"

"Always," he replied. "Do we have any waffles?"

I nodded and headed for the kitchen to refill my cup and make us both frozen waffles. We had some Vermont maple syrup left but were almost out. Which gave me a thought.

"Hey Liam, are you still interested in driving up to Vermont for a couple of days to snowboard? Mid-week prices right now. Beats sitting here playing video games all week while Cambridge turns to slush." I was a lifelong skier, as was Kathryn, but my kids tried both sports when they were little, and Liam had excelled at snowboarding from an early age. He wasn't bad on skis but preferred his board. Inga called herself ambisnowstrous. She could ski and snowboard equally well.

Liam was two steps behind me. "Can I bring Bash?"

Sebastian Fabron had been Liam's best friend since they were in the second grade. They did everything together.

"Yeah, as long as his parents are okay with being gone a couple of nights and he pays for his own lift tickets. I'll find us a couple of rooms at a Bed and Breakfast, and we can leave this afternoon, ski two days, and drive back Saturday. Give him a call."

He made a sound like a humpback whale breaching. I wasn't sure if he farted or that noise came from his mouth. "I'll text him."

Guess it was his mouth.

Liam eagerly went to his room, probably to get his phone, while I slid the waffles into the toaster.

While I waited, I checked my favorite travel website for some B&B's in Vermont and marked a couple that had rooms available for tonight but would wait for confirmation from Sebastian's parents before booking, just in case we needed to delay until tomorrow, or didn't end up needing a room that would sleep three.

I put bacon into a pan and thawed out some strawberries in the microwave. By the time I had the food and condiments on the table, Liam was back. "Bash's mom said it's fine for him to come with us. It gets him out of her hair for a few days. She said no rush returning him, and she'll give him money for lift tickets and food. Can we do three days on the slopes, not two? I checked the weather and it's going to be absolutely *perfect* up there for like the next four days." He rolled the word *perfect* like a cat.

"Sure. I found a B&B that has a room with a loft. It's in central Vermont, up by that resort you liked last year. But there are three ski areas near it, so you boys can check which has the best conditions while I drive. When you are done eating and loading the dishwasher, go shower and get ready. Tell Bash to be ready by two. We'll pick him up on the way."

Liam drank down his orange juice in one long gulp and pushed back his chair, grabbing his glass in one hand and his empty plate in the other.

"Cool. We'll be back by Sunday night, and Mom gets back Monday, right?"

Oh crap. I hadn't told him yet. "Yeah, about that, kiddo. Your mom is staying in Antarctica for another six months. Her research isn't done, and she needs the time."

"What the..." He bit off the swear that was to follow, remembering at the last moment that I did not take well to vulgar language out of children's mouths. "She's what? What is wrong with her?"

I let him rail for a few seconds before answering. "Liam, I'm pissed, too. But we'll survive. I guarantee it."

My words did not soothe him, so I let him vent his anger. It was a perfectly appropriate emotion for someone in his place. If I thought I could get away with a temper tantrum, I'd do it myself. Once he yelled himself into silence, he took the dishes to the dishwasher, loaded it, slammed the door violently, and stomped up the stairs. A minute later I heard the shower start.

Our historical house might have two and a half bathrooms, but if you tried to run both showers at once, one of you would be pelted by cold water, so I opted to email Kathryn first, before getting ready. After telling her how much I loved and missed her, I typed out a few sentences about the upcoming ski trip and how both she and Inga were the unlucky ones because they were missing what I was sure would be a fantastic trip. Snow, hot tub, someone else to cook us breakfast, all the good things in life.

Then I realized she had more snow than she knew what to do with down in Antarctica, and a childish little voice in my head felt a small twinge of glee before I guiltily pushed it aside.

Fast Facts

Every old civilization has a flood myth in its literature. In the Epic of Gilgamesh, waters so overwhelm the mortals that even the gods were scared. In India, Lord Vishnu warns a man to take refuge in a boat, carrying seeds. In the Christian Bible, God orders Noah to build an ark and save two of every living animal.

Some kind of major flood happened worldwide, and it left a lasting effect on the collective memory of mankind, which was preserved in these flood stories. That flooding would have happened at the end of the last ice age.

50,000 years ago, the ice sheets grew so large that they locked up so much of the world's water that sea level fell by roughly 400 feet. Beginning about 25,000 years ago, those ice sheets began to melt, and the sea level rose. Over the next several thousand years, coastlines receded inland by 100 miles (160 km). Hence, the flood stories of our ancestral memories.

Chapter 13
Inga – Miami

Winds whistled and a fire truck siren blared seven floors below us. I grabbed my earpiece from the nightstand, then keyed the button that brought the DPA to life.

"Lilith, visual only. What's today's weather?"

A virtual image floated in front of me showing a weather map of southern Florida and a text description from the National Weather Service. Tropical storm Alberto was brewing in the Gulf of Mexico, just west of Cuba, but it did not look like it would become a hurricane or that it would track east and come near Miami. But we would definitely get rain and wind over the next three days.

It was early Tuesday morning, and we were flying home on Saturday, so it appeared that the sunny part of our Florida vacation was over. With all the clouds that never broke up yesterday, I should have known that we were on the edge of a storm, but I was enjoying my time with Zoe, Caleb, and Jason so much that I never even thought to ask Lilith for a weather update. I should have instructed her to let me know of such things, but it was so sunny and warm after the long winter in Boston that it never occurred to me. Better late than never, I set up proper weather alerts.

I tried to go back to sleep but to no avail. By 9:30, I rolled out of bed and took a shower. At least I would get my paper done today, or maybe finish it tomorrow.

If the boys were interested, we could go to a movie this afternoon. There was a classic art deco movie theater that was on all the tourist websites as one of the top ten things to do in Miami. I loved art deco architecture but calling anything in Miami 'classic' rang strangely to my ears. The U.S. may not be an old country compared to Europe, but we did have historic architecture, and being from New England, I was accustomed to historic buildings being more like four hundred years old. To me, a century-old building was not historic. In Miami, it was ancient.

Zoe woke up as I was dressing and just in case she was deaf to the wind and rain outside, I updated her on the storm and my plans.

"Sounds good," she mumbled, dropping her feet to the floor, and padding off to the bathroom. A few moments later, I heard the toilet flush, and then the shower start.

I sent a message to Caleb about the movie and within moments he responded. *Has he been sitting at his phone, waiting for me?* The thought made me smile.

"Lilith, give me a list of movies and times for today at the Tower Theater." My DPA read off five movie names that I did not recognize as anything I had seen previews for.

"Lilith, do you have a description of the Tower Theater?"

Lilith complied with my request. "The Tower Theater is located in Little Havana. One of Miami's oldest landmarks, it first opened in 1926 and today serves cinephiles with independent and foreign films."

Well, that explained it. Cool as the venue might be, I was sure we would all be happier seeing a new action-adventure movie or sci-fi flick. I asked Lilith to list other art deco theaters and it turned out that all of them either showed only live theater performances or only movies that I classified as oddball.

I changed my tactic and asked Lilith to list the top-rated movies playing today and to provide me with the nearest location between 2 and 5 p.m. From the list, I settled on an action movie at the nearest theater.

Warrior Storm came out a week ago and had nothing but five-star reviews. It was two miles from our hotel, and since the guys were staying at a hotel a third of a mile south of us, it would still be a long walk in the rain and wind for them. Walking wouldn't be an option.

"Lilith, compose a text message to Caleb Milanov. '*Warrior Storm* at Cineplex 8 in city center starts at 3:45. Zoe and I will see if we can get our hotel van to take us, picking you guys up along the way. Let me know if that sounds like a good plan.' Lilith, send message."

I was towel drying my hair when Lilith informed me that Caleb had responded. "Would you like me to read his message?"

"Yes, please." I flipped my hair over and looked into the mirror. A square face stared back at me, the long, dirty blond hair looking brown because it was wet. My mother's face.

"Awesome, that sounds cool. I'll wait for your message about the van. If you can't get it, grab a rideshare, and we can meet you at the theater. Can't wait to see you."

Caleb's words sounded odd with Lilith's classic female inflection, and I smiled. I would probably never see him again after Saturday, so as long as there were no bodies in his closet, it didn't matter.

We'd had so much fun yesterday, playing tourist in the city after the early morning speedboat tour. Caleb liked to people watch, like Zoe and I did, and the four of us sat at a sidewalk cafe for hours just talking, drinking coffee, and making comments about everyone that walked past us. Afterward, Zoe and I stopped at the guys' hotel and hung out on the beach, playing Frisbee, and chatting until it got dark. The water was too rough to go in, which was fine since our bathing suits were still drying in our hotel. Jason ordered a pizza delivered right to our chairs on the beach, and Zoe had pronounced it "not quite New York style, but good enough." We didn't get back until fairly late.

Finally dressed, fed, and properly caffeinated, I pushed my daydreaming aside and sat down at the desk to start work on my paper. I'm not sure how long I worked, but I was well into the sixth page of how pop music was breaking down traditional cultural and geo-political boundaries when Lilith informed me that I had an incoming voice-only call from my mother. I looked at the time on my computer. 2 p.m. That made it 7 a.m. tomorrow in Antarctica. "Answer."

"Hi, mom! How are you?" Zoe stared at me from her bed where she was leaning back on the headboard, reading. The call was a surprise to both of us. I waited a couple of seconds for her response. This wasn't my first phone call from my mother over the last eight months and I knew the drill.

McMurdo bounced voice calls via satellite through Black Island Antarctica, to Sydney, then Colorado, and on to Miami. It was surprising there wasn't more of a time lag than the two or three seconds we were experiencing.

"I'm fine, sweetheart. It's been a few weeks since we spoke, so I thought I would call before my day got going. It's been really busy here lately." I could hear the urgency in her voice because she was speaking faster than normal. She usually had a professor's even cadence. "And I wanted to find out how upset you are with me that I'm staying here for the winter. I'm sorry I did that by email, not a phone call. That was a cop-out."

"Mom, it's fine. I mean, the email was definitely a cop-out." I gave a little laugh. "But it's okay. I understand why you are staying. Not like you can come home for a visit and then go back. Dad and Liam will survive, and me too. I'm kind of sorry I'm not home to help deal with Liam though. That kid has Dad's hands full."

Calling my younger brother a *handful* was giving him a huge benefit of the doubt.

"Yes, this is spring break week, right? I almost forgot you were in New Jersey with Zoe. Her family lives in the western part of the state, right?"

Oh damn, yeah, I was going to have to play this out as if I *was* in New Jersey. "They live just over the border from Philadelphia. Why?"

After a moment's delay, I heard my mother sigh. "Just something that came up in my research here. I guess I just wanted reassurance that you aren't anywhere near the ocean. Actually, in Philly, you are better off than in Boston."

"Why, mom? What's going on?"

She was making me nervous, not only because I was lying to her, but because nothing she was doing in Antarctica should affect me no matter where I happened to be in the U.S.

"I've made some startling discoveries here. It's another reason I'm calling you first thing this morning. I've been writing up my research and I have to spend a few more hours today fine-tuning it before I send it to the USGS."

"Wow! You're submitting already? But if your paper is done, why aren't you coming home? I'm confused," I admitted.

Zoe chimed in from the other side of the room, her Jersey accent clearly identifying her voice all the way to Antarctica. "I'll let you talk to your mom in peace. Gonna go get some water."

"Is that Zoe?" asked Mom, and then continued without waiting for an answer. "Say hi to her for me please and thank her parents for letting you stay there this week."

I ignored that and instead asked, "Mom, why is it safer for me not to be in Boston right now? What's going on?"

"Long story. There have been several large earthquakes and tremors at the edge of the Antarctic Plate over the last two weeks, and, in a nutshell, my research indicates that a high magnitude quake is impending, somewhere along the plate boundary in the next month. My paper isn't ready yet, but I've put together a summary of the findings and a warning for the U.S. Geological Survey to alert the scientific community. It could be weeks or months before this information makes it to the mainstream media, which makes you the first person outside of Antarctica to know."

"That's quite a breakthrough, Mom. Being able to predict something like that will really make your name in academia, won't it?" I was grinning proudly, even though she couldn't see me on the voice-only call. Video would take more bandwidth than McMurdo Station could afford.

"Inga, you misunderstand. This isn't merely about the research anymore. That quake could severely disrupt at least one or two extremely large, unstable glaciers, pieces of ice that hold back massive ice shelves. If any one of them collapses, chunks of Antarctica the size of U.S. states could crash into the ocean. Depending on what breaks off, and where it floats to, it will melt incredible amounts of freshwater into the ocean, raising sea level dramatically; five or ten feet, maybe more. The impact on sea level rise will happen in days. As the water rises, it will attack other glaciers from underneath, creating a chain reaction that could cause even more glaciers to subduct. This kind of rapid disintegration is a worst-case scenario, but if it happens, it could cause the sea to rise so fast that millions of people on the coasts would have to flee inland." I could hear the quick breaths between her rapid-fire sentences and the pitch of her voice rose at the end of each sentence.

"Mom, won't you and everyone there for the winter be in more danger than us up here? We are a long way from Antarctica."

The three-second delay was getting on my nerves, but I waited patiently for her reply.

"I've explained this before. What happens in the south affects the northern hemisphere more than the southern hemisphere. But listen, Inga, I didn't mean to frighten you. It's an extremely slim chance that any of this will happen, but I want you to be aware that this could happen. And in a few days, you'll be back in Boston, again by the coast. If anything happens here, you and everyone on the coast will have to get inland. It would be safer to stay at Zoe's, but of course, you can't do that. You have to go back to school."

If something happened and she found out I was in Florida...I had to fess up. I hesitated long enough for my mother to ask if I was still on the line. "Yeah, Mom, I'm still here. But 'here' isn't New Jersey. Zoe and I are in Miami for spring break."

My mom broke the time lag *and* the sound barrier. "What?! Are you serious, Inga? What the hell were you thinking?"

"I was thinking that it's damn cold in Boston and has been for months. We got the opportunity for a decent room, a block from the beach, at a good price, and found an affordable flight. Mom, if you could just postpone freaking out, Zoe's parents know where we are, and her mom approved the hotel. It's in a safe area."

I could hear her fury before it came out in words. "There is no safe area in Miami if the sea level goes up cataclysmically! We've discussed this before."

"Mom don't be melodramatic. It's only for a week. We are going home on Saturday. What are the chances of anything happening before that? I mean, other than the small storm off the coast. It's gotten rainy and windy here, but it's still a damn sight better than Boston in March!"

"Oh Inga, I wish you had told me you were going there. Do Zoe's parents think I know you went to Miami, or did you tell them you were lying to your parents? Are they supposed to cover for you if your father or I asked your whereabouts?"

"No! I would never put them in that position. Look, I'm sorry I lied, but if I told you, I know you would have forbidden me to come down here. You have a habit of catastrophizing everything."

As the old saying went, better to ask forgiveness than permission. I knew my mom would have said no. Dad too, because while he wasn't a total pushover, he almost always agreed with my mother when she laid down the law.

"Of course, I would have!"

I cut her off. "Mom, a month ago when we planned the trip, you had no way of knowing that there was any danger this far south. Your thoughts about a possible earthquake down there would not have changed my plans. It's unfair of you to be mad at me about this or expect me to change my actions based on an event that you said was extremely unlikely."

"Then why did you lie to me and your father? Or did you tell Dad the truth and only lie to the parent who is too far away to do anything about it?"

I started to reply but realized she was still speaking. "I'll tell you why you lied. You knew I wouldn't agree to this."

Well, more like yelling than speaking.

I knew she was worried and felt powerless, so I let her yell herself out before I even tried to respond again; only finally doing so once there was a four-second span of silence.

"Mom, I'm sorry. I really am. And I'll call Dad, like you asked, and tell him too as soon as we hang up."

"You will indeed! And make damn sure you get on that plane on Saturday and go home. I've already spoken to your father about contingency plans for getting out of Boston quickly, if need be, and he and Liam will be ready. Make sure you are there to go with them. Do you understand?"

"Yes, Mom." What more could I say other than that?

I said good-bye and hung up the phone, immediately placing another call to my father. This time I used video. Normally my father would be in class at this time of day, but the college where he taught, Northeastern, also had the week off. I wasn't sure what he and Liam were up to, but I was sure that he had his phone with him.

I had just hung up with my father when Zoe re-entered our room. She raised one eyebrow at me and said, "Couldn't help overhearing. Sorry. But...you are still breathing. How much trouble are you in?"

"Loads. Both parents. My dad and brother are heading up to Vermont for a couple of days of skiing and he just glowered at me and told me he expected more of me. I called just as he was picking up my brother's friend and he didn't have time to deal with me. He'll call me back tonight from Vermont to yell at me. I don't want to talk about it." I scowled and tried to get back to my paper but gave up in less than a minute.

Zoe rescued me from misery. "Let's see if Carlos can drive us downtown. So what if we're early?"

She was right. I grabbed my windbreaker and followed her to the elevator. The wind and rain outside were nothing compared to the shit storm I would face when I got home.

Fast Facts

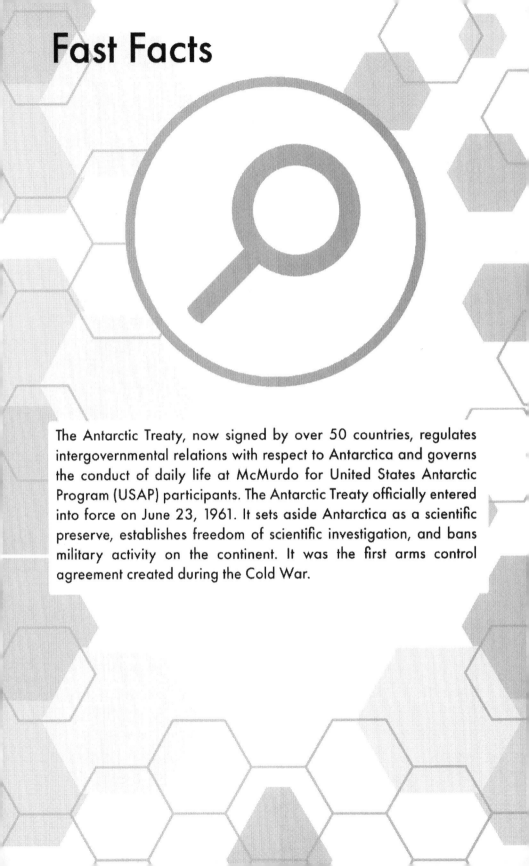

The Antarctic Treaty, now signed by over 50 countries, regulates intergovernmental relations with respect to Antarctica and governs the conduct of daily life at McMurdo for United States Antarctic Program (USAP) participants. The Antarctic Treaty officially entered into force on June 23, 1961. It sets aside Antarctica as a scientific preserve, establishes freedom of scientific investigation, and bans military activity on the continent. It was the first arms control agreement created during the Cold War.

Chapter 14

Nick – Boston

I disconnected the video call with Inga and almost threw my phone to the floor of the car. I couldn't believe her. As if I didn't have enough to deal with, with Kathryn gone and Liam being the trying child he always was. Inga was the one thing in my life I could count on to not screw up. Miami! What was she thinking?

I jammed my phone into its slot on the dash, backed out of Sebastian's driveway, and headed for the interstate.

"Dad?" asked Liam from the back seat. "You okay?

"Yeah, why?" I answered too quickly and too loudly.

"Nothing, just your nostrils are flaring like a dragon, and I can hear you breathing."

I hadn't realized I was doing that, and it figured that my son, who usually had some type of speaker jammed into his ear canal *would* pick this moment to not only be technology-free but also paying attention to the world.

"So, what's the matter?" he prodded. His friend, Bash, sat ramrod straight next to him. I could see both sets of eyes peering at me from the rearview mirror, silent, yet probing.

I answered in short syllables. "Your sister."

Liam immediately let out a guttural growl like a howler monkey but at the decibel level of a jackhammer. "Perfect Inga! Well, holy crap! What did she do?"

The grin on my son's face was remarkable. Somehow, by his older sister's indiscretion, he had come out on top, although not of his own doing. "She went to Miami."

Liam's readiness to revel in his sister's misbehavior was stopped short and his face fell. "So what? Why is that a problem?"

"This isn't your business, Liam. You only want to know because someone other than you has broken the rules." I pushed up the sleeves of my sweater, alternating hands on the steering wheel, and tugged at my collar.

"We have a rule against going to Florida?"

"That's not it!" I cut him off. "She lied about where she was going. She was supposed to be in New Jersey with her roommate, and instead, she got on a plane and went to an area that's not safe."

"Why not safe? Did she go with a boy or something? Besides, she called you and told you now, so obviously, she feels guilty and fessed up." He leaned back in his seat, so now I could only see his eyes and forehead, yet I knew he wore a satisfied grin.

"She didn't feel guilty. Mom called her from Antarctica and found out."

"Oh, so she got caught and Mom made her call you. So, what's her punishment for lying and going somewhere she wasn't supposed to?" The glee in my son's voice was scary. I had no idea if this was normal sibling behavior or if I should be worried about his emotional stability. Being an only child, I was never sure what the norm was for siblings.

"None of your business." I ended the conversation and Liam gave up. I focused on the road ahead, the interstate turning into State Road 2, heading west through Massachusetts. The boys spent most of their time playing a video game that, thankfully, I didn't have to listen to thanks to the aforementioned earpieces they now wore.

Once we hit I-91 and turned north, we quickly crossed the border into Vermont, and I shouted into the back seat to get their attention. "Liam!"

He pulled out his earbuds and asked, "Yeah, Dad?"

"Check conditions at all three ski areas for tomorrow."

"Killington and Okemo. What's the other one again?"

My son had been to every ski resort in southern and central Vermont since he was two but paying attention to minor details, like names, had never been his strong suit. "Bromley."

Researching stuff, on the other hand, was a natural talent. He could compare and contrast data in his head and make a good decision based on that research. I knew he was comparing prices, amount of man-made and natural snow, the number of lifts and trails open for each resort, plus the number of upper-intermediate and expert versus beginner trails at each location. Like me, my kids and Sebastian had grown up on the slopes, but both boys preferred the glades, while I liked the mogul runs. I knew Liam would consider that as well before making his determination.

"Okemo looks best, Dad," he decided. I didn't ask why, knowing I could trust Liam. I couldn't trust him to turn off electronics, get home on time, do homework, or show up to basketball practice, but this was a no brainer.

"Okay. Two more hours to go. Anyone need to pee?" I asked, peering into the rearview mirror.

They shook their heads, but Liam asked, "Can we stop at that country store over the border for dinner?"

I nodded. It had become part of our tradition. Drive to Vermont Friday after school, stop for food in Brattleboro, sleep at a B&B, ski Saturday, and do it all in reverse on Sunday. Kathryn and I had been doing this with our kids since Inga was three years old. It felt strange to make this trip without my wife and daughter.

Fast Facts

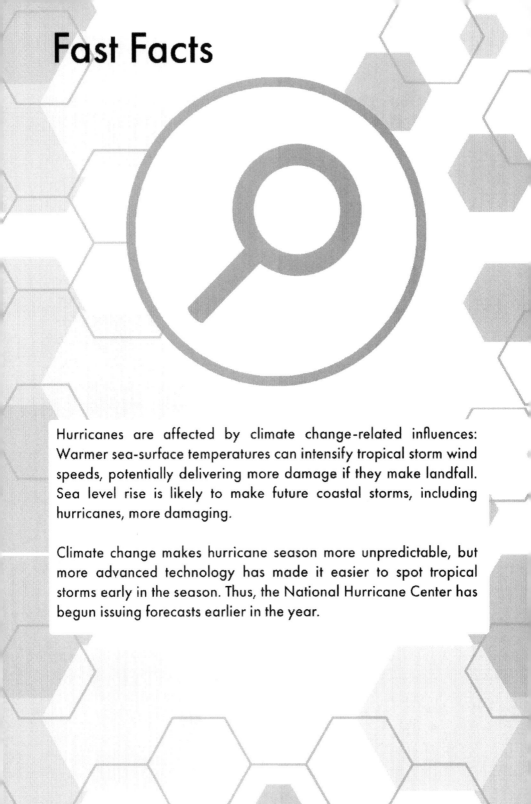

Hurricanes are affected by climate change-related influences: Warmer sea-surface temperatures can intensify tropical storm wind speeds, potentially delivering more damage if they make landfall. Sea level rise is likely to make future coastal storms, including hurricanes, more damaging.

Climate change makes hurricane season more unpredictable, but more advanced technology has made it easier to spot tropical storms early in the season. Thus, the National Hurricane Center has begun issuing forecasts earlier in the year.

Chapter 15

Inga – Miami

I clutched Caleb's arm as the final scenes of the movie played out and almost cheered with everyone else in the theater as the action hero defeated the villain, got the girl, and lived happily ever after. As formulaic as the plot was, the special effects were beyond fabulous, and the acting was superb. *Warrior Storm* would get a bunch of Oscar nominations.

I turned my DPA back on as we shuffled out of the Cineplex 8 and Lilith's virtual screen flashed a weather alert in my view. This was one instance where I preferred her disembodied voice in a crowd because focusing on the virtual screen while exiting the movie theater was tough. I was not that coordinated. "Lilith, audio-only," I said under my breath. I did not need to speak loudly for her to hear me.

It was just past six and ordinarily wouldn't be dark yet but as we emerged from the theater, the heavy gray skies made it seem like deep twilight.

Lilith's voice spoke in my ear. "You asked me to notify you of weather alerts. The current storm in the Gulf has intensified into a Category 1 hurricane and has also changed direction to an easterly path. It is projected to intensify into a stronger hurricane over the next 24 hours and to pick up speed, moving much faster than the models predicted. The current storm tracking models show Hurricane Alberto turning northeast, with an 80 percent chance of directly hitting Miami. The

National Weather Service has issued a warning to follow hurricane safety protocols and to take shelter in flood-prone areas."

The sky rumbled, and heavy rain bounced off the pavement. The deluge poured over the city with a roar as we huddled under the awning, waiting for our ride.

Jason was staring straight ahead, his eyes focused on the middle distance, which meant he was looking at a virtual screen his own digital personal assistant was showing him. "There! Our car is a blue, four-door Tour Electro, Florida plates beginning with UDJ." He pointed to an approaching vehicle which immediately pulled to the curb in front of us.

I stepped into the rain and in the seconds it took to reach the car door, my clothes were soaked. Caleb got into the car from the other side and smashed himself beside me as Zoe pushed herself in on my right. Jason was already in the front seat speaking with the driver as he pulled away from the curb. Inside the car, the rain hammered onto the roof louder than a rock concert drummer.

The flash river that ran down the street caught the car's tires and threatened to hydroplane even at the slow city street pace. The wipers could not keep up and visibility was reduced to a single car length. The wind was howling like the opening of a bad horror movie and the palm trees bent in the onslaught, taking the storm in stride, at least for now.

We sat in silence as the driver made his way out of the city center at a snail's pace, across the bridge that took us to the barrier island that was Miami Beach and the Palms hotel.

"You girls should stay here," said Caleb when we neared their hotel. When my questioning eyes met his, he continued. "It's a four-star resort. It's got to be stronger than your little hotel. You know, newer building codes and all."

I considered his logic because this *was* right on the beach and our *little* seven-story hotel was a block away from the churning ocean, but

Zoe beat me to the answer. "Absolutely. It's newer, probably tougher in bad weather, and it's squatter than our hotel."

As the car pulled up to the front entrance, Jason thanked the driver and told him to be safe out there in the storm, before getting out of the car and running toward the doors. We followed, battling the winds every step of the way.

Sodden, we crossed the opulent lobby, its high ceiling supported by tall, white columns and its walls covered in granite. It looked like it would withstand anything Mother Nature could throw at it, which boosted my confidence.

Caleb said, "It may be right on the water, but it has a lower level where there are conference rooms that serve as a hurricane shelter. They told us that when we checked in, but who would have figured we would need to use it in March?"

We passed a metal balustrade that surrounded the stairs leading down to the conference and spa level and dripped water across the terracotta floor all the way to the elevator.

Their room was on the third floor, and we could have taken the stairs, but as wet as we were, we might have slipped in our own micro-deluge as the stormwater streamed off our bodies.

The lights came on automatically when we entered their room, illuminating the heavy drapes pulled across the sliding glass door. "I thought we left the curtains open," said Caleb as he pulled them aside, so we could see the hotel grounds below.

Jason said, "There's a note on the nightstand. 'Dear guests: In preparation for the storm, all windows have been secured with clear plastic hurricane sheeting. Please leave the curtains drawn as a secondary security measure. In the event of a power outage or other storm-related event, please go to the lower-level meeting rooms for your safety.' It goes on, but that's the gist of it." He returned the paper to the tabletop and headed for the bathroom, returning with four large towels.

The exterior hotel lights illuminated the pool below, but every chair, chaise lounge, table, umbrella, and anything not made of concrete had been brought inside for safekeeping. Even the large tiki-hut-styled bar areas and gazebos had been disassembled, leaving brown skeleton frames, denuded of their faux-straw outer skins. Caleb closed the curtains against the inky darkness and driving rain in time to catch the towel Jason flung at him from across the room.

I looked down at my damp clothes and asked Caleb for a dry T-shirt, which he not only happily gave me but also brought me a pair of sweatpants and dry socks. "Thanks."

He kissed me in response, a full, wet lip smack that just about took my breath away. "You make these old baggy sweats look good."

I was so absorbed in Caleb's soft lips that for a moment I forgot about the storm, my mother's admonition, and even Zoe and Jason until I heard the TV in the background. They were sitting on Jason's bed, leaned back against the headboard as close as possible to each other, watching the news.

The satellite images on the television screen looked beautiful, a perfect swirl of white no more threatening than the circular designs on the hotel's fluffy white towels. The station was doing one of those 'man on the street' interviews and the guy talking was saying how he prayed the hurricane wouldn't come our way and that it would leave his home alone.

"That's ridiculous," I exclaimed. "It has to go somewhere. Praying isn't going to change anything. It might stay out at sea, but it's a fifty-fifty chance right now that its trajectory will hit the sunken everglades and keep coming inland. Just because it isn't supposed to hit Miami doesn't mean it can't turn right and come for us. It wouldn't take much."

Zoe translated. "Inga hates wishful thinking. That guy has no idea what this hurricane is going to do. He's just hoping his property will be okay and he thinks praying might help. She doesn't think God – if there even is one – plays favorites, so praying means that guy is asking God to spare him and hurt someone else."

She leaned into Jason next to her as if he could protect her from the hurricane. Zoe's sentiment toward Jason protecting her was about as realistic as the man being interviewed.

I couldn't fault my best friend though. I guess we all hoped for the best.

We huddled together, listening to the screaming of the wind and the rain pelting against the sliding glass door. We couldn't open that door anymore because the plastic sheeting the hotel management installed prevented it, but that would ultimately protect us if the glass cracked. Who wanted to walk out onto the terrace in a storm anyway?

The noise was almost unbearable, and this was only a Category 1 storm. I had to turn up the volume on the TV more than once.

I wasn't sure how watching the same news footage repeatedly could be so riveting but the four of us just sat there, watching for at least an hour until finally, Caleb said, "I'm hungry. Let's go see what the hotel restaurant has."

We were all famished and eagerly went to the lobby, but this time we took the stairs. Dressed in our borrowed sweats and t-shirts, Zoe and I were not exactly presentable in the elegant restaurant, so we hit the café. We took a table in the far corner, as far away from the windows as possible, mostly to get away from the sound of the wind and rain. Here too, the curtains were pulled across the windows, which were presumably covered with storm shutters on the outside, making it impossible to see outside anyway. I was quite sure that all hotels these days used shatter-proof glass, like in car windows, but Floridians were used to boarding up windows and drawing hurricane shutters across anything that opened.

It was nice that the guest rooms weren't shuttered. The newer high-tech plastic sheeting was just as strong as a storm shutter but allowed visibility.

The café smelled like cookies and roasted chicken, a combination that made me both hungrier and simultaneously wanting dessert first. We ordered sandwiches and salads, plus diet sodas, and this early into the storm, the hotel had not run out of anything yet, but I thought that would change in another day or so if the storm made it difficult for their deliveries to get here. But for now, we ate well.

"Do you think the hotel has bottled water and canned food for this kind of thing?" asked Zoe.

I nodded as I chewed my ham and cheese sandwich. It was my favorite since I was a little kid. "Probably dried and boxed stuff as well. And a backup generator," I added between bites.

The news played on every screen in the café. One station was explaining the cone of error, which was the weather graphic that they used to show where the hurricane's path might lead, but with a margin of error built in.

"Cone of Terror?" asked Zoe. "That sounds ominous."

A woman sitting with her family near us said, loudly enough for us to hear, "Cone of Terror is a nickname because anyone in the path is terrified."

When I nodded my thanks to her, she continued. "We're from Orlando, so we get plenty of tropical storms. Just thought we'd bring the kids to the beach for the week. No one predicted a winter storm of this strength, or we would have stayed home."

Her kids were fidgety, but I thought they were young enough not to be scared of the storm. They were just kids, with boundless energy.

I smiled at the children, and when I turned back to my friends, I realized that Caleb was staring over my head at a monitor. He said, almost too quietly to hear, "They just upgraded Alberto to Category 2. Geez, that's fast!"

Hurricanes weren't something I had a lot of experience with, since only a few had ever reached Boston. My expertise was with blizzards, which were the bane of every New Englander's existence. Every two or three years, we would get one of those "Storm of the Century" blizzards that buried the city, closed everything, knocked out power, and eventually forced our Governor to not only mobilize our own National Guard to dig us out but to request help from the Vermont Guard as well. Vermont had a lot of snowplows.

Swirling storms composed of liquid water were much more familiar to those in the south, and while Delaware wasn't the South, it was coastal, and Caleb and Jason had lived through their fair share of them, especially in the last few years as storms became more prevalent. Caleb continued, "And it's turning east. Toward us."

The newscaster said that as the storm swirled over the sunken Everglades, it would pick up massive amounts of water, which it would then dump on its easterly side. He also reminisced about the years when as a meteorologist, he could count on hurricane season starting in June. Everything was upside down the last few years.

"We should leave Miami," I said quietly. "It's going to get worse and maybe two hundred mile per hour winds don't mean much to locals, but for a girl from Yankeeland, I'm scared as crap. Pretty soon everything not nailed down – hell, everything that *is* nailed down – is going to start flying around like leaves in an autumn breeze, only it's going to be twisted metal and pieces of buildings big enough to flatten us. And that's before the floodwaters roll in."

The reality of our situation sunk in, and I completed my thoughts aloud. "We need to get out before we are in that Cone of Terror."

Three sets of eyes looked up at the images of the hurricane above us on the TV. Jason rubbed the back of his neck and Zoe fingered the skinny gold necklace she always wore. Caleb kept glancing at the ornate clock on the wall as if the sense of foreboding we all felt could be alleviated by slowing down time. Within seconds, all three agreed with me.

"We'll need to get back to our hotel and get our stuff tonight," said Zoe.

I pulled my phone out of my pocket and looked at the screen. It was almost eight. "And make plane reservations for tomorrow, first flight out," I added. "I'll have my DPA take care of ours to Boston." I asked Lilith if the airport was still open – the storm was only spreading wide bands toward Miami right now – and she confirmed that flights were still taking place.

Caleb nodded, swallowing the last bite of his sandwich. "Or anywhere available that is not here. My DPA will handle our flights to Wilmington. Or anywhere out of the path of the storm. Philly, or Newark, New Jersey, anywhere near Delaware is good enough. Inga, can I give Jax permission to interface with your DPA?"

Caleb wanted our DPA's to coordinate flights. I understood that, but...

"Jax? Your DPA's name is Jax?" I asked incredulously.

"Yeah, why?"

"Mine is Lilith." Anyone who had read my favorite series of steampunk novels by Ian Tregillis would know that Jax was the mechanical man who gained sentience and freedom from his human slaves, and Lilith was the captive robot he met along the way.

Caleb smiled at me with a sense of appreciation in a way only a kindred spirit could. "*The Alchemy Wars* have been my favorite novels since I first read them in eighth grade. I've read them at least five times."

I knew I liked this guy. "Six for me."

I turned my attention to the task of getting us out of the path of this hurricane. "Lilith, arrange a flight from Miami, Florida to Boston, Massachusetts, tomorrow morning, for me and Zoe. If no flight is available, arrange a flight to the nearest airport to Boston available. Permission to interface with Caleb Milanov's DPA, Jax, and coordinate departure times for Caleb's flight."

Within minutes, both Jax and Lilith notified us that we had departing flights just before and just after nine tomorrow morning. The boys had a flight to Newark, New Jersey, and Zoe and I were headed for Manchester, New Hampshire. Neither was getting directly home, and I wasn't sure how far Newark was from Delaware, but Manchester was the official alternate airport for Boston. It was just over the border, and about an hour north of my home in Cambridge.

"Come on," said Jason. "Let's get to your hotel and get your stuff." He was looking at Zoe in a way that was both protective and lascivious simultaneously and she caught it too.

As we took the stairs back to their room to get jackets, I heard Zoe ask, "Jason, why do you like me?"

He laughed, like this was the strangest question anyone had ever asked him, or perhaps it was just the most inappropriate timing. Eventually, he realized that she was serious and answered her. "Well, you are animated when you speak and use your hands a lot. It's cute. Plus, you smell fantastic."

Coming out of the stairwell, Caleb held the door for all of us and Zoe answered. "Those are really weird reasons to like someone."

Jason took her hand and walked quickly to their hotel room door. He swiped his phone across the keypad to unlock it and we followed him inside.

The storm winds were picking up. Stuff outside crashed noisily into the concrete hotel building, making me jump.

The four of us silently put coats on, though I wondered what use they would be against this rain. I envisioned all of it soaking through every piece of fabric on my body.

I had a ski jacket back at my hotel, which would be quite a lot more protection, but for now, my windbreaker was all I had. I zipped it up to my chin, patted the pocket of my borrowed sweatpants checking for my phone, and declared, "I'm as ready as I will ever be."

I could hear the wind through the concrete walls of the stairwell as we descended to street level.

Emerging into the storm, I almost turned back, but we had to get our things. I could live without most of what I brought with me, but without our IDs, we wouldn't get through airport security. Assuming the airport even stayed open much longer.

Caleb must have seen the look on my face because he shouted over the storm, "It's only half a mile. Come on, we'll make it!"

I swallowed hard, nodded at him, then ducked my head into the rain and followed him to the sidewalk.

My hair whipped so violently around my face I could barely see at all. In the darkness, the city had become a palette of gray and white, and different shades of in-between. Drops of water pelted us as we surged against the wind. I managed to lift my head just a bit and was rewarded for my carelessness with a face full of dirt and debris.

"Watch out!" someone shouted; I didn't know who. Perhaps it was Zoe, but the chaos around me washed away all but the loudest of her words.

A massive tree limb crashed down in front of us, its smaller branches reaching out gnarled fingers that grabbed our clothes and scraped our skin.

I clung to Caleb, holding onto the back of his jacket for fear of being separated by the sheer force of the storm.

I could feel Zoe next to me, never more than a foot away. One of her hands clutched Jason's arm, the other reached for my hand.

I grabbed it and we formed a human chain against the onslaught.

Fast Facts

The National Hurricane Center forecasts include a graphic that depicts the estimated track of each hurricane, including a cone that spreads out in front of the hurricane. It is called the cone of error but has earned the nickname "cone of terror."

People understand that the storm can go anywhere inside the cone, and one-third of the time outside of the cone, but the second they are no longer inside the hazy white funnel, they breathe a sigh of relief. They shouldn't. The forecast cone is not an impacts cone. The North Carolina Emergency Management Agency said people dropped their guard after Hurricane Matthew's cone of error moved away from the Carolinas in 2016. Three days later they were rescuing people off their roofs.

Chapter 16

Nick – Vermont

I was getting frustrated not being able to reach my daughter. I had tried her several times during the drive to Vermont and now that we had arrived and checked in, I'd gone from angry to worried to full-blown fear for her safety.

At 9 o'clock I tried again, and I let out a huge breath when she answered.

"Dad!" Inga all but shouted into the phone. "I'm really glad to hear from you!" She was breathing hard as if she had run a marathon.

"Hear from *me*? Inga, I've been trying to call you all day. Look, I'm not mad about you being in Miami, though I don't appreciate being lied to, but I'm really worried about you. I heard there is a storm on the way there..." I didn't even finish my thought before she cut me off.

"Yeah, it's coming this way. It's a Category 2 hurricane now, out in the Gulf. We've booked a flight out tomorrow morning. There were no flights available to Boston so we're landing in Manchester. Can you get us?"

"Yes, of course. Why are you so out of breath?"

My daughter gave me a long story about meeting some "nice boys" there and battling the rain to get to her hotel and pick up all their luggage, having decided to stay at the boys' newer, safer hotel and go to the airport with them. While I wasn't fond of my 18-year-old daughter staying with some guys she barely knew, at least they all had the sense to leave Miami early. My daughter had a good head on her shoulders, and I trusted her.

Though the pain of finding out she had lied to me about this trip was something that would take me time to get over.

Fast Facts

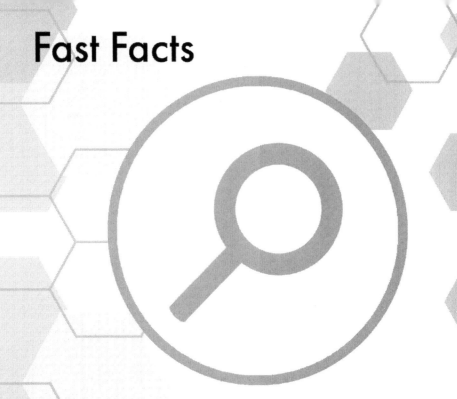

The United States Geological Survey (USGS) issues Earthquake Hazard Maps that show latest earthquakes, faults, and predict earthquake scenarios. Interactive graphic-rich story maps are available on their website at www.usgs.gov.

- The latest earthquakes maps show the past 24 hours from the ANSS (Advanced National Seismic System).
- An interactive fault map depicts comprehensive geologically based information on known or suspected active faults and folds in the United States.
- Earthquake scenarios describe the expected ground motions and effects of hypothetical large earthquakes.

Chapter 17
Kathryn – Antarctica

I held my head in my hands, mashing the temples between the heels of my hands, and then progressed to vigorously rubbing my eyes. I wished I could take my eyeballs out and run them under cold water. They were dry and tearing from staring at my monitor, but the hard work was almost over. I hadn't left my desk since I got off the phone with Inga this morning.

My report was done, proofread, and fact-checked twice. It was only two sheets of paper, as per USGS requirements. The earthquake hazard map with the key was on the front and the detailed, single paragraph on the back explained the figures.

I started reading it again, to verify all the data.

USGS Earthquake Hazard Map for Antarctica

Peak Horizontal Acceleration with 15 Percent Probability Exceedance in 1 year

By Kathryn Whitson, Massachusetts Institute of Technology, Earth, Atmosphere and Planetary Sciences Department.

March 2030.

A Mercator map of Antarctica, the Antarctic Plate, and its surrounding plates were positioned on the left side of the page. It was color-coded from light gray indicating the smallest seismic activity to red and dark brown indicating the most active. I had used the data on the USGS survey map for the Antarctic-Scotia Plate but updated it with data for the last two years, simply because their map was out of date. Then I added my data and circled it in red.

Earthquake Hazard Map for Antarctica

Peak Horizontal Acceleration with 15 Percent Probability Exceedance in 1 year

By Katrina Whitson, Massachusetts Institute of Technology, Earth, Atmosphere and Planetary Sciences Department.

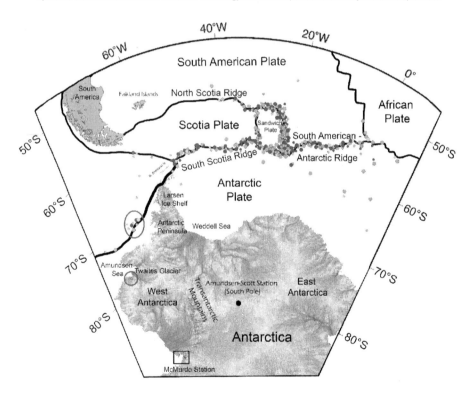

At the top of the key, I wrote an explanation:

"Locations of earthquakes with depths between 0 and 250 kilometers for the years 1975 to 2030 used in the hazard analysis. Circles are sized according to earthquake magnitude (M) and colored according to depth (h).

15 percent probability of exceedance in 1 year corresponds to a ground-motion return time of approximately 2500 years.

Incidence of new quakes detected in last 8-month period indicated in red-circled areas."

The explanation on the back was the most important part of the report:

Summary: Following a span of 8 months, ranging from mid-year 2029 to March 2030, seismic sensors recorded 6 quakes along the Antarctic Plate. Four were along the boundary of the Sandwich micro-Plate, and 2 were along the Antarctic Plate boundary, 50 kilometers west of the Antarctic Peninsula. All 6 quakes were between 4.1 magnitude and 5.3, with a duration of 9 to 28 seconds. A frequency of 6 incidents per 8-month period is typical for the region.

Beginning in the second week of March 2030, seismic sensors recorded a significant increase in activity, as follows:

- March 8, 2030: 3 quakes, with sequential magnitudes of 6.0, 6.2, and 6.3.
- March 9, 2030: 5 quakes, with sequential magnitudes of 5.2, 6.2, 5.0, 5.8, and 5.7.

- March 11, 2030: tremor of 2.3 magnitude, with epicenter 5 km south of the Amundsen Sea. Tremors on the continent of Antarctica are rare.

A frequency increase – even if not consistently incremental magnitudes – indicates that these readings are statistically relevant, with a 95% confidence level. Utilizing the predictive algorithm developed by the Berkeley Seismology Lab and used in the early warning system utilized by U.S. west coast states, combined with current readings of seismic activity from 3 volcanoes in Antarctica, the data shows that the seismic activity is measurably too high for an area with no volcanic activity, indicating a shifting of the tectonic plate beneath.

Predictive data: Based on the analysis using the Berkeley computer model and the new Whitson MIT Predictive Model, a quake of high magnitude will occur on the Antarctic Plate within 1 month, with a 95 percent degree of accuracy. The model shows that it will occur at the boundary of the Scotia and Antarctic Plates.

Situational Analysis: Much of the Scotia and Antarctic Plates boundary is at sea, and a large magnitude quake could have little to no effect on the continent other than potential tidal waves. Since Antarctica is mostly uninhabited, a tidal wave would pose little safety risk. However, if the quake occurs along the continental edge, especially in the northern section, it would be devastating. Currently, the Thwaites glacier has shifted by 3 meters, based on photographic evidence by Dr. Sylvia Rapp, Glaciologist, University of New Brunswick, Canada. Thwaites has become unstable.

Should a large magnitude quake disrupt at least 1 large, unstable glacier (sections of ice that hold back massive ice shelves), the ice shelf would collapse, and pieces of Antarctica the size of medium-sized U.S. states could crash into the ocean. Depending on what breaks off, and how much land ice follows it into the ocean, it will raise sea levels dramatically; 3 to 4 meters, perhaps even more. As each piece of land ice falls into the sea, it will immediately impact sea level. As the water rises, it will attack other glaciers from underneath, creating a chain reaction that could cause even more glaciers to subduct. This kind of rapid disintegration is a worst-case scenario, however, if it occurs it could cause the sea to rise so fast that millions of people on the coasts would have to flee inland. Potential total sea level rise could be upwards of 30 meters.

Recommendation: USGS should devise evacuation contingencies as flood and sea level rise mitigation tactics are planned.

I hit 'send' and my analysis was on its way to the USGS to warn the scientific community. I only hoped that my name, which was well respected in the field, would lend enough credibility that my somewhat outlandish prediction would not be scoffed at and ignored.

Fast Facts

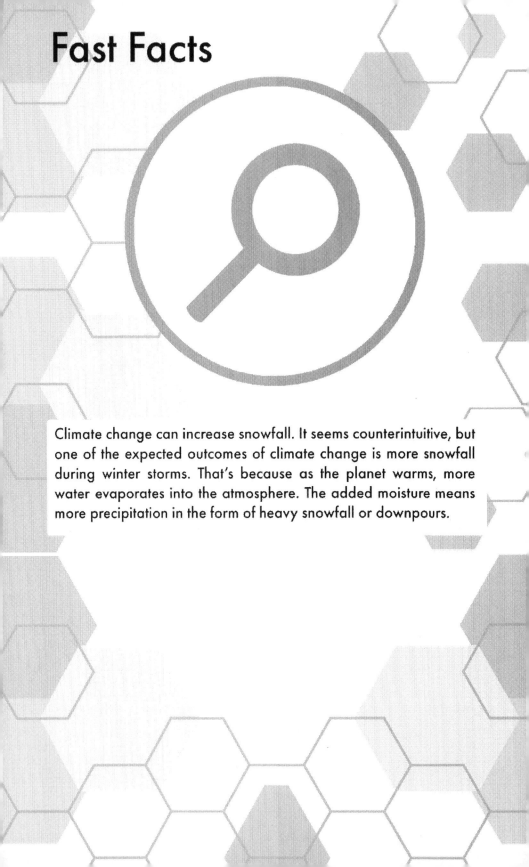

Climate change can increase snowfall. It seems counterintuitive, but one of the expected outcomes of climate change is more snowfall during winter storms. That's because as the planet warms, more water evaporates into the atmosphere. The added moisture means more precipitation in the form of heavy snowfall or downpours.

Chapter 18

Nick – Vermont

On the bedside table, my phone made a noise like a sound-bouquet of successively higher pitches in a musical line. It didn't so much wake me as incorporate the melody into my dreams until my brain sorted out the sound and differentiated the harmony from the dream state into the waking one.

When I saw the caller was my daughter, I came fully awake. "Inga, what's wrong?" I answered.

"Nothing, Dad, just that the storm is headed toward Miami, and they've canceled all the flights for today."

My stomach lurched, but before I could reply, she continued. "But it's still not predicted to hit the city directly or to grow much in intensity. It's headed north of Miami and moving fast. We'll be fine here, and we still have our flight for Saturday. Go skiing with Liam and Bash. Have a good time, and seriously, don't worry."

"How can I not worry about you? It's in my job description as a parent." I tried to give a little laugh, so she could hear that I was kidding, but of course, I wasn't. I was worried about my child, a thousand miles from me, and with nothing I could do to help her.

She sent a kiss through the phone, something she used to do when she was a little girl, told me she loved me, and hung up. My little girl was an adult, whether I liked it or not, and regardless of how worried I was, I could do nothing for her.

I tried to push the worry back to the far reaches of my mind and woke the boys.

It turned out to be an almost perfect ski day. Fresh powder coated the trails and the dove-gray sky showed momentary hints of cerulean blue peeking through the cloud layer. I rode the six-pack with Liam, Bash, and three snowboarders to the top of the chairlift that carried all the skiers up from the lodge, through the bowl into which every other trail eventually spilled.

This part of Okemo was a mixture of skiers, from raw beginners to the most seasoned veterans. Once at the top of the bowl lift, we skied down the west side toward the high-speed lift that would take us to the intermediate and expert trails on that side of the resort.

"Hey, Dad, Bash and I are gonna do the glades. Can we just meet you at the base lodge for lunch at like 11:30?"

I hesitated to let the boys go off on their own, not because they weren't good on the snow, but because they were fourteen years old. Two years ago I had less trepidation, but as second-year teenagers, they were more apt to get into dangerous situations than when they were younger. They were both fearless and adding the hormonally challenged early teen years to the equation invariably equaled turmoil.

"Let's do a couple runs together first," I decided.

They groaned, but that was the only argument I got. We headed off the lift to the left and they expertly threaded their way through the crowded bowl to the line for the express chair to the summit, which oddly, wasn't at the top of the western peak. Once on the lift, the boys talked to two other kids about the best trails and awesome tricks on the board, but my mind was on my daughter's plight until the boldness of the tall mountainous peaks drew my attention.

I had grown up skiing with my father. It was a generational thing on his side – his grandfather had emigrated from Norway and skiing was in our blood. From the moment I stepped into my first pair of skis as a child, I discovered the profound joy and unharnessed delight of gliding down a mountain, the sound of the snow crunching and squeaking beneath my skis.

As a parent, I had shared this blissful pastime with both of my children, passing along one of my small pleasures of growing up. I took my kids to the family cabin to ski the local hills, and when they got older, we started going to Vermont instead because the terrain was more challenging.

Nearing the top of the chairlift, I elbowed Liam next to me to get his attention. It was sometimes hard to hear through helmets. "Head left off the lift. We'll take the blue trail down and then we can go over to the south face and do a few runs there."

The morning was glorious. The snowy pines that lined the trails made a fairytale world as we cruised down the mountain, feeling the incredible rush of adrenalin that hits you when you catch an edge and almost go over, but right yourself and barrel down the slope. I liked moguls and wide-open cruisers, but the boys enjoyed the narrow trails through the trees, so we did runs on both types of terrain, although the narrow trails were difficult for me.

Four runs later my stomach was growling. The base lodge was inevitably a teeming mass of humanity.

"Lunch at the Summit Lodge, guys," I said as we boarded the quad lift. I could already taste the chili in my near future. Fifteen minutes later, we were standing our gear in a rack outside the lodge and lining up for much-needed sustenance.

"Get water," I reminded the boys. Staying hydrated was more important in the winter than the summer because out in the cold, you tended to forget how thirsty you were.

We shared a communal table in the lodge with other skiers, all in various stages of undress. You had to remove most of your cold-weather clothing to avoid overheating, but it was such a pain to put everything back on, that skiers tended to leave bits and pieces of their clothing dangling off their bodies. Bibbed pants hung low around waists, their straps reaching for the floor; unzipped jackets hung by an arm; boots almost always were unbuckled.

Hats, gloves, goggles, and helmets were strewn on tables, seats, and the carpet.

After lunch, I agreed to let Liam and Sebastian go on their own because they wanted to pick their way through trees while I wanted to attack some moguls before the end of the day. My skis were too long to traverse the narrow glade runs, while the boys' shorter snowboards would make quick work of it. "I'll meet you at our locker in the lodge at four. If I quit early, I'll be hanging out by the fireplace in the main lodge with a hot chocolate, so if you finish before that, come find me there."

"Okay, Dad," shouted Liam as he and Bash sat in the snow, buckling their bindings. I took off for a black diamond trail that I favored because it was steep and always had good bumps. In between runs, I checked for news alerts about the situation in Miami on my phone.

Two hours later the snow had lost most of its fluff and had transformed into a tougher path with an edge of ice. I was getting tired, and my old body was starting to make mistakes. *I should quit before I get hurt*, I thought, riding the lift to the top of the eastern-most peak that accessed a crossover trail that would get me back to the main base lodge.

I regarded the craggy steeps with their rocky outcrops coated in crystalline snow. The trees were stunted at this high altitude, like dwarves in a fantasy movie, and were coated in ice even this late in the season. As I neared the end of the lift, I put my goggles back down over my eyes and raised the safety bar, edging forward in the seat as I always did, ready for a quick getaway from my fellow chairlift riders.

I all but jumped off the lift, eagerly working my way through the crowd, and finally dropping into an intermediate trail that would take me almost sideways along the mountain, back to the base lodge. This trail was icy too, but it wasn't particularly challenging, and I backed off on my skis to take it easy.

It was then that I caught an edge.

I tried to regain my balance but hit a patch of slush that was refreezing in the shade of the mountain and went down. Hard.

The back of my helmet hit the snow and bounced before I could strengthen my head, limbs, and body, and come to a bumpy stop at the edge of the trail.

My breath was ragged and fast, and I fought to slow it.

"You okay?" someone asked as they skied toward me. I waved a hand to indicate I was fine, and they continued past me.

Stupid.

I wasn't hurt, except for my pride. A forty-something guy sprawled out on the snow was embarrassing. Skis, poles, even my goggles, were spewed across the slope. Total yard sale.

Reaching for my goggles, my phone rang in my pocket. I had set it to no calls except for my VIP list. Nervous Inga was calling with bad news, I fumbled to open my zippered pocket, tore my gloves off, and finally fished the device out.

"What's wrong, Liam?" I answered.

"Uh, Mr. Whitson, it's Bash. I couldn't get through to you on my phone, so I'm using Liam's. He's hurt." I could hear the teenager's voice cracking.

"How bad?" An adrenaline-fueled rush of terror surged through my body.

Sebastian's words were mingled with moaning in the background. That was Liam. "I don't know. Ski patrol is on the way. Someone stopped to help us. He's holding up Liam's head until they get here."

By this time, I had collected my gear and was ready to start toward the boys.

"Did he hit his head? What trail are you on? I'm on my way."

Bash replied, his voice now a little less shaky. "I think his head is fine. The guy is just trying to keep him calm. It's his right arm. He caught it on a limb, and it whipped backward as he brushed past it. Um, I think it's broken, Mr. Whitson."

"Okay, stay calm. Ski patrol is quick, and I'm sure they'll be there soon. Which trail are you on?" I asked again.

He told me, and I hung up the phone. I looked at the trail map and plotted out the best way to reach them, but it would take some time. There was no direct way from where I was to them without skiing down two-thirds of the mountain and then taking a slow quad-lift to the western mountain where they were. The ski resort had three main mountains and it was only by luck that I was already on the middle mountain and not still at the bottom of the eastern-most one when Sebastian called.

I tried not to panic racing to my child, but as a parent, my child getting injured was my worst nightmare coming true. I tried to reassure myself that a broken arm wasn't the worst thing that could happen to a kid.

By the time I arrived, ski patrol was not only on the scene, but already had my son on the stretcher, wrapped in a blanket, and was securing him for the trek down the mountain.

"Hey, kiddo," I said, releasing my ski boots from my bindings so I could bend down over my injured son. "Not your finest hour, huh?"

I flashed him a smile that was meant to be both calming and humorous.

Liam cringed and looked up at me from the stretcher. "Dad! I could hear the popping, ripping sound as my muscles tore away from my bones!"

"I'm his father," I told the ski patrol. This was obvious but required by law before they would give me information.

The smallest of the patrollers, a thin, young woman, said to me, "We splinted his right arm. It's badly wrenched but doesn't appear to be broken. An ambulance is waiting at the bottom, ready to take him to the hospital."

I grinned at my injured son. "Don't be melodramatic. You didn't tear any muscles, kiddo. It's probably just a ligament, and I know it hurts like hell, but you'll live. You're fortunate you didn't break anything."

Another of the ski patrollers nodded at me to indicate they were ready to begin the painfully slow trip down and I stepped back, out of the way.

Everything seemed to be going wrong. Both my children were in trouble, and I couldn't protect either one of them.

Fast Facts

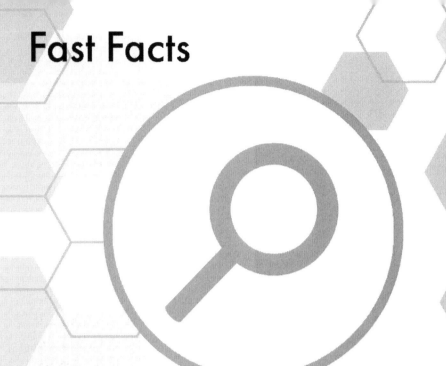

The Saffir-Simpson Hurricane Wind Scale rates storms based on sustained wind speed. The scale estimates potential property damage. Category 3 and higher are considered major hurricanes because of their potential for significant loss of life and damage.

- Category 1: Winds 74-95 mph (119-153 kph). Very dangerous winds will produce some damage.
- Category 2: Winds 96-110 mph (154-177 kph). Extremely dangerous winds will cause extensive damage.
- Category 3: Winds 111-129 mph (178-208 kph). Devastating damage will occur.
- Category 4: Winds 130-156 mph (209-251 kph). Catastrophic damage will occur.
- Category 5: Winds 157 mph or higher (252 kph or higher). Catastrophic damage will occur.

Chapter 19

Inga – Miami

Getting back to Jason's and Caleb's hotel last night had been just as harrowing and soaking an experience as the trek to the Miami Inn had been. It took us an hour, but at least we were in a sturdy, concrete structure that had been designed to withstand a Category 5 hurricane. We had all changed into dry clothes and tuned to a local news station for minute-by-minute updates of the storm. I'm not sure what time I finally fell asleep, nestled up against Caleb in his bed, but I woke hours later to the fury of the wind outside and a dark room. A minuscule amount of light was creeping in around the edges of the heavy curtain.

I nudged his sleeping form. "Caleb," I whispered.

"Umm, yeah?" he groaned sleepily and threw an arm over me in a hug.

I looked down the short hall to the bathroom where I had left the light on behind an almost-closed door in case I had to get up during the night. I didn't want to trip in an unfamiliar space. The hall and the bathroom were dark. "I think the power is out."

At that, he came fully awake. He used the remote but was unable to turn on the TV. "Crap."

I got out of bed and peeled back the curtain, craning my neck to look up and down the beach. "No lights in any of the other hotels either. I think the power is out everywhere."

"Great," came Zoe's sleepy voice behind me. "At least my phone is fully charged. The power must not have gone out too long ago. It's barely past dawn."

A moment later she groaned, and I already suspected why. Zoe said, "*Big* red message on the airline's website. 'Miami International airport is closed. All inbound and outbound flights are canceled. The runways are flooded, and the wind is too strong for flights. We will advise as soon as the situation improves.' Yeah, not surprising."

"Now what?" asked Caleb and Jason, simultaneously.

I left the heavy curtain open, as it was the only source of light in the room other than our phones, and the weak daylight Mother Nature was trying to provide. "My vote," I replied to the room, "Is to get ready and dressed, and then go down to the lower-level meeting rooms and see what the hotel is doing about getting us some breakfast. After that, we'll have to sort it out."

"Inga is right," agreed Caleb. "Food first."

It wasn't long before the four of us were trudging down the stairwell, lit entirely by emergency lighting, along with a few other guests and working our way toward the smell of coffee and baked goods. The lines were long, but we had nothing better to do all day, while we sat out the storm. There was some emergency power, and being one level below the lobby, we felt reasonably safe, even though that floor was not completely underground. A bank of windows that faced the beach on the east side was heavily shuttered.

We still had our original flight for Saturday. Today was Wednesday, so hopefully, everything would be back to normal by then, but I doubted it. The call with my father hadn't been traumatic. He was angry and worried, of course, but he would spend a couple of days skiing with the brats, while I muddled through a storm, and soon enough I would be back in Boston, and he could yell at me properly. Perhaps by then he wouldn't have any anger left.

By mid-afternoon, the storm was right overhead, and it was so loud we huddled with hands over our ears and still felt like our eardrums would burst from the screaming wind and rain outside. The steel beams of the hotel creaked and my blood chilled; suddenly being refugees crowded into the basement level with coffee and donuts seemed like the smartest thing we had done all day. The storm was moving fast as it cleared the sunken Everglades and made a beeline for the Atlantic Ocean. By late afternoon, the hurricane had grown to a spinning behemoth over the sea. One hundred and twenty mile an hour winds lashed the beach. We stayed together on the floor, watching the news until it stopped.

Then it was silent. Absolutely silent, like a cathedral.

The hotel manager ventured outside and most of the guests, including us, pushed behind him, through the doors that led to the beach. I could see the people ahead of me, already outside, bathed in sunlight. The storm was gone, like a bad dream, except for the wind. A gust blew by me, raising the little hairs on my arms. The eye had never come over us, so we must have been in the twirling outer arms of the storm the whole time. It probably wasn't the worst hurricane to ever hit Miami, but it was my first, and I'd been horrified.

I poked my head outside and the devastation hit me hard. This swathe of sand covered in garbage was the previously glorious Miami Beach.

The ocean waves still surged, even though the rain and wind had moved north. We followed the crowd and picked our way through the wreckage toward the road. Giant pieces of steel, concrete, and shredded plastic littered everything, except the low-lying roads, where the debris floated on new rivers. Buildings were stripped of their outer walls. There was a washing machine on the sidewalk, and a huge tree had broken into three pieces and was leaning against a concrete building.

The roads were completely consumed by water.

It had rained almost twenty inches in the last 24 hours and most of that rain occurred in the last five hours causing catastrophic flooding.

"It will be worse inland," someone near me said.

I turned and looked at a tall woman, about my mother's age. "Why?" I asked her.

She must have been a local because her insight was much more informed than most. "Flooding on rivers and streams can last for several days after a storm and rain-triggered flooding doesn't just affect coastlines. Hurricanes can cause deadly flooding inland, not just creating havoc and damage, but killing people along the way. As little as one foot of moving water can sweep a car off the road. Six inches of moving floodwater can sweep an adult off their feet. People who don't know better drive into floodwaters thinking they can drive through it safely. South Florida is prone to washouts whenever we have large amounts of rainfall."

"Yeah, but aren't people around here used to this? Don't they know better?" I asked.

She gave a short laugh before replying. "Take a look around you. How many people around here are from *around here*?" It was a rhetorical question. We all knew that most people in Miami at any given time were tourists. Tourists like us, and no, we didn't know any better.

She didn't wait for my reply before continuing. "With the sea level as high as it is, much of south Florida is already wet and vulnerable. These days, storm surges go many more miles inland than they used to when I was a kid, flowing up drainage canals. The airport shuts down with every major hurricane. Saltwater shorts out underground electrical wiring, leaving the area dark for weeks and contaminating drinking water, *that's* why the hotel has so much bottled water. Everyone does. I've never seen a hurricane this early before, but at least we don't have to worry about Zika virus mosquitoes in March."

"Yeah, great. One piece of good news," Jason groaned behind me.

I stopped walking and stared at the devastation in front of me. "Let's go back."

Once we began picking our way back to the Palms, most of the other hotel guests followed. There was nothing we could do out here until the relief services began organizing the cleanup. They had been staged just north of the city since before Alberto hit the state, and according to the knowledgeable woman walking with us, they would begin cleaning up debris and repairing downed power lines as soon as it was safe. Not much they could do about the flooding until the water ran off the surface into the canals on its own. The extensive, interconnecting network of canals and levees in southeast Florida were created in the early 1900s for drainage, flood protection, and water storage purposes, and with each hurricane or major rain event, they were an integral part of keeping Miami above the water.

But it would take days for all the water to flow down into the canals, and that didn't even consider the number of downed trees and power lines, which of course would leave a lot of areas without electrical power. No power meant no refrigeration, no freezers, no way to keep food and medicines cold. People would be in the dark, many without water as well, standing in line for ice, aid, and bottled water. I had seen this on the news many times but never lived through it.

Fast Facts

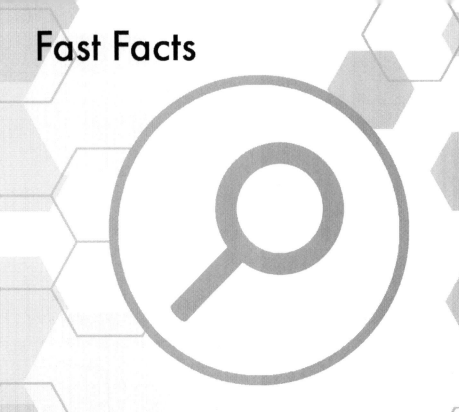

In many low-lying areas, especially in lower-income countries, water slums have arisen. One example is Makoko in Lagos, Nigeria. The community is made of floating structures and pole houses and shacks. It is an elevated community on stilts, shanties built of burlap and driftwood, connected by canals crowded with boat traffic. Poor people paddle boats full of rice and vegetables to sell to neighbors. In a water slum, it doesn't matter how high the water rises, the buildings can move with it.

In Makoko, people have learned to live with water, not fight it.

Chapter 20

Kathryn – Antarctica

I met Sylvia at our usual breakfast table like I had most days since we had arrived eight months ago. McMurdo Station had an international crew and I had developed a penchant for the eastern European custom of fresh bell peppers, sliced up and slightly salted, served alongside a generous hunk of bread with real butter, and thick-sliced pepperoni. I wasn't going to pass up the fresh veggies and served myself at least two full servings of the brightly colored peppers. Sylvia, being Canadian, ate a typical North American breakfast: carbs, carbs, sugar, and more carbs. Her plate of pancakes, smothered in Canadian maple syrup, with half a dozen sausage links alongside certainly fueled the Antarctic resident, but was only slightly healthier than a Tim Hortons' donut.

"Not to be a pest, but did you hear back from the USGS yet?" asked Sylvia before taking a sip of black coffee. She had a habit of prefacing her sentences. It made her sound hesitant, not the confident scientist I knew she was.

I nodded slightly, my cup already at my lips and not wanting to stop the previous flow of caffeine to my mouth. After a long swallow, I answered. "Yes, I got an email this morning."

"And?" she prompted me, stuffing a generous forkful of pancakes into her mouth.

"And nothing. At least not much. They acknowledge that since most of the fault line in my warning is at sea, a large magnitude quake will likely have no effect on the continent, and even if it did, the population here is currently so small as to be in such limited danger that they don't plan to issue any warning."

"That's ridiculous!" Sylvia shouted. "Didn't you tell them that if the quake occurs along the northern continental edge, it would be devastating?"

I nodded and continued chewing my buttered bread. Back home I would never eat like this, but here I burned enough calories just staying warm that I wasn't concerned about developing extra flab around my middle.

Sylvia spoke through her teeth with forced restraint. "Don't take this the wrong way, but didn't you tell them about my evidence that Thwaites is unstable?"

I nodded again, noticing people beginning to pay attention to us.

"Did they comment at all about a quake disrupting the Thwaites glacier and potential ice shelf collapse? Do they not care that enormous chunks of ice could break off if it's disrupted by an earthquake and potentially raise sea levels dramatically? It's not about the effect it might have on an almost-deserted continent; it's about the rest of the world!" She was getting louder, and the entire dining hall was listening now.

"Yes, I warned them about three, four, or even more meters of abrupt sea level rise if that should happen. And before you ask, the time frame was in my report as well. Weeks or months, not decades."

"And?" she prodded. I thought she would burst a blood vessel.

I tipped my head back on my neck to look at the ceiling. "And nothing. They thanked me for my due diligence, said that up until now my research has been exemplary and they do not discount my data, they simply do not feel I have presented enough evidence for them to issue a warning. They claim they have sufficient evacuation contingencies for coastal flooding already in place and in the event of an Antarctic earthquake, they will issue evacuation procedures for the Pacific, Atlantic, and Gulf coasts in the U.S. and advise other national and international agencies at that time."

Sylvia threw her hands up in an 'I give up' gesture. "Why aren't you more upset about this?" Sylvia could always see both sides of an argument and behaved well in public. This was not typical Sylvia.

I gave a half-hearted shrug. "It's what I expected."

"You did? Really? You seemed so eager to send your recommendation. I was sure you were confident they would consider it."

Pieter, the construction worker turned crawler driver, suddenly towered between us, and asked, "May I join you, ladies?"

I looked at my plate, empty except for three slices of pepperoni. "Sure, but we are almost done."

He ignored me and sat. "I couldn't help overhearing, but..."

Sylvia snorted through her nose, and I outright laughed. "You don't say?"

Sylvia might not have noticed the spectacle she was making, but once the handsome Dutchman sat down, a corner of her mouth lifted in a half-smile.

"You Americans are loud." He knew Sylvia was Canadian and I suspected he was trying to raise her ire on purpose, because the minute she tried to protest the insult, his eyebrows waggled, and realization dawned on her face. She smacked him playfully on the shoulder before leaning back in her chair, visibly relaxing.

"Okay, so do you have a better solution?"

"I admit I did not hear your entire conversation, but only because I wasn't in the room when you started, however, is anger a solution? So far, you have nothing."

I saw Sylvia's eyes narrow, and apparently so did Pieter, because he spoke faster. "Yes, I do have a solution to getting your warning out. Use social media."

"Are you serious, Pieter? We can't just make some posts and hope they go viral. This is serious." I knew enough about guerilla publicity tactics to know Pieter's idea sounded calamitous. "Millions of people around the world living on the coasts would have to flee inland if the sea level suddenly rises. We can't create an evacuation plan without the cooperation of the world's governments. All we would do with a viral social media campaign would be to spread panic."

He was undeterred. "My daughter does public relations for a living for some high-profile organizations, and I've learned a thing or two from her over the years. I think we could get your message out, without creating a panic, not by targeting the public, but rather the other world governments. Maybe social media isn't the word I was looking for. I meant public relations. All it takes is a few, and even megalithic countries like the U.S. will heed your warning if enough other nations start. There are island nations that will cease to exist if the sea level rises catastrophically, and I bet they all have flood and sea level rise mitigation tactics and evacuation plans already in place."

Sylvia nodded her agreement.

"We just need to find out which countries have plans and get your warning to them. You ladies are researchers, right?"

A smile danced on his lips. No one called female Ph.D.'s 'ladies.' Pieter had a knack for pissing off Sylvia, and he was doing it on purpose.

I thought it was an odd way to flirt.

I must have been wrong because Sylvia returned his lopsided grin and said, "Okay, so what nations would be good targets? China, Thailand, and Indonesia are no brainers, because large parts of Shanghai, Bangkok, and Jakarta would easily be submerged, but where else? Let's make a list."

We cleaned up our breakfast trays and followed Sylvia back to her office. It was the largest and had enough computers that we could start researching online. I said, "I'll start a group document on the main drive, and we can list the target countries there. As you find them, add columns for contact info for whatever government department seems to coordinate evacuation plans and sea level rise management. Names, phone numbers, email, whatever you can find. I've set it to auto-alphabetize so we can stay organized. Let's start with China, Thailand, and Indonesia."

An hour later we had identified almost thirty cities and countries that we felt were in imminent danger from a sudden rise in sea level. While every seacoast was at risk, not every country had huge populations that lived directly on the ocean. But those that did, totaled over 150 million people worldwide. In Asia, the worst hit would be Shanghai and Guangzhou, China; Mumbai, India; southern Bangladesh; Jakarta, Indonesia; and Bangkok, Thailand. The Pacific island nations of Kiribati, the Maldives, and the Marshall Islands would become coral reefs. In Africa, Lagos, Nigeria would be so overwhelmed, it would lose most of its population, and Alexandria and the Nile River Valley in Egypt would certainly be underwater.

In Europe, Denmark, Belgium, and the Netherlands were so low-lying that even with their famous flood mitigation, much of each country would be gone. The North Sea coast of Germany; Valencia, Spain; and London, England would be submerged. Ho Chi Minh City would be wiped off the planet, as would Venice and about twenty other smaller towns at the northern reaches of the Adriatic Sea. At the northern end of the Persian Gulf, the waters would rise in southern Iraq and Kuwait.

It took us the rest of the day to gather the contact information for these cities and countries, but we finally had our data. Now we needed a plan for what to tell them. The tremendous time difference between McMurdo and the east coast of the U.S. for Sylvia and me to contact our families turned out to not be quite as difficult for Pieter. His daughter in Holland was only eleven hours behind us, so after dinner, Pieter called her as she was waking up and explained the situation.

She promised to have a workable campaign put together by this time tomorrow.

Fast Facts

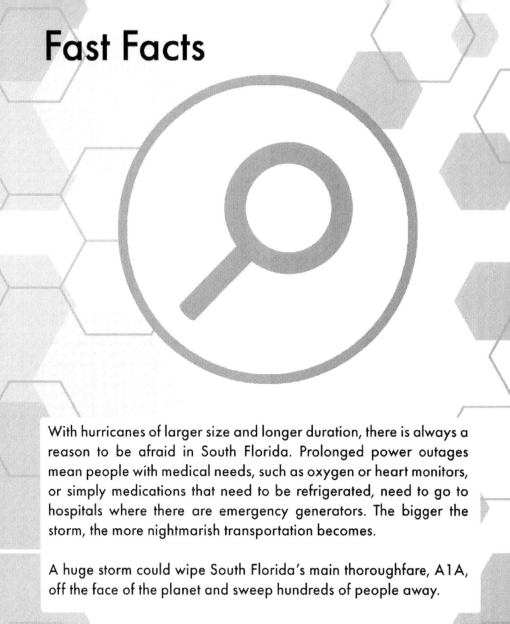

With hurricanes of larger size and longer duration, there is always a reason to be afraid in South Florida. Prolonged power outages mean people with medical needs, such as oxygen or heart monitors, or simply medications that need to be refrigerated, need to go to hospitals where there are emergency generators. The bigger the storm, the more nightmarish transportation becomes.

A huge storm could wipe South Florida's main thoroughfare, A1A, off the face of the planet and sweep hundreds of people away.

Chapter 21
Inga – Miami

The hotel management sent us back to our rooms for the night, even though the power was out. They said we could come back to the lower-level conference center for food and water at any time but wanted to avoid overcrowding when there were perfectly good rooms to use. It made sense, and we had all taken turns charging our phones downstairs off the generator power during the day.

When we woke Thursday morning, the power was still out, but with the sun shining, we had plenty of light in the room. We all showered and dressed since the hotel's water system operated from the generator, but we used bottled water to brush our teeth. The tap water might be contaminated from the storm.

"Are you guys finally ready to go down?" asked Zoe.

I nodded and followed everyone out of the room. The electronic lock would not close behind us with the power out, so it would be open to anyone who wanted to get in. Overnight, we had flipped the manual lock, but could not do that from the outside. The hotel was secured at the front and back doors by both the generator-powered emergency system and also by the bellman standing his post, so the only people who could get into Caleb's and Jason's room were those already inside the building. I didn't think the guests would start looting each other's rooms.

We may have been awake early, but we were far from the first to arrive in the emergency shelter room. There were about a dozen guests, most with children, already eating, drinking, and talking. We got ourselves some bagels and coffee and joined a group at a long cafeteria-style table. Caleb sat beside me, close enough to rub his arms against mine and his touch was comforting.

I stared up at the monitor in the far corner, the only one powered up on the limited generator power and watched the news broadcast. The volume was up loud enough, but the little kids were running around and making a racket, which made it hard to hear. Good thing for captioning beneath the video.

Just over half of south Florida's population was without electricity. Utility officials warned that it could take ten days or more for power to be fully restored. Most of the roads were severely flooded and people drifting back from shelters were finding their homes damaged or destroyed. The same went for businesses.

The city of Miami and surrounding Dade County had enacted a 9 p.m. curfew. Locations of shelters were reiterated from yesterday, for those who tried to weather out the storm and now were deciding that they couldn't stay home without power. The Salvation Army emergency disaster services had rolled trucks out overnight to areas hardest hit, and those trucks would hand out packaged meals and bottled water to anyone with the patience to stand in line. The addresses scrolled across the bottom of the monitor.

The news report went on to tell story after story of ways people had died. There were over fifty people dead and hundreds unaccounted for. The storm surge knocked buildings off their foundations and inundated the expensive mansions that lined this part of Miami. Dozens had drowned. Others lost their lives to falling debris that had crushed them. Another group of people were trapped inside of a municipal building that had collapsed from its foundation upward due to rushing floodwaters.

For all that devastation, the city of Miami had been spared greater catastrophe from the storm surge by Fisher Gate, but in unprotected areas, there was flash flooding. The water had risen in places from six to fifteen feet in half an hour. Warnings were issued not to drink tap water as contamination could cause leptospirosis, a bacterial infection transmitted through water contaminated with animal urine, and since the incubation period could be anywhere from two to thirty days, you wouldn't even know you had it until you were debilitated and suffering.

The storm had been brief, and even though people were getting used to larger and more frequent storms, by noon, we were all getting antsy in the shelter. Zoe checked her phone and declared that the airport was still closed.

Caleb leaned toward me, his eyes glowing and his hands fidgeting in his lap. "I desperately want to go outside and walk along the beach, even if it means dodging debris," he admitted.

"Ditto," I answered. So, we went.

We walked along the tide line where murky gray waves crashed. We weren't alone. Seagulls shrieked like spoiled children, swooping down for choice tidbits of seaweed and smaller sea creatures that the storm had washed ashore.

On the nearby roads and the Biscayne Bay side of Miami Beach, there were dangling electrical power lines and wrecked boats in the marinas, but here on the Atlantic Ocean, the damage was mostly beach erosion, along with trash and debris like shattered glass, wood, and other materials from the storm's destruction. The salty air tickled my nose as we picked our way through the mess.

Caleb interlaced his fingers in mine, and we walked hand-in-hand. I was starting to wish he didn't live so far away from Boston. I would miss him once we all got back to our respective homes. Not that Delaware was that far away, but still, I didn't think I wanted a long-distance relationship.

"I took an ecology class last semester as my science elective, and it's funny because, at the time, I didn't think anything I learned would be of practical use to me in life," said Jason, walking behind us with Zoe. "Even weirder is that I remember some of it. Beach erosion in particular."

"Really?" asked Caleb, turning to look back at his friend. "You remember something from a class. That's hilarious!"

"Seriously," scowled Jason. "Hey, if you don't want me to share, I'll shut up. I've got a gorgeous woman to look after and make sure she doesn't fall in the sand, after all."

"I can take care of myself!" Zoe punched his shoulder and he started laughing so hard, I thought *he* might fall in the sand. Zoe was not, and never would be, a damsel in distress.

Once Jason regained his composure, he continued. "When waves and currents remove sand after a storm, it makes the beach narrower and lower in elevation, just like it is here now. The hurricane's waves carry the sand offshore, storing it in sandbars. For months after the storm, the sand is slowly returned to the beach by calm-weather waves. Eventually, nature will put it all back if another big storm doesn't come along and start it all over again. But on populated beaches like Miami, they repair it faster with machines."

Caleb said, "Yeah, I saw something about that on one of those learning channel vids. They'll remove the large debris from the sand first, with tractors, and then lay the sand back on the beach. But some of that sand is contaminated, so they have to clean it while they are putting it back."

"Clean how? Like, disinfect it?" I asked.

"No, clean as in removing the junk. Rubble, garbage."

"Oh, like my little brother's room." Liam was a slob.

They all laughed and then Caleb continued. "They use surf rakes to remove smaller debris from the sand, the stuff that the tractor couldn't get. Then the rakes level the beach from rough like it is now, to a smooth beach. But it's a work in progress. Long after the hurricane is over, they have to keep cleaning it because the tides keep bring back the wreckage that washed out with the flooding."

I stepped over a large piece of metal that looked like it was torn from a roof and said, "Big job. It's a pretty place, but I couldn't live here. These storms are too scary. I'll take the occasional winter blizzard over a hurricane anytime."

We turned back soon after that. The once enchanting beach was depressing.

When we returned to the hotel's lower-level conference room an hour later, the news broadcast had turned into a discussion between analysts. A middle-aged Latino, identified on the screen as the Director of Disaster Services for the state, was discussing why the city was lucky. I found it strange that with all there was to talk about, anyone was spending time talking about what did not happen, but having nothing better to do, I paid attention to the broadcast.

The director said, "Luckily, the wastewater treatment plant on Virginia Key was not knocked out, because the city might have to dump its raw sewage into Biscayne Bay. We would have no choice. Garbage would litter the beach and the bacteria from the sewage would cause cholera. As I said, none of that occurred, and for that, we are thankful that nature has been kind."

The female anchor of the broadcast asked, "Dr. Acebo, I have to ask the question no one will. What would happen if the nuclear power plant at Turkey Point was heavily damaged by a storm surge?"

The director achieved a facial expression I have only seen after eating a raw lemon. "It would send a radioactive cloud over the city, but

Margaret, that could not happen. The utility has assured us the plant is completely safe, and its safety inspections from the Nuclear Regulatory Commission are completely up to date. The state of Florida takes nuclear power very seriously. Nothing like that can happen."

"Oh, that's encouraging!" said Caleb. I hadn't realized he was sitting next to me, but he had returned from the food station with sandwiches.

I looked around for Zoe and didn't see her. "Any idea where Zoe and Jason went?"

"Back up to our room," said Caleb, as if he wished he had thought of the idea first. A little privacy amid destruction wasn't a bad thing.

"So, what are we supposed to do here all day, in a city with no power and stuck in a hotel basement?" I mused aloud, not expecting Caleb to answer.

"Why don't we go volunteer ourselves to clean up the mess?"

Score another point for this guy.

"Why not?" We ate our sandwiches as we worked our way through the wreckage to the Miami Beach Police Department, two miles south. Caleb presented us to the woman at the front desk as two able-bodied people ready and willing to help in clean-up efforts.

She smiled warmly and said, "Thank you. That is wonderful, however, we cannot begin cleaning up until the utility company and the state declare the area safe. Have you ever helped clean up after a storm?"

We both shook our heads.

She continued. "Storm cleanup is different from regular cleaning. There are hazards including downed trees and power lines, broken sewer and water pipes, structural damage to buildings, roof damage, and broken windows. Disaster cleanup work is extremely hazardous. There are health concerns that require special tools and cleaning techniques, as well as protective gear like gloves, respirators, and goggles."

A look of concern crossed Caleb's eyes. "What kind of health concerns?"

Her answer was delivered completely deadpan as if she gave this speech daily to well-meaning but completely unprepared individuals. Like us. "Flesh-eating bacteria, chemicals released during the storm, and asbestos knocked loose from buildings, can create a toxic brew of chemicals and mold, which could cause debilitating and deadly long-term problems for those doing the work."

A shiver ran up my spine. "Oh. So, is there anything we are qualified to do?"

"Of course! Go to the Miami-Dade County mobile disaster unit at the Convention Center. They are providing housing and food to people who can't return to their homes and displaced visitors. You can help them distribute water, food, and relief supplies, or administer first aid if you are qualified."

We thanked her and left the police station, carefully picking our way through the wreckage, back to the beach to avoid the flooded roadways.

The Convention Center was closer to the Palms hotel than to the police station, only nine blocks south of where we started. If only we had known, we could have saved an arduous walk.

It was 3 p.m. by the time we made it to the building filled with those relying on the charity of the Red Cross, the city, and their neighbors. We joined the relief effort, handing out bottled water and provisions, then serving food at dinnertime, snagging bowls of macaroni and cheese for ourselves.

I saw a familiar face in the food line. Carlos Martinez, the shuttle driver from our hotel, stood before me, holding the hand of a boy about three years old.

"Hi, Carlos! I'm surprised to see you here." I was about to ask if everything was okay, but he wouldn't be in a hurricane shelter if it was.

"Hello, Inga. This is my son, Mateo."

The dark-haired boy smiled up at me as I prepared plates of macaroni and cheese with a side of green beans. I had not seen a wedding ring on Carlos and didn't imagine him as a father.

"Did the Miami Beach Inn get flooded out?"

Carlos flashed a smile that was meant for a silly child and answered, "We don't live at the hotel!"

I really wasn't very bright sometimes.

He continued in his charming, sing-song Cuban accent. "We lost power and it's not easy with a small child on the seventh floor of an apartment complex, so we came here for a hot meal. But I think we'll go home to sleep. This place is swarming with people and Mateo is frightened." He took the plates I handed him, gave the smaller portion to his little boy, and said quietly for my ears only, "I also worry that he could wander off in the middle of the night while I am asleep."

I nodded knowingly. Liam used to wander around at night when he couldn't sleep, at about that age. I could imagine this young child getting lost in row after row of cots. "Is Mateo's mom here?"

Carlos shook his head. "No, no, it's just me. His mom isn't with us anymore. Oh, we are holding up the line! Thank you, Inga." He nodded to Caleb who was serving the line beside mine, took hold of Mateo's hand and left.

"Must be tough being a single parent," mused Caleb.

"Why, because he's a guy? Mom's single parent all the time," I snapped.

"Yeah, and it's hard for them too."

"Sorry," I muttered my apology. I didn't usually snap at people.

Caleb scooped a serving of potatoes onto the plate of a young man. "Relax," he said to me. "This isn't so bad. I thought you said it was an adventure?"

"Yep. Partitioning stress into small compartment of brain now," I answered in a robotic voice, which made Caleb laugh.

By eight, we were both exhausted but felt good that we had helped a lot of people in need. Caleb took my hand in his as we worked our way down the road next to the canal, which was keeping this part of the city from flooding, back to the beach and the Palms hotel.

Fast Facts

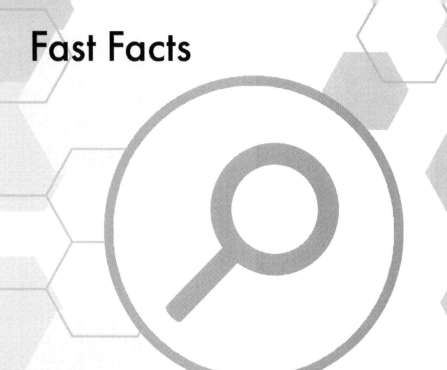

Operation Deep Freeze is the codename for a series of United States missions to Antarctica, that began in 1955-56. The annual sealift by cargo ships delivers eight million U.S. gallons of fuel and 6-11 million pounds (3-5 million kg) of supplies and equipment for McMurdo residents. U.S. Military Sealift Command operates the ships, but they are manned by civilian sailors. Cargo can range from mail, trucks, tractors, construction materials, dry and frozen food, to scientific instruments.

In January, U.S. Coast Guard icebreakers create a channel through ice-clogged McMurdo Sound in order for supply ships to reach Winter Quarters Bay at McMurdo. But ships aren't the only way to resupply the base. Additional supplies are flown into Williams Field from Christchurch, New Zealand.

Chapter 22
Nick – Vermont

The car engine started at the push of a button, and we set off to play tourist in the Green Mountain State. I had wanted to head back to Massachusetts but was overruled by two persuasive teenage boys. Liam's arm in a sling canceled our mountain adventure, but we could explore areas we had not seen before and revisit our favorite tourist traps. If Liam's arm started hurting too much and he was no longer having fun, we could always just head home.

From our Bed and Breakfast in the center of the state, we headed north to Waterbury, to make our annual pilgrimage to the Ben & Jerry ice cream factory, for a tour and free samples.

We had done this tour so many times that I was sure I could recite the process of how the ice cream was made, not to mention that I also knew every joke the tour guides regaled us with. Before we left, we walked through the Flavor Graveyard outside the factory, took photos of the boys with their heads stuck through the holes of the stand-up cutouts of the founders, plus had ice cream in the Scoop Shop, before driving to a nearby local pub in the quintessential Vermont downtown. I was dying for a good burger.

Liam's arm was aching even after a dose of Tylenol, so we opted out of visiting the cheese shops and apple cider store, even if there were free samples at each. We were stuffed from lunch anyway, and we had no way to refrigerate any cheese we bought anyway.

I turned the car north. As the car engine sang to the country roads, we ventured further than I had ever visited, to the Northeast Kingdom town of St. Johnsbury, or *Saint J* as the locals called it. We spent the afternoon in the town's elegant Athenaeum, perusing old books and looking at the art gallery.

"Why don't they just call it a library?" asked Liam. "*Athenaeum* is pretentious."

I mock scowled at him and said, "You uncouth barbarian!"

The boys laughed at my feeble academic joke. "It's more than a library or art gallery. It was founded as a cultural center, but along the 19th century belief in lifelong learning. It gets its name from the Roman school for literary and scientific study in ancient Athens."

Sebastian proved to me why I was grateful that he was my son's best friend. "The Victorian architecture alone is worth looking at, along with the wooden circular staircases. And the gallery that looks down on the first floor is just cool! There aren't a lot of libraries around anymore, since you can read almost anything online, but the books here are really old and they let you touch them! Thanks for bringing us here, Mr. Whitson."

Perhaps there was hope yet for this generation.

We ate dinner that evening in a decidedly unpretentious restaurant before driving south to our Bed and Breakfast. I decided to call an early end to our adventure regardless of the kids' complaints. I wanted to be home by Friday night so I could take Liam to our local doctor Saturday morning to have his arm rechecked.

Fast Facts

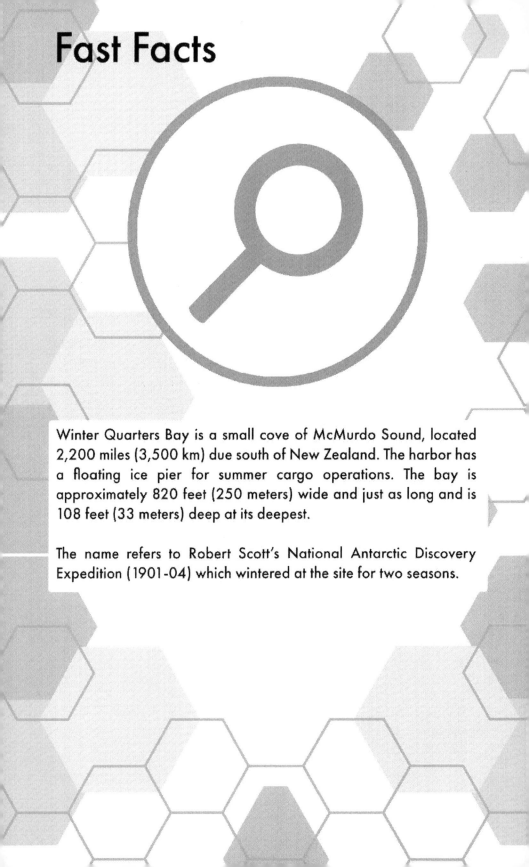

Winter Quarters Bay is a small cove of McMurdo Sound, located 2,200 miles (3,500 km) due south of New Zealand. The harbor has a floating ice pier for summer cargo operations. The bay is approximately 820 feet (250 meters) wide and just as long and is 108 feet (33 meters) deep at its deepest.

The name refers to Robert Scott's National Antarctic Discovery Expedition (1901-04) which wintered at the site for two seasons.

Chapter 23
Kathryn – Antarctica

I was sitting at the extra desk in Sylvia's office with my head in my hands, utterly exhausted, when Pieter announced that his daughter had our communications campaign ready. Her email said that she had a slow day at work and was able to devote time to it earlier than she expected. She provided us with a short but effective three-paragraph message that we would be emailing to every nation's appropriate contacts. We had stayed up the entire night pulling all that contact information together.

"Is it just me or is everyone starved?" asked Sylvia.

Without sleep, my body was spiraling into exhaustion, but I could not deny that I was also famished.

"We need to get some food before we send the emails. I for one need coffee and a clearer head before I start," continued Sylvia, and I nodded an exhausted agreement. Pieter just grunted like a caveman and followed us bleary-eyed.

Slumped in my usual chair in the dining hall, I ate a tray full of calories and drank two cups of life-giving caffeine.

Sylvia's breakfast today was much more protein than her habit, and I wondered if she was trying to be more European in front of Pieter, but I didn't care what her motivation was. I was simply happy to see her eating better.

"Let's split the thirty countries three ways and send personal emails to each contact, focusing on that particular nation's vulnerability if the Antarctic quake happened," Sylvia suggested.

Pieter nodded his affirmation, but his words denied her proposal. "I agree that focusing on each nation's potential risk seems to be the scientific way, but I think we need to just use my daughter's message as she gave it to us. There is too much chance for error that we could introduce in our sleep-deprived state."

"That, and the message will get too long," I added. "We need to keep it short and simple."

Sylvia acquiesced in the end. "For what it's worth, I concede that Pieter's daughter is the professional communicator and knows best. Let's use her message as is."

Refueled, we returned to Sylvia's office and set about sending the message.

SUBJECT: Urgent message regarding impending flood in your region

Dear [name],

Hello. We are Dr's. Whitson and Rapp, currently stationed at the Crary Science and Engineering Center, McMurdo Station, Antarctica, and we have an urgent message for you about a potential seismic event that could lead to devastating flooding in your nation. We need to speak with you immediately.

Sea levels began to rise ten years ago after the Walters-hausen glacier in Greenland collapsed. Now, a major earthquake is coming within the next month that has the potential to dislodge a huge piece of the West Antarctic ice sheet that will raise sea level by three to four meters. If this occurs, it will be catastrophic for coastal cities around the world, causing hundreds of millions of people to flee from the coastlines and submerging costly amounts of real estate and infrastructure. While we cannot prevent this seismic event, it is our duty as scientists to inform vulnerable nations so that your government can act swiftly to create an emergency plan.

We will be happy to provide the full report of our findings and advise your next steps. Time is critical. Please contact us by email and provide a phone number where we can reach you via VOIP satellite phone.

Sincerely,

Dr. Kathryn Whitson, Seismologist, Massachusetts Institute of Technology, USA

Dr. Sylvia Rapp, Glaciologist, University of New Brunswick, Canada

Once the emails had been sent, I looked at my companions. "Why don't you two go back to your dorms and get some sleep? I'll stay here and field phone calls and emails for the next four hours. Then Sylvia can come to relieve me. Pieter, your help has been immeasurable, but I don't think you can answer the technical questions I expect we will get. Please thank your daughter for her help, too."

"Already done," he replied with a nod. "If you need me, let me know."

Sylvia simply smiled at me before leaving her office.

I was exhausted, but I stared at the computer monitor, waiting for replies. Just to be safe, I turned up the volume on my notifications. I didn't want to nod off in the chair.

Fast Facts

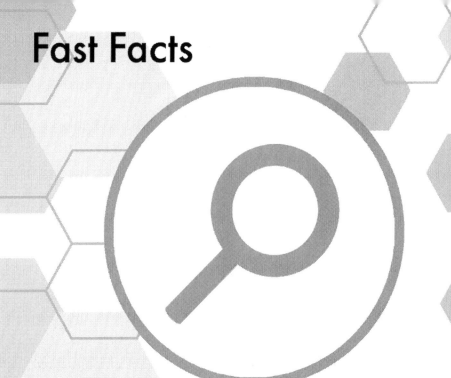

Despite the looming danger of wind and flood damage from a hurricane, many coastal residents refuse to leave their homes because they don't want to leave their pets behind. Nearly two-thirds of American households include a cat, dog or other pet, and these animals are family. You can't leave them behind.

As recently as 2012, it was nationwide policy to keep pets, except for service animals, out of human shelters. With climate change causing more and stronger hurricanes, shelters are now changing their rules. FEMA now has specific guidelines that include pets in evacuation and response plans.

One big change is that animal rescuers are included with human rescue teams. When they go in as the floodwaters are rising, rescuers are there to take the people in addition to the animals.

Chapter 24

Inga – Miami

I learned something on our second day volunteering at the shelter: shelter staff and volunteers did their best to make people comfortable, but a shelter was not a comfortable place.

Miami-Dade County had dozens of shelters set up in schools and public places, like the Convention Center where we were, with about 2,000 employees trained to run operations such as registering people, assigning sleeping areas, and distributing provisions. They used to rely on the Red Cross and the National Guard to staff the facilities, but those entities ran either on volunteers or personnel that could be doing something more useful than hand out bottled water, so about ten years ago, most counties in South Florida changed over to managing it themselves. Many of the people working here were county employees like janitors and cafeteria staff that knew these buildings and how they operated. Unlike volunteers, employees could be directed on what to do, and how to do it, so things were a lot more organized.

That didn't mean that there weren't volunteers, especially from among the people who were stuck in this shelter with their families because they had been evacuated from their homes. Assigning sleeping areas or assisting medical workers or food service beat sitting on a cot next to your family with literally nothing to do for days on end. There were volunteers at the information desk, handing out maps, telling people where to go for food, clothing, medical needs, you name it. The Convention Center was a large building and there were many services set up.

Caleb and I were placed with other volunteers: a high school student from Miami, a businessman whose house had been flooded, and a young woman who was a real estate agent. Our assignment was to walk down the rows of cots, handing out toiletries. Caleb pushed the cart. The realtor and I took the left side of the aisle, and the student and businessman took the right. Our cart was stocked with toothbrushes, small tubes of toothpaste, and travel size containers of deodorant, mouthwash, and soap. We spoke with each group of people and found out what they needed, spending a few minutes just chatting, which helped pass the time for both the evacuees and us.

Zoe and Jason had walked to the shelter with us today, having gotten bored at the hotel, but they had been assigned to a different section, so I was surprised when Zoe bounded up behind me, breathless. "Hey, Inga! We need your help!"

I turned around in alarm and asked, "What's the matter?"

"There is a group of animal lovers recruiting volunteers to rescue stranded pets. A lot of people won't leave their homes without their pets, and others were evacuated but need help going back for the animals. Cats, dogs, birds...it's heartbreaking. The floodwaters are rising, and if they don't get them out now, it will be harder later. And that's if they don't drown! Come on guys. Let's go help them."

Jason jumped on her last word without a breath. "They have enough help here. Let's be useful elsewhere. Caleb, I know you love animals. Inga? What about you?"

I exchanged a glance with Caleb, but we both already knew the answer. Of course, we would go.

Outside the Convention Center a middle-aged man in a red vest, emblazoned with a Pet Lovers First Responders logo, held a clipboard taking names of volunteers. We signed the form and then entered the van for the one-hour volunteer training session. They had specially trained staff to handle high-water rescues, but volunteers could help assemble small cages, guide animals out of the water once the trained staff rescued them, and feed and comfort the animals once they were rescued.

We were a small group of about a dozen people, sitting in an air-conditioned mobile training unit van, watching videos on the basics of animal rescue and the behavior of traumatized pets. I learned a lot, and while I had enjoyed being useful handing out supplies to people and chatting with them, I was looking forward to this task...wading through water; carrying out small, caged animals; leading larger animals on leashes. Each house we visited would be checked for pets, the staff would bring them out, and the volunteers would take over. We would bring the animals, either in a cage, terrarium, or on a leash, to the van and keep them safe. Based on the individual pets' needs, we would give them food, water, comfort, or all of the above.

Once we were full, the van would take the hurricane-rescued pets to the shelter across town until their owners could come for them. Each pet was tagged with the address of the home they had been taken from, so they could be reunited later with their human families. Some of those families were living in evacuation shelters themselves and would not be able to come for the animals for a while, but at least they knew their pets were safe.

In other homes, we would find people who were unwilling to leave because of their pets, and in those cases, we could take the animals to safety, so the people could also go somewhere until the water stopped rising and they could finally return home.

I never worked so hard in my life.

At one point later in the afternoon, Zoe and I were wading through thigh-deep water, carrying two small cages each, held high above the water, when she asked, "Who knew you could get sweaty walking through water?"

I longed to wipe the sweat off my brow, but my hands were full. "Seriously."

"Gggh…" and Zoe went under the water. Fast.

"Zoe!" I shouted, my hand a moment from releasing the cage in my right hand and reaching under for her when her head emerged, followed quickly by her body.

"Are you okay?!" asked Jason frantically, grabbing her elbow and making sure she was upright.

She spit water from her mouth, shook the water from her hair, and moaned, but still held on to the cages with two now-soaking wet rabbits. "Caught my foot on something. Tree branch, debris, I don't know. I'm fine, just need to pay more attention. I think I sprained something, not sure, but I'm good. I'll check it out in the van."

There were two people at the van door reaching out to take the cages from us, but instead of handing off our charges, the older one helped Zoe into the van. Behind us, a cat meowed its indignation at being in a box.

The Pet Lovers First Responder volunteer asked, "Did you swallow any of the water?"

"Yes, but I'm okay. I spit most of it out. I'm not going to drown in three feet of water." Her accent grew stronger when she was frustrated.

The volunteer replied, "I'm not worried about you drowning. I'm worried about the water. After a storm like this, it's polluted. A quarter of the homes in this area rely on septic systems, which aren't always maintained, and fecal matter leaks out when those systems are flooded. That causes waterborne diseases like cryptosporidium, giardia, and dysentery."

"So, you mean I'm likely to come down with the screaming shits!" Zoe was livid. She was rarely sick and the thought of it alarmed her.

The volunteer nodded. "You might. If you have diarrhea, please let a medical worker know immediately. Bacterial infections can be treated with antibiotics, but not all parasitical infections respond to all antibiotics, so you'll also need bed rest and lots of fluids. I suggest you start drinking as much bottled water as you can right away." He handed her a bottle from a plastic case on the floor.

She graciously took the water, sat down on a bench, and propped her left foot on another seat. A woman with a medical insignia on her jacket examined Zoe's ankle and pronounced it twisted but not sprained. "Can you stay in the van and help out cleaning up and feeding the animals please?"

"Yep, good idea," I said. "She's more trouble out there than useful."

Zoe punched me in the arm.

Fast Facts

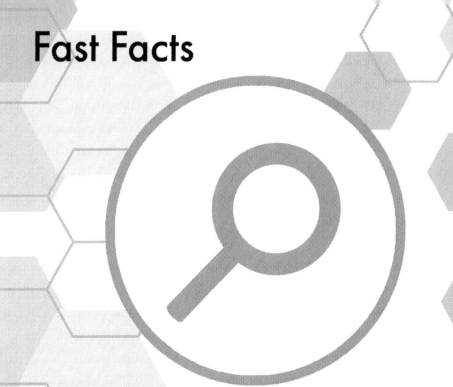

In 2009, the Maldives was the first island nation to raise the possibility of purchasing land in another country in anticipation of being gradually submerged. At the time the government looked at options in India and Sri Lanka.

In 2014, Kiribati, a group of islands in the Pacific Ocean particularly exposed to climate change, purchased 8 sq miles (20 sq km) on Vanua Levu, one of the Fiji Islands, about 800 miles (2,000 km) away. Kiribati has a population of about 110,000 scattered over 33 small, low-lying islands extending over a total area of 313 sq miles (810 sq km).

Crowding their population onto their property in Fiji would be a tight squeeze.

Chapter 25
Kathryn – Antarctica

In the end, I didn't have to hold my eyelids open with toothpicks as I had feared. Not only were the emails coming in quickly, but I had also responded to three of them by phone to environmental officials. Germany and Kuwait had plans in place to evacuate their populations from low-lying areas and simply thanked me for the warning. They would begin implementing existing plans immediately.

Kiribati was a different story. The small Pacific island had nowhere for their people to go within their own country, and they weren't the only island nation that faced the same plight. Luckily, Kiribati had seen the future ten years earlier when the Greenland ice sheet collapse inundated half their nation. I was pleasantly surprised to find that since then, Kiribati had purchased land in Fiji and had been setting up infrastructure there. Kiribati had a fleet of government-owned aircraft and immediately began flying their people over to their awaiting land.

Kiribati didn't need our help but was grateful for the forewarning.

Sylvia brought me a plate of food at 12:30. "FYI, I got a couple of hours of sleep, so it's your turn now. Eat, then go sleep for a few hours."

"Thanks, Sylvia. I need to send my boss an email and give him an update on our progress. But I'll type while I eat. Thanks for the burger."

My boss ran MIT's Earth, Atmosphere and Planetary Sciences Department. EAPS was the broadest of MIT's science departments. Our research supported many of the most pressing problems of our time:

natural hazards; climate and environmental change; natural resources; the origins of life, both here on Earth and elsewhere. We divided the research into eight distinguishable categories: atmospheric science, climate, geobiology, geochemistry, geology, geophysics, oceanography, and planetary science, but so much of our research was interdisciplinary so most of our people overlapped categories.

I wiped up dripped burger grease from my keyboard right after hitting send on the email to the boss, finished my meal, and headed off for some sleep. I had just arrived in my room when my tablet bleeped with an incoming personal email. Only three people set off that alert.

From: Whitson, Inga
Sent: Friday, March 22, 2030; 9:23 PM
To: Whitson, Kathryn
Subject: The joys of Miami after a hurricane

Hi Mom! I just wanted to check in quickly and let you know that everything is fine in Miami. Zoe and I have been volunteering with an animal rescue group today, saving pets that people had to leave behind when they evacuated. Some of these people were still in their flooded homes because they wouldn't leave without their animals. It's been hard work, and we just got back to the hotel with Jason and Caleb. The Palms is doing fine with generator power, and the city says they will have the power back on sometime during the night for any locations not flooded, which means us. So, we should be good to go tomorrow. Assuming the airport reopens, we have our flights booked to go home. I spoke with Dad just a few minutes ago and he's driving back to Cambridge with Liam and Sebastian later tonight. He offered to pick us up at the airport, but we left Zoe's car there, so we're all set.

I know you are worried, but you don't need to be. Other than Zoe being a klutz and tripping over something and getting a mouthful of water for her stupidity, we are all good. I'm more worried about you in the frozen Way Down Under. Hope all is well!

Love you,

Inga

Damn kid. Although I was glad she checked in, I was still worried about her in Miami. Not that Boston was much safer, but at least there she had her father and brother and if they had to run, there was higher ground to go to and they would all be together.

Nick would give his life to save our children.

I laid down in my bunk, thinking about what a selfish idiot I was for staying down here in Antarctica. I missed my family terribly. I wondered if they missed me at all. Maybe they'd gotten so used to me being gone after eight months they didn't need me anymore.

I fell asleep worrying, but before I knew it, it was 9 p.m. and Sylvia was knocking on my dormitory door.

Some of the countries took longer to acknowledge our email message, but the requests for calls kept coming steadily. We took turns in four-hour shifts through Saturday night. Sometimes Pieter came by and sat with whichever one of us was on duty. By noon on Sunday, we still had six countries that had not replied, so I re-sent the emails to them and immediately got replies from both Persian Gulf countries, Iraq, and Kuwait. Iraq said they had the problem in hand, thanked us for the warning, but did not wish to speak.

Kuwait's Director of Planning and Environmental Impact Assessment department was a different story. She sent her phone number, apologized for not seeing the first email, and asked for a call back immediately. They had no plan for evacuation from rising seas and she wanted to know more about the situation.

I rang Dr. Nourah Al-Baqsami, surprised but pleased that a woman held a high rank within the government of an Arab nation. "Dr. Al-Baqsami, this is Kathryn Whitson, calling from McMurdo Station, Antarctica. Thank you for taking my call."

Her accent was almost British. "Please, call me Nourah. We do not stand on ceremony at the Environment Public Authority in Kuwait. As fellow scientists, let's just start on a first name basis, if that is okay?"

I told her to call me Kathryn. "Nourah, may I ask why you do not have plans in place for moving populations in case of emergency? Frankly, I'm surprised that with the resources Kuwait has at its disposal, you don't."

Her laugh was more nervous than humorous. "Mostly our office handles environmental assessments and licensing requirements for development projects. Kuwait has done a lot of development over the last three decades, and all of it has been with the highest standards of environmental impact at the forefront. We are quite proud of our sustainability record. And honestly, we are a desert nation. An excess of water is not something that we have ever had to worry about."

I nodded before I realized she could not see me. This was a voice-only connection. "I've kept up with environmentally sound development around the world, and your country has an excellent track record. However, none of those developments that are at the northern end of the Persian Gulf will survive the rising waters, no matter how environmentally neutral they were built. I'm afraid that when this earthquake hits, the falling ice shelf will add megatons of freshwater to the ocean and within a few hours, the sea level will rise to a point that will inundate communities near the sea."

"But what if your prediction is wrong? If we evacuate hundreds of thousands and nothing happens? We will look foolish."

"I understand your concern, but isn't it better to be safe than sorry? The tidal waves alone would be good enough reason to protect your citizens. Besides, Kuwait is not a poor nation, and you are well respected on the global stage. You can afford not only the cost but the hit to your reputation. You can simply blame my research group." I thought but did not say: you won't be the only one.

"Alright Kathryn, I do understand, and of course I share your safety concern. But let me ask you, how are you so sure that your research is correct? How can you be sure that there will be a massive earthquake?"

I had given this speech a few times to other national representatives who had asked the same question. Nourah was an environmental scientist, so I didn't sugarcoat the data. "Long-term data from seismograph stations at the South Pole have added evidence to the theory that earth's solid inner core is spinning at a slightly faster rate than the rest of the earth. We've been monitoring seismic data at the South Pole since 1957. That's almost a hundred years of information. The different spin rate contributes to tremors and quakes and based on the predictive algorithm and past seismic data, my calculation is 95 percent accurate. The only question is *when* not *if*. But if you wait until the quake hits, you will not have time to move your endangered citizens. You will only have a couple of hours."

She didn't have any other questions and agreed to discuss this with her superiors and put together an evacuation plan. They could use buses to evacuate people to higher ground, at least thirty meters above sea level, and their military could set up tent cities in the hills above the bay.

It was no small undertaking, but if they intended to save their coastal population, they needed to act now.

Fast Facts

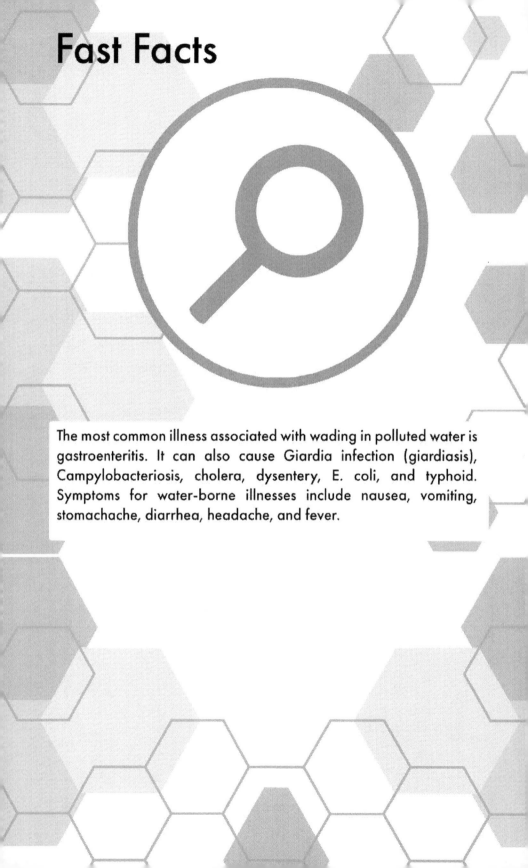

The most common illness associated with wading in polluted water is gastroenteritis. It can also cause Giardia infection (giardiasis), Campylobacteriosis, cholera, dysentery, E. coli, and typhoid. Symptoms for water-borne illnesses include nausea, vomiting, stomachache, diarrhea, headache, and fever.

Chapter 26

Inga – Miami

I woke in the middle of the night when I heard someone close the bathroom door. I could feel Caleb lying against me, his body comfortably warm against mine. I heard quiet snoring from the other bed, which meant it had to be Zoe in the bathroom. I was about to drift off when I heard the fan turn on. I sat up on the edge of the bed and waited for Zoe to emerge.

Quietly, I asked her if she was alright.

"Not really. Insides don't feel good and everything in me just left. I just want to go back to sleep." She moaned as she crawled into bed beside Jason. "G'night, Inga."

Before I fell back to sleep, Zoe was awake and in the bathroom again. This was not good. She generally had a cast-iron stomach, rarely bothered by anything from spicy foods to high levels of stress. She could down a ghost pepper while stressing over final exams and never once have ill effects.

Zoe groaned as she walked back to her bed.

"Remember what the animal rescue people said? If you come down with diarrhea, you have to let a medical worker know immediately," I said to her, secretly pleased for the darkness of the room so she could not see my worry.

"Yep," she replied. "But not at 2 a.m. They also said to get lots of rest and drink fluids. I'm trying to do that."

She was right. There wasn't much I could do for her at this hour. I knew she needed antibiotics for the bacterial infections she had clearly picked up in the polluted water, and even if whatever parasite coursing through her didn't respond to an antibiotic, we had to try.

Zoe was right about waiting until the morning. I closed my eyes and tried to get back to sleep but was worried about her and found myself lying awake listening to hear if she got up again. Outside the window, seagulls plucked through the hurricane debris like a child entangled in their disorganized room.

I must have fallen back to sleep because what seemed like only a moment passed before my eyes snapped open, woken by brilliant daylight streaming through the hotel window. A sound came from close by, but the first seconds of wakefulness did not clue me into what it was. A few moments later, once I was fully awake, I realized that the power was back on because Jason and Caleb were sitting in chairs quietly watching the news.

I yawned and stretched as I sat up in bed. Zoe was sound asleep in the other bed. She looked small huddled under the blanket. Her face was drained of color, and she seemed bone-weary.

"Is she okay?" I asked Jason. He slept beside her all night. He must have realized she was ill unless he truly slept like a dead rock.

One look at his face told me how stressed he was. Jason wore his emotions on his face and in his body language, and his voice exposed his quiet exhaustion. "She was up a couple of times earlier this morning. I made her drink a glass of water each time. We'll have to get her to a doctor, but for now, she should sleep as long as she can."

I nodded in agreement, sat up in bed, my back against the headboard, and watched the news. The airport was still closed, and travelers stranded there were sleeping on the floor and cleaning up in the bathrooms. It was Saturday and we were supposed to fly home today. It didn't take a genius to figure out that wasn't happening.

The news wasn't good. Floodwaters were still rising after the storm, even though the drainage canals had been upgraded only last year. There was a heightened fear of cholera caused by bacteria from sewage. And of all things, a municipal cemetery in Shorecrest, a low-income community on the east side of Miami, had coffins floating out! It was only four feet above sea level.

"*Night of the Living Dead* time?" I laughed, despite the gruesome reality.

I couldn't take another moment of watching the news and went to the bathroom, but before I was finished brushing my teeth, Zoe was at the door pleading to let her in.

"Sorry, Inga, but my stomach is lurching. I feel bruised inside." I spit the toothpaste in the sink and vacated the room quickly.

I ran a jerky hand through my hair. "Do you think she has cholera?" I asked Caleb and Jason.

"Not a chance," said Caleb, rolling his eyes to reinforce his disagreement.

Jason simultaneously asked, "Are you out of your mind?"

In a fit of anger for their dismissive remarks, I grabbed the clicker away from the two newshounds and changed the station to a cooking show. Nice, ordinary, non-storm-related, non-life-threatening background noise.

When Zoe emerged from the bathroom, she looked drained, physically, and mentally. Her face was ashen, and her shoulders slumped. She took one look at the monitor on the wall and groaned. "Gah! Anything but food shows!"

I changed it to a travel show.

I felt so bad for her, and I was worried, even if it wasn't cholera. An intestinal parasite or bug wasn't good under the best of circumstances. A bottle of water sat on the night table, staring at Zoe, but she didn't want it, claiming that even liquid left violently.

"Hey, turn it down please," I glared at the boys. "I need to call my father."

I punched the number for my dad, and he answered with video. He was in his study, and I knew what he would say before he opened his mouth. "I take it your flight isn't happening?"

I nodded. "Hi, Dad. I knew you'd already checked the airline's website before I called. I'm sorry about this. If I had any idea that we could get stuck in the aftermath of a hurricane in March – of all times – you know I wouldn't have come down here. I really am sorry."

His body showed none of his traditional anger signs. No flared nostrils, pulsing veins, or even his tell-tale knuckle cracking. Just parental concern. He cleared his throat and said, "I'm glad you are alright, at least so far. More than I can say about your brother."

"Why, what's with Liam?" I asked.

"He sprained his arm snowboarding, so we had to quit the mountain, though we did spend some quality time playing tourist in Vermont. We got home last night so I could take him to the doctor this morning. His appointment is in half an hour, so actually, I'll have to cut this call short."

I nodded. "It's okay, Dad. We'll be fine. We have power in the hotel now, and we've also spent some 'quality time' volunteering with the animal rescue group, so at least we are doing some good here. But Zoe seems to have gotten some kind of intestinal parasite from her clumsy fall in the water, and now she's pretty sick."

I saw the look on his face and cut him off before he could offer advice. "Yeah, I know. We are taking her to the Red Cross medical van this morning. Probably just needs some antibiotics."

My father responded with his usual stoic nod and said, "As long as you are safe, you can just ride it out, and eventually the airport will re-open. Take care of Zoe, and don't forget to email all your professors that you might miss classes on Monday and maybe even Tuesday."

I thanked my father and told him I loved him before hanging up.

I looked over at Zoe. She sat propped up in the bed with the covers pulled up to her neck. Her eyes were sunken and her skin sallow.

She saw me looking at her and said, "I feel miserable. I feel like waves of heat are coursing through my stomach and everything in my gut aches. It's all I can do not to run to the toilet every second, but honestly, there isn't anything left inside of me to leave."

I just nodded at her, not knowing what to say that wouldn't be absurd. But we had to get her some help. "Let me take a quick shower. I'll leave the door unlocked in case you need the toilet. We'll get dressed and take you down to the Red Cross truck and get some antibiotics."

She nodded wordlessly, the bottle of water still staring at her from the night table. I said, "Drink more of that," as I entered the bathroom and closed the door behind me. I managed to get my whole quick shower done and get dressed before she needed to use the facility again.

Poor Zoe.

Once she was done, the boys took quick turns in the single bathroom, and then we walked together to the mobile medical unit near the Convention Center.

She was hopping up and down in line as we waited, the pain evident on her face. "I have to go again," she whined, and Jason walked her to the bank of port-a-johns while Caleb and I held her place in the line; a line that stretched around the corner. Every once in a while, a woman dressed in a Red Cross shirt came with a clipboard checking for urgent cases. I gave her Zoe's name and symptoms and asked if we could go to the front of the line, but unfortunately, Zoe wasn't the only person in

Miami suffering and would have to wait her turn.

Eventually, we did get to the front with Zoe in tow, in a moment of reprieve from her intestines exploding and a nurse took her into the small examination booth inside the van. We waited outside.

Ten minutes later the back door of the van opened and two people in scrubs lifted a stretcher down hurriedly. A blanket-covered figure lay on it and we could see the person shaking from where we stood, an oxygen mask covering most of her face. The paramedics rushed the stretcher to a waiting ambulance whose emergency lights abruptly flared on.

"What the hell! Is that Zoe?" Sweat unexpectedly beaded on my forehead as quickly as the words poured from my mouth.

Caleb's hand on my shoulder stopped me from running after the stretcher just as Zoe came down the steps toward us with a bottle of pills in her hand. "They are handing out a broad-spectrum antibiotic to everyone with my symptoms."

I suddenly felt lightheaded and pressed my palm to my heart. She was alright.

Zoe continued unaware of my recent panic. "Whatever water-borne parasite this is; this miracle drug should do the trick but could be a week before I'm back to normal."

"Yikes!" said Jason lamely. "That really sucks." He couldn't find the right words either and none of us were going to tell Zoe what had just happened.

"Yeah, well, don't worry about it. I've had worse things happen to me than spending my days and nights sitting on a toilet! You guys should go back to the pet group and volunteer again. It beats sitting around doing nothing...which unfortunately is what I'm going to be doing, at least for a couple of days."

"Are you kidding?" I exclaimed. "I'm not going to leave you alone while you are sick. I'm going back to the hotel with you. You guys," and I turned to Jason and Caleb, "can go make yourselves useful..."

Before I could finish, Caleb cut me off, nodding his approval. "Inga, you are right. We don't all need to sit in that room. Jason and I will lend a hand today and meet you back at the hotel when we are done. If the airport opens up and you find out what flights we are rescheduled on, let me know. Otherwise, we will see you girls tonight."

He leaned in and gave me a quick but passionate kiss on my lips then grabbed Jason's arm and pulled him away. Muscles in my face that I had not even realized were tense, relaxed. I had a strong sensation of my heartbeat as I watched him walk away.

"Oh geez, don't be love-struck, you idiot," Zoe chided me. "Let's go back to the hotel. I'm not sure how long my intestines plan to remain stable."

She was right, as usual. Once we got back to Boston, I wasn't going to keep up a long-distance relationship – at least not seriously – so letting this guy steal my heart like a clichéd romance novel was stupid. Between my worry over Zoe and this feeling for Caleb, I was a mess. I was glad for some downtime, just staying in the room with the TV and my tablet.

By the time they returned to the hotel at 6:30 that evening, we had both gotten not only our schoolwork done for this week but read ahead for every class, although Zoe did much of her reading in the bathroom. My father always called the bathroom in our house *the library*. Zoe proved him right today.

"Hi honey, I'm home," announced Jason in a put-upon Cuban accent.

"Who are you, Ricky Ricardo?" Zoe rolled her eyes at him, then glared at me.

"Did you tell him about my little crush on Carlos?" she asked sotto-voce.

I grinned wickedly. "Indubitably! It's hysterical." At least I thought it was, but I don't think Zoe appreciated it.

"Just lightening the mood. How are you feeling?" Jason asked with true concern in his voice.

"Shoot me now. My stomach hurts from my diaphragm to my butt hole," replied Zoe. Her rigid body posture told me just how anxious about this illness she was even though her sarcasm tried to belie that to Jason. He didn't know her as I did, and her physical signs of stress probably weren't as obvious to him.

Nevertheless, Jason was sympathetic. "I know you hurt, Zoe. I really do. And I feel bad for you. This vacation has truly gone off the rails. With any luck, the airport will open again in another day or so, and we'll be home, but even then, you'll still be nursing this nasty stomach bug. It truly sucks."

Not one to accept sympathy, Zoe surprised me by saying, "Thanks, Jason."

"Okay, before this gets mushy," I interjected, "I know Zoe isn't interested in food, but I am. When I went down to the basement shelter a few hours ago to grab lunch, I saw a notice posted that they'll be running a movie there tonight, along with providing free dinner. And – apropos of nothing – it's a disaster movie, which sounds cool."

With little more discussion, we marched down to spend the evening with the other stranded guests. Zoe persevered, and while she only ate Jell-O, and missed a few minutes of the movie running off to the lobby bathroom twice, she was in as good spirits as possible, considering the circumstances.

Sunday morning, we woke to the news that the airport was still closed. With Zoe still running to the toilet every few hours, but hopefully on the mend, Caleb and I decided to go do the animal volunteer work and we left Jason with Zoe. It turned out that Jason had some schoolwork he was supposed to have gotten done this week – but of course, had bailed on that in favor of sun and fun – so he was happy to stay in the room, not only to act as caretaker for my best friend but his interests as well.

I hoped there would be a better movie tonight.

Fast Facts

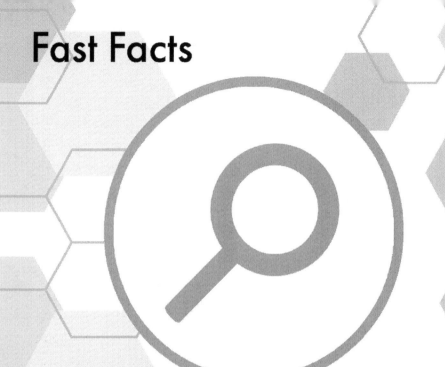

Icequakes are vibrations in glaciers and ice sheets. From small creaks and groans to sudden slips equal to a magnitude-7 earthquake, the shaking signals movement in the ice. High magnitude earthquakes, including Japan's 2011 Tohoku quake and Chile's 2010 Maule temblor, set off icequakes across Antarctica, just as they triggered earthquakes on land.

Icequakes can start after a rolling earthquake wave called Rayleigh waves, race through the frozen ice. As the ice shifts, icequakes can spike. Seismic signals involving ice-related phenomena (ice-quakes or smaller ice-shocks) are most frequently reported in association with glacially related mass movements of icesheets, or with sea ice, tide cracks, or icebergs. The shaking can adjust the ice above subglacial rivers or shift crevasses, both known icequake triggers.

Chapter 27
Kathryn – Antarctica

My feet dragged and my muscles ached as I walked across the passageway to the winter dorm pod after fielding phone calls all afternoon and immediately crashed on my bunk for a few hours. Sylvia was monitoring calls and emails at this point, but we had covered almost everyone by now, so we met for a late meal in the dining hall before retiring to our respective rooms.

I had just put on my pajamas and brushed my teeth, intending to catch up on some sleep when the world around me shook. The table next to my bed rattled like a freight train had gone by, and the surface of my water cup ruffled as if I had put it down too clumsily. It lasted only ten seconds, but it was strong.

Sylvia's door was open, and I walked in, plopped myself on her guest chair, and put my feet on her bed. "Did you feel that?" Though I'd been researching earthquakes my entire professional life, I hadn't experienced that many myself. It sent shivers up my spine.

"Well yes, of course. Tremor or earthquake?" asked Sylvia, more calmly than anyone else I know would have.

"Not sure, but I'm headed to my lab to check. Do you want me to let you know what I find out or will you be asleep when I get back? Shouldn't take me more than half an hour." It was almost midnight, so I didn't want to assume that just because I was awake, that the rest of the base should be.

"I'll be up. Stop in."

I made my way through the passageway to the Central Services Building. Not surprisingly, I didn't meet anyone along the way.

McMurdo Station was a little creepy alone at night. Our days were now down to about ten hours of light, and the base made up for some of that with indoor lighting to simulate a longer day, but at this time of night, it was truly dark, the kind of dark that exists only in remote wilderness regions. The windows in the passageway revealed a million beautiful pinpricks in an ebony black sky but the southern constellations were still a mystery to me.

It didn't take me long to check my equipment and return to the dorm pod and I entered Sylvia's room without knocking. I figured she would be asleep, and I would just give her my news in the morning, but she was sitting up in bed reading like she said she would be. I told her what the shaking was: a rolling earthquake.

She looked puzzled. "Okay, but are you sure that there haven't been any big earthquakes somewhere else along the fault line? Remember Chile's 2010 Maule quake and how it set off ice quakes across Antarctica? Could it be that?"

"I wish, but no. I just got a seismograph reading from East Antarctica that recorded a magnitude-5.2 quake. That's big for this continent, but around the globe, that's medium. East Antarctica is the most tectonically active area on the continent, so it makes sense that it was there. I hoped it was just a Rayleigh wave, but no such luck. This was a real earthquake."

"Do you think there will be more earthquakes or just ice quakes?"

It was anyone's guess, but I was fairly certain this was a precursor to more quakes. "The shaking definitely will shift crevasses and adjust the ice above subglacial rivers, triggering ice quakes across Antarctica. After the last three major temblors we had, ice quakes spiked, typically for a day or two as the ice shifted. But whether it causes more earthquakes is indeterminate right now. We just need to keep monitoring and see what happens."

"The way I see it, we need to be ready to evacuate if it continues."

"We do. Get some sleep. In the morning we will call the troops together and make a plan." I said goodnight and went next door to my bed. *I hope there aren't any more tremors*, I thought stupidly as I crawled into bed. I knew that was wishful thinking.

Five hours later I awoke, grateful I had slept that much. I had not expected to get any sleep at all, but exhaustion has a habit of taking its toll regardless of the amount of worry bouncing around in your skull cavity.

I took a quick shower and dressed just as swiftly, needing to get to my lab and review overnight seismic readings. I was also starving, so I swung by the dining hall on my way to the CSEC. As I walked from the dorm pod through the passageway to the Central Services Building, I peered through the glass wall to the darkness beyond. It was almost 6 a.m. but the sun would not rise until 8:30 today. The days were getting shorter but right now, we still enjoyed sunsets and dark night skies.

The sunsets here were the most magnificent on the planet, the cold air turning the weak rays of the sun into mango, indigo, and dragon-fruit hues. A month from now the base, and all of Antarctica, would be plunged into the five-month-long night.

I packed my breakfast in a to-go container, filled my oversized coffee mug, and left the dining hall through the east passageway to get to my lab. Suddenly, my coffee began to shake in my hand, then the floor turned sideways, and I was pitched off balance. My plastic food container was thrown from my hand as I fell on my backside. A cold wind chilled my back as the shaking ebbed and I saw a long, jagged crack in the glass wall, like a tear in the universe. Frigid air bled through.

Recovering both my composure and my food, I keyed my radio, attempting to contact the station master. "Martin, this is Kathryn. Do you read?"

Martin Howell's voice came through clearly. "Yes, Kathryn. Was that an earthquake?"

"Unless something huge exploded on base, yes, that's exactly what it was. I'm on my way to my lab where I will be able to determine the magnitude of the event. Meanwhile, there is damage is the east passageway. A four-centimeter-wide vertical crack extends from the base to a height of approximately two meters. Was there any damage in the control room?" The station master's office would collect all the damage reports and triage by order of importance and deploy maintenance teams to make repairs.

Howell's accent had the flat vowels of an upstate New Yorker. "Luckily, no. But it figures that we get a seismologist here as a researcher and we have an earthquake. I think I felt a smaller one last night too. For shit's sake, Kathryn! Antarctica doesn't have earthquakes!"

His language, on the other hand, was pure New York City.

"Howell, are you implying that my presence on this continent caused that?" My voice dripped indignation. He really was an asshole. How someone as small-minded as Martin Howell got into a position of authority in a place like this dumbfounded me. Station master served very much like a mayor would in a small town, only they were appointed not elected.

He replied in a syrupy-sweet tone. "Of course not, Kat, I'm only kidding. Glad you are okay. Is that crack a danger to anyone? Any sharp edges?"

No one called me *Kat*. I'd hated the moniker since I was a child. "No, I don't think so, but it's letting in a lot of freezing air from outside. You'd better inform everyone on the base to keep their outerwear handy at all times right now. There could be more tremors. I'm expecting a much larger quake to occur at some point in the next month."

"Larger?! When were you going to tell me about this? I am the station master, and you are supposed to keep me abreast of any and all information that is vital to this facility." I could imagine his pale face turning redder as he spoke.

"Today. I was planning on coming to see you this morning, right after I reviewed last night's seismic sensor data. I'll come by your office within the hour. I'm at my lab now, got to run." I wished I could just turn off my radio so I didn't have to hear his response, but if there were any emergency notifications, I would regret that decision.

So, I simply ignored the rest of his radio transmissions. None of them were nice anyway. Eventually, he gave up.

I poked the power switches on all the monitors at my workstation to wake them and the sensor data appeared on my screen. The tremor that just hit was a magnitude-4.5 with an epicenter on the mainland, about one hundred sixty kilometers inland, due east of Ross Island. That was a hundred miles. As a scientist, I was equally comfortable with miles or kilometers, and automatically converted in my head. I sat heavily into my desk chair and pored through the data in-depth, calculations converging in my mind.

A moment later, my coffee and breakfast were cold, and I realized that fifteen minutes had vanished from my life. I reheated both and scarfed them down as quickly as I could while printing out some charts and graphs.

I inspected the reinforced glass walls of the east passageway on my way to Martin Howell's office in the Central Services Building. There could be additional structural damage from the quake.

Martin's office did not look like a traditional mayor's office. It was a big room, filled with radio and satellite equipment, and five old utilitarian desks with computer equipment almost haphazardly distributed across them. The winter staff was limited to the station master and three assistants, one of whom worked night shift. McMurdo Station personnel provided support for operations, logistics, information technology, construction, and maintenance, but all of those departments had separate offices and were only loosely overseen by the station master.

Martin was alone in his office. I assumed his staff was inspecting the situation across the station.

Howell was an irritating man, with broad shoulders, and a rugged yet clean-shaven face. His tall figure and dark hair might have made him attractive if he had the personality to go with it. He sat behind a metal desk that looked like it had been in Antarctica since Robert Scott himself.

I sat on the only clean corner of his desk and dropped my printouts in front of him. "Here's the seismic sensor data I promised and a copy of the earthquake hazard map I sent to the USGS. I'll let you look over the report, but what it comes down to is that my research shows a clear prediction of a large magnitude earthquake hitting somewhere along the coast of Antarctica within the next month."

I gave him time to read the report.

Martin looked at me and raised one eyebrow. "You aren't serious, are you?"

"I am. And based on yesterday's and today's activity, I'm pushing up my prediction of a large quake to within the week, rather than within the month. I also believe it will happen on the coast or within the continent, not out at sea. The epicenter of this morning's tremor was inland of McMurdo by 156 kilometers," I explained.

Martin examined the earthquake hazard map. "But this shows most earthquakes happen out at sea."

I shook my head. "The shaking has shifted crevasses and will adjust the ice above subglacial rivers, most likely triggering icequakes across Antarctica. When this earthquake hits, the falling ice shelf will add megatons of freshwater to the ocean and within a few hours, the sea level will rise as much as three to ten meters, swamping coastlines around the world."

I gave him a couple more minutes to review the material in front of him. Martin was no scientist, but he was a fast reader and smart. Low pitched noises came from deep in his throat as he read. He frowned as he laid the report on his desk. "How much danger are we in here if your prediction comes true, especially if that doomsday glacier crashes?"

"A fair amount. If the glacier goes, it will cause a tidal wave as big as the one that destroyed Atlantis and I'm not talking mythology. The real Atlantis – the island of Thera in Crete – was destroyed by a supervolcano blowing its top in about 1450 BC and brought the Minoan empire to its end. This tidal wave would inundate our base the same way. We need to get to higher ground. We can get our entire staff up to the summit of Mt. Terror. Once the wave recedes, the sea level will be higher than before, maybe as much as ten meters. McMurdo is well above that mark except for the overlook, but everything here would be washed away by the tsunami. There would be nothing left to return to."

"Shit. Do you know how many millions of dollars are sitting on this base?"

I assumed that was a rhetorical question and didn't bother to respond. I just stared at him, waiting for him to continue.

He didn't disappoint. "Okay, obviously we will feel any quakes that happen, but how do we know if the glacier goes? Do we have cameras there? Drones?"

"Martin, Thwaites glacier is a thousand miles away. We can't remote control a drone from that distance...actually, maybe we can. This isn't my area of expertise. Let me get Sylvia down here."

He nodded. "I was just about to suggest that."

Of course, he was. I decided to let him do his job and think he was actually in control of this situation.

None of us had any control over this. The illusion that humans held any sway over Mother Earth was violently shattered every time a natural disaster took place, and Thwaites breaking apart would be the biggest disaster in recorded history. It would make the drowning of Atlantis look like a child's bathtub accident.

Martin hung up his phone and placed it back on his desk. "She's on her way."

Cell communications with the rest of the world didn't happen from the White Continent, but we had a local area network that we used to stay in touch with each other. It was easier than radios and allowed us to use a lot of the other functions on our phones, as long as it didn't involve actual internet access. Key personnel had radios, which only had twelve channels, each used to contact a specific department in case of emergencies. The station master's office was channel one.

McMurdo wasn't very spread out, and since the connecting passageways allowed one to get from the dorms to the Central Services Building without needing to dress for the tundra, it would not take Sylvia long to get here, assuming she was up and dressed. I busied myself with procuring a cup of coffee from the café down the hall and got back within the five minutes it took my friend to arrive.

"In here," called Martin from the small meeting room in the station master's office. Like almost everything at the base, it was a no-frills room. A round table was surrounded by six plastic folding chairs, one of which Martin had folded his lanky body into. My reports were spread out on the table. I nodded to Sylvia and took a seat beside her, cautiously sipping my hot coffee. The heat felt good on my hands.

Martin looked at Sylvia and said, "I've read through Kathryn's report to the USGS and reviewed her summary. I assume you already are familiar with this document?" He held it up for her inspection.

She nodded.

"Of course, you are." Martin was miffed that I shared that with her before him, even though our research often overlapped.

Sylvia gave him a simplified overview of the situation. "Thwaites is about one hundred twenty kilometers wide and isn't confined to a valley the way Pine Island glacier is, so there is potential for much larger releases of ice if the glacier's flow continues to speed up. Thwaites' melt would increase sea level by sixty centimeters; Pine Island by forty-five. But since together they provide critical support to the ice shelf, runaway disintegration of those Antarctic glaciers – and the entire ice shelf – would devastate the planet. Sea level could rise by three to ten meters, depending on how much ice gave way."

Sylvia was a stickler for using metric in scientific conversations, even when speaking with a lay person like Martin.

Martin nodded and said, "So I've heard. I agree with your assessment of evacuating coastal communities, and now I must consider the possible need of the same here at McMurdo and Scott Base. But evacuating this base, especially at this time of year, isn't an easy task, so we need data from your glacier to determine if it's even necessary."

Sylvia nodded again. She liked Martin Howell even less than I did and being quizzed at 6:30 in the morning by a pen pusher wasn't her idea of fun.

"I don't suppose you have any cameras on that glacier, do you?"

"I don't because surface-mounted cameras would not provide enough information to be of value." It was a stupid question and I had to give Sylvia credit for not biting his head off for even voicing it.

"What about a drone?"

"From where?" Sylvia asked. She rubbed the back of her neck before crossing her arms. "Thwaites is 1,600 kilometers from here. You can't fly a drone there by remote control. And no, we don't have anything anywhere nearby that we could pull out of storage remotely. Drones need to be set up on-site by a human being, Martin. With reliable satellite comms, we can fly them by remote control, but we can't unpack them from a crate in a warehouse that way."

Now he was as frustrated as we were, feeling impotent to do anything.

"What about Rothera or San Martin? Could either of them get eyes on the glacier?"

Rothera research station was the Brits' year-round base. They had maybe twenty people there in the winter. San Martin base was one of thirteen facilities in Antarctica operated by Argentina. It also had people who wintered over. Both bases were on the Antarctic Peninsula, north of Thwaites glacier, but they were both as far north of it as we were south. However...

Sylvia beat me to the punch. "Martin, you may have something there," she said. "Rothera might be able to help. Part of their research is in space science, and in the past, they have launched rockets from their base. Not only that, but they are the best funded base on the continent, so they have a lot of new equipment. They might be able to help get some visuals on Thwaites, even if glaciology isn't their usual area of study."

Howell looked through his directory and placed a call to Oliver Davies at Rothera. He put their station master on speakerphone, and we hashed out the details. Fifteen minutes later, we had an agreement from them to send an autonomous rocket-powered light plane over the glacier three times a day. The cost in fuel – and the simple fact that they had the fuel on hand – was a testament to their massive government and private sector funding. They would call us if the glacier did anything "interesting" and Oliver insisted that we owed them a huge favor.

"I think being first to know if the coastal research bases need to evacuate before a tsunami erases us from the planet seems like a valuable quid-pro-quo, don't you think?" pointed out Martin.

"Um, yes," replied the cultured Brit before disconnecting.

Martin Howell might be an ass at times, but he was amazingly good at negotiation. "Now we need to make some evacuation plans in case we need them. This isn't my normal thing. I've always relied on Josh to handle this stuff. Who would have thought we would need our Chief Evacuation Officer in the winter?"

I, for one, did not miss our Chief Joker. Together, Sylvia, Martin, and I spent the rest of the morning making lists of everything that would need to be taken to the top of Mt. Terror if the glacier crashed and caused a tsunami. People, temporary shelter, radio and satellite equipment, food, and supplies; our flying buses would begin this afternoon with temporary shelters erected for over 200 people. The twelve winterers at Scott Base, three kilometers up the road from us, would also need to evacuate. Since our helicopters could only fly about 400 kilometers, we would need to wait it out at the top of Mt. Terror until a ship could get close enough to meet us. It could be weeks, maybe even a month. Ice breakers move at a snail's pace, and even they can only come so far south at this time of year. There was a reason it was called wintering over. Leaving Antarctica this time of year was not normally an option.

It was ironic to think that sitting on top of an inactive volcano was our best chance to survive the disintegration of half the White Continent.

Fast Facts

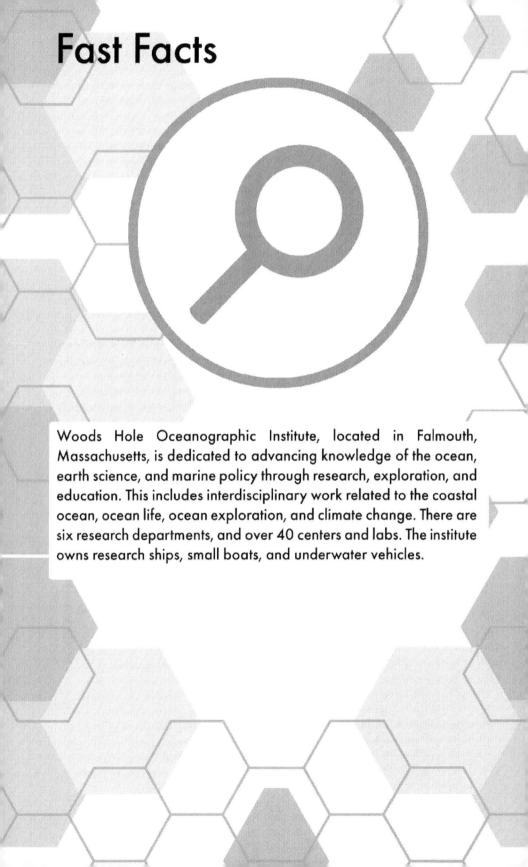

Woods Hole Oceanographic Institute, located in Falmouth, Massachusetts, is dedicated to advancing knowledge of the ocean, earth science, and marine policy through research, exploration, and education. This includes interdisciplinary work related to the coastal ocean, ocean life, ocean exploration, and climate change. There are six research departments, and over 40 centers and labs. The institute owns research ships, small boats, and underwater vehicles.

Chapter 28

Nick – Boston

Liam was moping around the house early on Sunday. His arm in a cast and propped up in a sling made sleeping difficult and he had been up several times during the night. I was surprised the day before when our doctor's office x-rayed it and decided to put him in a cast, even though the hairline fracture was not that bad. They advised that it would heal better this way, but Liam was not thrilled.

Eventually, I gave up on sleep, as well, and dragged myself downstairs to the kitchen for coffee. Liam had just turned on his video game, then realized playing it one-handed was almost impossible. "This sucks!" He shouted from the living room. The day went downhill from there.

By 2 o'clock, the kid was passed out on the couch, exhausted from lack of sleep, and worry about how he was going to survive this minor inconvenience to his life when my cell phone rang. It was Kathryn.

I answered eagerly. "Hello, my love! I'm glad to hear your voice, even with the three-second delay."

"I love you, and I wish this was a happy call." Her voice was strained and haggard.

"What's going on?"

"We've been having tremors here for the last day, some of them fairly big, even hitting magnitude-5, and McMurdo Station is prepping for an evacuation, in case the glacier goes," she said gravely.

"Good God! Are you going to be alright?"

I was not even sure she heard my comment with the lag as she continued. "The base has two large helicopters that can carry twenty-four people at a time, and we've got 212 here for the winter, including the New Zealand team at Scott Base. We also have two regular helos that can help out. The two flying tour buses will get the equipment and supplies we need up to Mt. Terror, if the time comes. The Brits are sending rocket drones over the glacier to record video, so we will know if the glacier collapses. Our station master has contacted the NSF home base to arrange for a ship and we'll meet it out at sea by helicopter. It can't come anywhere near the sound because it's frozen." My wife rattled off evacuation tactics like they were something she planned for every day.

When she took a breath, I asked again, "Kathryn, will you be alright?"

"Us? Nick, I'm not calling you to tell you to worry about us. We know what to do and have a plan to keep safe. I'm worried about you!"

"What are you talking about? We are thousands of miles away. A tidal wave from the crashing glacier isn't going to affect Boston." I was still trying to process all of her news and she was turning the danger back around on me.

"It's not the tsunami I'm worried about," Kathryn admitted. "I mean, it's an immediate danger for McMurdo, but I told you before, if an earthquake dislodges Thwaites glacier, and Pine Island next to it, the entire ice shelf could collapse. If that happens, enough ice will slide off this continent to raise sea levels by thirty to one hundred feet. Globally. Your chance of staying safe in Boston is about the same as the life expectancy of an ice cube in a volcano. And what about Inga in Miami? Is she home yet?"

She couldn't see me, but I shook my head anyway. "No. And the airport there is still closed after the hurricane. I've been checking in with her twice a day since it happened, and she texts me updates in between.

So far, she is fine. The hotel they are in got their power back, and other than Zoe getting an intestinal parasite, the girls are alright. They are just stuck."

I waited for the three-second delay and Kathryn said, "Shit. Okay, we'll figure it out. As far as you and Liam are concerned, you need to pack up all the essentials and follow our contingency plans and go to the cabin."

Years ago, my wife and I had made plans that if anything ever happened and we needed to get out of the city for some emergency, we would go to the three-season cabin we owned in the Berkshire Mountains of western Massachusetts. We vacationed there when we wanted a quiet weekend away.

"Kathryn, those plans were some weird crap we made back when we thought Armageddon could kill this planet. We were never serious about that! Good God, that was just a young couple's paranoia..."

She cut me off. "Nick, this *is* Armageddon! This is worse than a terrorist attack, or a war. This is a natural disaster that could change the way the world map looks."

"Katy...Katy!" I used my rare pet name for her when I needed to get her attention. "I can't just take off from work right after break to go to our vacation cabin. My department chair will have my head. I mean, what if nothing happens?" I took a long breath while I waited for the three-second delay.

"Are you saying you don't trust my research *and* the obvious evidence happening right now?" My wife tended to be indignant when you questioned her work. Kathryn was good at many things, but if there was one thing she excelled at, it was seismological research.

"Of course, I trust you. This is a national emergency you are talking about. Hell, a global emergency! But since no one has declared it such yet, my boss isn't going to trust your research. He trusts that I'm in my classroom educating students."

I took another deep breath. The time lag made irate arguments almost impossible.

My wife was incensed. "I don't care about your boss. I care about you and our children!"

"Look, once it is declared a national emergency, Liam and I will pack up and go to the cabin. In the meantime, I'll get the supplies that we'll need. I'll make sure the propane tank is filled so we have heat up there. I'll get food, clothing, and anything we need to survive and be ready to leave the moment we know."

This time she waited until I was done speaking before chiming in, and also did it at a cooler temperature. "Okay. And get our daughter out of Miami. Somehow, you have to get her out. Today if you can. You and Liam can drive away from the coast. Inga doesn't have that luxury. South Florida is so flat that there isn't anywhere safe within hundreds of miles of her location. It's a plane or ship. How can we get her out?"

"I had some thoughts on that. I might be able to get them on a Woods Hole research vessel. There are two ships out right now, and I'm fairly sure at least one is off the waters of Florida. I'll call Peter and see if he can arrange it."

Peter McAllister was one of the professors at the Woods Hole Oceanographic Institution that I had been friends with since my undergraduate days. WHOI operated two large research ships and several smaller boats to support oceanographic research. Although I taught biology at MIT, many of my master's students were in the Biological Oceanography Program at WHOI, so I worked closely with Woods Hole.

"Wonderful! I hate to cut this short, but I need to help with packing up things that need to be helicoptered out of here over the next few days.

We are going to set up our evacuation outpost complete with everything we need first, and then shuttle the most expensive gear up there to keep it safe. A lot of what we have is too big for helicopter evacuation, of course, but the most expensive research items tend to be the smallest. Anyway, you don't need the minutiae of our evacuation plans. I love you, and I miss you." Her voice caught on the last few words.

"I love you too, and you have no idea how much I miss you." I sighed. "Stay safe and keep letting me know what's going on." I knew she would but felt a need to reinforce it.

Fast Facts

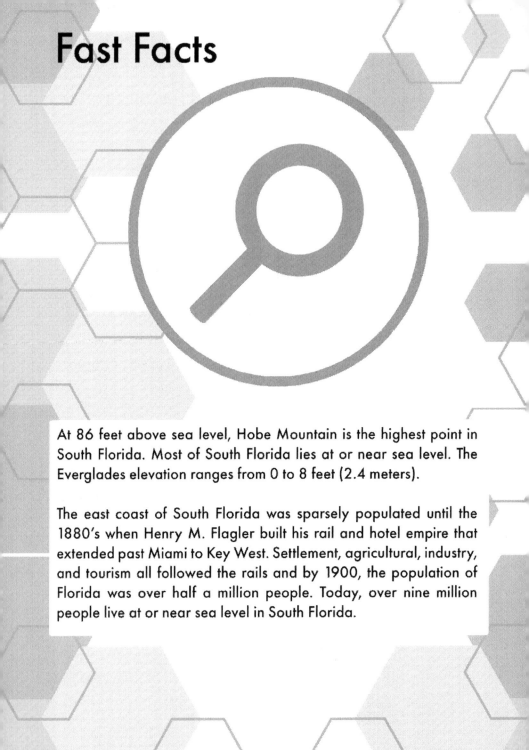

At 86 feet above sea level, Hobe Mountain is the highest point in South Florida. Most of South Florida lies at or near sea level. The Everglades elevation ranges from 0 to 8 feet (2.4 meters).

The east coast of South Florida was sparsely populated until the 1880's when Henry M. Flagler built his rail and hotel empire that extended past Miami to Key West. Settlement, agricultural, industry, and tourism all followed the rails and by 1900, the population of Florida was over half a million people. Today, over nine million people live at or near sea level in South Florida.

Chapter 29
Inga – Miami

Caleb and I were taking a short break in the rescue van when my phone rang. It was just after three and I was worried that it was Zoe, but it was just my father checking in.

"Hi, Dad!" I answered in good spirits. I was trapped in a flooded city but all in all, I was helping those in need, hanging out with a great guy, and having fun.

"Hey kiddo, you sound good."

"Yes, we are great. Caleb and I are working with the animal rescue group again today. Zoe is still sick, but she has some Red Cross issued mega antibiotics, so she should be better soon. How's Liam's arm?" Belatedly, I thought I should have asked him how he was as well, but my dad was always perfect. I don't think the man has ever been sick, depressed, or in any way under the weather his entire life.

My father gave me the rundown of my kid brother and my mother's urgent plea that we all get away from the coast because of the earthquake she was expecting. "Holy crap! Is it really happening this soon? Is she sure?"

Caleb was staring at me with a worried look. He couldn't hear my father's side of the conversation, but he saw my expression change. He started asking me what was wrong, and I held up a finger for him to wait.

"Dad, mind if I put you on speaker so Caleb can hear?"

"Is anyone else in earshot?" His voice had an edge of strain to it.

"Well, yeah, there are other workers in the van. Why?"

"Inga, as much as I would like to announce this information to the world, I would rather not cause a panic, and frankly, my greatest desire is to keep my family safe right now. Can you go somewhere that no one else will hear?"

"Not really. We are driving from location to location, rescuing stranded animals. All the houses here are flooded, only the road is above water, and there isn't anywhere private outside."

"Then you will just have to listen to me and tell your friends afterward. Listen carefully. Once the earthquake hits, if the ice shelf collapses into the sea, it will cause tidal waves and flooding across the globe. Everyone not at least one hundred feet above sea level will be in danger. Since there isn't anywhere in south Florida that's high enough to be truly safe, you need to get out. My friend Peter from Woods Hole has a small research ship currently moored in the Biscayne Bay Aquatic Preserve, about half an hour south of Miami. The ship's name is the *RV Barnstable*. They will be there only until tonight, then they are leaving. I want you on that boat."

"Dad, are you serious?"

"Yes, just listen, Inga. They are sending a skiff to Matheson Hammock Park, a family beach in Coral Gables that you should be able to get to. Get your friends and your stuff, then get a taxi or take a bus, whatever you need to, and get to that beach before dark. They will wait for you. Do you understand me?"

"Yes, Dad. Of course. What about you and Liam?"

"We will be fine. I am preparing everything we need to go up to the cabin. But we won't leave just yet. If things don't happen for a few days or weeks, I can't just leave my life. But if it happens, Liam and I can drive away from the coast. You can't do that. You need to get out of Florida. You get to the *Barnstable* and they will get you to their next stop which is Savannah, Georgia. From there, you will fly to Hartford. Not Boston. Understand?"

My response was more of a grunt than true affirmation, but my father continued. "I am putting money in your account so you can make the flight arrangements when you get to Savannah. You can use it for your three friends as well. I wouldn't advise those boys going back to Delaware or Zoe flying to Philadelphia either. Of course, the choice is theirs, but they should tell their families to get to higher ground, as well."

"Should they just fly to Hartford with me? We may not all fit in the cabin, but the mountains will be the place to be, right?" I assumed everything in the Berkshires and Connecticut other than the coast, and all the states north of it would be fine. Hartford's airport was well north of the city, almost in Massachusetts, and was the closest airport to our cabin.

"Yes, that's a good idea. Have them call their families but do it while you are leaving Miami. You only have about three hours to get to that park, so get moving. Let me know when you are on the research vessel."

I said goodbye to my father and hung up. I turned to the other two volunteers and said, "Sorry, family emergency. We need to bail." They nodded, understanding that family came before anything else.

I grabbed Caleb by the arm, and we left the van. I had Lilith call up all the rideshare apps, but she was unable to find one with a car closer than twenty minutes away, so we began walking briskly to our hotel, and I explained everything as we walked. We could see the Palms hotel in the distance when I finally finished my story and called Zoe, while Caleb called his parents.

"Zoe, we have an emergency. I'll explain when we get there, but right now I need you and Jason to pack up everything for all four of us and be ready to leave when we get there, which should be in about ten minutes." Before she could start to ask questions, I finished. "Just get off the phone and start packing!" To reiterate the point, I hung up.

Caleb was talking to his parents while we raced toward the hotel. He was out of breath because we were moving pretty fast, so I slowed my pace and he fell in beside me. He wasn't the runner that I was, but he had longer legs, and was in good shape.

"Lilith, arrange a rideshare from the Palms hotel to Matheson Hammock Park." A few minutes later, my DPA advised that there were very few rideshares operating in the wake of the hurricane, however, there would be a car at our hotel by 4:15. It was about an hour's drive to the park during normal circumstances, but I was sure it would take longer today.

Finally, Caleb got off the video call with his parents. I had only heard part of the conversation.

"Hard-headed Russians!" Caleb swore. "My parents are the most untrusting, skeptical human beings on the planet. They could not have been more amazed by this announcement than if I had told them aliens had just landed. But for shit's sake, I'm their son. You would think that they would believe me, even if they've never trusted anyone in their entire lives. My mother kept asking 'Are you sure?' and saying 'Impossible!' half the time in Russian; my father was worse. He stood there running his hands through his thinning hair and scratching his chin."

I expected disbelief and even denial. I had much the same reaction when my mother first told me this was even a possibility. "But did you get them to listen to you? Are they leaving Delaware?"

"Yeah, actually I did. Of course, my father wouldn't admit I could be right, but at least they are leaving. He just said they needed a vacation anyway. They are packing up everything important or valuable and driving up to the mountains in Virginia. Mom said it would be a second honeymoon. Ha! They never had a first."

A slow smile came to my face. "Well, let's hope after this 'honeymoon' you are still an only child!"

"Oh, gross, Inga! But I love the way you use humor to lighten a moment." He laughed as much as possible considering how winded we both were. We had covered the two miles from our volunteer location in just over thirty minutes and entered the Palms lobby.

I was glad the power was back on, so we didn't need to climb three flights of stairs.

As I propped my back and butt against the wall of the elevator, Caleb leaned in and kissed me. "You are amazing." It was a short kiss, but hard and passionate, and I was grinning when the elevator door opened. I smiled at Caleb as we hurried down the hall, hand in hand, and he shoved his phone at the keypad.

"After you." Caleb pushed the door open, and I walked in.

"What's going on?" asked Zoe and Jason, but I was pleased to see my suitcase and Zoe's standing near the door and two more on Jason's bed as he laid the last of his and Caleb's stuff into them.

"My mom is convinced that the big earthquake she's been predicting is going to happen soon, like in the next few days, and she wants us out of Miami before mountains of ice start falling off Antarctica. She says those two big glaciers are going to break up, and the ice shelf behind them will crash into the sea. If that happens, the sea level goes up. Fast. All of south Florida is too low in elevation, so she wants us out of danger, now, before it happens. My father has arranged for us to get on a boat and take us to Savannah, but we have to get to it now. Our ride will be here in a couple of minutes, so we need to get down to the lobby." I said that entire thing without taking a breath, which was amazing considering I had no breath left in me after our two-mile run-walk-jog.

Zoe had the good sense not to argue, but I saw Jason's mouth start to work and I shut him down with a look. "This isn't up for discussion. We are leaving now, whether anything happens or not."

Jason zipped his suitcase and his mouth.

Caleb had been pulling drawers out, looking under beds, and generally making sure we hadn't left anything behind; he found a sock under the desk chair, stuffed it into his suitcase, and zipped it. Throwing his backpack over his shoulder, he said, "Let's go."

The car was waiting with the trunk open when we got downstairs. Once our bags were stowed, we climbed in, again three of us in the back seat. It was cozy between the two boys. Zoe took the front seat in case we had to stop along the way to obey her intestinal parasite.

The driver told us that he would have to take the interstate across to the mainland because many roads leading to the A1A causeway were closed temporarily while crews restored power to that area and the traffic was terrible. We should get there by 5:30 at the latest, and the boat would wait at the dock until dark, so we had time.

Driving through Miami was an eye-opener for me. I had seen the devastation in Miami Beach, but the city itself was a shock. Somehow, they had fared better because there was less flooding, but there were road closures due to downed wires, flooding, and a few buildings that had collapsed from the winds. The lower-income housing, as always, was the hardest hit. I thought of Carlos and his young son, having to spend days at the shelter because they had no power, and the thousands like him. What would happen to all of them if the floodwaters came after an Antarctic earthquake, and those waters never stopped? At least after a hurricane, the waters receded. I needed to get in touch with him and let him know that he and Mateo needed to get out. Start driving north. I wished I had his direct number, but I only had the main number for the hotel.

"Zoe, Jason, call your parents and tell them what's going on. Tell them we are headed to Savannah, and then a flight to Hartford from there. Tell them that they need to leave home. They should try to come to our cabin. I'll text you the address. Send it to them."

The rideshare driver looked in the rear-view mirror at me, clearly wondering what was going on. He got an earful as both of my friends told the story to their parents, and I could see he wanted to ask questions, but with two conversations going on in the vehicle already, that was impractical. Zoe was off the phone in less than ten minutes and gave me a thumbs up and a smile. Her parents were the practical sort. Presented with facts, they would not argue, and I knew they were already packing. If they were anything like their daughter, they would just throw all their stuff into the trunk of their car without even bothering with a suitcase, grab the cat, and start driving. Under my breath, I asked Lilith how far it was from Mount Laurel, New Jersey to Great Barrington, Massachusetts, and was advised that it was four to four-and-a-half hours, depending on route and traffic.

Jason finally hung up the phone. "Well, my folks took some convincing, but in the end, I got them to agree to head north. We live in a small town in southern Delaware, almost two hours south of Philadelphia, and we are surrounded by water on all sides. They'll leave tonight. They'll stay on the western side of Philly and then head north to Allentown. They'll be fine there, but they agreed to drive up to your cabin once we let them know we are there. They'll also call my sister and let her know to head to higher ground."

By now the driver couldn't keep silent anymore. "Are you kids serious about this earthquake? You can't predict an earthquake, and all this crap about climate change melting the glaciers, it's just the Earth going through cycles. It's not going to all happen at once. Sure, the Greenland glacier melted, and we have higher sea level now, but it didn't happen overnight. People had time to move. You kids are acting like this is a disaster movie or something. So, a glacier in Antarctica falls into the water like what happened ten years ago in the arctic? It will be bad, but Miami is ready for another couple feet of sea level rise. We went through a lot, spent a lot of taxpayer money, to be sure of that. You'll be fine here. But if you feel you need to get home, of course, go."

He went on like that for a while, telling us all about the money his city spent, and from his diatribe, you'd think he single-handedly paid for Fisher Gate all by himself.

Well, at least we hadn't made him panic. That's why my father didn't want me to start warning everyone. Either they would panic, or they wouldn't believe it until someone in authority announced it. And by then it would be too late. I wanted to announce this to the world, save as many as we could, but I knew it wasn't that easy.

Our driver was proof of that.

Half an hour into the ride, Zoe started fidgeting. "Can you find the nearest bathroom please?" The driver gave her a look but pulled over at a fast-food restaurant a minute later. Rideshare drivers were paid by the distance, not the time, so the longer this trip took, the less money he made, so he was agitated. My worry was about making it to the boat on time. I really didn't care what this driver's paycheck looked like at the end of the day.

Zoe was back in the car in less than five minutes. She had these bathroom runs down to a science now.

"Ugh. I can't wait until this is over."

I was the one fidgeting as the traffic slowed to a crawl, and not because I had to go to the bathroom. We finally crossed into Coral Gables just after 6 p.m. and saw the sign for the park. We drove down the single-lane road to the public boat launch. I looked for the inflatable skiff that my father had described. A family was pulling a boat out of the water on a trailer, water gushing from the back end of it as the truck pulled it free of the bay, but other than that, all six of the public docks were empty.

"The park closes at 7 p.m.," said our driver.

"Does that mean a boat can't pull up to the dock?"

"No. Just means they close the gate at the park entrance and any cars left in here can't get out until morning," he replied.

I scanned across the small bay to the private docks on the other side of the park. There were nine piers, each housing about a dozen boats in slips. A sailboat was tied up in one slip, and a larger motorboat in another, but those were not our rescuer.

"Where is he?" I wondered out loud.

"Maybe he's just not here yet?" asked Zoe, anxiously biting her lower lip.
"Yeah," echoed both boys.

My face crinkled in consternation. "He's supposed to be here waiting for us, until dark, but yes, it's possible he just hasn't arrived. I guess we wait."

The four of us stood feverishly searching the water, now stranded at a public park, staring at the empty docks. We stood, we paced, we sat in the sand; Zoe used the porta-john. As the sun set, we were forced to conclude that the boat had left without us.

I hugged my shoulders and rested my chin on my chest. Not sure what to do, I called my father.

My father was livid. He wasn't an angry man in general, so it was odd to hear him get up in arms about anything. "I'll call Peter and find out what happened, but that won't help you right now. I'm not sure what else to suggest." We were sitting on the sand, my phone on my thigh, and my father on speaker so we could all be part of the conversation.

Zoe piped up. "I have an idea. That speedboat tour we took this week, those boats are probably just getting back into dock for the night. I'm sure if we get there quickly, one of the captains might agree to take us to Savannah."

I turned to Zoe and said, "And why would they do that?"

"We pay them, of course. Pay them enough to make it worth their while."

"You mean bribe them?" I asked, raising one eyebrow.

"Well, I wouldn't call it a *bribe* exactly," Zoe grinned. "Payment for services rendered."

My father's voice from my phone was loud and clear. "Yes, Zoe has it spot on. It's a great idea. Do it. Approach a boat captain and see if he or she will take you up the coast tonight before the official evacuation order is announced. Talk to each one of them until you get a yes. Use the money I put in your account." He told us how much to offer.

Zoe was already on her phone, setting up a rideshare to Miami Beach

Speedboat Adventures with whichever company could get here fastest, regardless of price. There was one ten minutes away and we walked to the park entrance to meet them and ducked under the gate blocking the road. When the car arrived, it was a small autonomous one, and Zoe and I sat silently in the cramped back seat. The boys sat in the front; one of the advantages of a driverless vehicle.

Thoughts raced around my mind like wild winds chasing themselves in a frenzied whirl until they coalesced into a plan. "Lilith, connect me to the Miami Beach Inn."

A moment later, a female receptionist's voice answered. "Hi, my name is Inga Whitson. I was a guest there until a few days ago."

"Yes, ma'am, how can we help you?" replied a young, high-pitched voice.

"I need to get in touch with your shuttle driver, Carlos Martinez. He was staying at the Convention Center shelter, with his son, because they had no power. I am a volunteer there." So, I was stretching the truth a bit, or at least the time frame, but I continued unhampered by my little white lie. "His boy left a stuffed animal there, and I would like the child to get it back. I could tell it was important to him."

"Yes, of course, Ms. Whitson. I'm sure Carlos would be happy to get Mateo's toy back. We cannot give out employee's numbers, but I can give him yours if that would be alright."

I gave permission and asked her to contact Carlos as soon as possible because I was leaving town tonight. That much, with any luck, would at least be true.

Within five minutes, my cell rang with an unknown Florida number, and I answered immediately. "This is Inga."

It was our van driver. "Hello Ms. Whitson. It's nice to hear from you, but Matteo did not leave anything behind."

"Hi, Carlos. Sorry about the fib. I had to get in touch with you urgently." He didn't sound perturbed by the falsehood. Probably thought

I was hitting on him. I'm sure he got that a lot from Spring Breakers.

"That's alright. It's not every tourist that volunteers to help those in need while she is on vacation." He laughed an almost nervous laugh. Maybe he *didn't* get hit on all that much.

"It was nothing. Listen, this is important. Do you remember when you took me and my friends downtown to the galleries, the story I told everyone about my mother and her research in Antarctica?"

"Of course, I do. Is your mother okay?"

"Yes, she's fine, well, mostly, but we may not be." I gave him a short summary of what my mother expected to happen and the time frame. "This will get out to the media eventually, but of course, not until the earthquake happens, because, well, that's the way the news works. But we have advance warning, and we are leaving Miami tonight. I wanted you to know because I want you and your little boy to be safe. You need to get out, but with the airport closed and many roads flooded or damaged, I'm afraid you might not be able to soon enough. It's a long way to drive to get to safety here. Nowhere in this flat state will be safe."

He made some noises and considering my apocalyptic announcement, he was likely also considering my sanity, and I was afraid he would chalk me up as a lunatic, thank me, and hang up. "How are you getting out?"

"We are going to the Speedboat Adventures dock right now and try to convince one of the boat captains to take us to Savannah. We plan on offering a hefty financial enticement. From there we will fly home. I'd like you and your son to come with us."

"Hold on." Carlos began speaking in Spanish to someone in the room, and I wished I had paid more attention in Mrs. Alvarez's Spanish class. His conversation was loud and fast, and if he was laughing with his buddies at the crazy girl on the phone, I wondered why he didn't just hang up and get back to his party. Instead, he said back to me, Cuban accent in full swing, "We will be there in *haf* an hour. *Don leaf wit* out us."

Fast Facts

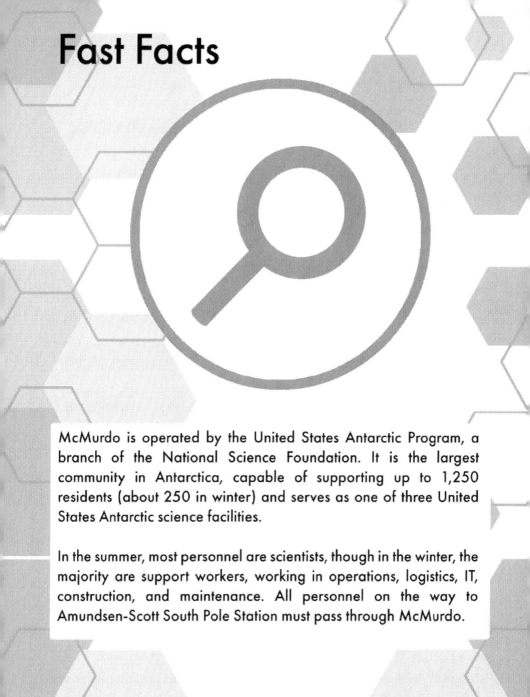

McMurdo is operated by the United States Antarctic Program, a branch of the National Science Foundation. It is the largest community in Antarctica, capable of supporting up to 1,250 residents (about 250 in winter) and serves as one of three United States Antarctic science facilities.

In the summer, most personnel are scientists, though in the winter, the majority are support workers, working in operations, logistics, IT, construction, and maintenance. All personnel on the way to Amundsen-Scott South Pole Station must pass through McMurdo.

Chapter 30

Kathryn – Antarctica

"Sylvia, could you hand me that tool kit?" It was a specialized kit for working on the seismographs I oversaw, and I would be lost without it in the field. I considered it vital equipment, and Martin had specified we only packed the bare essentials. I was determined to get the critical equipment in my lab up to the temporary shelter before I dealt with my personal effects.

Suddenly, the lights began to swing violently from the ceiling. Earthquake. No time to think. All at once, the lab was moved up and down with such a force that we dropped heavily to the floor. The framed photo of my family fell from my cubicle wall, glass shattering. Sylvia grabbed my hand and together we scrambled under the desk, pulling ourselves underneath while the very ground shook with more noise than an explosion. We didn't scream, we just waited silently under my desk. It lasted a long time. It *felt* like forever. But as the rumbles ceased, I read the data off my monitors. It had only been half a minute.

"Shit." I shook my head. "That was 5.9 and its epicenter was on the continent, less than one hundred and thirty kilometers from here. That's twenty-seven kilometers closer than the one early this morning. And neither quake was on the fault line."

Before I could say another word, the radio sounded on my hip. I grabbed it and keyed the mic. "Yes, Martin, that was another earthquake. It was a little closer than this morning's and quite a bit stronger." I listened to him swear for a moment before continuing. "They're called foreshocks, and the good news is that we get a warning that the bigger quake is coming."

"None of this is good news! Alright, so we have begun transporting temporary shelter, food, and supplies to Mt. Terror. I wanted to let you know that the dozen researchers at Scott Base will be here within the hour, ready to evacuate."

What he didn't say was that if Scott Base could pack up in an hour, why couldn't I?

I chose to ignore his unvoiced criticism. "Thanks. I do need to get my equipment packed up before I can evacuate. We must understand what is going on. I am fine with being on the last helo out of here if that helps. Have Rothan and Phil shuttle everyone else up there on the flying buses, get everything set up, and I'll be in the last group."

"Roger that," came Martin's voice through the reedy speaker. "We will have the radio and sat equipment up there in the next load of evacuation items, along with generators and portable heaters. Oh, one more thing. Oliver Davies reported that Thwaites was still stable on their last flyover, but there was some calving at the edge of the Pine Island glacier. Thought you and Sylvia would want to know."

"Thanks. She's right here with me and heard. Kathryn out." For once, I thought I would use official radio communications protocols, since the station master was, even if Martin only talked that way to show his superiority.

We got back to the task at hand, disconnecting equipment, wrapping what we needed to protect from damage, and placing everything into weatherproof storage boxes for transport. I could not disconnect my main computer until we were ready to go in case we had any more foreshocks. Two hours later we were in Sylvia's office doing the same with her gear.

Then the next quake hit. The building shook like a dollhouse, lab equipment tossed around like Barbie dolls. Sylvia's desk jumped over the linoleum like it had a mind of its own. Pieces of ceiling tile rained down in chunks and books flew off shelves.

I'm a research seismologist and I know earthquakes intimately, yet it was terrifying. This was no gentle 5-something magnitude warning. This was big. Maybe even The Big One.

The building floor moved, and the noise was like protracted thunder, only much worse because the vibrations were coming from beneath our feet. I felt rather than heard my radio vibrate and Martin's voice come from the speaker, but the world was shaking, and I couldn't answer and couldn't hear what he was saying, yet I knew. He was as terrified as I was.

As suddenly as if someone had flipped a light switch, it stopped. Sylvia sat beside me, panting for breath like a marathon runner. I grabbed my radio and keyed it. "Martin, are you all okay?" I was screaming into the microphone.

Silence. Silence for too long. I was sure the Central Services Building had collapsed. Crary Science remained upright above our heads, but I could only see this small section. The earth science pod was fine, but what about the other four? There were still people in the other pods.

I tried again. "Martin. Come in, Martin! Come on, Howell, answer me." A crackle was the only initial response, then finally his voice.

"Kathryn, yes, we are here. We are alright. What about you?"

I exhaled loudly. "That's a relief. Sylvia and I are alone in the earth sciences pod, but fine. I think people are packing in the atmospheric sciences pod, but I don't know their status. We'll go over to atmo and check that out. Let me know if you need us to go up to bio or down to the aquarium."

I signed off and we carefully threaded our way down the hallway that connected the earth sciences pod with the atmospheric sciences pod. Our offices were in the middle of the three buildings, which were built on a slope. The uphill pod – core and biology – was connected to the Central Services Building through a passageway. The three levels were connected by enclosed, outdoor staircases, so there was another staircase that led downhill to the aquarium pod.

The hallway was in shambles. Stacked boxes and crates had tumbled to the floor, blocking the way and we picked and climbed over objects, stopping to check each doorway. The fan room and boiler room were empty. We crossed to the atmospheric sciences pod, and I checked the six offices on the left while Sylvia inspected the photo lab, electronic labs, and computer storage and maintenance rooms. We met up in the multipurpose area glad that we had found no one in any of the rooms. If this were summer, most of these rooms would be full of researchers.

"I'll check the Lidar lab," I said. Sylvia nodded and went to the receiving office and loading dock. Lidar was locked and the lights were off. It didn't look like anyone had been in there for weeks.

Suddenly Sylvia shouted. "Kathryn! Come quick!"

I careened around the corner and saw crates strewn about the loading dock. The garage bay door was open, and Dakota O'Sullivan knelt at the edge of a crate, desperately hauling a heavy box. That's when I saw legs beneath the fallen box. Sylvia was beside Dakota, and said, "As we lift, try to pull him out."

Dakota and this trapped man must have been stacking boxes when the tremor hit and trapped the researcher beneath it. Arlen studied the south pole's auroras, and this was his third winter in Antarctica.

I reached under Arlen's arms and grabbed him firmly, nodding to Sylvia and Dakota. "Okay, lift."

As the box slowly raised, I pulled hard, and Arlen slid out. The trapped man, now free, cried out in pain. "My leg!"

Arlen was holding his left leg at the knee and trying laboriously not to scream or cry. "I can't move it." His voice quavered and his naturally golden complexion was ashen.

Sylvia put a hand on his shoulder and spoke comforting words, while I grabbed my radio and called the station master's office. "This is Kathryn in the atmospheric science pod. We have an injured man and need assistance."

When the response came a moment later it was one of the office staff, a young woman whose name I couldn't remember. "This is the station master's office. How badly is he hurt?" her voice was calm, like a 911 operator.

I looked over at Arlen, sitting on the floor with his eyes squeezed shut. "Dr. Arlen Novik's leg has been crushed by a steel box. He is conscious and in great pain. It's probably broken...or worse. We don't have anything to use as a stretcher. Can you send a medic?"

The woman's voice came again. Hannah, yes, that was her name. "We will have someone there within five minutes. Is anyone else injured?"

I told her we were fine and signed off.

Arlen spoke through clenched teeth. "Dakota...can you get those crates...up there?" He swallowed hard and continued. "Please. It's sensitive equipment. Make sure it's alright."

Fast Facts

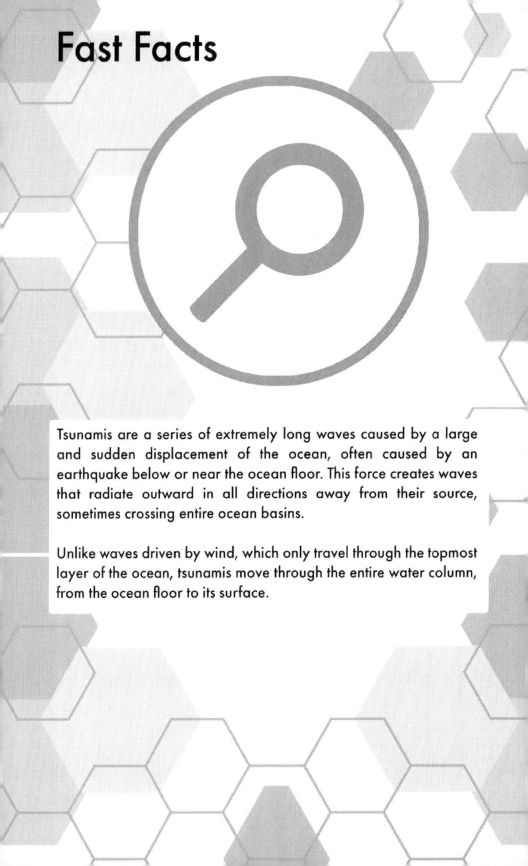

Tsunamis are a series of extremely long waves caused by a large and sudden displacement of the ocean, often caused by an earthquake below or near the ocean floor. This force creates waves that radiate outward in all directions away from their source, sometimes crossing entire ocean basins.

Unlike waves driven by wind, which only travel through the topmost layer of the ocean, tsunamis move through the entire water column, from the ocean floor to its surface.

Chapter 31
Inga – Miami

Carlos, Mateo, and a woman I didn't recognize stood waiting at Marketplace pier when the automated rideshare car dropped us off. They had two suitcases between them.

Carlos introduced his younger sister. "Alita, these are the young ladies from my hotel, Inga and Zoe, and their boyfriends, Jason and Caleb."

Zoe visibly bristled at the term *boyfriend*, as she and Jason were anything but; however, I didn't correct Carlos. Instead, I shook Alita's hand warmly.

Alita's smile was open and unguarded. "Thank you for taking us with you."

I shot her a surprised look. "I suppose I should thank you for believing in us. Can I ask why you don't think we are a bunch of nut jobs? After all, we are asking you to leave your home based on unpublished research from someone you don't even know."

"I trust my brother," she stated flatly. Her English held only a trace of Cuban accent, unlike her older brother. "Carlos is my only family since our parents died and he has always looked out for me. He believes you, and that's enough for me."

Carlos regarded his sister with endearment as she held her young nephew's hand. "I do believe you, and that's not because of your mother, Inga. You are right. I don't know her, or even you for that matter. But I have been worried about that sea gate and the ocean rising for as long as I have lived in Miami, and your story – your mother's theory – fits my own beliefs. So yes, I trust you. And we will go to Savannah with you. If nothing happens, then we will have had a nice adventure, and we will come home with some photos and memories."

"What about your job?" interjected Caleb.

"I took two weeks' vacation time. Now, let's go see about a ride."

All four of the giant catamarans were moored at the Speedboat Adventures dock but the office was closed. That did not deter Carlos. He knocked on the door until someone answered, and when they spoke to him in Spanish, I was glad he had taken the lead. This was his city.

Rapid, energetic conversation ensued, none of which I could follow. At one point, the man looked me up and down appraisingly, then smiled at Carlos and shook his hand.

"Why do I feel like you just sold me to this man?" I was kidding, but a part of my brain replayed human trafficking stories from the news.

"No, no, nothing like that. We were just agreeing on a price. I told him of your emergency – your sick aunt in Savannah, and how much it's worth to you to get to see her before she dies. She means so much to all of us, after all. With the airport still closed, he has generously agreed to *borrow* his employer's speedboat and take us there tonight. We must pay for the fuel, and his expenses."

Carlos stated the sum they agreed on and I almost shit a brick. It was almost all the money my father had deposited in my account. It wasn't like we had a choice, so I handed my card to the man, who swiped away nearly all my balance. I would have to get more from my father for plane tickets once in Savannah, but I would cross that bridge later. It was almost 500 miles away, and at top speed, we would not arrive until three in the morning.

The seven of us climbed into the open-air boat that could hold thirty-six passengers in long rows of seats. Tonight, we would stretch out on them and sleep as best we could, keeping out of the wind as much as possible.

"Hey, good thing for our winter coats," exclaimed Zoe, then looked pensive. "Is there a bathroom onboard?"

There was not.

"Oh jeez, me getting on this boat is like juggling in the dark. A special kind of stupid." Zoe scrunched up her face and said to the Spanish-speaking boat captain, "Okay, let's go."

"Yes, ma'am," he said in flawless, unaccented English.

I was glad I hadn't refuted Carlos' lie about my aunt now.

The catamaran slowly idled away from the wooden dock. It was high tide now, and completely dark, but lights coming from shops and streetlamps along the seacoast allowed us to take in a different view than on our last excursion. Fisher Gate was closed, completely blocking our view of Biscayne Bay. Behind it, behemoth cruise ships slept.

As we moved further from the pier and away from the city's innumerable docks, we edged cautiously around sunken bits of land that used to be islands. Our captain, Miguel González Flores, was methodical in the passage, avoiding submerged objects and those floating atop until we were far enough out to sea to pick up the pace. Flores pressed the engine for more speed, the catamaran's twin engines pulling the boat up out of the water until it almost floated on the surface.

Caleb and I sat in the front row, squinting into the salty spray, his arm wrapped around my shoulder. Zoe and Jason were in the row behind us, but the wind made it hard to hear anything they were saying, until Zoe shouted, "Look at the stars!"

Far away from the city lights, the sky was a blanket of twinkling, silver speckles, splattered across the black curtain of night. I rarely saw stars in Boston. Maybe just a dozen dim pinpoints in the night sky. But out at sea, a mile from the coast and a universe away from reality, there were thousands of them. Millions.

I leaned against Caleb and looked at the sky until the hull, bouncing with each wave, lulled me to sleep.

When a crick in my neck woke me, Caleb and I laid down across two of the narrow benches, bundled up in our coats. I saw Carlos on a bench behind me, his little boy snuggled into him. Alita and Zoe were asleep as well, but Jason was up front in the second driver's seat, chatting with Captain Flores, as much as was possible with the wind carrying away most of his words. I closed my eyes and let the droning of the engine and pounding of the waves lull me back to sleep.

A sudden jolt woke me just after midnight. I sat up momentarily confused as to where I was until a splash of cold water hit my face. The seas were getting rougher, rising, and falling in great mountains of choppy waves, unforgiving and tempestuous. Massive crests topped with white froth slid across the ocean. I longed for sleep by my mind battered me with worries and feelings of dread. The waves tossing the boat did not help and I stayed awake.

Forget about sleep, I would be glad to just not puke.

The sky was still full of stars so there was clearly no storm. Why was the ocean this rough?

Captain Flores glanced over at me. "Don't worry. Catamarans are extremely stable and naturally buoyant; virtually unsinkable."

At that moment, the catamaran was swamped by water.

I jumped off the seat, my coat drenched in saltwater from the mountains of tempestuous waves.

Captain Flores shouted, "Put on your life jackets, and seatbelt yourselves in!"

I had forgotten the boat had life jackets. We had worn them when we took the Fisher Gate Cruise, but no one had stuck by regulations on this unsanctioned trip. Caleb moved to sit beside me, and we extracted life jackets from under the bench seats, secured them, and found the retractable seat belts. Carlos had his little boy in a life jacket and secured before putting on his own.

As the catamaran tossed and heaved in the rough waves, I thought of all the times I had heard flight attendants telling passengers to secure their own breathing masks and life jackets before assisting others. That always confused me until I saw Carlos with Mateo. There was no way he would ever put his own life ahead of that child's.

Caleb held my hand for what felt like hours but probably was only twenty minutes when suddenly the catamaran took on an unnatural quiet in the noise of the lashing waves. The engines had stalled.

Fast Facts

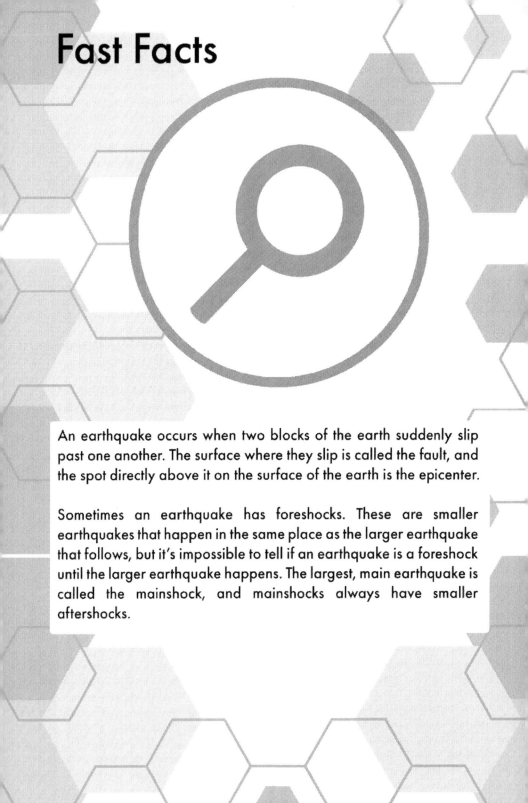

An earthquake occurs when two blocks of the earth suddenly slip past one another. The surface where they slip is called the fault, and the spot directly above it on the surface of the earth is the epicenter.

Sometimes an earthquake has foreshocks. These are smaller earthquakes that happen in the same place as the larger earthquake that follows, but it's impossible to tell if an earthquake is a foreshock until the larger earthquake happens. The largest, main earthquake is called the mainshock, and mainshocks always have smaller aftershocks.

Chapter 32
Kathryn – Antarctica

I had never felt so tired in my life. The muscles in my back ached from the effort to pack and move everything load by load to get the important items up to the temporary shelter atop Mt. Terror. Sylvia was no better off than me. More than half the winter staff was already up at the shelter. It was a huge undertaking to build winter quarters for over 200 people. Setting up electricity, heat, beds, cooking facilities, bathrooms, and storage of all the 'expensive' items that the scientists refused to leave behind would take a week or more.

I fell into my bed Monday night and was instantly asleep. I might have slept through another tremor or twelve, I had no idea.

With no rising sun to wake me Tuesday morning, I relied on my alarm. I spent much longer in the shower than I normally would, knowing there were no showers at the evacuation shelter, and was finally dressing when Sylvia came to get me.

"Have they packed up the kitchen yet?" I asked, hoping to get a hot meal, as unlikely as that was.

"Frankly, I have no idea. Let's go check."

The main cafeteria looked like a ghost town. I was not surprised to see Dakota directing the evacuation team. They were a dedicated individual who knew how to get a job done. I liked Dakota, and not just because of the fabulous food we enjoyed at McMurdo Station.

Dakota's sculpted cheekbones sat amidst flawless ivory bisque skin, but their unruly mop of ginger-red hair made them easy to spot a mile off. Dakota flashed us a smile as we approached. "Hey, you two! Thanks again for helping me get Arlen out after that tremor. I wish I had something better than cereal to say thanks with."

I did not want thanks for pulling a man out from a crushing load of crates. "It's me that should be thanking you for the great job evacuating all the kitchen supplies."

Dakota directed us to the one serving counter where the remaining foodstuffs were, and Sylvia and I filled up on cereal, ice-cold milk, and thankfully, a carafe of coffee.

Sufficiently filled, we spent the rest of the day packing more gear. My main equipment was ready to go so I made one helicopter trip up to the temporary base to move the seismograph sensor equipment before returning to McMurdo. The more time I had, the more I planned to take. We loaded crates and hauled everything with hand trucks out to the crawler at which point Pieter Nordling drove the equipment up to the helicopter pad. This went on until after seven when we finally quit for the night. Day and night hardly mattered at this point since the day length had shrunk to just a few hours.

Pieter, Dakota, Sylvia, and a dozen others, all as exhausted as me, gathered for a meal of makeshift provisions.

When the earthquake struck, the noise was at an intensity I'd never experienced before. At first, no-one moved, our brains unable to make sense of the input from our ears or the shaking under our feet. Fear overloaded us. All I could think was, get under the table and hold on for dear life. This was no tremor. It was full bore. The roar was many magnitudes louder than thunder. Dishes and glasses shattered. Then everyone moved at once, all of us in flight mode that all-consuming fear created. We held tight under the dining tables, clinging to the legs of the sturdy wood. Intelligent, educated adults panicked as the ground shook up and down as if the entire building had suddenly been tossed into the sky and fallen back to earth with a mighty impact. Cracks appeared in the ground beneath us.

Everyone scrambled to their feet but most of us immediately lost balance and were reduced to crawling as we rushed outside for fear that the Central Services Building might come crashing down on us. The lights flickered before going out. Our screams were lost under the deafening noise and as the shaking stopped, we reached out for each other in the frigid air. I grabbed Sylvia's hand and we half crawled; half walked outside as the building collapsed around us.

I looked around. The external lamp posts were illuminated, so our power center wasn't destroyed. There was chaos and wreckage everywhere, and large sections of the building were demolished. The two-story-high glass walls were so much broken glass scattered on the ground.

The rubble of civilization was strewn about the base. I lost sight of Sylvia as she let go of my hand, but then I saw Dakota and Pieter rushing from the Central Services Building to the nearest dorm pod. Pieter had a coat in his hands, and he caught up to Sylvia forcing her into it as they ran.

I was freezing without my Michelin Man outer gear. Outdoors unexpectedly in Antarctica in winter wasn't something you could do for long. The Antarctic air that blasted me was at least forty below. By the time I got inside again, my entire body was numb. Not just my extremities. I couldn't feel any part of my body. Someone held the door for me. I wouldn't have been able to work a doorknob.

As I slowly threaded my way to my room for a blanket, my frozen brain thought about the dorm pod surrounding me. The walls were made of a reinforced plastic resin that was almost impossible to break, shatter, or destroy. They could only be melted, so baring fire, it would never happen.

I found Sylvia and Pieter in her room, the door wide open. When I stumbled in, she wrapped me in a blanket, and I fell into her desk chair. Pieter had his down comforter wrapped around his shoulders. None of us had our coats in the dining hall, except whoever's coat Sylvia was wearing, thanks to Pieter. As the blanket started to warm me, my teeth began chattering violently.

The dorm pod had no central area to congregate, but people began to converge in Sylvia's room and the hall outside. Sylvia began taking a headcount to make sure everyone was accounted for while the rest of us warmed ourselves. It was then that I realized there was no heat coming from the ceiling vent. I was not sure what that meant. Either the heating plant had been damaged in the earthquake, or the dorm's connection to it had been severed.

"I hate to say this, but I've searched everywhere in the pod and there are at least three people not accounted for," said Sylvia, taking the radio from my belt. She began transmitting immediately.

"This is Sylvia Rapp to anyone on the channel. We have twenty-seven souls accounted for in the winter dorm pod. Station master Martin Howell, Hannah Anderson, and Billy Cranford, please report in."

There was no response.

Sylvia tried again and again.

A crackle finally emanated from the speaker. "This is Billy. I'm in Field Science Support."

Sylvia replied immediately. "Billy, are you hurt or in danger?"

"No, ma'am," came the young Aussie's response. "I'm okay. There is a lot of damage. The roof has collapsed on the western side where it connects to the CSB, but I think I can move enough rubble out of my path and get outside."

"Do you require assistance?" asked Sylvia.

"Not at this time. I'll let you know if I can't get to the dorm once I get out of the building. Billy out."

My teeth had finally stopped chattering and I asked Sylvia for the radio. "Go make sure everyone has outerwear. The heat's off and it's going to get colder in here."

She looked up at the air vent then grabbed her gloves from her dresser and left her room. Warmer now, I threaded my way through the gathered survivors and went next door to my room, dropping the blanket, and replacing it with my heavy-duty insulated jacket. I pulled a hat over my head and slipped into my gloves. They were thin enough to work electronics but the synthetic fabric recirculated body heat, keeping my hands comfortable.

I keyed the mic. "Martin Howell and Hannah Anderson, report please."

The silence that greeted me was disturbing. Even trapped, they should have been able to get to their radios, even if just to key the mic a few times. Unless they were unconscious. Or worse.

"Martin. Hannah. Come in please." I kept trying for fifteen minutes, and finally changed tactics.

"If you can hear me, we are coming to get you. Stay where you are; rescue is on the way."

Back in Sylvia's room, Pieter, our medic Levi, and two other men were waiting to leave with me to get Martin and Hannah. I saw the radio on Pieter's belt and realized they had listened to my pleas and the unnerving silence that greeted them.

The passageway to the Central Services Building was blocked by the collapsed ceiling, so our only access was at the other end of the dorm pod. That would make the overland trek to the CSB longer, but we had no choice.

I opened the airlock-like hatch at the far end of the long building and three of the five of us filled in, closing the door behind us. The vestibule was not built for crowds. The frigid air of Antarctica hit me hard in the face, and my lips were already bloody and cracked from my short time outside escaping the cafeteria. I pulled my goggles down then carefully descended the wooden steps, turning 90 degrees and working my way uphill toward the road, and across to the Central Service building. I heard the dorm pod hatch open again behind me, disgorging the last two members of our group.

The crack in McMurdo's main road that loomed ahead of me had not been there an hour ago. Suddenly my feet slid out from under me, and my ass hit the ground. Loose permafrost tumbled around me, and I began sliding toward the crack. I scrambled to my feet, but the earth shook beneath me again as an aftershock hit. I didn't know how deep the crack was, but it was wide enough to swallow me, and I was tumbling uncontrollably toward it. Chunks of rock and pieces of building debris tumbled past me and fell over the edge.

A strong hand gripped my wrist and clung to me until the earth stopped moving, then pulled me toward him. My gloved hand grabbed the wrist of my rescuer.

Pieter's grip was tight. "Hang on."

I didn't let go.

Scrambling to my feet, I felt like I was rolling on thousands of marbles, but I dug my heels into the slanted earth and Pieter pulled me toward safety.

"Try to avoid falling into anymore Grand Canyons," he admonished warmly.

"Will do," I breathed heavily, and the five of us worked our way over rocks and debris to the Central Service building. There was a gaping hole in the side where the passageway should have connected, and a large rift in the rocks that we had to get across to make it inside. It seemed that most of the hillside had come down around the building.

Pieter took the lead and slid down carefully into the crack, which was waist-deep for the tall man, then gave me a hand to cross. The other men in the group, all smaller than the Dutchman, navigated the crack as I had and followed me into the building. The men with me were the support staff that made up most of the base's population in the winter, rather than scientists, and I was glad to have them along. They were a hardy lot.

I radioed again to our missing people, but when I got no response, I began shouting instead. It wasn't far to the station master's office.

"Martin! Hannah! We are coming to get you!"

Perhaps their radios had been destroyed in the earthquake, but they should hear my voice now. We were close.

Rounding the corner, I saw the collapsed roof between the CSB and Field Science Support that Billy had reported. The two-story reinforced glass wall was gone. Shards of glass had exploded, covering the wide hallway.

A ceiling support beam blocked the way, and it took all four men to move it far enough away that I could squeeze behind it and through the office door. The building was dark, but my headlamp revealed the chaos and destruction and when I saw the bloody hand sticking out from under a collapsed filing cabinet I gasped.

"Got one! Help me out here," I shouted to the men behind me. Pieter wedged his large frame into the room and helped lift the metal cabinet.

The hand was small and female. "Hannah, can you hear me?" I was struggling to keep my voice calm while trying to be loud enough to get her attention.

She groaned in response.

"She's conscious," I said, and another one of the men lifted the cabinet with Pieter, while Cameron and I pulled her out.

"Don't move," I told her.

Hannah's voice was weak. "Couldn't if I wanted to. Did you find Martin?"

"Not yet. Just relax, we'll have you out of here soon."

Levi knelt beside her. "Can you move your legs?"

Her legs twitched as she tried, and her feet moved.

The medic put a gentle hand on her arm. "We've got to get you out of here to treat you, Hannah. You can move your feet so there isn't any spinal injury."

He nodded his head to me, and I grabbed her under her arms to drag her out.

The girl let out a short, sharp scream, then bit it off. "I think I've got a couple of broken ribs." Another sharp gasp and then we had her free.

Hannah managed to stand with assistance.

"Do you know where Martin is?" I asked as Cameron and Levi supported her and began walking towards the office door. I threw her coat to Cameron, and he caught it with his free hand. Pieter was already outside holding the ceiling support out of the way so they could get out. Cameron and Levi would get her back to the dorm pod where they could get her ribs wrapped until we were able to get her to the evac helicopter and up to Mt. Terror. We had moved most of the medical supplies up there at this point, and I had no idea what condition the medical center was in at this point anyway.

"He was downstairs."

I shuddered as they took her away. The Central Services Building was two stories with a large atrium that let in summer light, but today it was an eerie, dark chamber with the wide staircase that led down from the station master's office covered in huge shards of glass. Because the base was built on a hillside, the CSB's main floor was the upper level; the lower level faced downhill, with a view of McMurdo Sound.

Pieter held the beam as I emerged from the office and then let it fall behind me.

"We have to go downstairs to find Martin," I said.

I followed him down, cautiously picking our way through the rubble in the dark and ran into the back of the big man when he stopped. His headlamp swept the floor below us and stopped as abruptly as he had.

I gasped. "Martin!" I rushed past Pieter down the last ten steps but already knew that there was no way the station master could be alive. There was a man-size piece of window glass sticking out of his abdomen and the blood pooled beneath him was frozen from exposure to the Antarctic winter.

I knelt beside him and felt for a pulse. My hands trembled as I repositioned them to try again. Still nothing.

A moment later, Pieter was beside me, pulling me away. "Come on, we need to get the rest of the crew to safety."

"We can't just leave him here!" I was devastated. This couldn't be happening.

"We have no choice," said Pieter, his voice heavy with grief.

We made our way back to the dorm pods as quickly as we could with the injured girl.

I hated taking over as station master under these circumstances, but I had no choice. After Martin's death, and with most of the administrative staff gone home for the winter, those left were either too inexperienced or injured. Phil had flown all the frostbitten or battered staff to the evacuation base at the top of Mt. Terror, and now Rothan was piloting the last helicopter with myself, Sylvia, Dakota, and the young Australian Billy Cranford.

It had been three hours since the quake hit and there had been two more aftershocks, the last just moments ago.

I fidgeted in my seat as Rothan took us aloft from the helicopter pad. "Come on, come on," I muttered under my breath. I needed to check my relocated equipment to find out what the quake magnitudes were.

We cleared the squat buildings of McMurdo and I looked out at the frozen sea, illuminated by the halogen spotlights shining from the overlook tower at the edge of McMurdo Station. My breath caught in my throat and my words came as ragged squeaks. "Look at the ice!"

Not far from the end of the frozen pier at the edge of our island, the Ross Sea began cracking, jagged scars appearing across the pristine ice. Massive trenches materialized and the sea came rushing up between the immense blocks of sea ice.

"Higher, higher!" I yelled into my microphone. "We have to get higher!"

I didn't know if Rothan understood what was happening, but he accelerated, and the helicopter shot into the sky. Moments later the frozen sea pulled away from Ross Island in a cacophonic blast like a nuclear ex-plosion, revealing land that had not been seen since before the last ice age.

"What's happening?" shrieked Sylvia beside me, but I barely heard her over the deafening booms of ice blocks the size of skyscrapers falling to the exposed seafloor as the water receded from the coast.

"Tsunami. A tidal wave." My voice was calm. Tidal waves were just part of the science.

Suddenly the helicopter pitched sideways, and Billy fell toward me. Dakota lunged for his jacket and pulled him back into his seat. "Seat belt."

"Uh, yeah," said the young man as he secured his harness.

"Hang on everyone," shouted Rothan as he turned the helicopter 180 degrees. "Fighting the wind..."

That was when the giant wall of water came from the sea, growing as it approached.

"Higher!" shouted Sylvia needlessly, as our pilot expertly took the machine to a greater altitude. As a cohesive unit, we grabbed our seat bottoms and held on tight until we reached a safe height.

The massive swell, dark and menacing in the midnight sky, rolled toward the base. The wave exploded like an atomic shockwave and washed into McMurdo. It mowed down the town like it was made of paper mâché.

As the wave extinguished the spotlights, everything went dark.

Now blind to the events transpiring beneath us, we eased back into our seats, dazed, and shaken, and held on until the helicopter landed on the level plain at the top of the dormant volcano a few minutes later.

As Rothan powered down the helo, Billy opened the door and we stumbled toward the three insulated Quonset hut shelters. The long half-pipes with sloping sides were made of heavy plastic sheeting and PVC pipes that interlocked like tent supports. They were quick to set up, held in heat well, and kept wind and snow out. They were powered by solar panels which were becoming less and less effective as the winter sun was weakening day-by-day.

I immediately headed for the hut where the scientific equipment, comms center, medical station, and dining hall were set up and entered through the airlock-like double door vestibule.

When the sun rose for the few hours of daylight tomorrow, we would take stock of the damage, but I had no doubts that there would be nothing left of McMurdo Station. The sea had pulverized our town before dragging it to a watery grave.

Sylvia was recounting the story to those in the science hut, and I was certain that Dakota and Billy were doing the same in the two Quonsets set up as living quarters. I could hear the shocked responses behind me as I worked my way to the computer station that held my seismic equipment. Sobbing intermixed with swearing.

We couldn't survive here all winter and I was counting on an ice breaker from New Zealand coming to our rescue. As long as it could get within helicopter distance of us, which was about 240 kilometers, we could shuttle our people out to a waiting ship.

There was still a chance that I was wrong, and that the doomsday glacier would survive the shifting of the plates.

When I saw the seismic record of the last three hours on my monitor, I knew the chances of that were about the same as a snowball's chance in hell. The epicenter of the earthquake was along the fault line out at sea, exactly where earthquakes are supposed to happen. But it was a magnitude-8.9, and the two aftershocks were both in the magnitude-7 range.

That was not supposed to happen in Antarctica.

Fast Facts

Earthquakes are recorded by seismographs and the recording they make is called a seismogram. The size of an earthquake, measured in magnitude, depends on the size of the fault and the amount of slip on the fault. P & S waves each shake the ground in different ways as they travel through it. The P waves travel faster and shake the ground where you are first. Then the S waves follow; these shake the ground as well. If you are close to the earthquake, the P and S waves will come one right after the other, but if you are far away, there will be more time between the two.

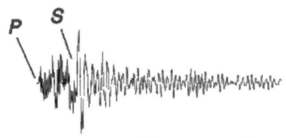

An example of a seismic wave with the P wave and S wave labeled.

Chapter 33
Inga – Off the coast of Florida

We bobbed at sea, tossed by waves so huge they dwarfed the boat. I fought to keep from throwing up and wished for solid land under my feet. The sea rose and fell like a roller coaster, my heart in my throat.

I hated roller coasters.

Mateo squirmed in his father's arms, crying that his stomach hurt. I looked back to see Carlos and Alita comforting the poor boy, but no amount of rubbing his little head and whispering soothing words was going to keep the boy from being seasick.

Captain Flores fought against the turbulent water, struggling against the tumbling sea until the waves died down. It was after three in the morning before the engine compartment dried out enough to crank the engine.

When the engine roared to life, the captain fist pumped the dark sky and we set off again. "I'm going to stay close to the coast, just in case. We are past the Georgia line, and it's fairly unpopulated here, especially in the middle of the night. We should make it to Savannah by sixish."

I must have fallen asleep because the next thing I knew, the sky had turned pink, and the sun was creeping above the ocean's horizon. I was about to ask Lilith what time it was when the DPA announced an incoming call from an unknown satellite phone number.

"Hello," I answered.

My mother's frenzied voice broke the silent morning air. "Inga, we have big trouble."

Fast Facts

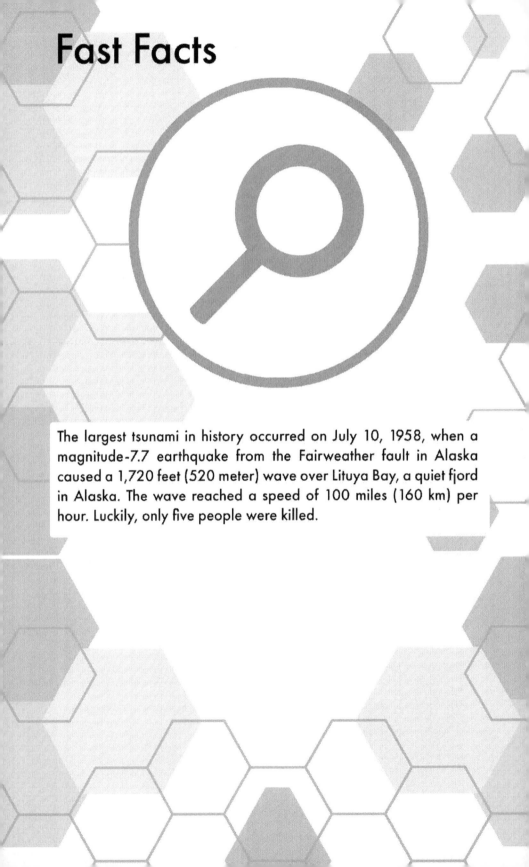

The largest tsunami in history occurred on July 10, 1958, when a magnitude-7.7 earthquake from the Fairweather fault in Alaska caused a 1,720 feet (520 meter) wave over Lituya Bay, a quiet fjord in Alaska. The wave reached a speed of 100 miles (160 km) per hour. Luckily, only five people were killed.

Chapter 34
Kathryn – Antarctica

Crossing to the communications center, I picked up the satellite phone and keyed in the codes to get an international line and dialed. It was 6:12 a.m. at home.

I was breathless by the time my daughter answered. "Inga, we have big trouble."

"Mom! What trouble?" She sounded odd. I expected to be waking her up, but there was something else in her voice. She wasn't simply tired. She sounded bone weary, exhausted.

"The earthquakes have started down here, but we evacuated McMurdo before the station was destroyed by a tsunami. We're up on a high peak, and we're okay."

"Destroyed! Tsunami? Do you mean tidal wave? Mom! Oh my God," she shrieked.

I could hear the terror in my daughter's voice, but also something else.

"Inga, please don't worry. I'm not in any danger. I'm safe."

The connection was clear, and I could hear her breathing slowing down as the initial shock of my announcement wore off.

I asked, "What's that noise behind you? Are you on the ship Dad sent for you?"

"Not exactly. But we are out at sea."

Inga filled me in on their evacuation from Miami, which in the end was much more arduous than my own. She had never been in as much danger as we were in Antarctica, but at least we had helicopters. This kid of mine, and her friends, had nothing but their wits, and some money from Nick. I felt pride in my smart and resourceful 18-year-old daughter.

I gave her an overview of what happened at McMurdo, trying to keep my voice calm. She finished by assuring me that she would be able to fly to Connecticut and make her way to our mountain cabin. She and all her friends would be there tomorrow.

"Inga, I'm so glad you got out of Miami. Please call your father and update him on your situation, and mine. I don't want him to worry. You know how he gets. I've got to go. It's almost midnight here and I've still got a lot to get settled before I can get any sleep. I love you."

"I love you too, Mom."

I ended the call before my voice broke and I let out an exhausted sob. She was alright.

I had not realized how worried about her I had been until this moment. I sat on the floor, dropped my head into my hands, and let the tears fall.

"Hey," said Sylvia, sitting down on the cold floor beside me, startling me out of my despondency. Without preamble, Sylvia hugged me. It took me a moment to notice that she wasn't speaking. So out of character for her. I sniffled up my tears and hugged her back for a long minute before finally pulling away.

I wiped the tears from my eyes and looked at Sylvia. "Call home and let your family know you are safe. Then I have to notify the NSF."

The U.S. Antarctic Program of the National Science Foundation ran McMurdo Research Station.

Or they did before the tsunami wiped it off the face of the Earth.

Fast Facts

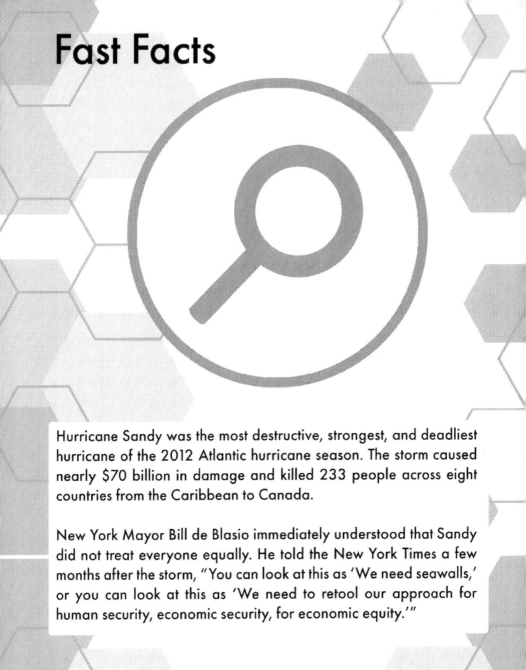

Hurricane Sandy was the most destructive, strongest, and deadliest hurricane of the 2012 Atlantic hurricane season. The storm caused nearly $70 billion in damage and killed 233 people across eight countries from the Caribbean to Canada.

New York Mayor Bill de Blasio immediately understood that Sandy did not treat everyone equally. He told the New York Times a few months after the storm, "You can look at this as 'We need seawalls,' or you can look at this as 'We need to retool our approach for human security, economic security, for economic equity.'"

Chapter 35
Nick – Boston

It was 6:30 a.m. when the phone rang. "Inga, are you alright?"

My daughter's tired voice came back to me in typical teenage sarcasm, but I was relieved to hear it. "We are seasick, drenched, and exhausted. Other than that, we are just peachy. Can you go to video, Dad?"

My phone was set to automatically answer in voice-only mode, but I quickly pushed the icon for video and held it up so I could see her face. She wasn't kidding when she described her situation. Even on the small screen with my blurry morning vision, I could see the dark circles under her eyes and her limp, stringy hair. "It's good to see you, kiddo. Looks like you are still on board the speedboat though. I thought you would have arrived in Savannah by now."

"Rough water all night swamped the boat and stalled the engines, but the captain got it going, and we are nearing Savannah now. We have been cruising up the Savannah River for the last half an hour. Captain Flores will drop us off at the public boat ramp just north of the city. It looks like a quick ride to the airport from there."

The boat engine roared behind her. My daughter took a deep breath before she went on. "The ride was expensive Dad, but it was the only way out of Miami. I'm going to need more money for the plane tickets."

I did my best not to sigh in relief that money was her only concern but had limited success. "Of course, honey. I'll make the transfer to your account as soon as we get off the phone."

My relief was short-lived when she continued. "Thanks, Dad. But there's more. Mom called from a satellite phone." She paused a moment and when I saw the drawn look on her face, my heart skipped a beat. Maybe three. "They evacuated McMurdo Station. It was destroyed by a tsunami."

"What? How can a town in Antarctica suffer a tsunami?" My brain tried to wrap itself around the concept and finally stalled as the flooded engine had on their boat.

"Dad, she's okay. She's more than okay. She's in charge now. They had one casualty, their station master. She didn't tell me how he died, and I didn't ask. They were on the last helicopter leaving McMurdo when the tsunami hit. She thinks it wiped out the entire base, but it's dark now so they'll do a flyover during daylight hours in the morning and know for sure." I could feel my face relaxing as Inga spoke, releasing the tension that I had not realized I'd been trying to hide.

I nodded at the screen then said, "Okay sweetheart. Let's hang up so you can get to the airport, and I can transfer you some money. I packed up yesterday, and Liam and I can leave at a moment's notice. I'll tell you; packing was a chore. With Liam's arm broken, he wasn't able to help, and I've got the vehicle so full, there is barely room for the kid and me to sit. I'm taking the T to work every day so I can leave our car in the garage ready to go. If we even need to. Maybe nothing will happen."

"Then why are we flying to Hartford, Dad? Why don't I just fly home?"

I swallowed hard and replied honestly, dumping my unrealistic optimism. "Because I know your mom is right."

Fast Facts

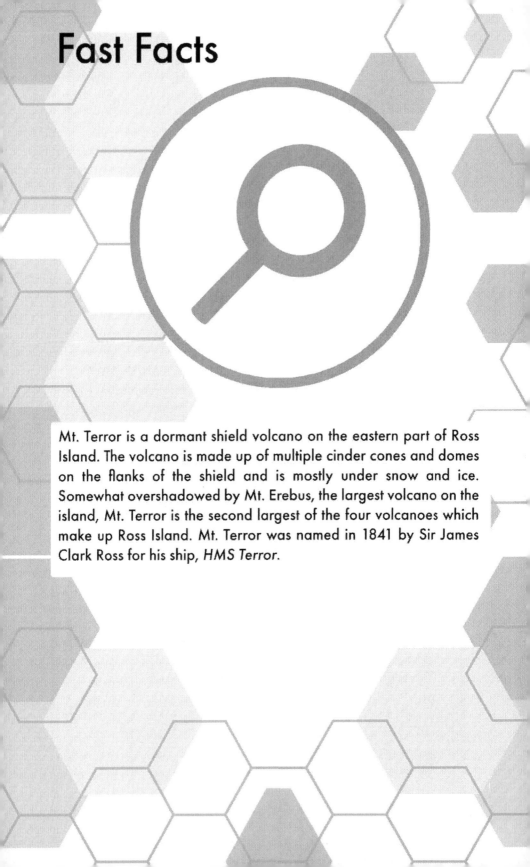

Mt. Terror is a dormant shield volcano on the eastern part of Ross Island. The volcano is made up of multiple cinder cones and domes on the flanks of the shield and is mostly under snow and ice. Somewhat overshadowed by Mt. Erebus, the largest volcano on the island, Mt. Terror is the second largest of the four volcanoes which make up Ross Island. Mt. Terror was named in 1841 by Sir James Clark Ross for his ship, *HMS Terror*.

Chapter 36

Kathryn – Antarctica

I only heard one side of Sylvia's satellite phone conversation with her husband. Their small town in New Brunswick was situated two hours north of Maine and twenty minutes from the Gulf of Saint Lawrence, in the northern reaches of the Appalachians. They were high enough in elevation that even if the sea level in the Gulf rose, they would be safe. It was just past 7 a.m. there. Her 14-year-old son, Pierre, was getting ready for school so she only spoke with him for a few minutes, but her daughter, who attended community college in Campbellton, did not have classes until later in the day and her husband did not mind being late for work if it meant a talk with his wife.

Obviously, her family was relieved that she was safe, but Sylvia was also able to make sure her husband and daughter understood that they needed to immediately drive home from Campbellton at the first sign of rising water in the Gulf of Saint Lawrence.

I hugged her as she handed me the phone, and as she left for one of the residential Quonset huts, she said, "I'll set up your bunk."

I dialed the home phone number for the director of the U.S. Antarctic Program at the NSF. It was only 6 a.m. there, but the phone only rang twice before he answered. "George Marshall."

"Hello, Director Marshall. This is Kathryn Whitson of McMurdo Research Station." There was a noticeable two-second delay, but the satellite phone connection was much better than our usual landline had been.

"Hello, Dr. Whitson. Where is Station Master Howell? Not that I don't enjoy hearing your voice."

I don't think I woke him, despite the hour; he sounded like he'd already had at least one cup of coffee. George Marshall and I were friendly colleagues, but not on a first-name basis. He was my bosses' boss.

"Director Marshall, we have had a major earthquake just off the coast and multiple before and aftershocks. We have evacuated to a temporary shelter at the top of Mt. Terror, and all are accounted for except for Martin Howell. I'm sorry to say that he was killed when a sheet of plate glass window crashed on him during the earthquake. We got everyone else out, but as the last chopper was leaving McMurdo, we watched a tsunami destroy the base. As far as we know, everything has been washed out to sea." I heard an audible gasp but did not let him interrupt me. It was easier for me to make a full report in one go.

When I finished, the director assured me that he would have an icebreaker come to rescue us at the earliest possibility as long as we could helicopter from Mt. Terror to the ship. "Director, I assure you that the ice is broken up in a way never before seen in an Antarctic winter. The ship can get in close but advise them to do it slowly because they will be dodging icebergs and debris all the way."

Director Marshall said to leave the details to him, and he would contact me as soon as he had any more information.

I thanked him, broke the connection, and gave the phone to Hannah, who had taken up the communications desk duty.

"My ribs are broken ma'am, so I can't do much else but sit. I'll be happy to man this post continuously. I think it's what Martin would have wanted."

I didn't think Martin Howell would have given two cents about her health or safety, but I wouldn't speak ill of the dead. I smiled at her and replied, "Yes, Hannah, that would be nice. I'll have someone bring you a cot. Turn the ringer up to high and get some sleep."

My watch read 1 a.m. when I finally fell onto a bunk near Sylvia.

Fast Facts

A new class of seismic events associated with the melting of large ice caps was discovered around Greenland. These glacial earthquakes generate long surface waves equivalent in strength to those radiated by standard magnitude-5 earthquakes and were observable worldwide. Glacial earthquakes mostly occur during the late summer.

Glacial earthquakes radiate little high-frequency energy, which explains why they were not detected or located by traditional earthquake monitoring systems. These large events are two magnitude units larger than any seismic events previously associated with glaciers, a size difference corresponding to a factor of 1000 in a seismic moment.

Chapter 37
Inga – Savannah, Georgia

The speedboat almost dwarfed the small community dock when Captain Flores pulled up alongside and threw out a line. There was a nip in the air, but after the open ocean, it felt almost tropical. March in Georgia was not Florida, but it was still better than New England could ever be. The air smelled of salt, sea, and blooming flowers.

Jason jumped out and secured the rope to a cleat on the dock while the rest of us gathered luggage and prepared to step gratefully onto solid ground.

I jumped down onto the dock. "Lilith, arrange a rideshare for seven to the domestic departures at Savannah airport." I had no idea what the name of the airport was, but the DPA was smart enough to understand even from vague commands, based on my current GPS location. Turning back to the speedboat, I reached for the suitcase Caleb handed me, then for his and Zoe's. It felt good to be off the boat, but my body was still swaying.

"How's your stomach?" I asked Zoe as she stepped down from the boat. She had held out the entire trip without a bathroom, so I assumed the polluted water virus had run its course.

"I'm okay, just need to pee." She looked around for a bathroom. The area was industrial. Plenty of buildings, oil containers, cargo ship storage, but I did not see anywhere we might find a bathroom.

"Don't we all," exclaimed Carlos as he helped his son down from the boat.

His sister turned to Captain Flores before debarking. "Won't you come with us? Florida will not be safe for much longer. You've heard everything Inga has told you. Don't you think you should stay now that you are here?"

The man nodded. "Yes. Honestly, at first, I thought you were all just crazy tourists because it didn't take me long to figure out that she doesn't have a sick aunt in Savannah." He pointed his chin at me. "But I have family in Ft. Lauderdale. I will go home and get them, and we'll head for the hills, as they say in the old westerns. We'll be fine. Thank you for doing business with Captain Flores." The man gave us a mock solute and pointed to the cleat at Jason's feet.

"Oh, yeah," said Jason, bent down, untied it, and tossed the rope up to the captain. I heard the boat receding behind us as we walked toward the road.

"Ha! Porta-potty!" exclaimed Zoe as she took off across the concrete to a green plastic stall on the other side of the parking lot. Thankfully, we all had time to take our turns before the van arrived.

Twenty minutes later, we walked into the terminal experiencing blessed warm air and ground that didn't sway beneath our feet. I almost kissed the tile floor.

"There don't seem to be a lot of shops here," said Carlos. "Maybe we should go through security first and once inside we can buy some towels and soap, you know, clean up a bit in the bathroom."

We had all agreed in the car on the way over that we felt like we had spent a week at the beach, covered in sand and salt from the ocean spray all night long.

Lilith had purchased our tickets, but the only direct flight to Hartford didn't leave until noon. We had over five hours to kill. "Yeah, agreed. I could do with a bathroom stall towel bath."

Carlos and Alita took Mateo through security in the longer line. As a child, he did not have a passport or an identity card, so they had to show his birth certificate.

The four of us were all security pre-checked so we went through the quicker TSA line. I was not sure why everyone who intended to fly didn't go through the paperwork, background check, and fingerprinting required for pre-check status. It was a hassle, but a one-time thing, and after that, getting through security at airports, train and bus stations, and schools was so much easier.

My father had told me stories of when he was a child before security measures like fingerprinting and background checks had been enacted. The senseless violence of it all made my heart ache. Metal detectors were just not such a big deal if it meant a safer society. My father saw it as an infringement on our freedom and rights. To me, it was just the way the world worked. I don't want to give up my life for somebody's freedom to shoot me.

"I'll hang back and wait for them, and then we'll meet you at our gate," said Zoe. I gave her a quick nod and headed for the nearest traveler's shop with Caleb and Jason, where we purchased small bottles of shower gel and seven towels. I couldn't wait to fish out my toiletries bag and brush my teeth and get the tangled knots out of my hair.

Half an hour later I felt cleaner than I had since before the hurricane. Zoe, Alita, and I beat the guys back to the gate, but of course, they also had little Mateo to take care of. Our bags in a line against the wall, we secured a row of seats and fell into them. But no sooner had I plopped down when my stomach began to rumble.

"Anyone want coffee and breakfast?" Both heads nodded and I went off in search of nourishment.

When I returned with a tray full of coffee, breakfast sandwiches, and napkins, everyone's eyes were glued to the television above our heads. "What's up?" I asked as I took a sip of the steaming, black liquid.

A middle-aged broadcaster on screen had a caption scrolling beneath him: "BREAKING NEWS. A series of strong earthquakes in Antarctica destroys McMurdo Research Station." The sound was off, or just too quiet to hear, so I followed the closed captioning.

"In a satellite phone call with George Marshall, Director of the U.S. Antarctic Program at the National Science Foundation, Dr. Kathryn Whitson, a research seismologist at McMurdo Station, reported that they experienced four large quakes, ranging from magnitude-7 to 8.9 as they were evacuating the base to a temporary shelter at the top of 10,600-foot-high Mt. Terror. We have a recording of Dr. Whitson's statement."

I moved closer to the television so I could hear my mother's voice. "Director Marshall, we have had a major earthquake just off the coast and multiple before and aftershocks." I listened to my mother's call, then as Director Marshall described the plan to send a Coast Guard icebreaker to retrieve the 200 plus people stuck on Ross Island.

The scene shifted to a news reporter standing on a Georgia beach. "We are told by NOAA that the earthquakes in Antarctica were the direct cause of the choppy seas in the Atlantic overnight from the east coast of North and South America to the west coast of Africa. NOAA advises that further tremors could continue to make seas rough for the next few days and has issued a small craft advisory for all of the Atlantic seaboard. Back to you in the studio, Natalie."

The news shifted to another story as I walked back to the group. "Choppy seas are going to be the least of our problems if that damn ice sheet gives way."

Fast Facts

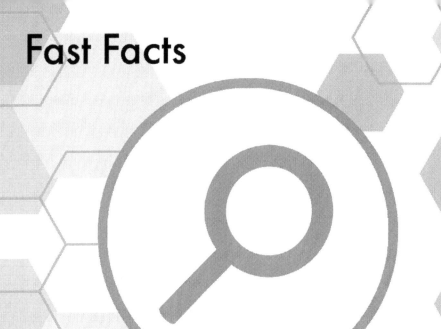

The geology of Antarctica is varied. The land is composed of sedimentary rocks, lava and deep magmatic rocks, a wide range of metamorphic rocks, not to mention both dormant and active volcanoes and glacial deposits. McMurdo base is built on the bare volcanic rock of Ross Island. Geologically, West Antarctica is similar to that of the Andes in South America. Extensive study of Antarctica's geology is hampered by widespread ice coverage.

The Antarctic Peninsula is the northernmost part of the mainland of Antarctica. The tip of the peninsula sits 800 miles from Chile. It is dotted with numerous research stations and multiple nations have made claims of sovereignty, including Argentina, Chile, and the United Kingdom. None of these claims has international recognition and, under the Antarctic Treaty System, the countries cannot enforce their claims. Argentina has the most bases and personnel stationed on the Antarctic Peninsula.

Chapter 38

Kathryn – Antarctica

For a brief moment, I had no idea where I was, and I jerked upright in a panic. Then reality rushed at me, and I saw the tsunami ripping away McMurdo. I pushed the memory away and dropped my feet to the floor as I sat on the edge of my cot, my head cradled in my hands. I rubbed my temples but the ache in my head would not abate.

Once I pulled myself together and sat up straight, I saw Sylvia eyeing me. She said what I was thinking. "We should call Marnie in Chicago before we see what the damage was to the base."

We both knew there would be nothing left of McMurdo anyway.

I had slept in my clothes, too emotionally drained and physically exhausted to bother with pajamas, for the few hours I had been asleep. It was 6 a.m., so I don't think I'd gotten even five hours. But it would do. Now I simply grabbed my toiletries bag and made my way through the connecting passageway to stand in line for the makeshift bathrooms. I sincerely hoped that the NSF would get a Coast Guard ship here sooner rather than later. Living in what amounted to a communal tent with one hundred other people, sharing three shower stalls and four toilets were going to get old fast. On the bright side, I felt like one of the original Antarctic explorers, but with better heat and food.

Sylvia had Marnie on the satellite phone by the time I got to the communications office. Hannah was asleep on her cot, still manning her station. I liked the girl. She reminded me of Inga in her determination and dedication. Sylvia held her hand over the receiver. "She wants to know if we think she should evacuate. Why don't you talk to her?"

I took the heavy brick of a phone. "Hey Marnie, glad to hear your voice. We miss you down here on the White Continent."

Her contralto voice came following a two-second delay. "Geez, girl, I haven't been home a week yet and now Sylvia tells me your ice shelf might come down soon, not in decades or centuries. Oh, and by the way, you made the morning news."

"What? How? Has word gotten out about Thwaites?" I simultaneously feared the panic it would cause, while also being worried that I would be laughed at and disbelieved by the scientific community for predicting what they considered to be an inconceivable long shot.

She laughed as if I'd said something absurd. "No! The earthquakes and tsunami. It's big news here. You might not know this, but neither of those phenomena is common in Antarctica."

This time it was me laughing hysterically. She was right. The entire situation was completely absurd and perfectly summed up by her sarcasm. "Funny, Marnie. But seriously, you and your family should be prepared to get to higher ground the minute you hear anything on the news about Thwaites."

"Kathryn, I'm not exactly on the coast. We'll be fine here."

"Not necessarily, Marnie. Chicago and all the cities on the Great Lakes will be in danger from sea level rise, too. It will just take longer to get to you. It's not as if those lakes aren't connected to the world's oceans. But it will take time for the St. Lawrence and the rivers that connect each lake to get to Lake Michigan." Marnie was a marine biologist, not a climatologist or oceanographer.

"There are three Great Lakes between me and the St. Lawrence River. But don't worry. We are okay. When you started telling me about the dangers of massive sea level rise, I started researching. There is a hydro station on the Ottawa River, between Quebec and Ontario, that will stop the flow of water from the St. Lawrence up to a thirty-five-meter rise. So, we really will be fine."

"You're sure? Sorry, stupid question. Of course, you're sure. You are a research scientist. Even if this isn't marine biology, I trust your data. Just be careful. There will be other dangers if the waters rise. Society goes crazy during disasters. People will want what you have. Stay safe, my friend."

Sylvia and I said our good-byes and I broke the connection. I desperately needed some food, and then we needed to get Rothan or Phil out of bed to do a flyover of McMurdo.

I was positive Dakota never slept because the area set aside as kitchen and dining looked like it had been there forever, not merely since yesterday. I saw their unruly mop of ginger-hair floating above the tables, as Dakota refilled a warming tray with scrambled eggs. I waved and with a nod of their head, Dakota continued serving food and making the evacuated staff of McMurdo feel safe and secure. Food had a way of doing that.

The sun didn't rise until almost eight this late in March, but as soon as the first rays of morning broke, Sylvia and I were aloft with Rothan as he hovered the helicopter over the base. If I had not recognized the contours of the land, I would have thought we were in the wrong place. The stark landscape below looked more like Mars than the former community of 2,000. There were no buildings. No massive steal wind turbines. No giant oil tanks. No snow. No ice. Not even debris.

The land had been scoured clean.

Although I had known this would be the case, I couldn't help but be as devastated at the loss. One lone tear rolled down my cheek and I hastily wiped it away with a gloved finger. I sat in stunned silence as

Rothan circled, listening to the sounds of Sylvia's camera whir as she snapped photos of the alien landscape.

The wind was furiously whipping around the top of the mountain, making our landing at the improvised heliport at Mt. Terror an event that normally would have made me seasick, but not today. Sylvia had to physically shake me out of my stupor when we landed. I ambled to the main Quonset hut, not caring about the cold or the wind that bit into me as only Antarctic air could.

The sea had washed everything away. Everything. There wasn't a speck of human civilization left at McMurdo.

"Excuse me, Station Master?" I turned to see Hannah walking toward me as quickly as she could with her broken ribs. I nodded for her to proceed. "You may not have felt it because you were in the air, but there was another quake while you were gone."

I shook myself out of my funk and followed her back to the small desk that now served as our communications station to look at the seismograph readings. I noticed Hannah's cot was still there, but the bedding was neatly folded and stacked.

My eyes flew to the readings on the monitor. The earthquake was out at sea, along the Antarctic Plate fault line, exactly where they should occur. For a moment I was relieved that it had not occurred on the continent itself, but only because those confused the crap out of me. This one at least I understood. Standard plate tectonics. Then I saw the data. It was a magnitude-9! I had never recorded a quake that large anywhere, much less on the Antarctic Plate.

A shrill sound behind me forced my attention away from the monitor. The phone was ringing, and Hannah answered it.

"Ma'am, Oliver Davies, the station master at Rothera Research Station. He says it's urgent."

I grabbed the phone from her hand. "Oliver. What do you have?"

"Kathryn, it's not good." His voice was rattled, even for a stoic Brit. "Our rocket-powered light plane flyover ten minutes ago showed massive fractures in Thwaites from the quake. Now we've got video footage of the sea receding off the coast. It's pulling away fast, Kathryn."

"Get your people up in the air now!" They had an evac helicopter that could hold twenty, the entire winter complement of Rothera. While they were hundreds of kilometers away from Thwaites, almost at the tip of the Antarctic Peninsula, the base wasn't much more than thirty meters above sea level. Unbidden, images of the denuded volcanic landscape of the late McMurdo Station flashed into my mind. "Get to high ground."

"Roger that. We're already in the process of evacuating." I could hear his breaths coming in ragged gasps as he walked through the frozen landscape, and then a dull sound in the background. Helicopter blades. "My people are on board, and we are taking off now. I've got the mobile sat phone fully charged, so I should be able to stay on the line for a while. We are still recording footage from the reconnaissance flight. It's relaying to my tablet from Rothera. At least as long as the base stays intact."

I took a deep breath. "Okay, I appreciate you staying with me. I can imagine what the quake did, but confirmation is better than guesses."

I put my hand over the phone and said to Hannah, "Can you get Sylvia, please?"

She nodded and a minute later, my glaciologist friend was standing beside me. I put the phone on speaker.

"Hi, Oliver, this is Sylvia Rapp. Thwaites has been loose and crumbling due to the subduction of warm water for the last two decades, and now the earthquake has caused more fractures in the glacier. We are standing by for your status report."

I swallowed hard, waiting on the line with him until he received further visuals. It was a few minutes later when Oliver began speaking again.

"The rocket plane is over the glacier again. The photos are not as zoomed in as I would prefer, but I can make out what's happening. The water is definitely receding from the glacier. There appears to be a bump in the seabed that is now exposed."

Sylvia nodded although he couldn't see her. "That's called the grounding line. Is there any ice on top of that bump?"

"Negative."

"Shit." That was not good. Not good at all.

"The ocean has pulled the ice off the grounding line. That's what protects the main part of the glacier from the sea. How far back from the glacier does it look like the water has receded?"

A moment went by as Oliver estimated measurements on his small tablet screen. "Kathryn, I'm no expert, but the sea appears to be approximately twenty-five or thirty kilometers from the glacier. I am seeing the ocean floor. If it weren't so dangerous, I would marvel at the alien beauty of it."

"That's what we saw before the tsunami inundated McMurdo. Damn, I wish I could see your footage. Is there any way you can tie that feed into the sat phone? No, sorry. I don't know why I asked. Lack of sleep. I know the satellite phone doesn't have image capability." My stomach began turning flip flops. Even without the visuals, I knew what was going to happen next.

"I believe the water looks like it's coming back. Give me a second for another measurement." Oliver was silent for so long that I thought the connection had died, but then his voice filled the room again. "Kathryn, the measurement shows the water is now ten kilometers from the glacier."

"Then, the tsunami is indeed headed back to Thwaites," said Sylvia. "Tell me, can you see a second bump, or ridge, that looks like the grounding line? That second bump is called the Ghost Ridge, and it's located seventy-two kilometers behind the grounding line."

"I can see a rise in the ice on the glacier at that point, but nothing to determine if it's an underground ridge. Why?" Oliver had been quite calm and cool during these last few minutes of our conversation, but I could sense his fear.

"The Ghost Ridge is what holds back the ice shelf behind Thwaites. As long as that holds, the shelf will remain mostly intact even if the glacier completely crumbles into the sea. Losing Thwaites will be disruptive to the world's seacoasts. Losing the entire ice shelf, well, devastating isn't a strong enough word. Terrifying is more like it. Keep your eye on that spot."

"Roger. The water is now five kilometers from the base of the glacier. Another couple of minutes and it will hit the ice."

"Okay. Thanks for staying on the line with me, Oliver. Are your people alright? Do you have supplies packed and a place to evac to?" I was concerned. Rothera base hadn't had any intention of evacuating – were they screwed?

"Yes and no. We hastily packed a few days' worth of supplies and four winter tents and will wait it out in the Chilean Antarctic territory."

The mountains in the interior of the Antarctic Peninsula were over 4,000 meters tall. They would be safe there. Safe, but frigid.

Oliver continued. "The coastal and island Argentinian and Chilean bases are evacuating as well. Together we will wait until a ship arrives from Argentina. It is on its way right now from the Falklands. They estimated four days, but that was based on expected ocean navigation before the massive waves kicked up by the quakes. No telling what the iceberg situation will be between the peninsula and the Falklands. By then...hold on, I've got something on the monitor. The water has reached the edge of the glacier."

I heard Oliver take in a sharp breath and wanted to ask him if the ocean was stopping once it hit the frozen mountain of ice but before I could, he continued.

"It's continuing to flow over the glacier, but I'm not sure exactly what I'm seeing. Shouldn't the tsunami rebound and go back out to sea?"

I thought for a moment, wave vectors and angles materializing in my head. "It should. Do you not see the wave backtracking over itself, away from the glacier?"

"No. It's as if it's disappearing. Like the water is diving into a black hole." His voice was difficult to hear over the helicopter noise, and he had been speaking loudly to overcome that. Now his voice was getting hoarse from overuse and stress.

Oh, crap. "Not a black hole," said Sylvia. "The tsunami is rushing under the glacier. That's why it's not bouncing back. The subsurface must have subducted enough at this point that the water from the tidal wave is flowing *under* Thwaites. Shit."

"Why is that bad?" asked Oliver.

In lieu of an answer, Sylvia was pleading now. "Can you still pinpoint the place where the Ghost Ridge should be? Can you see it on the monitor?"

"Yes, it seems fine, but...bollocks! It's cracking. The glacier is cracking, just behind the Ghost Ridge! It does appear that the tsunami rushed under the glacier all the way to that ridge. Wait, I've got another photo transmitting now. Bloody hell! Thwaites is lifting upward. It's as if a world of ice is rising into the sky. The ice is massive."

"If it's the entire glacier, that's a piece of ice the size of Rhode Island or Hawaii. How low does your rocket plane fly? Will it be in danger from the ice?" I had no idea how high the sheet of ice would rise before the tsunami finally hit a dead end and rushed back into the Southern Ocean.

"We had it at a low altitude to get better photos, and I have no way to communicate with it now to change its flight path. I'm afraid the images from the onboard camera are one way. Alright, I've got another photo coming now. They are being taken at twenty-second intervals. This one shows the glacier at a higher altitude than before. We will just have to wait and see what the next few photos reveal. Bloody hell, Kathryn. This is not how I planned to spend my last stint in Antarctica, watching a flying glacier! Okay, another shot from the aft camera. It's dropping. Thwaites is dropping in altitude. It is falling back to the sea below it." His voice was gaining volume as well as speed.

"What goes up must come down," I stated calmly. Calmer than I should have. I was powerless to change anything.

"Yes," he replied flatly. "But what happens when something the size of a small state crashes into the sea?"

"Nothing good, Oliver. Nothing good. The last time something that big landed in an ocean it wiped out the dinosaurs. But this chunk of ice didn't come from space, so its velocity is minuscule compared to 66 million years ago. Still, tsunamis will form around the world. Coastlines will be inundated."

"Quite right." Oliver's voice was tense. "Nothing good at all. One moment, Kathryn."

I heard him breathing but nothing else. Then he was back. "The feed has been lost."

Either the rocket plane was destroyed by the flying ice, or the wave from Thwaites falling into the sea had destroyed Rothera Research Station.

Fast Facts

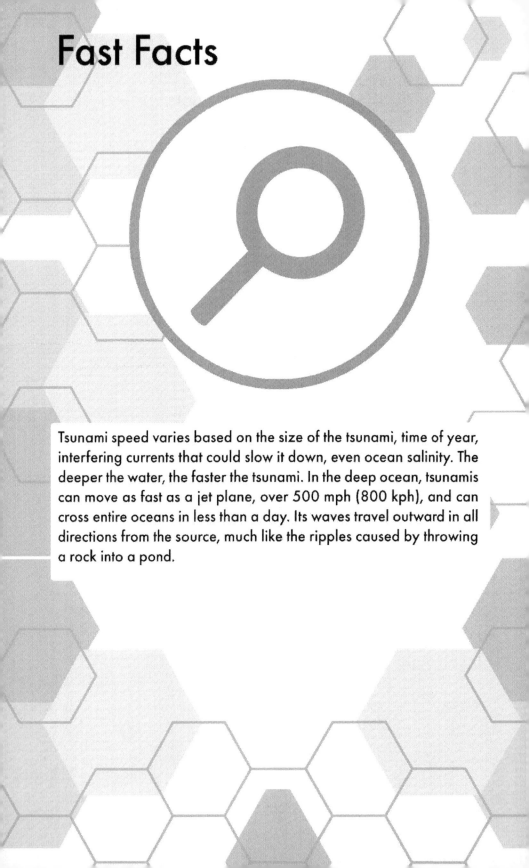

Tsunami speed varies based on the size of the tsunami, time of year, interfering currents that could slow it down, even ocean salinity. The deeper the water, the faster the tsunami. In the deep ocean, tsunamis can move as fast as a jet plane, over 500 mph (800 kph), and can cross entire oceans in less than a day. Its waves travel outward in all directions from the source, much like the ripples caused by throwing a rock into a pond.

Chapter 39
Inga – Savannah, Georgia

11:59 a.m.

I sighed. We should have boarded twenty minutes ago, but there had been a delay in our flight due to a maintenance issue with our aircraft. The airline was sending another plane, but it would not arrive until 3 p.m. They assured us that they would board us quickly and get us in the air as soon as it arrived. We rushed to get out of Miami and now we were stuck sitting hundreds of miles further north but still barely above sea level in the river city of Savannah.

And now my stomach began rumbling again. "Hey Zoe, fancy a slice of pizza, southern style?"

"Hell no!" She snapped, and I grinned. I was aware of how picky her taste in pizza was. New York – or better yet, New Jersey – style only. There was a place in Boston, a block from Fenway Park that had pizza that Zoe agreed was 'decent.' I missed that place. I missed all of Boston.

I was afraid I would never see my home or my favorite city ever again. I sighed for a second time.

Caleb put his arm around me. "Hey, don't worry. We're all going to be okay. Let's get some lunch, alright?"

I nodded, swallowing my sadness past the sudden lump in my throat.

By 3 o'clock I was napping on Caleb's shoulder when an announcement on the loudspeaker above my head woke me. "This is a gate change announcement. United American flight number 5743 to Hartford, Connecticut will now be departing from Gate G11. The aircraft is here, and we will begin boarding momentarily. Departure time is now 4:20 p.m. I repeat…"

"Well shit! And why the hell are they moving us in the world's smallest airport? There's one damn terminal with fifteen gates. What's the point? Now we have to pick up all our stuff and relocate." I was angry. I didn't care why they were moving us, I simply wanted to yell at the world.

As I began angrily grabbing my roller case and backpack before storming off toward the other end of the small terminal, Lilith's voice sounded in my earbud. "You have an incoming call from the same satellite phone that called you earlier. Should I answer?"

"Yes, damn it, yes." I heard the call connect and some static then shouted into the phone, "Bad timing, mom. They are moving our gate."

"Inga," my mother's voice was insistent yet difficult to hear over the airport terminal announcements and the noise of passenger conversations. "Where are you? I expected you to be in the air already."

"Then why are you calling if you thought I was in flight? Whatever. I don't care. We are still in Savannah, but our plane is finally here. Why?"

"Thwaites just collapsed into the sea. It was thrown into the air, then bounced into the ocean like a rubber ball." Her voice was barely audible over the background noise, but her fear came through loud and clear.

"Oh my God, Mom. Are you alright? You weren't near it, were you?"

I could hear the frustration and worry in my mother's voice. "Inga, it's a thousand miles away. When does your plane take off? Savannah is too close to the ocean, honey."

"Less than an hour. How long does a tidal wave take to get to Georgia from there?" I was somewhat worried that people around me would hear and panic, but there was too much noise, and delayed travelers changing gates were notoriously oblivious to anything not related to their flight. But my friends heard me loud and clear. I looked into their shocked faces and more than one raised eyebrow of my companions as I listened to my mom's reply.

"That varies by the size of the tsunami, time of year, interfering currents that could slow it down, even ocean salinity. But this is the largest splash the ocean has seen since the death of the dinosaurs. It could be quick, perhaps an hour, but probably longer."

"Oh shit. Should we tell the airport, airlines, whatever? I don't know, shouldn't they get everyone into the air?" I looked around at the milling passengers, all oblivious to what was happening on the bottom of the planet, and I felt guilty not shouting out the danger to every one of them.

"Do you think that a gate attendant is going to listen to a bunch of teenagers, honey? Just get on that plane. I love you, Inga. I'm going to call your father now and make sure he and Liam are on the road inland ASAP. Then I'm calling the director at the NSF and make sure he gets this story out to the media. I know it will cause panic, but maybe some people can get away from the coasts. But my priority is my family. Get yourselves out. I love you, Inga."

The line went dead before I could tell her the same.

I retold my mother's short description of what happened to the glacier as we walked toward our new gate and happened to glance up at the monitor as we went by. The news was on, and there were images of Thwaites, combined with 'expert' commentators talking about what was happening.

"Hey, that's my mom's boss!" I shouted as we stopped beneath the TV screen. "She hasn't even called him yet. How did he find out...oh." I stopped as I read the caption beneath the footage, clearly taken from well up into the atmosphere.

It was a fifteen-second video playing on repeat. Director Marshall's words were written in closed captions beneath the video.

"Satellite footage shows the Thwaites glacier being broken up by the tsunami created by the magnitude-9 earthquake on the Antarctic Plate at 2:05 p.m. eastern time. The water rushed underneath the ice, separating the glacier from the land, and lifting the ice into the air. As the momentum of the tsunami stopped and the water flowed back into the Southern Ocean, the glacier, which is 5,400 square kilometers in size, roughly the size of all the Hawaiian Islands put together, was plunged into the sea. The waves created by this event are massive, as seen in this image from NASA." The screen cut to satellite video.

"We expect tidal waves from this crash to begin hitting every coast along the Atlantic within hours. South America already has seen tidal waves, as seen in this footage from the International Space Station," said Director Marshall's voice off camera.

We watched the video of a giant wave washing away the east coast of Argentina. Suddenly everyone in the airport terminal started crying, screaming, or rushing about. Gate attendants began speeding up the boarding of every flight.

Director Marshall was still talking on the screen, although few were watching him anymore. Everyone knew that there were tidal waves headed to Savannah, and we all knew what that meant. We had to get out of here.

Marshall's words scrolled across the bottom of the monitor as the wave destroyed the Argentinian coast. "Thwaites glacier is the keystone that holds the West Antarctic ice sheet together. The area of the entire ice sheet is 2.2 million cubic kilometers, or in layman's terms, 580 million gallons. That's enough ice, once it melts, to raise sea levels, worldwide, by thirty meters, or one hundred feet."

Standing at gate G11, the gate agent announced that we would begin boarding immediately. Departure time had been moved up, and we proceeded through the gate as quickly as we could. Larger luggage was tagged and taken for loading onto the plane and within fifteen minutes, our flight was loaded. I noticed that both of our gate agents were also onboard and that there were no empty seats.

Glancing through my window I saw the plane to our right backing out of the gate. I nudged Zoe. "Wasn't the flight at G9 not taking off until 3:55? Look, it's headed out now."

She swallowed hard and replied, "I think they are getting every aircraft off the ground, and it looks like they are putting airport personnel on the flights too."

She was right. Three baggage handlers were sitting among the passengers.

They were evacuating Savannah-Hilton Head airport.

The front exit closed with a heavy thud, the flight attendant latching it in place as the plane backed away from the terminal before the flight attendants even began their safety demonstration. The pilot's husky female voice came from the speakers. "Welcome to United American flight number 5743 to Hartford, Connecticut. Please secure your seatbelts. We are number three for take-off."

Moments later, the flight attendants completed their safety demo, and both of them strapped into their jump-seats, one at the front and one at the rear of the plane. We taxied out from the small terminal and rolled toward the runway.

"Aren't we moving a little faster than normal?" I asked Zoe.

She nodded, swallowed, and closed her eyes before saying, "Small airport. Not far to the runway. This pilot is in a hurry. Air traffic control must be having a fit." Zoe's hands held the armrest in a death grip. She was as terrified as I was.

The engines roared and we accelerated down the runway. I leaned back as the g-forces pushed me back into my seat. A minute later we lifted, and I felt the landing gear retract into the body of the aircraft with a thump before looking out the small window. We were banking right and the wing on our side dipped downward. I could see the ground beneath us as we climbed. "Zoe, look!"

There was a wall of water coming toward us! I heard screaming, then realized the voice was my own. I grabbed Zoe's hand and held my breath as if we were diving into the ocean. Others were screaming or crying. The plane climbed sharply as the wall of water enveloped the ground below us. My nails dug into Zoe's arm as the plane climbed sharply.

I was too young to die. That's what counted in a survival situation. Your will to live. I had nothing else on my mind but clinging to every second of life I could grab.

I turned my head to look out the window and saw the water swell beneath the aircraft and engulf the airport and the city beneath us.

A moment later the aircraft began leveling out and I unclenched my teeth. The pilot's voice came on the speaker. "Thank you all for remaining calm. We are safely in the air, as are the two planes that took off before us and one more behind us. I'm sorry to report that all other aircraft caught on the ground, well, we don't know since the control tower went silent. Rest assured, this flight is safe, and we will pick up instructions from air traffic control momentarily from Augusta. Our flight to Hartford will take us up the coast. Please remain calm and stay in your seats. Thank you."

I held Zoe's hand as we shared the small window, looking down on the drowned city of Savannah. Caleb's hand reached over the seat back and I felt it gently resting on my shoulder, comforting me.

As we flew north, we saw tidal waves hitting the east coast everywhere. People were crying or staring in shock out the windows.

I had no idea if my father and brother made it out of Boston.

Fast Facts

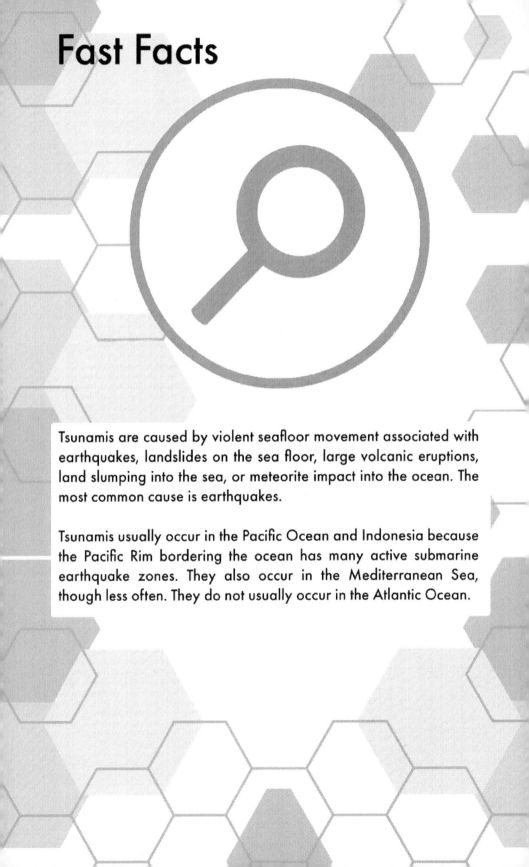

Tsunamis are caused by violent seafloor movement associated with earthquakes, landslides on the sea floor, large volcanic eruptions, land slumping into the sea, or meteorite impact into the ocean. The most common cause is earthquakes.

Tsunamis usually occur in the Pacific Ocean and Indonesia because the Pacific Rim bordering the ocean has many active submarine earthquake zones. They also occur in the Mediterranean Sea, though less often. They do not usually occur in the Atlantic Ocean.

Chapter 40
Nick – Boston

More than two decades of marriage meant that Kathryn and I knew each other's schedules as if they were our own even if we were separated by a day and a half's worth of time zones, so I was surprised when my phone lit up on my lectern showing "Kathryn McMurdo sat phone." The volume was off, as always, while I was lecturing.

If Kathryn was calling me at three in the afternoon, it was life or death.

"That's all for today, class." These kids were just back from spring break; they were happy to get half an hour of their lives back.

I answered on the fifth ring. "Kathryn, what's going on?"

My wife's voice was hurried. "Nick, Thwaites crashed a few minutes ago. The entire glacier, it didn't just fall into the ocean. It was lifted up by the tsunami and *flung* into the sea. We lost the British base's reconnaissance photos immediately afterward, so I don't know the total devastation, but in a matter of hours, tidal waves are going to hit every coastline along the Atlantic."

"Okay, slow down. Kathryn, I'm prepared." I looked at my watch. "Liam should just be getting home from school. I'm already walking out of the building. I'll be home in half an hour. I packed the car yesterday, so we are ready to jump in and take off."

She exhaled loudly. "Nick, you've got to get out of Cambridge."

"Katy, sweetheart, I'm moving as fast as I can. I am quite literally running down the stairs. I even took the train in today rather than driving because our car is in the garage, packed and waiting. The T is the fastest way out of Boston anyway. I will get home, get Liam, and get away from the coast. Trust me. Sweetheart, are you safe?"

"Yes, I'm fine. No change since yesterday. We are secure at Mt. Terror and will wait it out. We've got supplies and heating fuel to last a few weeks. I've got to go call the NSF. Please call me when you are on the road, okay?"

"I will. I love you."

She replied in kind and disconnected as I reached the T station at the edge of campus.

My luck for once held, and the train was just pulling in. I even got a seat. I punched Liam's contact card and he answered moments later.

"Hey, Dad, what's up?"

"On my way home. Be ready to go when I get there."

My son's voice went solemn. He knew I was talking about the mountain cabin, not some trip to run errands. "Roger that, Dad."

Nineteen minutes later I exited the train station in Cambridge and ran the seven blocks to my house. I passed Sebastian's family's house as they finished loading their vehicle and his father, Gabriel, gave me a wave. I was tiring and slowed to a fast walk the rest of the way to my house and rushed inside. "Liam?"

"Yep, all set," Liam said as he stuffed his tablet into his backpack. "I loaded up road food and soda from the fridge. It's in the canvas bags by the garage door." His gaze was serious, something I rarely saw unless he was lost in a video game.

I grabbed the two bags and we hopped in the SUV. As I backed out of the driveway, I saw Gabriel pull out behind me. I was grateful that he and his wife believed me when I warned them about Kathryn's theory and concerns. It would have been easy for him to brush aside her worries as a simple academic exercise that she got too caught up in.

Most of the world didn't understand the damage humanity had done to our climate and environment. Even though the earthquake was what finally caused Thwaites to come undone, the warming ocean waters beneath it had caused subsurface damage. Perhaps if the ocean had been cooler all these decades, perhaps the glacier would have survived the earthquake.

I called Gabriel and updated our travel plans. I intended to stay off the interstate until we got out of the city limits, then push forward as fast as we could to the Massachusetts Turnpike and head west. It was a four-hour trip to the cabin in the Berkshires, but we only needed to get about twenty miles west before we were high enough in elevation to be in the safe zone from a tidal wave, should it hit Boston.

When we hung up, I turned on the radio to find a news station, but I didn't need to. The story was apparently on every station, even my default top forty channel which never broadcast the news. The Atlantic coast, beginning in the southern part of South America and traveling north up the coast was being inundated by waves of water. Some larger than others, depending on the ocean depth in each latitude, but major cities were being wiped out. Buenos Aires and São Paulo were covered by a 50-foot-high wall of water moments after the crash of the Thwaites glacier in western Antarctica.

As the waves moved north, they devastated Miami, all of Florida, and the southeast. Waves were headed for the mid-Atlantic and New England and were expected to hit within the next hour to two hours depending on latitude. The good news, if there could be any from this earth-shattering event, was that the waves were getting smaller as they headed north, and by the time they reached Canada, it was expected to mimic nothing more than a 10-foot storm surge. Based on the height of the waves – because there were more than one – experts estimated that any elevation less than one hundred feet above sea level was expected to have damage.

Everyone was asked to remain calm but to move to higher ground immediately. We were told that skyscrapers were not a safe refuge because the force of the water could collapse buildings.

Liam shouted, "Dad, can you drive faster? We need to get ahead of everyone before the traffic backs up!" I noticed he was looking in his visor mirror, using it as a rearview. At first, I thought he was just watching the see if Bash and his family were still directly behind us, but then I saw his eyes. Big and round like marbles, as wide open as could be. I looked in the rearview mirror, too.

As we crossed into Framingham, roughly twenty miles west of Boston, I saw what had my son mesmerized and put my foot to the floor. I was just barely ahead of the traffic, having had advanced warning. I took my eyes off the sight behind me and concentrated on the road ahead, my foot jammed into the accelerator.

Liam screamed. "It's a wall of water, Dad, behind us! It's coming fast. Go faster Dad! Hurry, hurry! Move move move move move!" His one hand gripped the panic handle, the other broken arm in a cast clasped firmly to his stomach.

I moved as fast as the SUV would go, its supercharged engine almost red lining. Like cars on a racetrack just given the green flag, most of the cars ahead of me did likewise. Any car slower than mine, I left in my dust. I sped around cars, the speedometer passed one hundred, then 120. After that, I stopped looking and just concentrated on dodging cars. I climbed the hill ahead of us, still accelerating. As I neared the top, I chanced a glance in the rearview mirror again, relieved to see the nose of Gabriel's pickup truck behind me. I began to slow down and finally came to a stop on the side of the highway at the apex of the hill.

We were still far from the mountains, but we had reached its foothills and the small hill had finally contained the rush of water. I sat in the driver's seat, taking deep breaths, trying to slow my heart rate. Liam jumped out of the car, pumping his good fist into the air, yelling, "Hell yeah! My dad is awesome!"

I sat in the driver's seat for ten minutes before I had the strength to get out of the car and join my son and the Fabron family. I felt the adrenaline slowly dissipate in my body, all but a small, warm puddle in my heart. My son's words bounced around my heart. He'd never called me awesome.

Other cars had also stopped all along the Mass Pike and traffic was pulling over on both sides of the road. People stood around looking at the water downhill of us, watching as it receded, flowing back toward the ocean, toward Boston, toward a devastated mass of urban life. People cried, adults and children alike, and they clung to each other, thankful to be alive, but devastated at what had been lost. I heard people crying about family and friends that they knew hadn't made it out of the city.

Eventually, some cars started up and drove west, continuing away from the metropolis. I turned to Sebastian's father. "Gabe, I'm going to Bradley to meet my daughter. With any luck, she will land right about the time we arrive." I'd called her repeatedly, but it just went to voice mail. I had no idea if she had taken off from Savannah before it was consumed by the ocean. All I could do was operate under the assumption that she had.

I handed Gabriel a key. "Go on to the cabin. Lock the doors and don't let in anyone except the parents of Inga's roommate, Zoe Walsh. I...I don't know their first names. Stay safe."

We shook hands, then he pulled me into a hug. "Nick, you and your wife saved our lives. I can't begin to thank you. Be safe. Go get your girl."

Bradley International Airport was two hours from our home in Cambridge, and Inga was returning home with six friends. They would never fit in my overflowing SUV. Liam and I barely did. But it didn't matter. I would be there when she landed.

If she landed.

Fast Facts

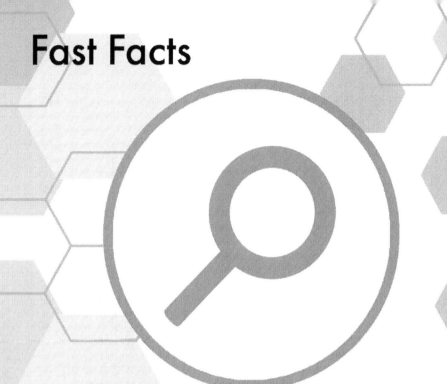

Groups of activists, academics, and government officials have proposed nonbinding guidelines for the treatment of climate refugees, but these do not have the force of law. Before the Paris Climate Agreement of 2016, there had been a move to create a group within the United Nations that would recognize and help with relocations, as well as provide compensation to those who lost their homes due to climate change. But Australian negotiators put an end to it. During the Paris talks, the issue of climate refugees was so politically explosive that it was hardly discussed.

During the 2021 United Nations Climate Change Conference, whether deliberate or inadvertent, the issue of climate refugees was once again overlooked.

Chapter 41
Kathryn – Antarctica

It was almost noon, and I was sitting at the communal dining tables in the Quonset hut we'd dubbed Q1, my head in my hands. I had a tray of food in front of me, thanks to Dakota, but I was so tired I couldn't keep my eyes open.

Since I got off the satellite phone with Oliver Davies, every member of the winter over team was taking turns calling home to tell their families of the situation and warn those on the coast. We learned that the news was all about the tsunamis.

I gave precedence to those who lived on coasts to call home first. Luckily, many lived in the center of the US, with a few from mountainous New Zealand. The handful of Australians were all coastal residents.

Even limiting the calls to one minute each, with 212 people, it was still going to take almost four hours for everyone to try to reach their families. Some had been lucky, but there had been more unanswered calls than not. We didn't know if those families were safe and the phone service was simply overloaded, or if they'd perished.

My heart raced uncontrollably, and my entire body was vibrating. The calls home were sending me further and further into a state of utter despair I never knew I was capable of.

They were also keeping me from hearing from Nick, so I didn't know if my husband and son were dead or alive. I didn't know if my daughter's flight took off.

Lunch was the last thing on my mind.

It would be at least an hour before we cycled everyone through their calls, and then I'd try to reach Nick again. Those who had not reached their loved ones would stand in line for the single satellite phone to try again, after me.

I picked up my tray and walked to the communications desk. Hannah was sitting in the lone chair, monitoring the calls, making sure everyone got their chance, but that they kept the calls to the allotted one minute. I handed her my food. "Hannah, when we get home, you are getting a promotion."

She smiled her thanks and looked back at her watch, timing the current caller.

There was a cot in Q2 calling my name and I sank onto it, exhausted. Just a quick nap. I had an hour.

Fast Facts

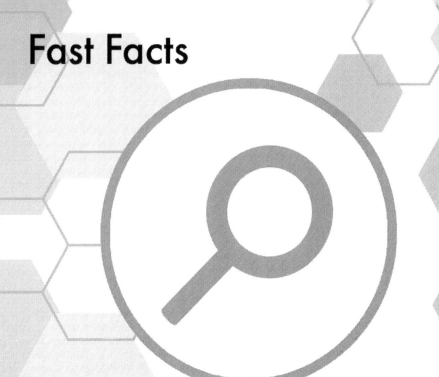

In the Netherlands, flood control is an important issue, as about two-thirds of its area is vulnerable to flooding. The country is one of the most densely populated on Earth. In modern times, flood disasters combined with technological developments have led to large construction projects to reduce the influence of the sea and prevent future floods. The Dutch have a solution to rising seas. They take a multi-layered approach: prevention (using dunes, dikes, barriers, and dams); spatial planning behind the dikes to limit the effects of flooding; and emergency management.

Climate change has become a big business in the Netherlands, with delegations from as far away as Jakarta, Ho Chi Minh City, New Orleans, and New York visiting the port city of Rotterdam. They often wind up hiring Dutch firms to mitigate their own cities water management and flood mitigation issues.

Chapter 42

Inga – Hartford, Connecticut

My head had been leaning on Caleb's shoulder since he switched seats with Zoe halfway through the flight. I couldn't bear to look out the window anymore.

Caleb was tracking our flight by GPS on his phone and kept me updated on where we were. Suddenly he sat up in a hurry and leaned over me to look out the small window. We were over the Delmarva peninsula, but I wouldn't have known if I hadn't looked at the screen. The peninsula was a flat and sandy area with absolutely no hills. Where the map on his phone showed land, there was only gray water. Delaware was under the Atlantic Ocean. Caleb sniffled, then caught himself.

I squeezed his hand and leaned my head back on his shoulder as he settled silently back in his seat.

Half an hour later, the pilot's voice came over the speaker. "We are twenty minutes out of Hartford and air traffic control has put us fifth in the queue to land. All conditions at Bradley International Airport are stable, but flights to many nearby airports have been diverted to Hartford, so we will have to circle and wait our turn. The tower assures us that it will not be more than a ten to fifteen-minute delay." Her voice was calming and the passengers, many who had spent the entire flight in tears, settled down every time she addressed us.

I tried to empty my mind and relax, but thoughts kept flashing in unbidden. Did my father and brother get out of Boston? Was Boston even still there?

A bump jarred me awake as the wheels touched down. I must have dozed off because forty minutes passed in a moment.

I sat up straight and looked out the window. A nice dry runway was rushing by as the plane decelerated.

I turned on my phone as soon as the plane started taxiing to the gate, and moments later, texts started popping in. Six new messages. I clicked the icon. All were from my father! A smile a mile wide broke across my face as I read them. They were okay. I couldn't contain my enthusiasm.

"My dad and little brother made it out of Boston and are on their way to Hartford to get us!" Judging by the time stamp on the last text, they would beat us to the gate.

The aircraft neared the terminal and Zoe shouted behind me, "My parents are at the cabin, Inga! They made it. They can't get inside because it's locked, but they are there and safe. They say they'll hang out on the porch swing and enjoy the evening." She was beaming.

I looked at my watch. "Zoe, at 7:30 in the mountains in March, they are going to freeze to death sitting there." I had to laugh. Zoe's beatnik parents would probably curl up in sleeping bags – made of all-natural fibers, of course – and wait out a blizzard just to be outdoors. "Tell them to wait in the car." But I was laughing. My family was safe, and so was Zoe's. In the midst of all the devastation, I couldn't be happier.

I had never flown into Hartford before, and while the terminal was much larger than Savannah's, it was easy enough to follow the signs toward the exit and ground transportation. We looked and felt like seven refugees. Exhausted and wearing two-day-old clothes, we made our way out of the secured area into the main terminal.

Someone jumped on me from behind, grabbing my waist in a death grip half made of plaster. I turned, about to deck my assailant and saw Liam. My swing morphed from a punch to a hug in an instant. "Hey, slob! Aren't you a sight for tired eyes!" I looked around. "Where's Dad?"

The kid, who was almost as tall as me now, pointed with his chin. "He's renting a van. There isn't a lot left. You might have noticed; this airport is busy!"

"Yeah, no shit, Sherlock. All the airports on the coast are rerouting flights here." And to other inland cities as well.

"Oh my god, Inga, you should have seen it! This wall of water, like a million feet high, raced in from the ocean, chasing us in the car. It was like a disaster movie. But Dad was amazing; he drove like a race car driver, swerving around slower cars and pushing the SUV as fast as it would go. And Bash's dad was on our rear bumper the whole way. Shit, those old guys can drive!"

Then his mouth took a visible downturn. "Inga, it's all gone. Boston. It's gone. I've been watching news broadcasts on my phone since Dad outraced the tidal wave. It's bad."

Didn't I know it.

I introduced Liam to my new friends, then told him how Savannah had been washed away as our plane took off. By the time I finished, we were at the car rental area, and I pushed my way to the front of the line to my father standing at the counter. I wrapped my arms around him, never so happy to see anyone in my life. I couldn't help it, but tears welled in my eyes. I wasn't crying, just...leaking.

Thirty minutes later we were cruising along in a seven-passenger van, following my father to the Berkshires, Carlos at the wheel, and Mateo already asleep in the rearmost seat, nestled into a car seat next to his aunt.

With all the dangers in the world at this very moment, my father still had forethought to rent a car seat for a toddler he didn't even know. I had never understood how my father kept it all together; everything organized and in its place. He had superpowers. Organization Man!

Caleb wrapped his arm around me, and I snuggled into him. His mother had sent him a text that she and his stubborn father were safely in the mountains, and his dad thanked him for the warning.

Zoe was texting her mom because when she tried to call, the lines were busy. Her mom said that the Fabron family had just arrived, and they were unpacking and making sleeping arrangements for a crowd in the small, three-bedroom cabin.

Jason sat up front, next to Carlos, making call after call trying to reach his parents. When he finally got through, he discovered they were in Allentown, Pennsylvania, prepared to drive up to our cabin to pick him up whenever he was ready. But they had not been able to reach his older sister, Nadia, who lived on the coast in Connecticut. Was she safe? Would Long Island protect coastal Connecticut from destruction, or would the water just come up the Long Island Sound and devastate it all? No one knew and Jason was torn up. He idolized his older sister.

I wished that everyone I knew and everyone they knew was safe and accounted for. It's easy to get lost in the act of living and believe things will always go on as they are but everything comes to an end.

I just never expected it to happen this week.

Almost everyone I had known my entire life in Boston, all the people we met in Florida, and everyone my friends knew and loved along the coast was dead or missing.

Fast Facts

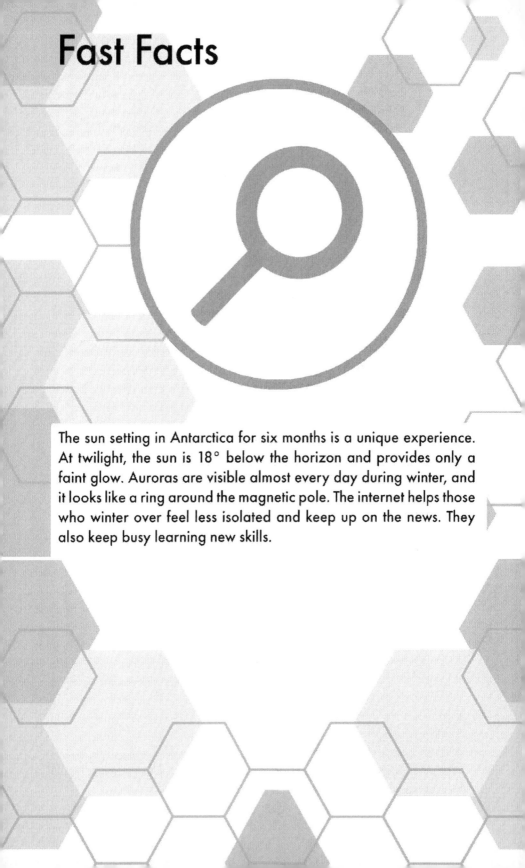

The sun setting in Antarctica for six months is a unique experience. At twilight, the sun is 18° below the horizon and provides only a faint glow. Auroras are visible almost every day during winter, and it looks like a ring around the magnetic pole. The internet helps those who winter over feel less isolated and keep up on the news. They also keep busy learning new skills.

Chapter 43

Kathryn – Antarctica

Billy stood above my cot, his hand on my shoulder, shaking me hard. "Ma'am, wake up please." His voice jittered.

"I'm awake. What's the matter?" The young Aussie had not been able to reach his family yet and I was worried he came bearing more bad news. Or perhaps it was another earthquake and I had slept through it.

Instead, he said, "Hannah sent me. There is a call for you. Come quick."

I raced to put on my outdoor gear. At negative forty, even the twenty steps between Quonset huts would give you severe frostbite. I asked him who the call was from, but a gust of wind ripped away my words.

Maybe it was Nick or Inga. Was my family finally safe? I passed through the double entrance to Q1, stripping my outerwear off as I walked through the vestibule. Lunch was in full swing, and the place was crowded since most people had diddly squat to do, except eat, sleep, try to call home, or worry.

Hannah handed me the satellite phone. "It's Director Marshall, ma'am. Sorry, we had to wake you, but he said he would only speak with you."

I grabbed the phone with a jerk. I really could have used another hour of sleep, but I couldn't ignore his call, and not just because he was my boss. "Director. What's the news?"

His voice was calm in a way that only a man watching dangerous situations unfold from a position of total safety could be. His office in Alexandria, Virginia was only forty feet above sea level, though quite a distance from the Atlantic Ocean. Neither Alexandria nor Washington DC had been wiped out from the tsunamis. But once the flooding began, the story might be vastly different.

I wondered if George Marshall was aware of that.

"Kathryn, we are getting live footage from the ISS and from satellites that show the Thwaites glacier is breaking up into a million icebergs. The space station crew said the massive fragments appear to be spreading northward in all directions, carried by the currents and the waves. We are estimating that it will melt in weeks, raising sea level by over ten meters."

Yes, he did know. "I'm aware of that danger, Director. I've been espousing that position for years, and –"

He cut me off. "I'm aware of your predictions. You are not the only one who has warned of that eventuality. Hundreds of renowned climatologists have said the same. No one thought that it could happen this quickly, or suddenly. Kathryn, I wanted to let you know that we have plans for an orderly evacuation of Washington, Alexandria, and all lower-lying municipalities along the Potomac and Chesapeake over the next week. Right now, the country is dealing with coastal tsunamis up and down the Atlantic. It will take time to get everyone to high ground. As you can imagine, it's a massive undertaking."

It was my turn to cut him off. I was glad to get news of the situation but had other, more selfish concerns. "Director, I'm aware of what's involved. I know that 212 people aren't your highest priority, but have you made arrangements for a vessel to come get us?"

"That's why I'm calling, Kathryn. I've tried, I really have. The Coast Guard icebreakers are all moored in Seattle or up in the Arctic. There is nothing far enough south than I can divert to you, no matter how many favors I call in. But I had a thought. What about the British ship down in the Falklands? It's headed to evacuate Rothera and the Argentines. It's due there in two days. It can reach Ross Island five days later. Can you hold out up there for another week?"

"Maybe, Director. Yes. We'll make it work. Can you fill me in on coastal damage? Have the tsunamis run their course?"

"It seems that they have. Canada is still experiencing rough waves. As you probably already guessed, Florida is a total loss. The entire peninsula was washed away from tidal waves coming at it from both sides. The Gulf states fared better, with higher-than-normal tides and flooding. And while every community along the Atlantic was affected to some degree, those that suffered the worst were Savannah, Charleston, Atlantic City, New York, and Boston."

He took a deep breath before finishing. "Kathryn, they are all gone. Completely washed out to sea."

Savannah. Boston. Both gone.

My resourceful daughter had made it out of Florida only to wind up in a city that was destroyed just hours later. My husband and my son knew the danger about Boston but may have waited too long.

My family was all I had. My research paper would never be published now, the reality of my research coming true before the wheels of academia could bring it to light. My city was gone, which meant everything of value, including my career, was destroyed, washed away by the ocean.

I had to know if my family made it out.

I signed off from the NSF Director and gave Hannah the phone. "Let people start trying to reach their families again."

"Yes, ma'am."

I looked around the crowded room and whistled loudly then addressed the suddenly silent room. "We expect evacuation with the help of the British in seven days. We just have to hold out." Cheers battled tears; the McMurdo crew relieved to have rescue coming yet expressing it in different ways.

I turned back to the bruised and battered young woman who was so dedicated. I knew she had been close to Martin and how sad she was at his death; I wasn't sure how she continued. "Hannah, have you called home yet? You should take your turn. Where is your family?"

I'm not sure how I missed the fact that her eyes were red and swollen, and it had nothing to do with her injuries from the CSB collapse.

"Florida, ma'am. I don't need to call home."

Fast Facts

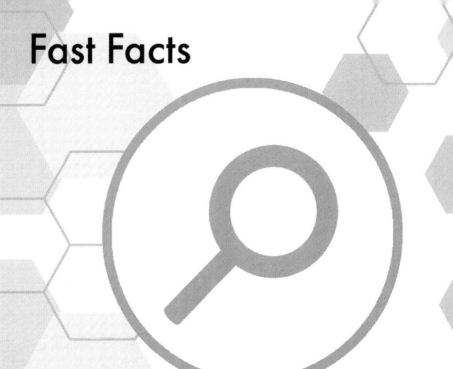

Most of the world's megacities are located in the coastal zone and roughly 40 percent of the world's population lives within 100 kilometers of the coast. That's about three billion people. As the population and economic activity along the coasts grows, so does pressure on coastal ecosystems. Coasts are highly vegetative and provide rich biological resources like fisheries, so people have always settled in those areas. Historically, this has been advantageous for survival.

The downside of living near the coast is they are prone to many natural hazards such as erosion, large storms, harmful algal blooms, flooding, tsunamis, and sea level rise.

Chapter 44

Inga – The Berkshire Mountains, Massachusetts

By 9 p.m. we were unpacked and settled in. The cabin had been furnished with groups in mind. My parent's bedroom was the smallest, with just a queen-size bed, but my room and Liam's both had two bunk beds; those cheap metal framed ones from the discount box store that had a full-size mattress on the lower bunk and a twin up top.

Dad gave his room to Zoe's parents and took a top bunk in Liam's room above Bash's parents. Carlos shared the other lower bunk with Mateo, with Alita on the top bunk. That left my room for me, Caleb, Zoe, and Jason, with Bash and Liam taking the two top bunks. Neither Dad nor Zoe's parents were thrilled with their daughters' sharing bunks with these new boyfriends, but they were not so naive as to think we had not done "that" already, and Dad's only comment was, "No hanky panky with your brother and Bash in the room."

I gave him the evil eye. That was just gross.

I was exhausted and went to bed as soon as I had my pj's on. Outside, the world might be flooding, but for now, it just felt nice to be back in my childhood vacation cabin.

When I awoke in the morning, Caleb snuggled in beside me. I crawled over him, slipped into my fuzzy slippers and warm robe that lived at the cabin, and went out to the kitchen to put on a pot of coffee. The cabin was cold. The heat was on, but the walls were uninsulated and leaked like a sieve.

Jason was asleep at the table, his phone in his hand, with its low-battery light flashing. I sat down beside him, and he lifted his head instantly from the table.

"What?" He snapped, but as soon as he realized it was me and where he was, he apologized. "Sorry. I spent most of the night trying to reach my sister. I've called and texted, even gotten through a few times, but only to voicemail."

I nodded in sympathy. It was difficult to not know where your missing family was. My mother was still in danger, but at least for now, I knew where she was. I knew she was alive and alright.

"Have you talked with your parents? Maybe they've had better luck finding out something."

"Haven't gotten through, but my mom texted late last night that they still had no word. After that, I didn't want to bother them. Let them sleep if they can." He looked at his nearly dead phone, then got up from the table and pulled his charger out of his backpack.

I put the coffee pot on, and Jason came over to the kitchen to find a plug for his phone. I asked, "Why does your sister live in Connecticut? I thought your family was from Delaware." Maybe I was being too nosy, but the words came out before my brain engaged.

He shook his head. "Only my mom's family is from Delaware. My dad's grandparents live in West Haven and when my sister got into Yale, my father encouraged her to go. She lived off-campus with my grandparents because she didn't get a ton of scholarships and Ivy League schools are expensive. But she loved living with our grandparents. She learned about the Chinese side of our family from our grandfather, and she thrived there. After graduation last year, she stayed." He plopped down on the couch in the small living room, and I joined him.

Suddenly, realization dawned on me. "So, it's not just your sister you are worried about, is it? Your grandparents, too?"

He nodded affirmation. "But my parents called them and warned them after I told them to get out of Delaware. I was sure they left the coast."

"Then I'm sure they got out; all the phone lines are just tied up. And networks are down everywhere after the tsunamis. Why don't you crawl in bed and get a few hours of sleep? When you get up, they'll be food ready, your phone will be charged, and maybe you'll even have a message from your sister or grandparents by then."

Again, he nodded agreement, too tired for words, and quietly padded into the bedroom.

An hour later, the troops started to stir, and I had breakfast ready. We didn't see Jason until almost noon, and he looked a lot better, though he still had no word from his family.

It was a quiet day at the cabin, everyone just watching the news on their phones, learning about the destruction up and down the east coast. There was some Pacific coast damage, but no major tsunamis. The Thwaites glacier had been aimed straight at the Atlantic. The west coast had hurricane-size tides but the destruction of marinas, boats, and some expensive ocean view houses, wasn't the same scale as the loss of entire cities.

As we watched and learned more about how lucky we were that we were high and dry, I realized that the world would never be the same again.

I had stopped wearing my DPA earpiece in the cabin because it was just a waste of battery power and nothing was going on that required my attention, so I was surprised when my phone rang. I had gotten used to Lilith's voice in my left ear announcing calls. I grabbed the phone from the couch next to me and answered quickly. "Mom!"

"Inga, it's so good to hear your voice. I've been trying to get through for half a day, and I finally had to get some sleep. I just woke up. Are you at the cabin? Did your father and Liam make it?" She sounded more worried than I expected her to be. I knew she was safe, so I had stopped worrying about her, but it never occurred to me that she did not have the same confirmation about us. She must have felt like Jason had, not knowing.

"Yeah, we are fine, and Dad and the brat are here, too. So are Bash and his parents, and Zoe and hers, and our new friends who came up from Florida. It's super crowded in the cabin." I let out a little laugh as I saw Dad gesticulating in the background, and added, "Dad wants to talk to you. I love you, Mom." I handed my phone to my father who took it to an empty bedroom.

Liam shouted after him. "Hey, I get to talk to her, too, before you hang up!"

Dad was back in less than a minute, handing the phone to Liam. "Keep it short. I've got news for all of you when you're done."

Another minute later, Liam hung up, and I pocketed my phone as my brother plopped down, cross-legged on the floor. "So, Dad, what's Mom's news? She wouldn't tell me. Said you would fill us all in. Oh, and Bash, she says hi."

Bash fist-bumped Liam. He liked my mom. She always gave him extra snacks.

Zoe and Alita had been in my bedroom but came out to the living room to hear what my father had to say. He cleared his throat and announced, "Kathryn spoke to her boss at the NSF."

Greeted by blank stares from Carlos and Alita, he clarified. "National Science Foundation. Director Marshall says the media will have coverage of it shortly, but there is a satellite video of the Western Antarctic ice sheet sliding into the ocean. It's happening right now. It will probably take a few days, so it won't do immediate damage like Thwaites crashing, but he doesn't think it will stop. Says there isn't anything holding it back and he expects the entire ice sheet, all the ice west of the Transantarctic Mountains to slide into the ocean over the next couple of days. Experts are saying that's enough fresh water to raise the oceans 150 to 200 feet."

The room was as silent as a morgue.

Most of the world's megacities were located in the coastal zone and more than 50 percent of the world's population lived near coasts – coasts that would be inundated.

The world indeed would never be the same again.

Fast Facts

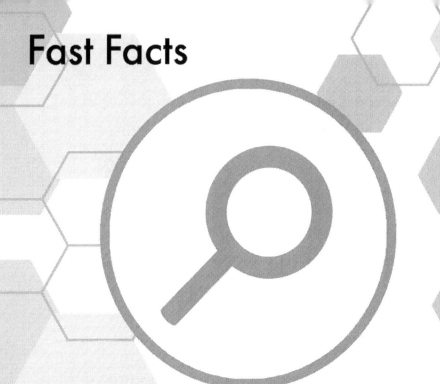

The Amundsen-Scott South Pole Station is a scientific research station at the South Pole, the southernmost place on the Earth. It is located on the high plateau of Antarctica at an elevation of 9,301 feet (2,835 meters) above sea level and is administered by the Division of Polar Programs within the National Science Foundation under the United States Antarctic Program. The Amundsen-Scott Station has been built, rebuilt, torn down, expanded, and upgraded several times since 1956.

The number of scientific researchers and members of the support staff varies seasonally, with a peak population of about 200 in the summer season from October to February. The winter population is generally around 50.

Chapter 45

Kathryn – Antarctica

A day and a half later, I got a call from Oliver Davies. Their rescue ship had arrived, and they were en route by helicopter to reach it. By now more than half of our group of 212 people had been able to reach their families, but many had not, and of those who had, many had lost people and still more were unaccounted for. The call from Oliver was a welcome respite from the non-stop bad news from home.

"I miss your photo monolog, Oliver," I said as we shouted over the rumble of his helicopter blades. "It's hell not being able to see what's going on."

"Can't you figure out some way to tap into the video feeds from media satellites? You are a bunch of scientists, aren't you?" I could hear his dry chuckle and was glad the man and his small team were getting rescued. They had been surviving inside their two helicopters at the top of the nearest mountain. It had been a cold couple of days for the twenty British researchers. "See you in five days, Kathryn. It'll be nice to meet you in person."

"Same here. Safe travels." I broke the connection and gave the phone back to Hannah. She had been living on that cot next to the communications desk since we arrived. Her family was presumed dead and the man she worked for had been killed when the Central Services Building collapsed. She should have been the most miserable person at the base, but she always had a smile for everyone and kept at her comms duty non-stop except when she slept, used the facilities, or ate.

I was grateful that my family was all alive and safe in the Berkshires. I was one of the lucky few.

I spent my time analyzing and writing up the data coming in from the two seismographs still operating, the one at Amundsen-Scott South Pole Station and the one in East Antarctica. All my offshore equipment had stopped sending data as they fell into the ocean with the ice shelf.

Oh shit. Amundsen-Scott Station. How could I be so stupid?

"Hannah, can you raise the South Pole Station on the sat phone please?"

Fifty people were wintering over at Amundsen-Scott, and we had no way to get them out.

It took less than five minutes for Hannah to get me connected to the station master at the South Pole. Emily's voice was as sunny as her current living environment was dark. "Kathryn, a pleasure to hear your voice. Director Marshall filled us in on what's happened at your station, not to mention what we are seeing on the internet. Are you all okay there?"

I had to laugh. "I was calling to check on you! Yes, we will be alright until the rescue ship arrives. But Emily, what about you? There isn't any way that we can come get you."

This time she was the one chuckling. "Kathryn, that's been the case since February. Anyway, right now this might be the safest place on the planet. We are 2,800 meters above sea level, on the other side of the Transantarctic Mountains from the failing ice sheet and have provisions to last for six months. I can't think of anyone better equipped to deal with this catastrophe than the South Pole, even if it is negative 65 degrees outside and pitch dark. We've got a beautiful aurora going on right now and you know what we don't have? Riots, looters, and refugees desperate for shelter. No, we are good."

She had an excellent point. "Agreed! But I have no idea what the situation will be at the NSF once the winter is over. What happens if the resources aren't there to come get you?"

There was a moment of silence before she answered, her voice losing all humor. "Who knows what anything will be like six months from now."

I tried to analyze seismic data for a couple more hours, but then finally gave up. What was the point? The "big one" was a fact now and no matter what I discovered; nothing would change the situation. I was just grateful that the aftershocks had stopped. Finally, I called Dr. Nourah Al-Baqsami, Kuwait's director of Planning and Environmental Impact Assessment Department, and although she did not answer, I left her a voicemail with the satellite phone number where she could reach me. I was quite surprised when she called me back four hours later.

"Hello, Nourah. How is your evacuation going?"

"Kathryn, it is so wonderful to hear your voice. I saw everything on the news and heard how McMurdo was destroyed. I am glad your team is all right. Our evacuation plan has been proceeding well, and we were able to get most of our coastal population moved up to tent cities in the hills above the bay. I wish it had all been for nothing. I would have rather blamed your research group for a false alarm than deal with this nightmare." I could hear the exhaustion and stress in her voice.

"Me too Nourah, me too." We talked for a few minutes but then I let her get back to her work. The evacuation area her military had set up was only temporary, but the bay area where her nation's capital had been just days ago was gone forever. Kuwait had a long road ahead of them to recreate a new capital city after theirs was swallowed by the sea. Her country, indeed, all countries around the globe, had a lot of work to do to reconfigure their population, their government, their entire infrastructure.

I stayed up until midnight so that I could check in with my family as they awoke. I needed to hear each one of their voices for a few minutes before I went to bed. Stranded on top of a mountain in Antarctica, I realized just how lucky I was.

Fast Facts

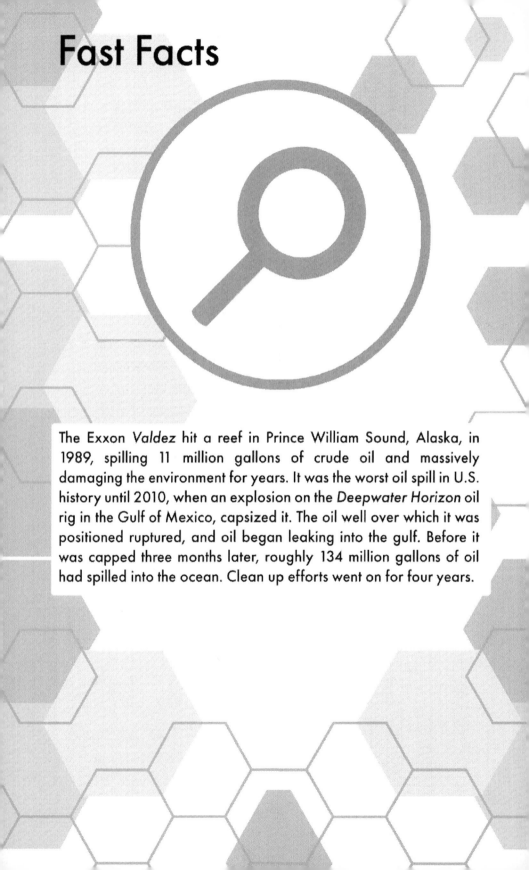

The Exxon *Valdez* hit a reef in Prince William Sound, Alaska, in 1989, spilling 11 million gallons of crude oil and massively damaging the environment for years. It was the worst oil spill in U.S. history until 2010, when an explosion on the *Deepwater Horizon* oil rig in the Gulf of Mexico, capsized it. The oil well over which it was positioned ruptured, and oil began leaking into the gulf. Before it was capped three months later, roughly 134 million gallons of oil had spilled into the ocean. Clean up efforts went on for four years.

Chapter 46
Nick – The Berkshire Mountains, Massachusetts

Our large group was in a kind of groove now, surviving in the small cabin in the woods. We took turns for showers, cooked, ate, and tried to reach extended family. I was getting to know Zoe's new boyfriend, Jason, and was able to console him as he continued to reach out to his grandparents and sister in coastal Connecticut, but the boy had not yet managed to find out anything about them. Every hour, every day that went by made the chance that they were still alive slimmer.

We watched the news on multiple media channels, every hour hearing new stories of how high the ocean was rising, and how the coasts were being pushed further back from the ocean. More areas were being evacuated as more Antarctic ice crashed into the ocean. The ISS sent images to the world of half a continent denuded of immense quantities of ice, all of it swept north into the Atlantic and Pacific oceans, the currents carrying massive icebergs into ever warmer waters. The sea was rising by tens of feet a day. But today, some experts were finally announcing that the greatest part of the ice had already broken off and at this point, the ice that remained on the continent appeared to be holding its own.

The major part of the crash was over.

The sea had risen over fifty feet in some parts of the world, and higher in others. The ocean wasn't uniform, owing to the Earth's rotation and tides. There was also the problem of massive chunks of ice that wouldn't melt for years and would remain shipping hazards during that entire time. It all depended on how far into the warmer waters the ice was carried and how quickly. Debris from the drowned cities didn't all stay drowned, and there were areas of the world's ocean where floating garbage coalesced. Plastic bags, fast-food wrappers, and crushed plastic bottles all pushed together from the oil slicks from the submerged cities.

At 2 p.m. on Friday, Kathryn called, and I was excited to hear her voice. "Katy, you have no idea how much I miss you!" I answered excitedly.

Her voice was measured, serious. "Oh Nick, I miss all of you, too. I'm afraid I have news that's not particularly good."

I had to laugh. "Like any news has been good for the last week?"

"This bit is personally terrifying. The rescue ship that picked up the Rothera team disappeared off the radar and has not been heard from for the last two days. It is assumed that they are lost in the frozen, iceberg-filled Southern Ocean. We have no way to get home now."

My heart sank and I fell heavily into a chair.

"Nick?" asked Kathryn. "Are you still there?"

"Yes, Katy, I'm here. Just thinking. There has to be a solution. After all, you are a VIP. You foretold this nightmare."

A tinny, nervous laugh came from my phone speaker. "Hardly. No one believed me for years, and by the time I had solid evidence, it was rather late."

I told her how much I loved and missed her and assured her that I would come and get her myself if I had to. I would move heaven and earth to get my wife home.

Then a thought struck me. I didn't need to move celestial bodies, only one old friend. "Katy, I think I have a solution. I'm going to call in a favor from Peter McAllister. He owes me."

"You mean the Woods Hole professor who was supposed to get Inga and her friends out of Miami? What makes you think he can get 212 people off a mountain top when he wasn't even able to get two teenage girls out of Florida?"

"Peter is the cousin of the CEO of Blankendahl Petroleum. When we had lunch last week, God it feels like a month ago, anyway, they have an icebreaker in the Southern Ocean, traveling from the southern tip of Argentina where they were drilling offshore for oil. He told me all about it during lunch. Completely monopolized the conversation, as he always does." At the time I'd just rolled my eyes and ate my lunch, but now I was glad I'd paid attention and not bothered trying to get in a word edgewise.

Kathryn interjected, "I thought all the major oil companies switched their energy manufacturing activities to renewable energy years ago."

I grunted. "Most did. Offshore drilling has been illegal in most countries since 2025. But Blankendahl is the last hold-out. They have oil wells in the Southern Ocean. Not close enough to Antarctica to break the Antarctic Treaty, but close enough for our needs. I can see if Peter can convince his cousin to send their ship south to rescue you and your team. I'll present it as good PR for the last major energy company still drilling to mount a rescue of the woman who predicted this fiasco. It's not like many people think fossil fuels are a good idea at this point. And ever since the Exxon *Valdez* oil spill in Alaska's Prince William Sound, no one has thought ships carrying oil through frozen seas was a great idea."

I told my wife how much I loved her and hung up, dialing Peter's number a moment later. It didn't take more than a few minutes to explain to him what I expected from him for reneging on his deal to pick up Inga. He left her there to die, all so that he could be on his way to Aspen for some spring skiing. He had not believed that she was in real danger. It was only by Inga's ingenuity and sheer luck that she and her friends escaped the doomed city of Savannah. I laid the guilt on thickly.

Within an hour Peter heard back from his cousin at Blankendahl. They were sending their ship to Ross Island.

The tanker owned by the last oil drilling company on Earth was called *Prince William's Revenge.*

Fast Facts

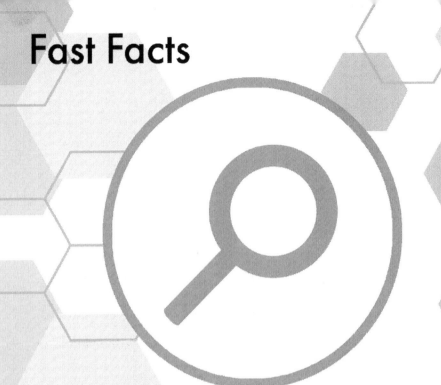

Three million years ago, global temperatures were about as warm as today. Oceans were dozens of feet higher. Then the last ice age hit, roughly 2.5 million years ago and ended about 11,700 years ago. Glaciers covered huge parts of the planet. This is the first ice age that humans were around to experience.

Since most of the water on Earth's surface was ice, there was about half the rainfall that we have today. At the height of the ice age, average temperatures were 9-18°F (5-10°C) below todays.

Currently we are in a warming cycle, called an interglacial, but the Earth will turn cold again, possibly within the next several thousand years. Until then, temperatures will continue to rise, glaciers will melt, and seas will rise. The human contribution to the rate at which temperatures are rising is part of the science of climate change.

Chapter 47

Inga – The Berkshire Mountains, Massachusetts

Just after dinner on Friday night, Zoe's parents organized a memorial service for everything we had lost. We gathered in the living room and stood in a circle. Mrs. Walsh had brought some emergency candles from home, and she lit three of them and placed them on the carpet in the center of our circle.

I reached out for Zoe's hand next to me, and Caleb's on my other side, and that prompted everyone else in the group to hold hands, though not without a look of disgust from my little brother. Holding hands with his best bud, Sebastian, freaked him out so he quickly moved to a spot elsewhere and took dad's hand on one side, and Bash's moms on the other.

Properly arranged and with head bowed, Zoe's father cleared his throat. Travis Walsh's voice was sudden and precise, and everyone stopped their conversation. "I want to start by saying how lucky I am to be in this cabin right now. We all are. We escaped the deadly fate that befell millions around the world, with a great deal of work on Kathryn's part, and a good bit of luck. But we've also lost a tremendous amount as a group, as a family, as a society. So, let's go around the room and acknowledge all that. If you don't wish to speak, you don't have to, just nod, and let the next person go. I'll start."

Mr. Walsh was in his late forties which put him a few years older than my father. His curly brown hair, just like Zoe's, had a mind of its own and he had to push a lock of it back behind his ear before retaking his wife's hand and speaking again. "I want to say how thankful I am that my wife and only child are here with me, safe in a world that will never be the same again. We lost so much, and I know that we'll never get back to New Jersey, our home has most likely been inundated by the ocean by now. If it hasn't, it will be with the coming sea level rise in the next few months. But that doesn't matter. I'm happy to make a new start with those that I love."

He squeezed Zoe's hand and she took that as her cue to speak next. "Ditto, Dad. I'm also thankful for Jason, who I never expected to be in my life, and of course Inga, my best friend for the last year, and the rest of forever. I'm sad to think that everything we had is gone. My college, my stupid old car, and everything we saw in Florida. All those people we tried to help down there after the hurricane, the animals we saved, and the rescue group. The Wynwood Walls murals, the art deco architecture. Everything. I can't believe it's all underwater. But it is. We are lucky, and as soon as we get Inga's mom home, I'm going to hug the crap out of her in thanks for saving our lives." She gave a little giggle, way too girlish for Zoe, and then squeezed my hand.

I guess that had become the cue to switch off. "So, that thing about squeezing the crap out of my mom...Zoe, didn't you have enough crap after the cryptosporidium?" I grinned at her, thinking back to her comment about the screaming shits. She suffered for her good-natured offer to help the stranded animals.

Perhaps we always suffer for our good deeds. My mom certainly was.

Zoe kicked my ankle gently and I faked an "ouch!" before continuing. "Like Zoe, I came home from Florida safely, thanks to my mother, all her research, her perseverance, my dad's guidance, and yeah, a little luck. I also gained a wonderful guy, Caleb, and some new friends." I looked up at Carlos and Alita across the circle and smiled at them, holding little Mateo's hands between them. "But I lost my town of Cambridge, my adopted city of Boston, everything I had at home and school, and everything I prepared for and planned for my life. A degree in music right now seems frivolous. I plan to dedicate my life from here on out to helping the world and everyone in it, to the best of my ability. I felt the best when we volunteered to help Miami deal with the hurricane. So, I'm rededicating my life to the betterment of humanity. I'll figure out how later."

Caleb spoke next, and I was surprised that he professed his love for me right there in front of my father and everyone. It made me think we might have a future together even if my face flushed in embarrassment. But then my father gave me a smile that said he was alright with it. My father didn't approve easily.

Caleb passed the baton to Sebastian, and we went around the room like that for twenty minutes.

When we got to Carlos, he brought a different viewpoint to the memorial than the others in the room. "Ever since I left Cuba with my little sister, and immigrated to Miami as a teenager, I have felt like a piece of my life was missing. I never went back to Cuba, not even for a visit, and I regret that. Now it's too late. Like Miami, Cuba is gone. To think of all the extended family we left behind in Cuba...well, it's sad. I'll probably never even know what happened to some of them. But in the end, I consider myself lucky. I lost my wife to cancer, but she left me with my wonderful son Mateo, whom I love more than life itself, and my little sister. I promise both of you that I will always take care of you."

His Cuban accent was particularly thick right now; something that I noticed happened whenever he got nervous, upset, or sad. Although he professed his good luck, it was sadness that prompted it now.

Mateo hugged his father's leg and Alita went on to add to her brother's sentiments. "I had a lot of friends in Miami. I was going to community college and had a part-time job. I lost all that, all those people. My life may have started in Cuba, but I barely remember that. I miss Miami. I miss the food, the beach, even that giant Fisher Gate which didn't save us in the end." Her shoulders drooped and I heard a sniffle.

There was no denying Jason's emotions. It wasn't just sadness, but true rage. From the news stories, we knew that nothing remained of Connecticut's coast for ten miles inland. I had looked up the elevation of West Haven yesterday. Just thirty-three feet. His nostrils flared and his eyes were wide, showing their whites.

When he spoke, Jason's words were clipped. "My sister and my grandparents are most likely dead. I can't confirm it, but after a week, we would have heard something. Anything. I haven't mentioned it yet, but my parents will be here tomorrow to pick me up and we are going to search for them. I don't know how close we can get, but we are hopeful that the emergency services they set up in Hartford might have some information. I won't rest until I know what happened to her. Nothing I lost – my home, my school, my whole damn state – none of that matters right now."

He broke from the group and went to the bedroom. Zoe let him go. She knew he needed to process his loss, and if that meant driving around Connecticut, not being able to even get close to the town where his family lived, then that's just what he needed to do.

Fast Facts

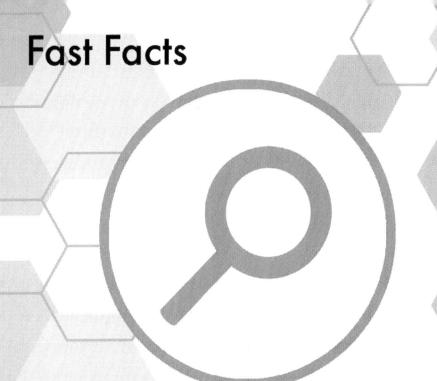

In 1773, James Cook and his crew crossed the Antarctic Circle for the first time and while they discovered nearby islands, they did not reach Antarctica itself. His ship was probably as close as 150 miles (240 km) from the mainland.

On January 27, 1820, the Russian expedition of Bellingshausen and Lazarev became the first explorers to see and officially discover the land of the continent. Three days later, the British expedition of Edward Bransfield sighted Trinity Peninsula. The first landing was possibly when American sailor John Davis' ship's log claims to have set foot on the ice on February 7, 1821, while looking for seals. They did not find any.

In the early 20th century, several expeditions attempted to reach the South Pole during the "Heroic Age of Antarctic Exploration." Following a dramatic race with Robert Scott, Norwegian Roald Amundsen finally reached the Pole on December 13, 1911.

Chapter 48

Kathryn – Antarctica

The world had seen more panic and death in the last week than in both World Wars combined. Hundreds of millions of people around the globe had lost their lives or were fleeing from the rising sea. Any coast not destroyed in the initial tsunamis would be flooded. The east coast of Argentina, the west coast of Chile, New Zealand, Hawaii, and Japan were all heavily populated areas that needed to permanently relocate their coastal populations to higher ground. Evacuations were in process on every coast.

Flatter countries and islands in most cases had no higher ground to move their people to and that was creating a disaster refugee situation that few countries could assist with while they were facing their own problems.

Worst of all were the landlocked countries in the interior of continents. These nations now had the opportunity to be heroes to the coastal lands, yet most closed their borders and blocked refugees from entering, in fear of being overwhelmed, their resources stretched too thin for a massive population influx.

Panic swept the world faster than the water. It wouldn't be long before the situation devolved into war in many areas of the world. The last week had seen riots, gun battles, and looting.

All we could do was learn about it secondhand. We had lost our satellite communications when McMurdo was destroyed so we had no internet. We only had our sat phone, and that wasn't video capable. I knew Oliver thought we scientists could rig something up, but none of us were that kind of scientist. Besides, without equipment, it wasn't possible to MacGyver something together in real life.

Four days after Nick's promise, we got a call from the *Prince William's Revenge*.

A rather high-pitched British accent came through remarkably clear of static. He sounded young. "This is Captain Wellington of the *BP Prince William's Revenge*. Does anyone read me?"

Hannah took the radio call. "McMurdo Station here. Stand by for our station master."

She passed me the microphone with a wide grin. Our rescue had arrived. "Hello, Captain Wellington. This is Kathryn Whitson, acting station master. You have no idea how happy we are to hear your voice!"

The captain continued. "Happy to hear from you, as well. We understand you are in need of evacuation. We are nearing Ross Island and will anchor off the coast where our navigator feels the ocean is deep enough and from where we are in less danger of icebergs. We have a helipad and are expecting McMurdo survivors."

"You do know there are over 200 people here, right?"

"Yes, ma'am. It will be tight, but we will make it work. Keep your gear to a minimum. I was told that your Antarctic Program will return in the summer to assess the damage and potentially rebuild. In the meantime, perhaps you can secure your equipment."

"Understood Captain. We will only bring personal possessions. We have two helicopters to ferry people. Expect the first in thirty minutes."

I had no idea if the NSF would consider returning to this continent for quite some time, but it was a pleasant thought to hang on to while we packed.

Phil and Rothan made several trips to the *Prince William's Revenge* beginning with the injured, then the support staff, while the science teams secured the equipment we would be leaving behind. I was amazed at how quickly the temporary Mt. Terror outpost of McMurdo Station emptied, and it wasn't long before Sylvia and I were on the last helo ride to the ship.

As Rothan skillfully executed a half-sideways takeoff in blustery winter winds, I looked down at the three Quonset huts, the snow already piled up against the sides. I keyed my radio mic on the public channel. "Do you think we will ever return to Antarctica?"

Sylvia shook her head. Pieter Nordling, who had spent five winters at McMurdo Station, was the only one on the crowded helicopter to reply. "Someday. No matter how much the world changes, you can't keep the spirit of discovery down."

Epilogue

Inga – Hartford, Connecticut

I felt the wheels of my plane touch down on the runway at Hartford's Bradley International Airport, glad to be back in New England after three years in Indianapolis.

The world was a different place. The coastlines had been reshaped by the flooding. Just last week, NOAA had announced that the sea level had not changed appreciably in three consecutive months, and they were putting the final tally of rise at 162 feet. Of course, the globe was still warming, though much slower now, and that left potential for more ice in East Antarctica to melt, but the world's governments had put severe restrictions on anything that could raise carbon dioxide levels; from clean energy to cattle ranching and cutting down trees. While a massive earthquake was the precipitating event for the destruction of the West Antarctic ice, scientists had confirmed that if the Earth had not been heating up for almost two hundred years, the likelihood that the quake would have done the damage it had was slim to none.

My family, the Fabrons, and Zoe's had stayed in the Berkshires for a year and a half after the world flooded, but eventually, Zoe, Alita, and I had enrolled in college in Indianapolis. We lost a year of school but got things back on track. Alita had become our third bestie. We joked that a tripod was stronger than a pair and together the three of us would face whatever the world threw at us. Carlos and Mateo moved to Indy with us. Carlos wanted to be far away from the ocean.

Jason never found his sister or grandparents and eventually, he and Zoe drifted apart. They stayed in touch for a few months, but long-distance relationships, especially in our new high-stress world, never worked. Zoe and Carlos had been dating for the last three years and I suspected that he was going to ask her to marry him soon. She might even say yes.

My parents both left academia and began working for the Federal Disaster Relief Agency. They spend months away from the cabin, traveling to various parts of the country to help resettle people and build new infrastructure for the displaced. Caleb's story of the entire Delaware town that relocated to a cornfield in Indiana became the model for the survivors.

Liam went to a boarding school not too far from the cabin but was able to stay there when our parents were traveling. Surprisingly, he thrived there and graduated at the top of his class.

My mother kept in touch with the rest of the McMurdo survivors. Her friend Pieter and his daughter in Holland now lived in the mountains in France. Like the U.S., European countries like the Netherlands, Belgium, and coastal Denmark were almost entirely lost.

In the U.S., most people now lived in the center of the country. With the loss of New York and Los Angeles, Chicago was our largest city and Denver became our new capital after they evacuated Washington.

The GDP of the entire globe was about $100 trillion each year and we lost about 40 percent of it when we lost the coasts. One saving grace was that manufacturing tended to be inland, or it would have been higher. The world spent at least half of its GDP for the last five years rebuilding, and it wasn't done yet.

Indianapolis, St. Louis, and other Midwest cities have grown exponentially. Once the survivors from the coasts resettled, the breadbasket of America began feeding much of the western world, helping Europe and Africa as best they could. Wars were starting to abate, and coastal populations had finally blended into countries in continental interiors, especially in Africa and Asia, though not without ongoing culture clashes and political turmoil. Half a billion people around the world had perished in the initial tsunamis and the slow rise after, but more than two billion later died from famine, disease, and war.

The world was indeed a vastly different place than I grew up in.

As my luck usually had it, I was near the back of the plane, but eventually, I made my way off and worked my way through the crowd to the main terminal. Caleb stood waiting for me, holding a goofy, hand-written sign. "Marry me, Inga."

A border of irregular, hand-drawn pink hearts framed the sign.

I ran into his arms.

I thought I might like the name Inga Milanov.

Maps

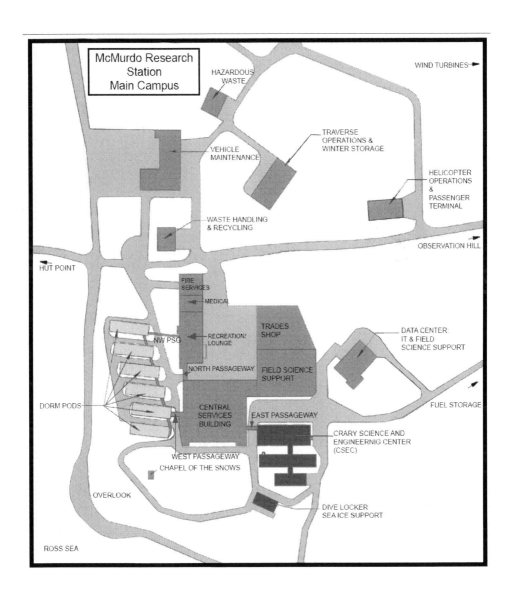

McMurdo Research Station Main Campus

HAZARDOUS WASTE

WIND TURBINES

TRAVERSE OPERATIONS & WINTER STORAGE

VEHICLE MAINTENANCE

HELICOPTER OPERATIONS & PASSENGER TERMINAL

WASTE HANDLING & RECYCLING

OBSERVATION HILL

HUT POINT

FIRE SERVICES

MEDICAL

TRADES SHOP

DATA CENTER: IT & FIELD SCIENCE SUPPORT

NW PSG

RECREATION/ LOUNGE

NORTH PASSAGEWAY

FIELD SCIENCE SUPPORT

DORM PODS

CENTRAL SERVICES BUILDING

EAST PASSAGEWAY

FUEL STORAGE

CRARY SCIENCE AND ENGINEERNIG CENTER (CSEC)

WEST PASSAGEWAY

CHAPEL OF THE SNOWS

OVERLOOK

DIVE LOCKER SEA ICE SUPPORT

ROSS SEA

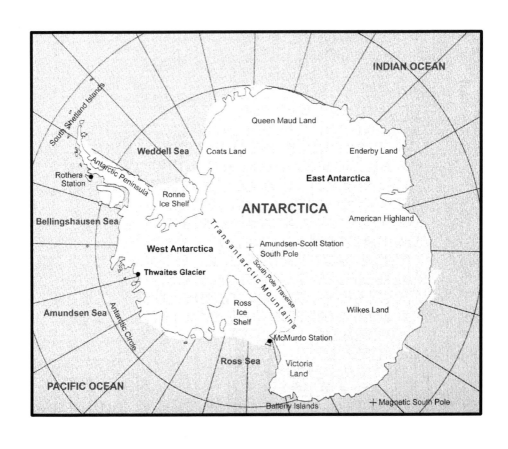

Acknowledgments

I've been interested in sea level rise and global warming for years and tackling that notion in a disaster novel format was challenging. I thought I was well-versed in the topic but learned so much more researching it. While the characters and events are fictional, the facts presented in the novel are all factual, or extrapolation of facts. All Fast Facts entries are non-fiction.

Special thanks to Jeff Goodell, contributing editor at *Rolling Stone* and author of *The Water Will Come: Rising Seas, Sinking Cities, and the Remaking of the Civilized World*, whose insightful explanation of sea level rise provided valuable background science for this novel, as did his *Rolling Stone* article *The Doomsday Glacier*; Eric Holthaus, meteorologist and contributing writer for *Grist*, the *Wall Street Journal*, and *Slate*, for his insightful articles on climate science and policy; Jon Gertner, *Wired* magazine; Peter Brannen, author of *The Ends of the World: Volcanic Apocalypses, Lethal Oceans, and Our Quest to Understand Earth's Past Mass Extinctions* for an education on how the climate shifts of today have analogs in the planet's five past mass extinctions; Ian Tregillis, author of *The Alchemy Wars*, one of my favorite sci-fi series of all time; my beta reader team; my wonderful family and friends – who all too often are roped into becoming beta readers; and, of course, the constant support I get from you, my readers.

My thanks to all of you!

For more information, check out www.lyndaengler.com

Made in the USA
Coppell, TX
21 February 2022

73883740R00190